ERIKA KIMPTON was born and raised in Switzerland where she studied Interior Architecture before she came to Australia in 1967. Since then she has enjoyed a successful career as an interior designer before taking to writing fiction. This is her first novel. She continues to work in her profession, travels extensively and is currently working on her second and third novels. She lives in Melbourne with her four children.

Tansie

Erika Kimpton

SPINIFEX

Spinifex Press Pty Ltd,
504 Queensberry Street,
North Melbourne, Vic. 3051
Australia

First published by Spinifex Press, 1994
Copyright © Erika Kimpton, 1994

Typeset in 11/14 pt Sabon by Claire Warren, Melbourne
Printed in Australia by Australian Print Group, Maryborough
Cover design by Liz Nicholson, Design Bite
Wigs courtesy of The Individual Wig
    402 Chapel Street, South Yarra 3141
    Shop 4, The Park, 16–32 Oxford Street, Darlinghurst 2010

National Library of Australia Cataloguing-in-Publication entry

CIP
Kimpton, Erika, 1945–
    Tansie.

    ISBN 1 875559 34 5.

    I. Title.

A823.3

This publication is assisted by the Australia Council, the
Australian Government's arts funding and advisory body.

For Sylvia who spent many hours reading and correcting numerous drafts and for my children, Nina, Todd, Sari and Lara who often wondered whether their mother would ever return to the hot stove where she rightfully belongs.

Chapter 1

The rain splashed loudly on to the tin roof over the front verandah and Alix ducked under it for protection. She stopped at the door and rang the bell with characteristic impatience. She ran a hand through her short blonde curls and then buried both hands in the pockets of her jeans. Her light-grey, suede flier jacket was casually draped over her shoulders and her feet were thrust into a pair of short fine-leather boots. Although her attire was casual, there was a cool elegance and confidence about her.

When the door suddenly flew open, Alix was taken by surprise. Her green-grey smouldering eyes opened wide. Nothing had prepared her for the woman who now stood in front of her. And, she had not the slightest inkling of what lasting impact this woman would have on her life in times to come.

Tansie's heavy fringe was swept sideways across her forehead, barely showing her large almond-shaped eyes. They were a translucent honey colour, matching the trim on her navy blue, woollen jacket. Her finely chiselled cheekbones, straight narrow nose and full red lips were perfectly shaped and proportioned. Her skin was smooth and had the luminous glow of pure alabaster. The tight faded jeans accentuated her thinness.

It wasn't just the physical beauty Alix noticed though. With her head inclined slightly forward, her arms dangling by her sides and her shoulders stooped, Tansie exuded an aura of fragile vulnerability. At the same time, the scent of

1

her exotic perfume suggested that there was a sensual woman underneath the shy childlike exterior.

"Hi . . . I'm Alix Clemenger," Alix said.

"Hiii, I'm Tansie Landon," Tansie drawled and curved her lips into a smile. Her voice had an undertone of seductive huskiness, but the words which followed indicated otherwise. "I can't start to tell you how grateful I am to be going away with you." When Alix didn't respond, she continued, "You look as though you expected someone different."

"I did," Alix said with an air of blatant honesty, trying to interpret Tansie's smile which was both shy and provocative.

"Oh? How so?" Tansie asked, nervous now.

"In fact, you're not at all what I expected," she confessed, unwary. "After I spoke to you on the telephone, I envisaged you as the twin-set type, checked pleated skirt and pearls, prim and proper, you know what I mean?"

Tansie laughed. "I've been called many things in my time but never prim and proper."

"One day you can tell me what those things were," Alix responded with ease. Laughing together now, their eyes locked for a moment or two. After a short pause, Alix continued. "Let's go. The girls are waiting," she said and reached for Tansie's leather overnight bag and skis.

As soon as everything was stowed in the boot of the silver Range Rover, Alix climbed behind the wheel. Tansie slid into the back seat and slammed the door.

"I'm sorry, I didn't mean to . . ." Tansie stammered. A wave of embarrassment coloured her cheeks bright pink.

"Don't worry. The kids do it all the time and I'm quite prepared for the day when the door will simply fall off," Alix laughed and went on to introduce Tansie to the other two women, Jackie and Cherryl.

Having left the engine running, Alix manoeuvred the car

away from the curb and into the early morning, heavy stream of traffic. As they drove through the Melbourne suburbs, no one spoke for a while. It gave them an opportunity to study one another.

Judging by their appearance, they were a group of well-dressed and finely groomed yuppie women in their late thirties. On the surface, there was nothing particularly unusual about them.

Jackie, although intelligent, didn't use her intellect often. She was attractive, placid and unruffled and had no trouble idling away her days. She felt no guilt even when preparing a Weetbix dinner for the children was too bothersome.

Alix was her direct opposite: bright, energetic and with a catching sense of humour. She was generous and warm but her temper could flare from time to time and on a moment's notice. In her view, idleness was a crime. While she tolerated it in others, the standards she set for herself were often punitive. It came as no surprise to anyone that she was accepted worldwide as a serious composer and accomplished concert pianist long before she turned thirty. Still, she had remained unpretentious.

Cherryl had a bubbly personality, talked incessantly but without substance. She appeared empty-headed and with no original thought of her own. Alix didn't suffer fools gladly and, in her view, Cherryl fell into that category. Her bright red hair reinforced Alix's assessment.

In the end it was Jackie who broke the silence. "I'm dying to know whose Jaguar was parked in your driveway early yesterday morning," she said, glancing at Alix. "Haig drives a Benz, doesn't he? And," she continued with a wide grin, "Haig would never be seen driving a battered old Jag anyway!"

"Who knows?" Alix laughed. "However, what were

3

you doing driving past my house at some ungodly hour?" Taking her eyes off the road, Alix cast her friend a sideways glance.

"I obviously wasn't in bed!"

"That is quite obvious! Not even you can be in two places at the same time," Alix replied with a smile on her lips and a nonchalant shrug of her shoulders. Haig's car had gone in for a service that day, hence the Jaguar. Had he driven his own car, Jackie would have known who her visitor was. Nevertheless, she saw no reason to volunteer that information, least of all while there were two virtual strangers in the car. She believed that having a lover or lovers was an entirely private matter and, despite her high profile, she had generally managed to keep it that way.

Jackie knew full well that any further questions would be useless. Instead she settled for their usual jocular banter.

From time to time, Alix glanced into the rear view mirror so as to observe Tansie.

Tansie appeared to be different from most women Alix was acquainted with. She was timid and only spoke when spoken to. But, it was her childlike charm Alix found quite fascinating.

A few days earlier, Jane, a mutual friend, had asked Alix whether there was room for one more person to go skiing. Tansie had only recently left her husband and needed to get away for a few days, Jane had explained. Alix's friend Mary had cancelled the ski trip on short notice, and she told Jane, she would be happy for Tansie to come instead.

As they neared their destination, Thredbo, Alix had to concentrate on a mixture of rain, sleet and snow that was blurring her vision. She only half listened to her companions' conversation. She liked Tansie's voice, low and mellow, and thought if it were trained properly it would make a lovely singing voice.

When the women had filled in the hotel registration forms, they reached for their assortment of bags and suitcases and headed for the stairs. At the landing, Alix glanced over her shoulder and announced rather than asked, "Tansie and I will share one room . . . you two take the other."

"Fine with us," they replied in unison, followed by what sounded like a sigh of relief from Tansie.

Alix had looked forward to sharing a room with Mary, as she had for several years now, and to catching up on all the news they never seemed to have time for in town. She was a little disappointed but consoled herself with the thought that Tansie would probably make a pleasant change.

Alix unpacked her own neatly packed leather suitcase and caught a glimpse of Tansie's. She drew her eyebrows up and wondered how on earth Tansie could find anything at all. Her bag was chaotic. It was in greater disarray than Alix's teenage son's sports bag. The Reeboks she had just taken off had definitely seen better days, Alix noted. But the snow suit Tansie put on moments later looked expensive and brand new. The price tag still dangled from the sleeve.

When they returned to the change room downstairs, Jackie admired Alix's shiny emerald-green jacket and matching pants with the delicate gold embroidery and Tansie's burgundy one. "What outfits!" she exclaimed.

"You're welcome to borrow mine anytime," Alix replied.

"I wouldn't dream of it!" Jackie laughed. "Out there on the slopes I want to be inconspicuous!"

Alix chuckled softly as Tansie said with some trepidation, "I take it you're all accomplished skiers?"

"I wouldn't say that. I'm pretty hopeless," Jackie responded. "Cherryl's not bad and Alix, you'll soon find out . . ." She let her voice trail off and rolled her eyes. "What about you?"

"I never had a chance to learn to ski when I was a child," Tansie muttered. "I only skied a little after I married Alan, so, you can just leave me if I fall behind. I'll manage."

Alix gave her a curious stare but didn't say anything. Reaching for her skis, she clumped across the tiled floor and went outside. She squinted against the bright sunlight which had made a miraculous appearance. The heavy clouds had disappeared into nothingness. Alix always felt good when the sun was out and she let her gaze wander over the rolling hills and the numerous snow-gums. Given the earlier snowfall, the trees now seemed to be breaking under their heavy load as a light breeze gently swayed their branches.

As a child, strapped to her father's back, Alix had gone skiing long before she could walk. It had soon become a lifelong passion. Each winter, as the weather got colder, Alix began to miss the European mountains, the clean, crisp air, the massive glaciers, the soft powder snow and the smell of burning pine-needles in the open fireplace. Over the years she had learnt to appreciate Australia's rugged beauty. But, in her heart, she longed for the quaint European village resorts, their exclusive shops and restaurants and the surrounding alps.

Having arrived at the top of the ski slope, Alix impatiently slid back and forth. Without waiting for her companions she pointed her skis straight down the hill and, using her stocks, pushed herself off with a flourish.

"Had I known you skied that well, I would have stayed home," Tansie cried in awe when she came to an unsteady halt next to Alix.

"I just started a little earlier than most other people,"

Alix said. "And attending boarding school in Switzerland helped."

"That explains it of course," Tansie replied with more ease. It also explained Alix's slight accent; Tansie had wanted to ask her about it but wasn't quite game enough to. "I suppose you also speak several languages?"

"A couple," Alix smiled.

"To be more precise, she speaks five, including Russian," Jackie said, thinking that part of Alix's charm was her modesty.

After a few runs with her companions, Alix left them to have a private ski lesson. Not because she was bored skiing at their pace but rather because she believed that there was always room for improvement. Much to her friends' amusement, Alix had studied the photo display of all the available ski instructors. Trusting that he was also the best skier, she settled for the most handsome one. She could not imagine herself settling for anything less than perfect.

Tapping her gloved finger on to the notice-board, she drawled as though in a dream, "Just look at his eyes." She disappeared in a cloud of snow seconds later.

Back at the Arlberg Bar, the three women had already downed a couple of drinks when Alix returned from her lesson. Her face flushed, she dumped her cap and gloves on the table and shook her curls back into shape.

"That was quick! No tête-à-tête under a tree?" Jackie raised her eyebrows, mockingly.

"Such frivolities were Michael's specialty . . . God rest his soul . . . and he never even caught a cold," Alix exclaimed without malice. Her husband had died four years before, but painful memories of their troubled marriage lingered.

Sipping her drink rather faster than the others, Tansie

sat and listened to her companions' comfortable chatter. She enjoyed their easy banter, and as she started to relax a little, she soon joined their conversation. She could not have wished for nicer and more interesting women to be with. Tansie very much liked Jackie's droll manner of speaking and her easy-going attitude. Even though, like herself, Jackie too had recently left her husband, she seemed philosophical about the imminent divorce. It was not something she had done lightly, but ultimately realised she simply had no other option. For the sake of keeping the family together, Jackie had tolerated Peter's womanising as long as she could. But when she found out that his longtime mistress was pregnant, she asked him to leave.

It was Alix though that Tansie was most fascinated with. On the surface Alix often appeared flippant, but Tansie quickly realised that underneath that cool facade was a very passionate woman, a dreamer and a romantic. When she spoke, she tended to use her hands to emphasise a point she felt strongly about. Long, elegant hands, Tansie noted.

As Alix and Tansie got to know a little more about each other, they were amazed that their paths had never crossed in the past. They discovered that they had mutual friends, other than Jane, and moved in much the same social circles.

Later when Tansie had begun to feel more at ease, and finding herself alone with Alix in the powder room, she said, "I know it sounds dumb but Jackie is a very lucky woman to have someone like you in her life. A real friend who cares for her, and . . ." She didn't finish, and turning to the row of basins, began to splash her face with cold water.

"I think so too." Alix's reply was flippant but she wondered what Tansie was really trying to say. In her view, a life without close friends, would be intolerable. Yet Tansie seemed to imply that she didn't have any. She could not think of a single reason why a woman as exotically beautiful, bright and playfully charming as Tansie was, could be so alone. From what Alix had observed so far, she seemed to draw people towards her quite naturally.

"I'd like us to stay in touch after this holiday," Tansie continued, looking at her mirror image.

"Sure," Alix replied. Only later did she wonder about her response. This was not like her at all. She was normally more wary of instantly befriending people. Over the years, she had learnt that people often sought her company only because of her celebrity status and the glamour she could add to their lives. She decided in the end that Tansie seemed to be genuinely looking for a friend.

Jackie and Cherryl were waiting in the hotel dining room when Alix and Tansie entered to join them for dinner. In their own way, they each looked quite breathtaking.

Alix's stride was purposeful and her manner aloof. Yet she exuded an aura of warmth, compassion and a mystery which most people wanted to explore. She wore a pair of black fine-wool evening pants and a green shirt a shade or two lighter than her eyes.

Tansie, in comparison, was nervous in her elegant surroundings although, after marrying Alan, she had come to experience a more luxurious lifestyle. Her eyes darted from place to place without focusing on anything or anyone in particular. Her insecurity was so deep seated, she seemed oblivious to the many appreciative looks she was given by some of their fellow diners.

"I feel as though everyone is undressing me. It feels weird going into a restaurant without a man!" she whispered over Alix's shoulder.

Alix put her hand on Tansie's arm and smiled. "There's

nothing wrong with going into a restaurant with an attractive woman, you know," Alix assured her with ease and sat down next to Jackie.

Jackie wore a pair of navy slacks and a cream top. A multicoloured silk scarf was casually wound around her neck. But it was Cherryl whom Alix rolled her eyes at. She wondered not for the first time why many redheaded people had no sense of colour. They seemed to be drawn towards bright red and orange. Cherryl was no exception. Tansie in comparison looked elegantly subdued in a black rollneck sweater with gold buttons on one shoulder and black pants. The sleeves were pushed half-way up her arms, revealing her slender wrists.

The four women settled into a round of easy small talk as they studied the menu and sipped the cold white wine.

Lighting one of Alix's Davidoff cigarettes which she loved but never bought for herself, Jackie asked, "How is Felix? Is he . . ."

"Which one, Mendelssohn or Santini?" Alix interrupted dryly.

"Mendelssohn?" Cherryl asked, raising her finely plucked eyebrows and flicking her hair off her forehead. "That name rings a bell. I'm sure I've met him somewhere."

As Jackie noticed the immediate glimmer of impatience in Alix eyes, she gave her a light kick under the table. It was to no avail.

"You look extremely well preserved considering the man died nearly a hundred and fifty years ago. What's your secret, Cherryl?" Alix asked in a nonchalant manner. She did not hide the intolerance she felt at such ignorance. Normally, she enjoyed meeting new people and the intellectual challenges they might offer her. In Cherryl's case, she thought differently.

"After all this, I still don't know how Santini is," Jackie exclaimed before Cherryl could reply. "My mouth waters at the mere thought of his spaghetti marinara!"

"Isn't he one of those famous Italian opera singers who is also supposed to be a wonderful chef?" Cherryl asked.

Alix shook her head in exasperation. "What have I done to deserve this?"

"Probably plenty if I thought about it," Jackie teased. "Cherryl, Felix Santini is Alix's housekeeper."

"Nobody has male housekeepers," Cherryl said, a note of insolence in her voice.

"Female chauvinism? What a pleasant change!" Alix smirked and popped another plump oyster into her mouth. Even if the conversation was not particularly scintillating at this point, she could still enjoy her meal. As for Cherryl, Alix thought, she'll learn not to spar with me.

"How are his talents as a lover?" Cherryl asked sweetly.

"I'll introduce you, dear. You can find out for yourself," Alix smiled, cringing inside. She hated calling people dear, but in Cherryl's case, it seemed fitting. "Although," she added, "real ladies wouldn't dream of ever sleeping with the hired help. It is simply not done!" The words rolled from her lips as though the Queen herself had spoken.

Jackie began to choke on a piece of bread and Tansie burst out laughing. Tansie had never heard anyone deliver such a barb with quite the same aplomb.

"What exactly do you do, Alix?" Tansie asked, catching her breath.

"I'm a composer. And I perform occasionally," Alix replied. With a fiendish smile playing on her lips, she added, "Perhaps you've seen the ads on television for 'Mum's best loved washing powder' or 'Naturewide compost bins'? They're just some of my creations!"

"I've never noticed the music, I'm sorry!" Cherryl said.

For once, Alix was glad when the owner of the hotel came up behind her and kissed her on both cheeks.

"Darlink . . . how are you? It is wonderful to see you," Ernest gushed. As he withdrew an immaculately starched handkerchief from his pocket, he sighed and wiped his forehead with it. He looked affluent in a portly sort of way and a little overdressed in the dark grey suit. "Please, excuse me, it is very hot in here," he added.

"Change of life perhaps?" Alix inquired politely.

Jackie grunted something under her breath and Ernest rolled his eyes upwards as though he was looking for help from high above.

"Why do we love her so?" he exclaimed. "I will forgive you, darlink, if you play the klavier for us."

"For you, darlink . . . anythink!" Alix mimicked and followed him across the restaurant, smiling and nodding at a few people she knew.

Ernest instructed the pianist to go and have a drink. To the audience he announced, "Ladies and gentlemen, I give you Madame Alix Clemenger!"

Alix gave him a playful frown. "As a man of the world, Ernest, you should know that no self-respecting 'Madame' would tolerate being 'given' to her customers!"

A round of applause drowned out her voice. As soon as her hands touched the first key, a hushed silence fell over the crowded room. The lights were turned off, except for one spotlight which remained on Alix.

As the first few notes rang out, Tansie's heart began to thump beneath her ribcage at an alarming pace. The wild and wicked mannerisms Alix had displayed earlier on the snow fields and in her conversations had all but disappeared. Tansie was so enthralled by Alix's serene beauty and her mysterious reserve, her breath caught in her throat.

More than anything, she wanted to stretch out her hands and run her fingers over the flawless skin of Alix's face. She wanted to look deep into those green-grey eyes which forever twinkled with amusement, flashed with impatience or smouldered with passion.

She was in awe of Alix's talent and felt a touch of envy. Obviously Alix had experienced a life and opportunities Tansie could only have dreamt about.

Tansie could not remember the last time she had felt so strongly attracted to another human being. There was nothing about Alix she didn't find enchanting. From the dignified way she held her head to the playful way she frowned and let her gaze wander dreamily into the distance.

Tansie shook her head as a tight grip began to clutch at her heart. Such feelings for another woman were not new to her. But what frightened her was their intensity. She took and discarded lovers much like other women bought and discarded stockings. She decided she had to have Alix. With an inward smile, she acknowledged that Alix would be a challenge. Not least of all because she believed Alix had never had a female lover.

Alix played two Chopin études in rapid succession, followed by a short Beethoven sonata and finished with one of her own sonatas. It would have been hard for anybody to imagine a finer performance, despite the less than perfect tone of the piano.

"Wonderful, wonderful, darlink," Ernest cried when she dropped her hands into her lap. "Now tell us *Herzchen*, what was it you played last . . . perhaps Rachmaninoff?"

"It was Clemenger," Alix smiled.

"Such talent . . . such wonderful talent," Ernest exclaimed and reached for both her hands.

"Thank you," Alix smiled graciously and thought, talent and hard work.

She remembered only too well just how hard she had worked at her academic studies and her musical education. At the age of thirteen she had given her first performance with the Berlin Philharmonic and at sixteen she had passed her matriculation. Immediately afterwards, she was accepted at the Conservatorium in Vienna to study under Randolf von Habkern. During those years, she periodically gave concerts around Europe, sometimes on her own and sometimes with her Aunt Hanna, also a concert pianist, but always under the baton of Siggy von Allmen. He had been one of the world's leading conductors and Hanna's husband.

Nobody ever knew what had motivated her to excel in the adult world at such a young age. She had always been able to draw upon enormous resources of energy and strength.

Later when they walked back to the hotel, Tansie instinctively held on to Alix's arm. She felt just a little unsafe on the slippery surface of the hard-packed snow. It also gave her an opportunity to be a little closer to Alix without being obvious about it. "Do you really have a male housekeeper?" she asked.

"Actually, he is much more than just a housekeeper," Alix confirmed. "He's both father and nanny to the children, he's a marvellous chef and runs the whole house like clockwork."

"How many children do you have?"

"I had four," Alix said. "Rhys, my first one, died before he was two years old."

"I'm sorry," Tansie replied, and recognising an undertone of sorrow in Alix's voice, didn't ask any more. "Looking after Alan was quite enough for me! Now of course, I'm glad I never wanted any. I'm not sure I could cope on my own."

"You would if you had to," Alix said.

"Anyway, getting back to Felix. Where did you find such a jewel?" Tansie chuckled. "And, why did you choose a man for the job? That's a bit unconventional, isn't it?"

Alix smiled, a smile Tansie could not see in the dark. She had always leant towards freedom of thought and spirit, with a healthy sense of adventure and a strong need to explore the less conventional aspects of life in general and of music in particular.

"In the past," Alix finally said, "I had many women who helped me with the children and the house. Some were excellent and others were hopeless." After a short pause she continued, "When the Swedish nanny ended up in bed with my husband, I gave up employing female household staff."

"That must have been awful for you," Tansie said with sympathy.

"It was," Alix confirmed. "So when Felix came along, I grabbed him."

"Where did you find him?"

"On safari in the Serengeti Wilderness."

"Oh, really?" Tansie remarked, although she was not sure whether Alix was pulling her leg.

Chapter 2

Most evenings, after dinner at the hotel, the four women strolled through the village to Max's piano bar. Alix and Jackie knew many people who, like themselves, were regulars on the mountain. Others recognised Alix from photos they had seen. Of all the alpine villages, Alix thought that Thredbo had some of the European charm she often missed.

Alix only half-listened to her companions' conversation as she let her eyes roam over the dimly lit cellar room. For a change, she was quite content to just sit and let the world go by. As she relaxed, a tall and lanky redheaded man leaning against the bar caught her eye.

He promptly sauntered towards her and, reaching for her hand, lifted it to his lips.

"My heart breaks at the thought of being unable to bed you this very moment," he drawled in his Irish twang.

"Ohhh? Do you have a problem in that department?" Alix asked without blinking an eyelid.

For a split second, he stared at her and then burst into raucous laughter. "You're not just a pretty face. Witty too! I like that in a woman," he grinned. "By the way, my name is Kennedy. John Fitzgerald Kennedy . . . what's yours?"

"Monroe . . . Marilyn Monroe!"

"Whatever your name is or whoever you are, you'll do me just fine," he cried with amusement. "The real JFK might have been better lookin' an' more famous than me but if it's an excellent lover you want, I'm your man!"

"I'll take your word for it!"

Alix was not looking for a new lover, her current arrangement suited her well enough. Still, she enjoyed their humorous and playful interlude. In the end, she let him down gently without bruising his ego. He soon scanned the room for his next prey.

Swivelling Tansie around on her barstool, he gave her a critical glance before delivering the same speech he had delivered to Alix. He added, "Just before I take you home and make passionate love to you, I think it's only fair to tell you that I have a good little woman and several lads of all sizes at home."

A glance passed between Alix and Jackie. Knowing so little about Tansie, they were curious to find out how she would react.

Tansie's eyes blazed momentarily as she drew her narrow shoulders back defiantly. Then she seemed to change her mind. "I think not," she laughed. "I don't go out with married men!"

"Who said anything about going out?" he exclaimed with mock exasperation. "All I want is a woman for a night or two!"

"Better luck next time," Tansie replied and, reaching for her purse, made a sudden, hasty departure.

"What a shame, she's got real beauty and yet . . ." John said ruefully as he watched her leave.

Alix too made a move to go. "I'll see you back at the hotel," she said to Jackie and left.

Slipping and sliding on the hard-packed snow, Alix caught up with Tansie who seemed to be in a hurry to get back to the hotel. With her head bent down and half-buried in her jacket, she didn't see that she was heading straight for an ice patch. Before Alix could warn her, Tansie's feet flew out from beneath her. Seconds later, she was sprawled out flat on her back.

"I doubt that the missionary position would do for JFK! I'm sure he'd prefer something a little more exotic!" Alix commented and extended her hand.

"God, he was ugly!" Tansie muttered and wound her arm through Alix's for support.

"At least he was honest. And, I thought, rather entertaining."

"I'm glad someone saw the funny side," Tansie replied. After a short pause, she chuckled, "Could you imagine having several children all with red curly hair like him?"

"You'd never lose them in a busy supermarket!"

"I hadn't thought of that," Tansie laughed.

When they got to their room, Tansie said, "I'll finish unpacking if you want to go to the bathroom first."

"Okay," Alix replied. She undressed to her underpants and shirt, and grabbing a T-shirt, disappeared into the adjoining bathroom.

Tansie followed her with her eyes. She smiled when she noted that she could see Alix's mirror image through the half-open door. She watched Alix remove her make-up, brush her teeth and then pull her shirt over her head and unfasten the bra. For the moment or two before Alix slipped her T-shirt over her head, Tansie took in her slender body and her small round breasts. She is even more beautiful without clothes, Tansie thought, but then averted her gaze. She didn't want to be caught out.

Once they were tucked up in their beds, Tansie gave her companion a sideways glance. "How do you do it?" she asked.

"Do what?"

"Joke when some guy makes such a blatant pass at you like the Irishman did," Tansie said. She had become wary of men and the promises they seemed to make and break so easily. "It's not that I mind," she continued more slowly, "I mean, a guy making a pass, I'd just prefer it if it was done with a bit more finesse. He made me feel very cheap."

Alix took some time to reply. "You shouldn't ever feel cheap," she eventually said.

"I wish I had your confidence," Tansie sighed. She leant across the edge of her bed and lightly kissed Alix on the cheek. With a chuckle, she added, "Maybe if I stick around you long enough some might rub off, do you think?"

"Maybe," Alix smiled.

After a brief silence, Tansie asked, "Have you thought about getting married again?"

"I have my moments," Alix said. From time to time she had entertained the idea. In the end she had done nothing about it. She had come to like her single status and the freedom it gave her. "What about you?"

"At this stage, I really don't know. Maybe after Alan, who was really quite untrustworthy, I don't want another husband," Tansie replied. What she didn't say aloud was that, in her mind, the separation from Alan was not per-manent. She was only teaching him a lesson. "But in any event," she chuckled, "while Alan is looking after me well enough financially, there is no need to rush into another marriage. It would just be my luck to end up with another one who'd complain if I stayed in bed all day instead of doing his washing!"

"I suppose not," Alix replied evenly. She could neither imagine being financially dependant on a husband nor staying in bed all day. But, if Tansie chose to do so that was entirely her own business.

"I'm going to sleep. Good night," Tansie murmured and dived under the covers.

"Sleep well," Alix said, switched off the small lamp and folded her hands underneath her head. Tansie's idiosyncratic and contradictory behaviour had been puzzling Alix for a couple of days.

Alix had watched her on more than one occasion quite openly charm whatever man happened to be around. Given her unusual beauty, she had no trouble attracting them. But as soon as they got a little friendlier, she would put them back into their place. Alix wondered whether Tansie was frightened of men or whether it was just insecurity. Or whether she was guarding something, her past maybe? The most simple explanation Alix could think of was that, given Alan was untrustworthy, she had simply lost confidence in men.

As she now thought about her companion, she realised that Tansie had divulged very little about herself other than about more recent times. She had, however, made passing comments such as, "Where I come from this or that was frowned upon" or "I have little contact with my mother in England and my sister up north" but without ever explaining why. And since it was always said in a cut-off manner, Alix never asked for more information. It stirred her curiosity though.

At the end of the week when Alix dropped her off at home, Tansie said with a slight blush to her cheeks, "Thanks for a lovely week, Alix. I had a lot of fun. You were a wonderful companion and most entertaining."

"I enjoyed it too," Alix smiled. As her gaze now held Tansie's, Alix noted a sparkle in her eyes that had not been there at the beginning of their holiday. Alix thought it to be most charming.

Tansie gave her a hug and kissed her cheek. She had wanted to do this all week but given that there had been no real opportunity or reason, she had restrained herself. "Can I give you a ring next week?"

"Hmmm, that's fine," Alix replied and meant it. Although she had no real idea why, she felt very comfortable in Tansie's company.

Tansie watched her leave and then, without bothering to unpack, she ambled into the sitting room. She rewound the tape on the answering machine and pressed the play button. She wanted to hear Alix's voice and hoped that her message was still on the tape and had not been wiped out by another one. Tansie pulled her legs up on to the couch and poured herself a neat scotch from the decanter on the side table.

"Tansie? It's Alix. I'll pick you up at seven o'clock tomorrow morning . . . bye."

Tansie smiled. She liked to hear Alix's voice with its soft melodious tone and the slight trace of an accent. She wondered what it would sound like if Alix ever spoke words of endearment, particularly when in an intimate situation. Would it sound soft and sexy and seductive? She decided that it would.

Barely registering the rest of the messages, her thoughts remained with Alix.

Alix was everything she herself would like to be. Strong and independent and with a keen sense of direction. Not even the fact that she was widowed at an early age seemed to bother her or hinder her in any way. But then, Tansie reasoned, Alix had the three children, a highly successful career, many friends and, for all Tansie knew, even a new man to take her husband's place. As for Alix's privileged upbringing, which she had mentioned in passing, Tansie didn't even dare to contemplate that.

She sure has everything, Tansie now thought. As irrational as such thoughts were, invariably they were followed by thoughts of her own past.

At the age of five Tansie had become a 'child migrant'. She was shipped to Australia with many other British children, outcast and rejected by a seemingly inhumane society. She learnt many things during that long and torturous boat journey. A kiss on a sailor's lips would earn her a piece of chocolate and for a cuddle she was promised a penny or two. A promise that was never kept. Compared to what awaited them in the orphanages once they arrived in Australia, the trip was heaven.

Tansie would never forget the taste of watery cabbage soup and the stench of antiseptic solution, the desolate look of the concrete playground and the high brick walls surrounded by barbed wire. She had never forgotten the terror of the endless physical and emotional abuse she had endured. Even now, thinking about it, she felt the same nausea in the pit of her stomach as she had then.

Days had rarely passed without some sort of punishment. Wetting the bed meant sleeping in a wet sheet for a night. Lying was generally punished with an hour in the pitch-black, mice-infested cellar. But the punishment was rarely consistent with the offence. She lived in terror of being hauled into the Mother Superior's office. There, at least two other nuns watched as Tansie pulled up her skirt and bent over the desk. The bamboo stick was so thin it cut into the soft flesh like a sharp knife. After each beating, she staggered from the room, unable to sit for days. As she grew a little older, she became very cunning in order to evade such punishments.

Although the physical injuries eventually healed, it was the humiliation and helplessness she had suffered which shaped her character and remained deeply embedded in her psyche.

To this day, Tansie never slept alone without a light on. She still feared that some sort of abuse would be heaped upon her in the dark.

As a teenager, she had clung to the hope that one day it would all be over. Happiness would somehow fall into her lap as it had for her older sister Arlene who, after nearly twenty years, was still contentedly married to a wonderful man.

After many traumatic failed relationships with both men and women, Tansie had married Alan at the age of nearly thirty. Finally she had what she had craved for: through marriage to the right man she had made herself acceptable. She had thrived on the respectability that marriage bestowed upon her. That the separation was anything other than temporary never crossed her mind. She was no longer a freak with a background too horrible to speak about and an outcast without a father. A father unknown even to her mother.

Shaking her head as though waking from a deep sleep, Tansie turned her thoughts back to the present.

On impulse, she decided to accept the invitation Alix had extended during their stay in Thredbo. It was to the Melbourne Symphony Orchestra's annual ball that Saturday. Tansie used to like such large and elegant gatherings but, after leaving Alan, she had become wary of them. Without a husband at her side she was a nobody once again. But, because she wanted to see Alix as soon as possible, she decided to go.

"Do I look all right?" Tansie asked as soon as she opened the door for Ian, her escort for the evening of the ball.

"You look stunning," Ian confirmed, adjusting his white silk bow-tie.

She had needed Ian's compliment, but the confidence

it had given her sapped right out of her the moment they arrived at the ballroom. As she passed a few people she knew, she gave them a brief nod. To be with a man other than her husband made her uncomfortable and she hoped that nobody would tell Alan. But she also felt a little intimidated by the pomp and glitter and clung on to Ian's arm as she took tentative steps towards Alix's table.

Alix turned and, as their eyes met, they gazed at each other for a moment. Tansie felt a rush of colour on her cheeks and her heart missed a few beats. She's even more beautiful than I remembered, Tansie thought. The delicate eye make-up highlighted the green colour of her eyes and gave them a dreamy expression. The carmine lipstick accentuated the perfect curve of her lips.

"Hiii . . ." Tansie muttered.

"I'm so glad you came. Let me introduce you to my other guests . . . Jackie, you've already met," Alix said with genuine warmth as she noted how seductively elegant Tansie looked this evening. Her rich, dark chestnut-coloured hair which had obviously been styled for the occasion, was piled up on the top of her head into a mass of curls. It accentuated her fine features, especially her high cheekbones, Alix thought. "You look lovely," she added, taking in the body-hugging sequin top and wide, royal blue gathered skirt. "I like that colour on you . . . you should wear it more often."

Tansie lowered her eyes. "Thank you . . . so do you."

"May I join the admiration society?" Kate asked in the blunt manner her friends loved her for. "I'm Kate Hilton," she added. Casting Tansie a glance, she continued, "Karl Lagerfeld is my favourite designer. This dress looks superb on you."

"Oh, it's not mine. I only borrowed it for the night."

"Who cares as long as it looks great," Kate responded

breezily and motioned for Tansie to sit down next to her.

Before Alix could take her seat again, her escort reached for her hand and drew her to her feet. Towering over her by nearly a foot, Haig slipped his arm around her back as they joined several other couples on the dance floor. They easily picked up the rhythm of a Vienna waltz. The men looked most handsome in their silk evening tails, spotlessly laundered shirts and white starched waistcoats. The women were colourful in their sedately elegant gowns. As the couples swept across the polished floor with the flamboyant gestures a Vienna Waltz required, they all seemed to be engulfed by an air of romance and of times long gone by.

Not sure how to start a conversation with Kate, Tansie let her gaze wander over the dance floor. As her eyes fixed on Alix and her companion, again, her heart took on an erratic beat. Mesmerised, Tansie continued to stare. She admired the fine cut of her sleek emerald-green dress and the way it fitted her tall well-proportioned body. As for Alix's legs they seemed to go on forever. She moved gracefully and confidently to the music as though dancing was all she ever did. Whether it was the way she looked at her partner or the way her hand rested on his shoulder, Tansie didn't know, but the air of sensuous seduction which surrounded Alix was quite breathtaking. The thought of what Alix's fine hands would do if they were ever to touch her, sent a tantalising shiver down her spine. But she also wondered what position Haig took in Alix's life. Judging by the comment Jackie had made during their drive to Thredbo, Tansie could safely assume that he was Alix's lover. What she didn't know was how Alix felt about him. Had Alix been deliberately evasive when they had talked about re-marrying? She would just have to find out in due course, she decided.

"Alix is very beautiful," Tansie said aloud, not addressing anyone in particular.

Kate had heard it but decided not to respond. Instead she let her hand run over the smooth fabric of her pale grey Christian Dior creation. As usual, Kate looked immaculate, right down to her manicured hands. The big diamond earrings which dangled down the sides of her neck, further enhanced her elegance.

"How was your holiday?" Kate asked, taking a generous sip of champagne. "Quite frankly, I'll never understand why anyone would want to go and get their tits frozen off on the top of some rotten mountain."

"It was wonderful," Tansie replied politely. Kate's exuberant manner made her nervous and she too reached for her full glass. "The girls were very kind to me, especially Alix."

"She's tops with a heart of gold. Too good for her own good, if you know what I mean," Kate confirmed.

After a moment's silence, Tansie said, "Haig's a very attractive man . . . Alix is a very lucky woman."

"She deserves the best," Kate replied, but wondered nonetheless whether there was some sort of inquiry behind Tansie's statement. Had Tansie taken a fancy to Haig? He was, after all, a most eligible man, Kate thought. What was obvious, though not surprising, was that Alix had told Tansie little about herself. Kate did not always agree with Alix's need for privacy but respected it nevertheless. Maybe if she were as famous as Alix she might feel the same, Kate acknowledged with a smile and without envy.

A short while later when they were all on the dance floor, Kate observed Tansie dancing first in Haig's arms and then with Jackie's partner. Tansie gazed at both men with large luminous eyes as she lightly ran her hand over their shoulders. Kate even heard an occasional seductive chuckle as it emanated from Tansie's throat.

"I hope she doesn't have anything serious in mind," Kate muttered and drew her eyebrows upwards. Tansie's earlier interest in Haig did not sit well with her. Kate knew that Alix and Haig had been friends and lovers for many years and, although there had been no talk of marriage, Kate believed that it was still a possibility. The thought of Tansie trying to move in on Haig made her shiver. Something about Tansie bothered her. Kate recognised that Tansie was quite timid, but provocative at the same time. She also saw how easily her unusual beauty attracted people and how easily they seemed to respond to her. For Alix's sake, she hoped that Haig would not be one of them.

When Kate went to the powder room to freshen up her make-up, she caught the tail end of a conversation about Tansie. She smiled. She would never talk from behind a closed lavatory door, nor for that matter at the beauty parlour. She was not generally interested in gossip but, now, she couldn't help but hear what was said. She had noticed earlier that Tansie knew a few people and Kate was curious to find out a little about Tansie's reputation. Kate stood in front of the large mirror, and gazing at her image, pretended to decide what colour lipstick to use. She always carried three in her purse.

"Sue, do you know any of the people Tansie's with?" Kate heard one woman ask from behind a closed cubicle door.

"Other than Alix Clemenger, no," Sue replied. "I haven't seen her for months and . . ."

"Neither have I, but you know what Tansie's like," her companion interrupted, adding slowly, "she's always finding new friends and dumping them again."

"Yeah . . . strange, isn't it?"

How interesting, Kate thought. Whoever the two women were, they obviously had been Tansie's friends once upon a time and had suffered the fate they described. Not wanting to be there when the women emerged, Kate settled on the soft pink lipstick and quickly applied it. Moments later she returned to the ballroom, putting the conversation she had overheard to the back of her mind.

After the ball, Kate invited everybody back to her house for a night cap. Only Tansie and Ian declined.

Alix watched Tansie leave and smiled when she saw her bending down and taking off her shoes. The gesture reminded her of her children. They always walked around in barefeet even in the middle of winter.

"What do you think of Alix?" Tansie asked as soon as Ian had taken off his tail coat, deposited it on the back seat and pulled out of the parking lot.

"She's got great legs!"

"You men are all the same! If the legs and tits are good, nothing else seems to matter," Tansie groaned with some distaste. "What about Haig . . . isn't he one of the most handsome men you've ever seen?"

Ian laughed. "I didn't notice." He gave his companion a sideways glance and added, "Don't you women have a rule that you never go after someone else's boyfriend or husband?"

"Who said anything about going after Haig!" She chuckled seductively.

"What? You mean you and Alix?"

"No darling, I mean you of course," she said and let her hand slide over his thigh.

Chapter 3

Haig sat down on the bed and reached out for Alix's hand. He drew her towards him so that she came to stand between his legs. As he curved his hands around her slim waist, she bent down and kissed him. Their lips met and Alix felt a shiver sweep down her spine and lodge at the base of it.

They undressed, slipped between the crisp sheets and moved into each other's embrace. Even after nearly twenty years, Haig still excited her as much as he had in the beginning but, now, the hesitancy of the first time was long gone. There was no uncertainty as to what each wanted. Their bodies were finely tuned.

Later, with small beads of perspiration on his forehead and his eyes closed, he rested his head on her chest.

"Have I made up for my bad performance last week?" he drawled in the semi-American accent he had acquired.

"Bad performance?" she drawled in the same manner. When he winced, she ruffled his hair and added, "You have . . . champagne?"

Haig watched her retrieve a bottle from the small refrigerator in his wardrobe and wondered whether he had made a mistake years ago in not asking her to marry him. He had always been aware of how passionately she had loved him and of how much he must have hurt her. Yet, something had always prevented him from asking her. To this day he did not know what it was. But then, he rationalised, he had never asked anyone else to marry him either. Now, she seemed as content with their arrangement as he was.

Sitting cross-legged and opposite each other, they drank champagne and chatted, catching up on the news. A feeling of comfortable intimacy engulfed them as an occasional laugh rippled from their chests.

After a while, she snuggled back into his arms. When his lips gently trailed down to her nipples, she held his head in both hands. The feeling he evoked in her was so exquisite she didn't want him to stop.

Alix curled closer into his arms and sighed. Her lips slowly formed into a half-moon when she murmured, "I chose well all those years ago when I decided to make you my first lover."

"You didn't say that a few days ago," he teased.

"There's always room for error," she quipped.

As Haig continued to fondle her, Alix let her thoughts drift back to when they had met.

She had been introduced to Haig at a bankers' dinner in Zürich. She had just turned twenty-one and had only recently returned from Vienna. With fondness she now reflected on their very first meeting and the conversation they had had.

Alix remembered commenting on his rather unusual first name, to which he had replied, "Knowing how much my mother loved Scotch, it could have been worse. She could have called me 'Dimple'!" Whether it had been his sense of humour or his handsome elegant looks which reminded her of her father, she didn't know. She had fallen instantly in love with him.

Their love affair had continued for nearly three years. As turbulent and traumatic as their relationship was, mostly caused by their infrequent meetings, she was prepared for the first time in her life to surrender her freedom. But not so he. The day finally came, however, when she could stand it no longer. When she was invited to the Juilliard School of Music in New York, she accepted.

A year later she was invited back to Australia to compose the music for a documentary film. Haig was still very much on her mind but she forced herself not to contact him. Although her love for him had not wavered, she married Michael Clemenger six months later.

Some five years into her marriage, a marriage which was already on the brink of disaster, she met Haig again. Though she struggled with herself for a long time, she eventually embarked on another wild and passionate affair with him. Alix despised cheating, whether it be on a lover or a husband. In that instance and because she had felt so neglected both physically and emotionally by Michael, she had been able to justify it in the end. She had made sure, however, that Michael never knew about it. He had never given her the same respect and his liaisons had always been, not common knowledge, but conducted with less than utmost discretion.

Years later when she found out that she was pregnant for the fourth time, she once again refused to see Haig. She felt she owed it to herself and the children to make one last attempt to keep the marriage going.

After Michael's death, however, it was only a matter of time before she and Haig resumed their relationship. She still loved him and could not imagine the day when she wouldn't. They now shared the sort of love that comes with maturity. The often destructive and raging desire she had experienced when she was young was no longer there. Since Haig spent most of his time overseas, they only saw each other intermittently, which suited them both. It allowed Alix the freedom she needed but still gave her the comforting knowledge that someone somewhere in the world genuinely cared.

31

Alix was brought back to reality when, having gone to sleep, Haig moved away from her. She shivered and, pulling the sheet up to her chin, she too drifted off. The following Monday Alix drove him to the airport. He was returning to New York via Hong Kong. Knowing that they would not see each other again for several weeks, maybe months, they kissed languidly and only drew away when it was time for Haig to leave.

Before that week was out, Tansie rang Alix to ask if she would meet her for a coffee in the Toorak Village where she had a hairdresser's appointment later. Alix too had an hour or so before she was due at the concert hall and said she'd be at Romano's within a few minutes.

Alix was there first and, after ordering a cappuccino, sat down at the small corner table. Seemingly far away with her thoughts, she studied her hands and wrists. They were long and slim, their skin soft and the nails polished with a light red colour. The jewellery she wore on her wrists and fingers was simple. She was dressed in her favourite pair of Valentino jeans, a pale blue cotton shirt and a delicately checked Escada blazer. On her feet she wore Italian leather slip-on shoes of which she had a pair in almost every colour. Her light tan trenchcoat was flung over the back of an empty chair.

Alix was so engrossed in her musings, she didn't hear or see Tansie when she arrived moments later.

"You have beautiful hands, Alix," Tansie murmured, and bending down to kiss her on the cheek, casually let her own hand rest on one of Alix's. She wore the same jeans and sweater she had worn the day they went to the snow, Alix noted with a smile.

"Thank you." Alix lifted her gaze as she instinctively withdrew her hand. Tansie's simple gesture of affection and familiarity unsettled her just a little. She was not uncomfortable with such gestures but rather taken aback, especially when they were made by a woman she barely knew.

She reached for her packet of Davidoff cigarettes and lit one. Although they always seemed to be quite casual, Alix had observed on previous occasions that Tansie was generous with her affections towards her. She wondered whether that was simply the way Tansie was or whether she had been singled out.

However, before she could dwell on it further, Tansie started to chat about their recent ski holiday and how much she had loved it.

"I hope you didn't mind too much that I didn't ski too well and that you often had to wait for me," Tansie concluded a little shyly.

"Not at all," Alix responded. "In fact, I was most impressed with the improvements you made during the week. At that rate, you'll soon fly down the mountains."

"I doubt it," Tansie laughed. "But thanks for saying so. You're very kind."

"My patience is normally minimal when it comes to teaching other people skills I've learnt years ago," she admitted with a smile. "But, somehow you seemed to have been able to stretch it just that little bit further."

"So I've noticed," Tansie grinned.

As they were leaving the coffee shop and were walking to Alix's car, Tansie hesitated briefly before she asked, "The Rivoli is showing a movie I'd like to see, would you be interested in coming along?"

On impulse, Alix wanted to turn her down. She didn't have enough time to spend with her friends, let alone with someone she barely knew. "Why not," she eventually said. "I haven't seen a film for ages." Mentally checking what free nights she had available, she added, "How about Wednesday next week?"

"I'm free," Tansie confirmed.

Revving up the engine of her white Mercedes sports car, Alix said, "I'll meet you at the theatre half an hour before the movie starts . . . okay?"

Tansie nodded and watched Alix back out of the car park and drive off. Now she had something to look forward to, she thought as she ambled towards the hairdresser's. Two hours later when Alfredo had finally finished with her hair and Maria had polished her nails, Tansie stood up and briefly glanced at her mirror image. Her dark chestnut-coloured hair was now much shorter than she had worn it for some time. It was perfectly cut and waved and gave her a more youthful appearance. The eye make-up she had applied earlier in the day was bold but immensely becoming. The lips were painted a rich red colour to match the polish on her fingernails.

Although she was satisfied with what she saw in the mirror, her thoughts turned to Alix. Alix seemed to gleam with confidence and exuded an air of such worldly sophistication and youthful flamboyance, she could not help a feeling of insecurity taking hold of her. She wondered how she could measure up to Alix. She would find a way, she decided then and there. Her step had a light spring to it when she left Alfredo's.

The following Wednesday, Tansie arrived at the cinema before Alix. She was waiting outside when Alix came flying around the corner, out of breath, her elegant cashmere coat flapping around her legs.

"I'm sorry I'm late," Alix apologised as she took in Tansie's new hair style. "Your hair suits you like that, you look terrific." Raking her own short mop of unruly curls, she said, "Unfortunately there's not much I can do with this lot."

"You look cute," Tansie grinned and only just stopped herself from ruffling Alix's hair.

With some amusement, Alix rolled her eyes at Tansie but didn't reply. She couldn't remember the last time someone had called her cute but thought it was probably at least thirty years ago.

During the movie, Alix and Tansie periodically glanced sideways at one another, but their eyes never met. As Alix became more and more mesmerised by Tansie – her unusual beauty and her ready laughter at most things Alix said, Tansie became more and more aware of Alix – the subtle sexuality she exuded and her own strong reaction to it.

Much to Tansie's chagrin, Alix had to leave straight after the film. She only felt better when Alix agreed to have lunch with her the following week. As she ambled to her own car, Tansie acknowledged that where Alix was concerned, she was not feeling very patient. But, she reminded herself, rushing things would probably get her nowhere.

It wasn't until much later that Alix asked herself why she had so readily agreed to have lunch with Tansie. She didn't like going out to lunch and resented the time she had to be away from work. Why had she made an exception for Tansie and even cancelled a couple of appointments for the early afternoon? Alix had no explanation other than that she enjoyed her company.

Shortly before lunch, Alix returned to her office after another harrowing board-meeting with Michael's family's company, Clemenger Pharmaceuticals.

Jenny, her long-time secretary, handed her a bundle of telephone messages and said, "John would like to see you when you have a minute. And Svetlana rang to ask if you were free to have dinner with her and Boris this evening."

"Am I free?" Alix asked, hoping that she was. She always enjoyed the evenings she spent with Svetlana and Boris Rostoff. In fact she had a very soft spot for both of them. Boris, because he was one of the best conductors she had ever worked with and continued to work with whenever possible. He was currently the visiting conductor for the Melbourne Symphony Orchestra. And Svetlana, because Alix loved her unpredictable and highly charged gypsy temperament.

"You are," Jenny confirmed with a smile.

"Would you ring Svetlana back and tell her that I'll be there?" Alix replied absent-mindedly and read the first message. 'Can't make it for lunch but call in for a drink after work if you can – Tansie'. With impatience, she crushed the piece of paper in her hand and threw it into the rubbish bin. She disliked being stood up. On impulse, she wanted to ask Jenny to ring Tansie back and tell her that she was too busy. Moments later, she decided to think about it.

Reading the next message, she smiled. It was from Laura informing Alix that she was ready to quit as the Managing Director of Atrix Recording if she had to put up with another temper tantrum from Johnny-Superstar. Alix received such messages almost weekly. Still, they never ceased to amuse her; mostly because Laura was as dramatic and temperamental as was her wiry mop of wild black curls. Even some of the pop-stars Laura dealt with paled in her shadow, Alix thought.

Alix had hired Laura the same day she bought the down and out Atrix Recording company. She smiled as she now recalled their very first conversation. Even before Alix had a chance to tell Laura what the job entailed, Laura had brazenly informed her that she lived with Mia. Alix had assured Laura that this was entirely her own business. In her view, this was not even an issue for discussion, neither then nor now.

Just before she entered her own office, Alix looked over her shoulder and said, "Jenny, would you ring Laura and tell her that I'll see her first thing in the morning. The Clemenger boys were quite enough for one day. By the way, has the travel agent delivered my ticket yet?"

"Yes, it's on your desk," Jenny replied.

Taking off her grey pin-striped jacket, Alix folded it neatly over the back of the couch and kicked off her high-heel patent-leather shoes. She rarely wore those shoes for any other occasion than for board-meetings with the Clemenger boys. She knew she could take them on, on an intellectual level – theirs were quite limited, but to compete with their burly figures she needed the extra height.

Despite the miserable winter's day, her music room was bright with its french doors and expansive windows overlooking the vast manicured lawn and swimming pool. The room itself, painted a light yellow colour, was elegantly furnished and everything was arranged in an orderly manner. The concert grand piano assumed a prominent position near the windows. The antique writing desk stood in front of the wall-to-wall bookshelves. A large oil portrait of her father hung over the open fireplace and numerous photos of her children stood scattered on the mantelpiece. They included several pictures of her first-born child, Rhys. He had been a beautiful baby and when he had suddenly died from complications after minor surgery just before he turned two, she too had wanted to die. Soon after his death, when she found out that she was pregnant again, she had seriously contemplated having an abortion. If anything should happen to this baby, she knew she would not survive it. Without Kate's help and encouragement, Alix knew that she would never have had another baby. Now, of course, a life without children was unimaginable.

A smaller oil painting of her aunt Hanna hung on the wall between the French doors. It was always on that picture that Alix's eyes rested for just a bit longer. Even before Alix's mother had died, Hanna had occupied an important part in her life. Years later when they had toured the concert stages around the world and performed together, Hanna had become her friend, her mentor and the mother Alix had never really had. Hanna was passionate, warm, outgoing and selfless whereas her mother had been withdrawn, cold, selfish and passionless. When Alix was much younger, her mother's indifference had caused her a great deal of pain. But so had her own feelings of resentment towards her mother. As Alix had grown and become a woman herself, Alix's feelings changed to immense sorrow for the woman who had never felt real love, passion or pain for that matter. When Alix came to truly understand what an emotionally lonely, isolated and miserable life her mother must have lived, through no fault of her own, Alix eventually found it in her heart to forgive her. And with that forgiveness, Alix set herself free from all the resentment and guilt she had suffered.

After depositing her slim burgundy briefcase on the desk, she wandered into the studio of her writing partner. She found him balancing his tall willowy frame on his high stool behind the electronic keyboard and talking on the telephone. Every time she caught him in that position, she wondered when he would topple over and crash through the glass doors behind him. Alix believed it was only a matter of time.

John gave her a languid grin and into the telephone he joked, "Gotta go, love . . . the boss's arrived . . . I'll see you soon."

His conversation was not lost on Alix. "Don't you ever get tired of chasing women?" she asked.

"Not as long as they make it worth my while," he responded smartly as he stroked his blond moustache. His pale blue eyes reminded Alix of an early morning winter sky. "You should see this one," he added longingly as he rolled his eyes. "She has just joined the Victorian State Opera and, oh boy, has she got breasts!" He indicated the size of her chest with both his hands.

"What's her voice like?"

"How would I know?" John grinned. "We do many things together but we don't sing in the shower!"

Alix nodded with unusual patience as she let her gaze wander over the chaos in John's studio. Sadly she thought what a brilliant musician and composer he could be if only he put his life and mind into some sort of order. Over the years she had hoped that one day he would, but that day never came. Yet, she had to admit that over the years they had composed some of the most wonderful film music. The numerous trophies on the side-bench were proof of that.

They worked on John's latest composition until Jenny buzzed him to remind him of his luncheon date. He left moments later and Alix returned to her own studio.

She sat down at the piano but before she could strike the first key, John's blond head appeared around the door.

"By the way, remember the film score we wrote for Ralph Schönberg's movie *Let Yesterday Be*?" John said playfully, "it received an Oscar nomination for best original music score a couple of weeks ago."

"And you forgot to tell me? After all the effort we put into composing the music?" Alix cried, picking up a bundle of sheet music and throwing it in his general direction. "You keep that up and you'll get yourself fired one day," she added in jest but he had already gone.

Still shaking her head, Alix collected the scattered notes, put them back on the music stand and sat down again on the piano stool.

To warm up, she played a few scales and then ventured into some Chopin études. Her hands moved gracefully over the shiny keys and, with her head tilted to one side, she silently formed the tunes she was playing on her lips. Normally, she soon lost herself in the music. For a reason she could not immediately think of, today her mind seemed to be cluttered with thoughts of Tansie. Was it perhaps the light and charming tunes of the music she was playing that reminded her of Tansie's easy laughter? She acknowledged that there was certainly something about Tansie that she felt herself drawn to. Just what that something was, she didn't know and neither did it particularly matter to her. By the time she moved to playing one of her own compositions that still needed some work done on it, she decided to accept Tansie's invitation for a drink that evening. Tansie lived only a few streets away from Boris, which meant she wouldn't have to cut her working hours too short.

Later, Alix showered, applied her evening make-up and changed into an elegant but slinky white jersey dress. Then she went in search of the children. They were all in the cosy, French provincial kitchen, waiting for Felix to serve dinner.

"How is Frau Mozart this evening?" her older son Drew asked. He reached across the kitchen bench for a hamburger, but withdrew his hand when Felix gave him a tap with a wooden spoon. With a playful frown, Drew added, "No violence in this house, please, Felix."

"Quite right, sir," Felix joked.

"She's fine, thank you," Alix replied to her son's question and gave Felix an approving smile. She was respectful of the work he did for her and the compassionate care and understanding with which he treated the children. So far she had never had a single reason to undermine his authority and she knew that the children shared her feelings. They were much more attached to him than they had ever been to their father. Michael had always treated them with indifference, at best, and blatant disrespect for their feelings, at worst.

Felix was a rugged man of above-average height with alert, intelligent blue eyes and black curls which had started to go grey at the temples. He too spoke several languages fluently, including Arabic and Bantu which he had learnt during his many years in North Africa and Kenya. He always looked distinguished. The dark suits, white shirts, discreetly coloured waistcoats and bow-ties he wore when shopping or taking the children to school were tailormade from the finest fabrics. His looks were masculine yet sensitive and he instilled confidence and trust in everybody he met.

To prepare and serve dinner to the children, he always took off his jacket. He put on an immaculately laundered floor-length apron much like the waiters wore in Parisian restaurants.

Turning her attention back to Drew, Alix asked, "How's school?"

"I don't know why I have to go to school!" Drew grumbled in response. "Dad never finished uni and he still made millions."

"He did at that." Alix readily agreed with her son but sighed.

Drew looked and behaved more like his father every day. He had the same sparkling blue eyes, broad shoulders, narrow hips and long muscular legs. As for his mannerisms, they were very much like Michael's. This frightened Alix at times. She didn't want him to grow up to be as shallow as his father and never find real happiness. Nor did she want him to take to the superficial world of the idle rich like Michael had.

Alix bent down to kiss her younger son, Christian, when her daughter came flying through the door.

At nearly twelve, Sara was still petite and her body had not yet started to fill out. Her dark brown hair was in its usual disarray around her delicately boned face. Her soft green-grey eyes smouldered like her mother's.

"I just scored the title role in the school play," Sara announced, blinking her long black eyelashes in a dramatic manner.

"Congratulations, darling. That's wonderful," Alix replied and gave her a hug. She was pleased for her daughter and had no doubt that one day she'd be a great actress. Or perhaps an opera singer, Alix thought with a smile.

"Can I take drama lessons now? Please, Mum?" Sara asked.

"What for?" Drew chirped. "You'd be dangerous if you were any more dramatic!"

"Why don't you mind your own business . . . you . . ." Sara responded but Alix interrupted her.

"I'll make some inquiries," Alix promised and kissed them one after the other. To Felix she said, "I'll be at Boris' if you need me."

"Ahhh . . . having dinner with your favourite 'Ruskie' conductor," Drew grinned and gave her a knowing smile. "Why don't you marry him? Then you can drool over him all day and all night long."

"Since he's happily married to Svetlana, I'll give him a miss but thanks for the suggestion," Alix laughed good-naturedly and left.

Chapter 4

It was weeks since Tansie had even noticed the packets of wet clay, the numerous pieces of different sized and shaped wood, sandstone and marble she kept scattered on the kitchen floor. Her working habits had always been erratic even at the best of times. Certainly in the past, she had blamed Alan for this. He often demanded she spend time with him when he was home. But then he never showed any real interest in her creativity, nor did he ever understand it. His mind was geared to making money and not to appreciating art. However, in more recent times, it was either her lack of self-discipline or her low mood that kept her away from her work. When one of those moods really hit her, she even went so far as to destroy some of the sculptures she had created. Afterwards, she always regretted it.

However, since returning from her week's holiday in the snow, she seemed to have more energy and was in higher spirits. If Alix was going to visit later, she wanted to at least look as though she was busy. It was bad enough that she had let it slip on one occasion that she often stayed in bed all day. Alix didn't have to find her there.

As her slim fingers now worked the soft clay statue in front of her, she smiled. She was making excellent progress with it, and once it was cast in bronze, she was sure it would look fantastic. She was very pleased with her effort and she hoped that Alix would be too.

Tansie had given a great deal of thought to what she could possibly create that would appeal to Alix. She had decided on a statue of a conductor. She had never been to a concert and therefore knew little about conductors, hence the local library reference books that lay open on the bench beside her.

As she continued working, her thoughts turned to Alix. For some time now, she had contemplated making a portrait of Alix. Although she had little experience working with marble, she knew that to do justice to Alix's image, she had to make it from a stone that was as flawless as Alix. She could feel excitement rise inside her at the thought of creating Alix's beautiful face. A face so smooth, lovely and warm, she could almost feel it come alive under her fingertips. No, she suddenly decided. She wouldn't start this creation just yet. There was no rush and she wanted to savour the anticipation just a little while longer.

Tansie was pleased that her creative energy had taken an up-turn. Having met some of Alix's friends who held powerful positions or were raising several children or even doing both, her own inadequacies had begun to distress her. It turned out, however, that this distress was just the sort of push she needed. She too had a talent, she decided, and could keep up with any of those women despite her limited education.

She wiped her fringe from her forehead with the back of her hand. A few clumps of clay caught in her hair and stayed there. Her denim overalls and red T-shirt looked as though they hadn't seen a washing machine in weeks. Only her work tools were kept in some sort of order on the bookshelf behind her.

When she heard footsteps on the floorboards in the hall, she called out, "I'm in the kitchen." Moments later, Steven wrapped his arms around her.

"What're you doing here?" Tansie asked with a touch of

annoyance and pushed him away. For the first time since she'd taken him as a regular lover, she thought that the moment had come to get rid of him. He was married, after all, and could offer her nothing more than what all married men could, sex.

"What I do most days on my way home from work," he grinned, trying to pull her into his arms.

"I'd rather you left. I'm waiting for . . ."

"I know . . . that new mate of yours," he grunted in a less than friendly manner. "Ever since you met this dame, the infamous Ms Clemenger, you've talked about nothing else but her! You don't even like classical music, so what does . . ."

The sound of a discreet cough made them both spin around.

"I didn't mean to barge in on you but the front door was open," Alix said, looking from Tansie to her companion.

"What a beauty!" Steven whistled, taking in Alix's elegant figure.

"Don't be disgusting," Tansie scolded, adding, "Steven was just leaving . . . I'll be right back." She gave him another push and shoved him out the door.

Left alone, Alix stood in the middle of the room and let her gaze wander curiously from the big old-fashioned kitchen through the open double doors into the sitting room and the hallway beyond. Suddenly she felt very cold and drew up her shoulders. There was no heating but that was not the cause of her discomfort. Glancing around again she noted that, other than the basic furniture, both rooms were virtually empty. The bookshelves and walls were bare too. Alix couldn't imagine what it was like to live in such a dreary place. Depressing, she thought. Why would anybody want to live in such sparse, cold surroundings? Certainly in

Tansie's case, she knew that it was not because of lack of money. Alan gave Tansie a very generous allowance. What Alix couldn't know was that this house, in Tansie's mind, was only a temporary abode as was her separation from Alan.

Alix took off her coat and went to collect some firewood from the front porch. When Tansie came back, the fire was lit and soon spread some real warmth through the room.

"Thanks for lighting the fire," Tansie said, and collecting some drinks and glasses from the kitchen, returned to the sitting room.

For a little while, Tansie did most of the talking. She was nervous about having cancelled their lunch date and now didn't want Alix to ask any questions about it. She was good at making plausible excuses and made them frequently. However, she wasn't sure whether Alix would be as easily convinced as most other people.

Tansie took a large sip of straight scotch and sighed. "I needed that," she said. "How is the new movie score coming along?"

"Fine," Alix replied just as her eyes caught sight of a few statues which stood on the table in the large bay window. Approaching the table, she asked, "Did you make those?"

"I'm still learning . . . they're not very good," Tansie replied.

"They are exquisite," Alix exclaimed, casting them an admiring glance. She picked up each piece, studied it and then carefully put it back. Some were finely carved wood statues, their surfaces highly polished and shiny. Others were crafted from sandstone and some were bronze casts. There was something vibrantly energetic about all of them but in particular the two ballet dancers. "Have you ever had an exhibition?" she asked, turning towards Tansie and studying her for a moment.

Tansie looked particularly lovely this evening, Alix thought, despite her grubby workclothes. The light from the small lamp which stood on the table next to her cast delicate shadows over Tansie's face and gave it a soft glow. Her hair too seemed more glossy and lustrous than Alix remembered it. She smiled, thinking that if she were an artist she would want to capture Tansie and the mood of that very moment without delay, probably in water colours and in soft shades of blue and grey. However, she remembered just how useless she was with a paintbrush and discarded the thought.

"Good God no!" Tansie cried, flabbergasted at the mere thought. She remembered only too well the disparaging comments Alan had always passed. She didn't need any more from people who'd understand more about art than he did.

"I'm on the board of the Fundraising Committee for the Blind Institute," Alix said. "Why don't I get you an invitation to submit some of your work for consideration for the next exhibition?"

"Please don't . . . I'd die of embarrassment to have all those people staring and laughing at them!" She took another generous sip of scotch and then continued. "One of my friends, Julie Pizzy, tried and was knocked back. She's much better than I am . . . even Alan said so."

"I remember her sculptures," Alix mused. "The committee decided unanimously that they were not good enough."

"Don't ever say that to her," Tansie giggled. "She doesn't like you much anyway . . . she thinks you're a snob!"

"Fair enough." Alix gave her a hint of a smile. She was not in the least perturbed by what other people said or thought of her.

"Julie was a typist at the modelling agency I used to work for," Tansie volunteered. With a raise of her eyebrows, she added, "It wasn't until she started living with Margret that she decided to try her artistic talents."

"Maybe she should have stayed a secretary," Alix commented without malice. "Anyway, think about the exhibition. In the meantime I've got to run or I'll be late for my dinner date."

"How's Haig?"

Alix smiled. The question was not very subtle. "He's fine and, I expect, back in New York by now. I'm having dinner with Boris Rostoff."

"Am I supposed to know who this Boris guy is?" Tansie asked. There was a distinct tremble in her voice but Tansie hoped that Alix wouldn't pick up on it. She was frustrated that she still knew so little about Alix and her private life in particular. Was Boris another one of her lovers?

"No, not necessarily," Alix laughed, totally unaware of Tansie's feelings and thoughts. "He's the visiting conductor for the Melbourne Symphony Orchestra."

"Now you'll really think I'm dumb!"

"Not at all. At least you knew who Mendelssohn was."

"I did at that," Tansie grinned.

As the two women walked to the front door, Tansie draped an arm around Alix's shoulders. Turning to her and taking in Alix's already familiar scent, Tansie felt a shiver run down her back. She felt exhilarated in Alix's presence and smiled. She wanted to touch her. She wanted much more than to just put an arm around her shoulders. Alix was so beautiful, her hair golden in the bright porch light and her eyes sparkled like two stars in the dark sky. Tansie wondered how long she could bear not to kiss her, not to embrace her.

Tansie's smiling, sultry gaze held Alix's for a moment. Her gaze said more than any words could but Alix didn't recognise the message. Tansie's voice was soft but husky when she said, "Somehow I feel as though I have known you for a long time . . . my life isn't so empty any more." After a short pause, Tansie continued, "It's strange, I know, I mean I've only known you for a few weeks and yet . . ." she let her voice trail off. Although she found it very difficult not to go on, she knew that it was far too soon to say more.

Although Alix thought the remark was a trifle strange, she didn't say so. She wondered, yet again, how such an attractive, charming and intelligent woman could possibly be so alone. On impulse, she wanted to put her arms around her much as she would with a small child. She wanted to comfort her, tell her that nobody should feel this alone. She didn't, reminding herself that Tansie was an adult woman.

"You know that music you played in the car when we drove to the mountains, it was one of your compositions, I think. It was beautiful and will always remind me of you," Tansie said thoughtfully.

"It was my Symphony No. 1, the *Children's Symphony*," Alix confirmed. She had started to compose it soon after Rhys' death and finished it during her second pregnancy. The *adagio*, the first movement, was as slow and sorrowful as her son's death. The grief had poured out of her like a waterfall and had become a strikingly original composition. The piano solos were as amazing as they were unusual. The *allegretto*, the second movement, was a lively dialogue between herself and her unborn child, between the piano and the orchestra. And the *allegro*, the last movement, had all the speed of a baby arriving into the world with considerable impatience.

"Unfortunately," Tansie continued, "music was never part of my upbringing. Except for the stodgy hymns we were forced to sing in church!"

"If it's any comfort, my education stopped short of the church. I believe in dial-a-prayer if necessary," Alix said.

Chuckling and kissing Alix on both cheeks, Tansie asked, "You're very entertaining . . . how about having lunch soon? Maybe sometime next week?"

Alix was about to remind her that she had already cancelled one such date but thought better of it. "We can, but not for at least a couple of weeks. I'm leaving for Europe on Thursday."

"How wonderful," Tansie cried. "You don't need someone to carry your bags or something, do you?"

"It's mostly business," Alix laughed. "I'll be lucky if I get half a day off to go shopping." Or, she thought, to spend a night with Haig. When she spoke to him a couple of days earlier, he had promised to try and meet her in Paris for a day or so.

"What a shame," Tansie said, a tone of sadness in her voice.

Alix was about to say that perhaps one day Tansie could go with her but stopped herself in time. She couldn't think of a single reason why that thought had entered her head. It flustered her just a little. Instead she said, "I'd better go or I'll be really late for my dinner date. I'll see you when I get back."

"Okay," Tansie replied and watched Alix stroll down the driveway to her Mercedes sports car. She waited until Alix had pulled away from the curb and the tail lights had disappeared into the distance before she closed the door.

The thought of Alix away in Europe left her feeling sad and empty. Without another thought, she padded into the bathroom, swallowed three sleeping tablets and went to bed.

Closing her eyes and snuggling into the soft pillows, her thoughts returned to Alix. The scent of Alix's perfume – Oscar de la Renta, Tansie thought – still lingered in the air.

Although she regularly took men to bed, her real desire was for women. She could not remember a time when making love with a man had been particularly pleasant or satisfactory. Men were there to give her an identity, to give her a sense of belonging, to make her whole. Without a man she was nothing. She remembered only too clearly her childhood when she had been ignored. Just another child without a father, without a name.

Tansie's real longing was for Alix. So far nothing Alix had said or done had indicated even the vaguest interest in having a relationship with her. In fact, the more she knew of Alix, Tansie was sure that Alix was quite naive in such matters. And, Tansie suspected, Alix would possibly take quite unkindly to the idea.

Over the two weeks Alix was in Europe, Tansie had bouts of highs and lows. Some mornings, as she woke, she dived right back under the covers. On those days nothing could induce her to get out of bed. The thought of another endless day and another one after that without Alix was almost unbearable.

Other mornings, she bustled about long before daylight and worked on her sculptures. She chiselled away at the marble portrait of Alix she had now started or she worked on the statue of the conductor who began to look more and more like Boris Rostoff. After Alix had mentioned Boris, Tansie searched for some photos of him as well as of Alix from newspaper archives. Both statues were coming along exceptionally well. She was most pleased with her efforts.

In the evenings, she saw people she hadn't seen for a while and read all the books on classical music she could lay her hands on. Since music appeared to be at least one love in Alix's life, she wanted to try and learn something about it. At the local music store she bought half a dozen discs.

But early one morning, when she couldn't stand Alix's absence any longer, she tracked her down in Paris.

"Hello?" Alix said when she answered the telephone in her suite at the George V Hotel.

"Hiii . . . it's me," Tansie drawled a little shyly.

"How are you?" Alix gave Haig who was standing in front of the mirror a quizzical look. "Is something wrong? Are you okay?"

"Yeah . . . I'm fine," Tansie replied. "I just wanted to say hello. Did I disturb you . . . are you busy?"

"Not really," Alix said. "But what are you doing up at this hour? It must be six o'clock in the morning."

"I couldn't sleep," Tansie muttered, loving the sound of Alix's voice. "I'd better let you go. You must have a million things to do. I'll talk to you when you get back."

As Tansie hung up the telephone and rolled on to her back at her end of the world, Alix slowly replaced the receiver.

"Strange," she said to herself.

"Is everything all right at home?" Haig asked, concerned rather than curious. "Nothing wrong with the children, is there?"

"No," Alix replied. "That was Tansie."

"Ohhh?" Haig drew up his eyebrows. After a moment's consideration, he added, "I don't know what she's all about but when she danced with me at the ball, she . . ."

Alix laughed. "She made a pass at you?"

"You could call it that."

53

"She's got excellent taste, I must give her that," Alix teased. "While she might have flattered your ego, I'm sure there's nothing to worry about. I think she's just lonely, maybe even a bit depressed. She told me that she hasn't come to terms with the separation from Alan. She'll sort through all that in due course, I suppose."

"There's something about her that seems to be getting to you," Haig continued, having picked up on an undertone of uncertainty in Alix's voice. "I hate to sound unfeeling, but she is a grown woman and, I expect, perfectly capable of taking care of herself."

Alix put her arms around his neck and snuggled against his broad chest. Although she didn't know why, she now needed the warmth of his body. "You're probably right," she murmured. "But still, she reminds me of a child who's . . ."

"If it's another child you want, let's get to it." His dark amber eyes flashed with anticipation when he reached for the shoulder buttons on her dress.

"Oh no you don't," she laughed, flew from his grasp and went into the bathroom. Another baby was the furthest thing from her mind. She was already bringing up three children on her own and didn't need any more. She certainly didn't need another globetrotting father!

As Alix began to apply her make-up, her thoughts returned to Tansie. It wasn't for the first time that day that she'd thought of Tansie. In fact, she had thought about Tansie during most of the afternoon. Tansie would love Paris, Alix was sure of that, and she could almost see that special twinkle in Tansie's eyes whenever she encountered something new. She smiled to herself as she acknowledged that she had come to like many things about Tansie. The way Tansie brushed her fringe off her forehead when she wasn't quite sure about something or the way she let her arms dangle down her side when she was embarrassed. They were childlike gestures, but Alix found them most charming.

But, for the first time ever, Alix missed not having a companion to go shopping with. She didn't know whether this was purely because she actually had time to stroll around rather than rush from shop to shop or whether she wanted someone to share the afternoon with. She acknowledged that it would have been nice to sit down with a friend, have a cup of coffee and a chat while they watched the world go by on the Champs Elysées. It was then and there that Alix decided to ask Tansie to accompany her on the next trip to Europe early in the new year. She would have to attend to some business but she would also take time off for a real holiday. A luxury she rarely allowed herself or in fact had time for.

Having made that decision, Alix continued with her make-up. When Alix returned to the sitting room where Haig was waiting for her, he drew in his breath.

"You look ravishing! The shopkeepers on Rue de Rivoli must have had a wonderful day," he said admiringly, and taking Alix's elbow, started to walk toward the door.

"They saw me coming and put up the prices," Alix replied, unperturbed.

Suddenly Haig stopped and looked at her. "She seems to have become very attached to you, in a strange sort of way," he stated thoughtfully.

"Who?" Alix gave him a blank stare.

"Tansie."

Alix laughed and hooked her arm underneath his. "Your imagination is not fit for a serious banker! You'll lose your reputation if you don't watch it," she quipped.

That same evening, Alix and Haig dined with Boris and

Svetlana at Maxim's. Boris was also in Paris to finalise some of his guest appearances for the following European winter season.

They had just finished dinner when Boris said, "Alix, I would like you to perform with me in Zürich in February. It would be . . ."

Alix smiled as she let her hand run over Boris' cheek. "My dear friend," she said. "Thanks for the offer but you know how I feel about concert tours. I'm away from home often enough as it is."

"Who said anything about a concert tour?" he asked, looking around himself. "All I want is one performance . . . maybe two," he grinned.

Alix laughed and made the second decision for that night. Since she had already planned a trip to Europe, she could quite easily give a concert as well. "One performance, Boris," she said.

Chapter 5

As winter became spring and the days grew longer and warmer, Alix and Tansie's friendship began to blossom. A deep and special understanding had rapidly developed between them.

Tansie knew why it was special but didn't say so. Instead she pursued Alix with such childlike charm, Alix in turn began to think of Tansie as a breath of fresh air in a world even Alix found ratty at times. She very much enjoyed Tansie's enthusiastic company and her often spontaneous and innocent affection. At the end of a hectic day, once or twice a week, Alix was happy to sit over a quiet dinner in a small restaurant and chat.

Until Tansie had come along, Alix had either worked well into the night or spent time with one or other male friend or lover. She enjoyed their company but now she suddenly became aware that she had missed socialising with women. During the day, she was mostly too busy to spend time with her girlfriends. At night, they were too busy with their husbands and children. Tansie who had neither husband nor children not only seemed to be available but provided her with a warm companionship she had not had for some time from a woman friend. It never occurred to her that her desire to be with Tansie meant anything more than this.

One day when Alix all but despaired about her workload and the fact that she had so little time to do other things, Kate pointed out the reason.

"I'm not surprised. Tansie has become quite demanding of you," Kate said, adding without drawing breath, "and to be quite blunt about it, I don't trust Tansie. She's . . ."

"I appreciate your concern, Kate, but what can she possibly do to me?" Alix was bewildered, not sure what Kate was trying to say. In her view, Tansie couldn't hurt a fly and why would she even want to.

"She could just disappear!" Kate said. "Remember, I told you about the conversation I overheard in the ladies' powder room at the symphony ball?"

"I do," Alix confirmed.

"You put a lot of effort into your friendships and if she did that to you, you would be devastated."

"Why would she do such a thing to me?" Alix could genuinely not think of a single reason why anybody would want to do that to her. She was not conceited in the sense that she thought other people could not live without her, but she knew her worth as a friend.

"Who knows?" Kate shook her head and took another sip of champagne. Suddenly it struck her. "She is in love with you and sooner or later she's going to make a pass at you," Kate blurted out.

"Don't be absurd, Kate!" Alix's voice was impatient. She shocked herself. She had never spoken in this tone to her friend.

"It's possible. It happens." Kate remained firm.

"Of course it happens but not to me it doesn't," Alix said casually. "Anyway, at the rate she's running around town with all manner of men, I hardly think she's interested in women."

"You don't know that, Alix."

"You're right, I don't." Alix readily accepted that she had grown very fond of Tansie, but she could not imagine herself taking it any further. Whether Kate believed Tansie capable of such a relationship or not, Alix certainly didn't. While she acknowledged that they had a special friendship, it hardly meant that they were going to fall in love!

After a short pause, Kate asked, "Hasn't any woman ever made a pass at you?"

Alix almost choked on her drink. Catching her breath, she croaked, "Not that I am aware of."

"There you are, you wouldn't even know," Kate exclaimed smugly.

"I most certainly would!"

The conversation with Kate was forgotten as soon as it ended. The idea was simply too absurd to give it even one more thought.

Towards the middle of spring, Alix finally extracted a promise from Tansie that she would exhibit some of her sculptures at her art class showing. She genuinely believed in Tansie's talent. It wasn't quite the start Alix had wished for her but it was better than none at all. Maybe once Tansie made a start, it might well give her the confidence she still lacked and would ultimately lead to bigger things.

"How is it going?" Alix asked when she ambled into Tansie's workroom a few days before the sculptures had to be submitted. The room was even more chaotic than usual but Alix didn't notice. She was more interested in the statues. One in particular had caught her eye.

Tansie's eyes lit up. "Thanks to your relentless encouragement, I think I'll get there," she cried and drew Alix to her side. "What do you think of this one?" she asked, running her fingertips over the neck and brushing off some fine dust that had settled there.

Alix gasped as she stared at her own portrait. Several studio photos of herself were propped up against a small stand behind the full-size bust. She was momentarily rendered speechless.

"You're very kind . . . I've aged at least ten years since those photos were taken. By the way, where did you get them from?" Her voice was light but deep inside she felt uneasy.

"All the newspapers have them on file," Tansie giggled.

"I should have known!"

Scrutinising the bust and running the tip of her index finger along its finely curved lips, Tansie asked, "Anyway, what do you think? Am I capturing the real you?" Although her gesture was meant to be seductive, Tansie was disappointed when she noticed that Alix seemed oblivious to it.

"More than I care to admit," Alix muttered.

Tansie had indeed captured all of her. This was quite evident even in its unfinished state. The very fine stubborn line which at times ran from the corners of her lips down the sides of her chin, and the critical aloof gaze in her eyes.

As it dawned on Alix how carefully Tansie must have studied her to produce this sculpture, she began to feel a little uncomfortable. For a brief moment she wondered whether it was her need for privacy which was now threatened. I've got to get out of here, she thought. Although it was most unlike her, her head seemed suddenly muddled.

"They're great," she managed to say. "But I can't stay, I've got . . ."

"I know we didn't plan it but I hoped that you might stay for dinner," Tansie interrupted. She looked crushed and made no pretence at hiding her disappointment. But she pulled herself together and asked, "Would you mind if I exhibited your portrait together with my other sculptures?"

"No . . . I don't mind . . . that's fine," Alix mumbled. "I'll meet you at the exhibition on Friday." Seconds later she slammed the door and fled down the driveway. Something was happening, Alix felt it. But whatever it was, Alix didn't think she would want to know about it.

It took Alix most of that night to convince herself that she had simply overreacted. Other artists had painted or photographed her, so why should Tansie's portrait be any different? She remembered the portrait Josh White had painted of her some years back which had won him the prestigious Archibald prize. She had felt the same discomfort then. Later, she had realised that it had meant nothing more than an artist capturing just a little more of her true self than she wanted to expose to the world. No doubt it was the same with Tansie.

The night of the exhibition was the first warm evening of spring and Alix scanned her wardrobe for something suitable to wear. Should she wear a skirt, a dress or slacks? Her eyes began to glow when she remembered the cream suit she had brought back from Paris. It would be perfect, she decided. The military style jacket reached half-way down her thighs, with large buttons down the front. The skirt was just a couple of inches longer. She put it on and noticed with pleasure that it fitted her like a glove.

When Alix arrived at the exhibition hall she headed straight for Tansie's statue of the conductor. She had watched Tansie create it and had seen it at various stages of completion. The last time Alix had asked her about it, Tansie had said it was at the foundry. Now, here it was.

The nearly two-feet high bronze statue looked remarkably like Boris Rostoff. With his heels raised just a little off the stand, his left arm bent at the elbow and his right hand holding the baton stretched towards an imaginary eternity, he oozed all the vibrant energy that was so typically Boris. Alix was rendered speechless for a moment. She wondered how Tansie could possibly know Boris so well. Tansie had never met Boris and had only used photos for reference. Did she have insights into people Alix had not been aware of? It was possible she decided as a sudden calmness swept through her. If she could capture Boris with such intimacy then she could most certainly capture Alix in the same way. She gave her own portrait a brief glance. She noted that it had a small sign, 'Not for sale', attached. Alix figured that Tansie was either going to keep it or give it to Alix. Either way was fine by her.

Alix turned away from the statue and ambled towards the small desk just inside the door.

"I want to buy statue number seven," Alix said to the young girl. She retrieved her fountain pen and filled in the cheque with a flourish.

The transaction completed, Alix turned to go. She was looking for Tansie when she collided with a tall man and dropped her handbag. Its contents spilled over their feet.

Bending down to pick up her belongings, she heard the man say, "I was about to buy that statue!"

Alix recognised the voice and, looking up, she said, "It was beyond your budget, Geoff."

"Cruel as always," Geoff responded.

"Some things never change, Geoff." Alix gave him a disarming smile and left him standing gaping after her.

Geoff was the social editor for one of the local tabloids and in the past had stretched the truth once too often to Alix's disadvantage. She accepted that publicity would always be part of her life, but she didn't have to accept it if it was gossip, idle or otherwise.

When Tansie appeared at Alix's side, looking radiantly excited, they strolled through the vast hall, stopping to take a closer look at various pieces of art. Although the general standard was quite remarkable, Alix thought Tansie's were the most charming. They also showed not just talent but exceptional talent. Even in the few months since Alix had met her, each new piece she had created had been an improvement on the previous one. She was more convinced than ever that Tansie could achieve great success.

As well as the conductor and Alix's portrait, Tansie had exhibited the bronze cast of the two ballet dancers in a classical *pas de deux*; both dancers stood tall and straight with the male behind the female, their slim graceful bodies just touching. The two wood carvings, one of a young girl and one of a woman holding a baby in her arms, were more abstract with fewer details but their womanhood was beautifully depicted. Alix no longer felt disconcerted by or uneasy with the intimacy implied by any of the statues. She put it down to Tansie's unusual talent.

"The girl at the desk told me you bought the conductor," Tansie said when they stood right in front of it. "Why didn't you tell me you wanted it?" With a shy smile, she added, "I did make it especially for you, you know."

"I figured that," Alix said breezily. "But I preferred to buy it."

"Thanks," Tansie said and dropped her head on to Alix's shoulder. "That means a lot to me, provided you didn't do it because you felt sorry for me."

"Rest assured that wasn't the reason," Alix said and smiled. "It's a beautiful sculpture. Don't you think it'll look superb on the side-bench in my music room?"

"It will indeed. Did you see, only three of my statues haven't been sold? Everybody else only sold one or two," Tansie beamed and, without drawing breath, continued, "will you at least let me give you the portrait of you?"

Alix smiled. "Yes, I'd like that very much." She took

Tansie's arm and added, "Let's go and have dinner somewhere, shall we?" She didn't want the evening to be over just yet. Tansie's success had to be celebrated properly, she thought.

"What a wonderful idea."

As they were driving out of the parking lot, Tansie suggested a small Italian bistro in South Yarra. She had been there a couple of times before and liked it.

Over dinner, the mood between them slowly changed from the earlier excitement over the successful exhibition to a warm and comfortable intimacy. An intimacy between friends that normally only became evident after a long time. Alix noted it but didn't give it too much thought. They had simply become close friends a lot more quickly.

As Alix momentarily studied Tansie's face, over which the flickering candle on the table cast intricate lights and shadows, she thought how truly beautiful Tansie was and how good she felt in her company.

Tansie also watched Alix and she too felt good except, unlike Alix, she knew what those feelings really meant. She reached across and briefly touched Alix's hand. She loved the feel of Alix's skin, smooth and warm. "What are you thinking about?" she asked.

Tansie's spontaneous and gentle affection no longer bothered Alix. Tansie often made such gestures and, although they implied some intimacy, Alix had accepted them as simply being as much a part of Tansie as any other gesture she made.

"I just thought how good it feels to be with you. This has been a lovely evening," Alix said softly. She took a sip of champagne and then continued, "When I was in Paris a couple of months ago, Boris asked me to give a concert with him in Zürich in February, I said I would and . . ."

"That's wonderful," Tansie cried excitedly. Then she suddenly became timid. "Do you think I could go with you? I'd love to hear you perform."

Alix smiled. "I was just going to ask you that," she replied and held Tansie's gaze. "After the concert in Zürich, and some business I have to take care of in Vienna, I intend to take some real time off. We could go skiing, would you like that?"

"Would I like it!" Tansie exclaimed enthusiastically. "I'd love it Alix."

"Well then let's do it," Alix laughed. She was enchanted by Tansie's response and knew that they would have a great time together.

Chapter 6

Half an hour after storming out of yet another Clemenger Pharmaceuticals board-meeting, Alix flew into her studio and slammed the door. Her briefcase landed on the sideboard with a thump as she slumped into her desk chair. Where her integrity was concerned she never made any compromises, no matter what was involved. Today, Michael's brothers, Andrew and Jason, had finally pushed her too far. She would instruct her stockbroker to buy enough shares in the company to give her a majority shareholding. Then she would appoint her own managing director.

Moments later, John put his head around the door and gave her a curious stare. Jenny had warned him that Alix had looked like thunder when she arrived.

"What's up love?" he asked.

"Nothing I can't fix!"

"I take it the Clemenger boys have something to do with your mood?" he gave her a wide grin. "Just to add to your aggro, Laura wants to cancel Johnny-Superstar's contract."

"I thought we sorted that out months ago?"

"Obviously not," John continued. "He hasn't shown at the recording studio for three days and she's had enough." When Alix didn't respond right away, he added, "I think Laura's mood has more to do with her friend Mia! You know, lover's quarrel."

"You would at that," Alix said and rolled her eyes at him.

"What are we going to do about Laura's problem?" John

asked, bringing her back to reality.

"What's our friendly attorney's advice?"

"Sally doesn't think it's a problem," John informed her. "Little Johnny-Primadonna didn't read the fine print . . . a special clause she put in his contract when it was drawn up."

"Smart lady!" Alix smiled. "I'll ring Laura later and tell her to go ahead and cancel his contract. Now, can I have some peace and quiet?"

"Sure," John said and left.

Alix sauntered over to the piano, played several scales in rapid succession and then moved on to whatever tune came into her mind. Mozart, Beethoven, Chopin, Schumann and even some Clemenger thrown in.

Later, just as Alix stepped out of the shower in order to get ready for her dinner date, Tansie rang.

"Hiii," Tansie drawled in her usual childlike fashion. "Would you come over and have dinner with me this evening?"

"I'm sorry, I can't. I already have a dinner engagement," Alix replied.

"Ohhh? Is Haig back in town?"

"No," Alix said.

"It must be some other chap I don't know about," Tansie chuckled.

"It is!" Alix chuckled in a similar fashion.

"Strictly business I take it?" Tansie asked. Before Alix could say anything, Tansie continued with a giggle, "What's he like in bed?"

On first impulse, Alix wanted to tell her to mind her own business, but for some reason she couldn't quite bring herself to do so. "Pierre?" she said, smiling to herself. "He's very good."

"I had no right to ask," Tansie immediately apologised. "Forget I did!"

Alix replaced the receiver after she had arranged to have dinner with Tansie the following evening.

Tansie's question, as much as her tone of voice, continued to puzzle Alix as she drove into the city to meet Pierre at the Windsor Hotel. It wasn't that she had never been asked about her love life before. Invariably, Alix only had to mention a man's name and Kate would ask that same question. But then, Kate was naturally curious and also believed that no good-looking woman should spend even one single night without a companion. Alix didn't agree with that philosophy but when it came from Kate, she took it in her stride. With Tansie though, she wasn't sure whether it was just curiosity or something else.

As Alix slammed the brakes on at the next traffic light, she heard Kate's voice as though she was sitting right next to her. "Tansie's in love with you." Haig had implied much the same.

"At that rate, I'll soon believe it myself," Alix muttered aloud. But even more daunting was the thought that she herself could fall in love with another woman, any woman. "Now you're being positively absurd," she said and moved on with the traffic.

Pierre had just finished filming in Hong Kong and, given the close proximity, decided to come to Melbourne to discuss the movie script, *Patrick*, with Alix. He planned to film it some time in the new year. He was pacing the hotel lobby when Alix came through the swing door. As usual he looked the typical debonair Frenchman, casually attired in grey gaberdine slacks, pale grey shirt and suede bomber jacket. His dark blue eyes began to sparkle when he spotted her. Moments later she was in his arms. They kissed leisurely for a while and it crossed Alix's mind just how much she loved being kissed by him.

"Are you hungry? Shall we go and eat?" he eventually asked, linking his arm with hers.

On impulse she said, "No . . . let's go to your room. We can always get room service if need be."

As he bent down in the lift to kiss her again, she remembered their first encounter. They had met in Paris only a few weeks after Michael's death. He had invited her to come and discuss the music score for his movie, *Toujours Et Jamais*. When their business had been completed, she had accepted his invitation to spend a few days in the French Alps with him.

It was dark when they arrived at his chalet. The moment their bags had been inside and the front door was firmly shut against the bitter cold wind, Alix had moved into Pierre's arms. Until the moment she was alone with him, she hadn't realised just how much she needed the physical comfort only another human being could give. She needed to be held, caressed and made love to.

"Make love to me, Pierre," she had said.

When she had returned home with very clear memories of their love-making, she had indeed composed the music for the film, *Toujours Et Jamais*. The following year the movie had won the prestigious *Palme d'or* at the Cannes Film Festival. At the same time, the jury had also awarded her the *Lion d'or*, an award specially created for the brilliant and outstanding music Alix had composed. Within days of the announcement, the album sold out around the world.

The precious memories still lingered in her mind even after several years. And although she was very attracted to Pierre, she now had an ulterior motive for wanting to go to bed with him. She needed to prove to herself that even if

Kate was right that Tansie was in love with her and was to suggest a relationship, Alix would most certainly turn her down.

When Pierre asked if she had to go home that night, she shook her head and curled her body into his. With a smile on her face, knowing that her life was under control, she went to sleep.

The following day, Tansie arrived at Alix's offices unannounced. When she entered, she could hear the mellow sound of a male voice coming from the studio.

Agitated, she said to Jenny, "I have to talk to Alix." Without waiting for an answer, Tansie knocked on the door and opened it. Having tried to ring Alix for most of the night without success, she knew that Alix had spent the night with Pierre.

Alix was sitting at the piano, smiling and listening to the man who was standing behind her. The man was huge, at least six and a half feet tall, with shoulders like a bear. His straw-blond hair curled over the top of his black rollneck sweater. A violin was tucked under his left arm, the other rested on Alix's shoulder. Although he was not strictly handsome, he had the same vibrant irresistible energy and charm as Alix.

Tansie recognised him from the photos she had used to sculpt the conductor. It was Boris. Now that she had seen the two of them together, she was convinced that Alix and Boris were lovers. The two seemed made for each other.

The thought made Tansie gasp, alerting Alix and Boris to someone's presence. Their heads turned simultaneously.

"I didn't know you had company," Tansie blushed with embarrassment.

Alix noticed the blush and thought how well it suited Tansie. "That's okay," Alix smiled. "Boris and I were just about to finish anyway."

Boris too gave Tansie a smile and said, "I'm glad you came. My young friend works me far too hard." Packing up his violin, he continued, "I will see you tomorrow, Alix." He kissed her lightly, gave Tansie a nod and left.

"He's very compelling, your Boris," Tansie blurted out the moment the door had shut behind him.

"He is," Alix agreed. "But he's not mine!"

"Is he married?" Tansie asked. In order to sculpt him, she had studied many photos and newspaper clippings but had seen no reference to a wife. Now she needed to know.

"Very much so," Alix replied.

After her night with Pierre, Tansie's remark no longer rang alarm bells in Alix's head. They had a good, solid friendship and nothing would change that.

"Let's go up the road and have a coffee," Alix said and closed the piano lid.

"I can't," Tansie replied. "I've got to meet Lorenzo."

"Lorenzo?" Alix asked with an amused glint in her eyes. "What happened to Ian and Steven?"

"They were farewelled a long time ago," Tansie said, hiding her disappointment at Alix's casual question. She had hoped to get some sort of reaction from her; indifference and amusement were not what she'd hoped for. "I just came by to ask you something," she added.

"Sure."

"Could you take a weekend off so that we can go to your country house?" Tansie asked. "You promised some time ago."

"You're right, it's time I delivered my promise," Alix agreed, vaguely recalling that they had talked about going away for a weekend some time ago. Noting Tansie's child-like demand, she smiled to herself and thought how charming it was. "How about this weekend?"

"Oh, I'd love it," Tansie exclaimed and spontaneously gave her a hug.

"Then it's a deal," Alix said.

Once Tansie had left, Alix went back to work. If she were to go away at the weekend, she could not afford to take time off now.

She returned to the composition she and Boris had worked on, a sonata for piano and violin, and thought of the old masters who had had the luxury of weeks, months and, in some cases, even years to compose a piece of music. But, as that thought surfaced, she reminded herself with a smile that she made a very handsome living out of it. Most of the old masters didn't.

Three days later, Alix drove Tansie up the mile-long driveway which led to Alix's house just past Yarra Glen. The sun was out and the new growth on the trees gave everything a feeling of freshness. Alix brought the car to an abrupt halt in front of the large Victorian homestead.

Tansie looked a little shaken but Alix was laid-back about such matters. She wouldn't drive a fast powerful sports car if she wanted to go slowly.

Together they unloaded the car, opened doors and windows and then stepped outside on to the verandah.

Alix took a deep breath and leant against the freshly painted balustrade. Only now that she was actually here did she realise just how much she had missed the place.

Despite Michael's opposition at the time, she had bought the property soon after Sara's birth. She had wanted a place to get away from it all. He had wanted one at the beach where the action was. In the end, they both got what they wanted. Except Michael had sulked for weeks afterwards and never set foot on Alix's property.

After many months of restoration, it had finally become the haven she had craved. It was big enough for friends and children yet still offered Alix solitude when she wanted it. Together with the architect, she had worked hard until it had exactly the feel she wanted: her very own unique combination of simple elegance and informal luxury. The upholstered furniture was large and comfortable with each loose cushion stuffed with soft luxurious goosedown. The fabrics she had chosen were of the finest wools, cottons and linens in tonings of blue and yellow. The rugs on the polished floorboards were imported from Turkey and Pakistan. She had never wanted a house to impress but, rather, had achieved the beauty she wanted with clean, uncluttered forms and lines.

The two women stood close to each other as they surveyed the lush green paddocks and sprawling fields in front of them. The gently sloping hills rose beyond the river. The dam at the bottom of the property was just visible from the main house, as was the small cottage Alix had rented out to the local school mistress. The many huge weeping willows, oaks and fir trees which surrounded the house seemed to protect it with their massive crowns.

Alix suddenly felt an unusual contentment sweep through her whole body. It was unusual to her because, more often than not, she was restless and wanted to get on with whatever she was doing. She looked at Tansie and wondered whether it was she who had that calming effect on her. She thought that was entirely possible.

"This must remind you of Europe," Tansie commented.

"Not quite, but it was the closest to it I could find," Alix replied. "Anyway, you'll see for yourself in a couple of months."

"I can hardly wait," Tansie exclaimed excitedly.

Alix was more than ready to take a holiday and she was glad to be going with Tansie. She enjoyed her company and the childlike enthusiasm Tansie displayed for anything new. She particularly wanted to show her all the places she herself loved so much. Paris, Vienna, maybe Italy and certainly the alps. In the past, she had mostly travelled on her own or with the children. To now go away with a female friend would make a pleasant change, she thought. It had at times crossed her mind that to have a travelling companion to share things with would be very nice. Until now, she had never done anything about it.

As Alix seemed momentarily lost in her own thoughts, Tansie observed her. She smiled and thought how beautiful and serene Alix was right now. Tansie didn't often see her like this. More often than not, Alix dashed from place to place, played the piano at a frantic pace, gave impatient instructions over the telephone or heatedly discussed a piece of music with fellow musicians. She didn't know anybody else who could keep up such a relentless pace. It wore Tansie out just watching her.

Tansie wanted to capture this moment of tranquillity. But she wanted even more to reach out and take Alix into her arms. The moment passed before she could move.

Alix, quite oblivious to Tansie's thoughts, suggested they make the most of the early summer sun and work on their tan. Returning to her bedroom, Alix slipped on her bikini bottoms. She always sunbaked topless and to do it any other way regardless of whose company she was in, never crossed her mind. She grabbed a couple of magazines from the bedside table, two fluffy towels from the linen press and then called out to Tansie that she would meet her at the pool whenever she was ready. She fetched the sun lounges and cushions from the shed and then stretched out.

What bliss, she thought and folded her hands underneath her head. When she heard Tansie's feet on the wooden steps that led down from the terrace, she turned in Tansie's direction. She smiled. Tansie too was topless.

Alix wanted to look away – after all, she had seen other female friends in the nude – but found she couldn't. Gazing at Tansie, she noted that Tansie's body was much like that of a young girl, thin and angular and yet, overall, there was something very seductive about her. It took her a moment or two to work out just what it was. It was her breasts, Alix thought. They were a little larger than one would expect, round and firm but still well-proportioned compared to the rest of her body. It was a beautiful sensuous body, Alix decided. She was about to avert her gaze when the thought of what it would feel like to let her hand run over Tansie's smooth skin struck her. She shivered involuntarily and looked the other way. Either you're being totally absurd or the sun is getting to you, she scolded herself and lit a cigarette. Such an idea did not deserve to be entertained any longer.

Tansie smiled as she lowered herself on to the sun lounge. Alix's gaze had not escaped her notice and she wondered what the brief flicker in Alix's eyes meant. She hoped that it was what Tansie wanted it to be: desire.

Over the next couple of hours, Tansie periodically allowed her eyes to gaze at Alix's body. Again, she wanted to reach out and touch it. Although with considerable difficulty, Tansie held back. She recognised an aloofness and ambivalence in the way Alix flicked the ash from her cigarette into the nearby garden bed and decided that if she were to make a move now it would probably send Alix running.

Alix didn't look at Tansie again. Her earlier thought had rattled her too much for her liking. Now she wanted to forget that she had ever had it. As the afternoon progressed, Alix slowly started to relax again and enjoyed the blissful luxury of simply sitting in the sun and doing nothing at all.

After some hours of soaking up the sun, Alix suggested a short horse ride. They changed into T-shirts, jeans and boots and strolled to the back of the house where the stables were. With the afternoon breeze billowing their hair, they rode past the grazing cows and down the hill. When they reached the dam Alix prepared to jump the fence a few lengths ahead of her. Moments later, her horse catapulted into the air and floated over the railing. Her heart raced with the jump. She had not ridden for some time. Her moment of insecurity passed when the horse landed safely on its hoofs.

Tansie had watched Alix take the jump but decided that the opening in the fence would do her just fine. As she drew alongside Alix, she asked, "Where on God's earth did you learn to ride like this?"

"In Argentina when I was quite young," Alix replied. "My father played polo . . . he taught me."

"I can't even start to imagine what sort of a life you must have had from the day you were born!"

"Most of the time it was wonderful," Alix confirmed.

After a short pause, Tansie said, "You don't talk much about your childhood, do you?"

"No," Alix smiled, adding softly, "neither do you for that matter."

Tansie smiled too but her smile was sad. "Who'd want to know!" she exclaimed tightly. "It's nothing to brag about."

Alix instinctively stood up in the stirrups and leant across. She put her hand over Tansie's and said, "Why don't you try me?" It was not a challenge but rather an invitation to talk about something which obviously distressed her. As though she suddenly saw Tansie for the very first time, Alix felt a deep need to know everything there was to know about her. It was not idle curiosity. She was genuinely interested in who this woman really was.

"Let's go and sit under the oak tree over there," Alix added and dismounted her horse.

Chapter 7

The horses were let to graze. Alix sat down and then, stretching out, rolled onto her stomach. Tansie sat down less than a foot away, and leaning against the massive oak tree trunk, drew her knees up and wrapped her arms around them.

For a moment, Tansie let her gaze wander into the distance. When she finally looked at Alix, an uncertain smile crossed her face. "Are you sure you're ready for this?"

"Until I know what it is, how can I know whether I'm ready or not?" she replied softly.

"I suppose so," Tansie said. Then suddenly the words began to spill from her lips.

Tansie spoke of the day when she was taken from her mother's grubby council flat and marched onto a huge boat with a hundred or so other children. She told Alix how she had been terrified and clung on to the hand of her older sister Arlene, barely leaving her side; how she had been abused and suffered in the orphanage; how she had never eaten fresh bread or worn a brand new dress until she left the institution. She spoke of her longing for a happy marriage and a house of her own like her sister's. She described how Julie had become her very first true friend (she left out the bit about her being her lover); how Alan had swept her off her feet and how the marriage had eventually gone sour because, as Tansie said, Alan was untrustworthy (again she omitted to say that she thought the separation was temporary).

During the whole of Tansie's narration Alix remained silent as her feelings alternated between shock, anger, sympathy and compassion. How anybody could inflict such mindless and soul-destroying brutality on helpless children was beyond Alix's comprehension. From time to time, Alix averted her gaze as she absentmindedly chewed on a long blade of fresh grass. Even in her wildest imagination, she could not have dreamed of such an horrendous life. Except in Tansie's case it was not a dream. It was very real.

When Tansie fell silent for a moment, Alix reached out for her hand and held it firmly in her own. What could she say, she wondered, that would not sound hopelessly inadequate? Alix had no words.

As tears began to fill her eyes, Tansie continued. "The worst part of all is that I don't know my father's name or his identity! All I have is a single photograph of my grandmother, holding me in her arms soon after I was born." She stopped and wiped a few tears from her cheeks. "When I visited my mother the one and only time, nearly twenty years ago, she gave me a couple of brown faded pictures. They were of men in uniforms, either one of whom, according to my mother, could have been my father. One, she remembered, was called Harry. She had no idea about the name of the other!"

Tansie stopped again and, after fumbling in her pocket for a tissue, blew her nose. "For some years my mother wrote to me but, when I didn't write back, she gave up. Now, we have virtually no contact. That's fine by me too. Once I came to terms with what she had done to me, I simply forgot that she ever existed."

On impulse, Alix got to her feet and, kneeling down in front of Tansie, quite naturally folded her into her arms.

She noticed how soft and vulnerable Tansie felt as she held her. She stroked her hair to soothe her. She was so immersed in Tansie's story that she didn't think of what Kate had said or of what she herself had felt earlier: that there might be something more to the strength and tenderness with which she now held Tansie.

Alix continued to hold Tansie and let her cry as her own heart started to feel something of the pain Tansie must have been through. And yet, she wondered whether she would ever really understand what it all meant to Tansie. Giving her a tight hug, Alix silently promised that she would try.

Slowly Tansie calmed down and, lifting her gaze to meet Alix's, she gave her a weak smile. "I told you it wouldn't be pleasant." Her voice quivered when she added, "Maybe now you don't want to know about me any more."

"Don't even think such a thing," Alix replied softly and let the back of her hand run over Tansie's cheek. "Nobody can choose their parents and, one way or another, we all have a past. Some are just worse than others, that's all." She fell silent for a moment and then asked, "Where is your sister now? Do you see much of her?"

"No, she lives up north on a large property with her husband and three children," Tansie said.

"That's too bad," Alix replied sympathetically.

"Thanks for listening," Tansie smiled without moving out of Alix's embrace. She wanted to savour their closeness for a little while longer.

"I'm glad you told me."

The sun had started to set and it was getting colder when they finally got up. As Tansie started to walk towards the horses, she said, "Now that I've told you my life story, it seems only fair that you do the same, don't you think?"

Alix smiled. "I will, one day, when the time is right." As

she said it, a brief flash of the day when her childhood had come to a sudden halt went through her mind. She would tell Tansie but not right now. Alix mounted her horse and, as she gave it a touch of the heel, she motioned to Tansie to do the same.

As they neared the forest and the dirt road which would lead them back to the house, they slowed to a canter and followed the narrow trail through the dense bush. Finally the open fields were once again in front of them. Exhilarated after a fast gallop towards the house, they dismounted in the home paddock.

Since the evenings and nights were still cold, they ate their dinner in front of the open fire. Tansie had volunteered to cook knowing that if Alix prepared the meal a boiled egg would probably be all that was on the menu. Learning to cook had never been on Alix's list of priorities.

Almost as soon as Alix had finished the meal, she lit one of her Davidoffs and sprawled out on the couch. Closing her eyes, she sighed.

"Although I despise idleness," Alix said lazily, "Lying here, well fed and all, I could almost make myself believe that a less vigorous lifestyle has some merit."

"You wouldn't dare to suggest that I'm lazy," Tansie cried, flinging herself on top of Alix and beginning to tickle her.

Alix couldn't help but laugh. But as she became acutely aware of Tansie lying on top of her, her body pressing her down, Alix felt uncomfortable. It was just a little too intimate for her liking. She wriggled until Tansie lost her balance, fell off and landed on the floor with a thump.

"That'll teach you to take me on," Alix said lightly as she helped Tansie back to her feet.

Alix sprawled out on the couch and Tansie curled her

body into one of the large armchairs. For some time, they both sat in silence as they watched the logs crackle in the fireplace. The mood of the moment seemed precious and neither felt the need to talk.

It was towards midnight when Tansie started to yawn. She gently drew Alix to her feet and said, "Time for bed."

Together they made their way into the west wing where the bedrooms were. Alix just stepped out of her bathroom when Tansie appeared.

"Can I sleep in your room?" Tansie asked timidly. "I don't like strange houses much."

"Sure," Alix replied. A brief flicker of surprise appeared in her eyes, but she said nothing. Instead she took two extra pillows from the wardrobe and pulled back the bedspread.

Alix read the paper for a while but when it fell to the floor and her eyes began to close, Tansie reached across and switched off the light. Drifting off to sleep almost instantly, Alix barely noticed that Tansie had slipped her hand into her own. The next morning, their fingers were still clasped together. Alix noted it but thought little of it, other than it was probably just another side of Tansie's character she had not yet seen. Alix got out of bed as quietly as she could and pulled an old football jersey over the top of the T-shirt she had worn during the night.

When the coffee was ready, Alix poured a cup and carried it into the sitting room. Opening the French doors, she filled her lungs with the fresh air. Sipping the steaming brew, her thoughts turned to Tansie. It was only now that she began to wonder why she had allowed her to sleep in her bed. Was it simply a sympathetic reaction on her part to Tansie's life story? She thought it entirely possible.

"It's no big deal anyway," she said aloud. As though she wanted to convince herself that it meant nothing, she added,

"Other girlfriends have slept in my bed."

Only after some reflection did she think about how she actually felt about Tansie's physical presence. She had felt as good about it as she felt on a sunny day, she thought. No matter how hard she tried, she could not deny that she had liked the warmth of this other human being in her bed.

"At that rate, you'll soon wonder what it would be like to kiss Tansie," she muttered to herself. The words had barely left her lips, when her emotions went into a spin. She had not felt quite this vulnerable for some time.

"You have control . . . all you have to do is exercise it," she said and, with an energetic stride, returned to the sitting room. Comforted by that thought, she sat down on the couch and started to work.

Immersed in the sheet music, scattered all around her, Alix was ensconced in a composition when Tansie came padding across the room. She looked up startled when she felt Tansie's hand run through her as yet uncombed curls.

"Good morning, did you sleep well?" Alix asked lightly.

"I haven't slept so well in months," Tansie reported. "What about you? I heard you grind your teeth a few times."

"Michael hated it but when I suggested we have separate bedrooms, he almost choked on his steak. Needless to say, he never mentioned it again," Alix admitted. What she didn't say was that she only ground her teeth when she was disturbed about something.

"What are you thinking?" Tansie asked, having noted the sudden change in Alix's expression.

"Hmmm? . . . Nothing!"

Since the weather remained warm and sunny for the rest of the weekend, the two women did little else but laze in the sun and take the occasional dive into the pool.

Alix only worked when Tansie was bustling around the

kitchen and preparing their meals. She was not only aware that time meant nothing to Tansie but that she herself found it difficult to work when Tansie was around. She was continually caught between the desire to spend time with Tansie and the recognition that to do so was a luxury she could not afford.

When they had to shut the house up and go home, Alix noted a sad and lost look in Tansie's eyes.

"What's up?" she asked.

"I'm just sad we have to go home so soon," Tansie replied in a shaky voice, adding, "especially since we won't get another chance to come back for quite some time, I expect."

"Why won't we?" Alix gave her a puzzled glance.

"You told me that as soon as the children go on holidays, you'll take them to Portsea until they go back to school in February," Tansie reminded her. "That's only a couple of weeks away, you know."

"I'm glad someone remembers what I'm doing," Alix joked. "Why don't you come with me?"

"Do you really mean that?"

"Of course, the house is plenty big enough," Alix confirmed. "But let me warn you, it'll be more like a circus than a picnic! The house'll be full of children."

"That doesn't matter," Tansie cried and headed towards the garage with a new spring in her step. Now, at least she had something to look forward to. She had dreaded the holidays and Alix's absence. Although she was horrified at the thought of all those children Alix had warned her about, she would deal with them somehow. To this day, any more than half a dozen children together made her cringe. She would never forget the lack of privacy and dignity she had experienced in the orphanage.

Chapter 8

By the time Alix's guests arrived for the Christmas Eve party she gave in town every year, the whole house had an air of festivity about it. The candles on the fir tree in the garden were lit and even Mitterand, the family Basset Hound, ran about excitedly.

Just before she called in her guests to take their seats at the dining table, she thought of Michael. This was their fourth Christmas without him. She had to admit that they had been more peaceful. Michael had paid little attention to celebrations such as birthdays and Christmas. Family life had never been high on his list of priorities. In the end he died very much as he had lived: flying high by the seat of his pants. He had crashed his Cessna in the mountains and his life had been over in a matter of a few short moments. She knew that, had he been given the choice, that was the way he would have wanted to go.

By the time Alix had realised just how shallow he was behind his bright suave appearance, it was too late. She was well and truly ensconced in supposed matrimonial bliss. After a short time, she had retained few illusions about their relationship. She felt it was doomed. Had it not been for her extreme loyalty, she had no doubt that in time she would have called an end to this charade of a marriage. She had mourned her children's father and her marriage, but not her husband.

Returning to the present, Alix straightened a napkin she had previously overlooked and went to fetch her guests.

Alix was attentive towards everyone present. But occasionally she caught Tansie's eye across the vast dining table. As they held their gaze, a special glow would cross each of their faces. Despite their short friendship, Alix could not now imagine Christmas festivities without Tansie.

When it was time to open the presents, everyone assembled in the formal sitting room. Alix's friends were used to her extravagant generosity and were aware that she thought money was only useful when it could give pleasure to other people. Tansie was overwhelmed.

"How can I ever thank you for all this?" Tansie said, giving Alix a hug and glancing at the several gifts she had just unwrapped. Among them were a complete set of compact discs of Beethoven's symphonies and a set of Alix's own works, a set of silver napkin rings and matching coasters and a box of handmade stationery with Tansie's name engraved on it.

"I had a lot of fun Christmas shopping," Alix smiled, adding, "had you not outgrown tricycles, tip trucks and dolls, I would have bought those too."

After lunch the following day, Felix packed the children up and took them to the beach house. Alix was to follow the next day after a party at Haig's mother's house.

As usual the party was a lavish affair but, from time to time, Alix's thoughts drifted to Tansie. Here she was amid some of the wealthiest and most powerful people in the country and, still, she thought of her friend. Alix missed her easy laugh and the now familiar comfortable gesture of Tansie draping an arm around Alix's shoulder and whispering some nonsense into her ear.

The next day, Alix picked Tansie up and together they drove to the beach. When Alix's car came to an abrupt halt in the circular driveway of the limestone summerhouse, several children appeared seemingly from nowhere. Once they had greeted their mother and introduced their friends, they vanished as quickly as they had arrived.

"You really meant what you said," Tansie cried, horrified. "Do they all live here?"

"There's a fair chance!" Alix was nonchalant.

She knew that at least half of them would be house guests. But that prospect did not bother her a great deal. Since Alix's father had been a diplomat, she had moved from place to place until she went to boarding school. This had made it difficult for her and her brother Tom to form close or long-term friendships. She had promised herself that her own children would not suffer the same fate.

Alix unloaded the car and Tansie took her time wandering around the huge house. Most people didn't have one house this size, she thought. Alix had three.

It stood majestically on the cliff top amid tall cypress trees and overlooked Port Phillip Bay. Built in the shape of a boomerang, each room had a view over the water. On calm days the waves lapped onto the beach but, in rough weather, they crashed on to the nearby rocks and sprayed water high over the cliff. Despite its size, the house had an open, friendly and inviting atmosphere about it.

The two women installed themselves in the north-west wing which housed two bedrooms, each with its own bathroom, and a music room. After Michael's death, Alix had made some minor alterations which would allow her privacy and solitude even if the house was full of children.

Within a day of their arrival, the women settled into an agreeable routine of holiday activity. Most mornings Alix worked for a few hours, then they played tennis and later sunbaked around the swimming pool and waterskied in the afternoon. Towards evening, they played another few sets of tennis with Alix's friends who had houses nearby. Occasionally they packed a picnic lunch and ventured to the local riding school for a day in the bush.

On those days, Alix often reflected on times long gone by when she used to ride with her father, and on the time Tansie had related the story of her childhood. Neither memory was particularly pleasing. She could do nothing about her father. He was dead. But she could at least try and make up for Tansie's lost childhood. That thought comforted her.

At the end of each day when the house was eventually quiet, Alix and Tansie enjoyed its tranquillity. More often than not, they took a stroll along the beach. They would grope their way down the steep wooden steps and then slowly walk along the deserted beach. Even the cool wet sand which found its way between their bare toes felt comfortable.

Sometimes they talked. Other times they walked in silence. Tansie was well aware of her intense desire for Alix. She was in love with her, she knew. Tansie felt as though she had known Alix for ever and that all that was missing between them was physical love. She had often observed Alix's behaviour and wondered whether Alix was aware of her feelings and whether she returned them. Tansie had noticed Alix staring at her at different times but didn't think that sufficiently indicative. Alix was naturally reserved and aloof and Tansie knew that Alix would never make the first move. And she knew that, in Pierre, Alix had at least one male lover. Since Alix had never actually said so, Tansie could only assume that Haig and Boris were lovers too. Would Alix now consider a female one? Tansie did not know.

Late one evening Tansie sat silently on the beach, her mind occupied by thoughts and desires she could barely contain. Tansie looked down at Alix who was lying flat on her back. Her hands were crossed behind her head and, to Tansie, she looked more desirable than ever. Her long legs were stretched out and her slim ankles crossed. The full moon in the clear sky emitted enough light for Tansie to see Alix's chest rise and fall with each breath she took.

Suddenly Alix opened her eyes. She was momentarily dazed. Had she been asleep and dreaming, she wondered and shook her head. The night was warm and windless and yet, deep inside, she felt cold. She shivered. How could she be cold? As her earlier dream pushed itself to the surface, she flew to her feet. A swim would do her good, she thought and, with an impatient tug, she pulled the T-shirt over her head and dumped it at her feet. Alix was about to say something but the words died in her throat. She began to shake inside and felt as though she was losing control of her mind. Her gaze, as she fixed it on Tansie who was sitting at her feet, was bewildered. What the hell was going on?

Tansie knew what was going on. She rose to her feet, smiled and drew Alix into her arms. Tansie gently pressed her lips against Alix's. At last, finally it was happening, Tansie thought, overwhelmed with joy.

Alix didn't know whether it was shock or excitement but she felt her legs go weak at the knees the moment Tansie's lips touched hers. Alix shivered in Tansie's embrace and broke into a cold sweat. She wanted to push Tansie away, tell her to stop and then run like hell. As though paralysed, she remained motionless. She couldn't take a single step as her heart started to pound wildly in her chest. This was not a dream she could later forget and pretend it never happened.

Still embracing, they dropped down on to the warm sand and stretched out alongside each other. Tansie slipped her arm underneath Alix's head and cradled it in the crook of her elbow.

Alix felt Tansie's warm breath float closer and closer over her face. Rigid, tense and fearful, she wanted to break away. At the back of her mind the thought that she would not get another chance to escape briefly registered. And she didn't. Within seconds, all conscious logic was abandoned and she lost herself in a kiss so deep it took her breath away. She felt as though every ounce of control she might still have had slipped out of reach.

No . . . no . . . you can't do that! Alix's head began to pound. Yes . . . yes . . . you want to do that! And then, without directing any of her movements, Alix lifted her arms and wrapped them around Tansie.

Tansie drew away a little, and whispering, "I won't hurt you," planted tender kisses all over Alix's neck and shoulders, cheeks and eyes.

With their lips tightly clasped together again, they slowly began to probe and savour as their hands began to caress each other's smooth bodies. Tansie's movements were controlled, she knew exactly what she was doing. Alix's were more tentative. But much to her surprise, her feelings were no longer tentative. She wanted to be held, caressed and made love to. That thought sent immediate and tantalising currents right down her spine and to the very tips of her toes. Had she ever really thought about such an encounter, she could not have been forewarned of the intensity of her own feelings. She had become a body without a mind in a matter of seconds. Alix responded to every one of Tansie's tender touches and her own deep stirrings soon matched those of Tansie.

The rest of the world was forgotten and making love became absolutely inevitable.

Much to her own amazement, Alix suddenly knew what she wanted to do and how to do it. Knowing her own body well, she also knew what gave it the greatest pleasure. She was now prepared to give that same pleasure to Tansie.

When it was all over, Alix's heart beat furiously and she collapsed next to Tansie. As they recovered, Tansie raked her hand through Alix's damp curls. Softly, she muttered, "I love you."

Tansie's words did not register in Alix's mind immediately. Her whole body still tingled with the after-glow of making love. Then, as Tansie's words sunk in, Alix's body tightened. No, she thought, this was all too much. This was most certainly no dream! What on God's earth have we done, she cried silently and scrambled to her feet. She vaguely acknowledged that, in the past, she had always liked to stay in her lover's embrace after making love, savouring the moment for a while longer. But this wasn't just any lover, she reminded herself. This was different, exceptional, she thought and dashed towards the water.

Tansie too sat up and stared at the naked body silhouetted in the moonlight. With a twist in her heart, she knew she had never loved anyone quite like she loved Alix. If Alix walked away now, she would welcome death over life. Her eyes were still fixed on Alix when Alix arched her back and dived into the dark water.

Within seconds, Tansie too was at the water's edge and began to shout, "Alix . . . come back . . . Alix!"

But Alix didn't hear her. With her head under water, each arm glistened in the moonlight as it came up and disappeared again. Her strokes were powerful but silent. They barely rippled the water's surface as she rapidly put distance between herself and the beach. When she thought her lungs would burst if she swam another metre, Alix reached for the nearest anchor-chain and let herself float on her back.

Still gasping, her mind, confused as it was, turned back to Tansie and to what had happened between them. The only clear thought was that another woman had made love to her. And, she had reciprocated. How could she have allowed this to happen and worse, without a struggle?

Later, Alix had no recollection of how long she had been in the water. When she eventually struggled to shore, Tansie was waiting for her with a towel.

Rubbing her down, Tansie said, "I'm so sorry, Alix, I didn't mean to upset you like this . . . I don't know what came over me . . . I . . ." She let her voice trail off and allowed the tears which had brimmed in her eyes for some time to mingle with the salt water on Alix's face.

"I never thought that two women could be this close," Alix murmured, catching her breath. Groaning as though in pain, "Oh, God . . .", she collapsed into Tansie's arms and wept like she had not wept for a long time.

Tansie traced Alix's lips with her forefinger and hushed, "Let's go back to the house, you're frozen through."

Alix followed Tansie in a dream-like state. She allowed Tansie to run a hot bath for her, towel her dry and then tuck her into bed. Tansie slipped into bed beside her and gathered her into her arms. Within seconds, they kissed and touched again and lost themselves in each other. Alix's mind kept saying you can't, but her body kept saying you can and I want to.

When Alix woke early the next morning, she felt as though she hadn't slept at all. Her eyes were gritty and every muscle in her body ached. She vaguely remembered having nodded off into a light slumber, only to wake again covered in perspiration. Guided by what little light filtered in through the shutters, Alix reached for the cigarettes on the bedside table. She lit one, looked at her trembling hands and inhaled deeply.

Tansie was sound asleep. She was curled up like a baby with her knees drawn up almost underneath her chin. Her dark hair was swept across her face, all but obscuring it.

Alix felt her heart miss a few beats. Surely this was all wrong, her head told her. But there was no mistaking what her heart felt.

An uncharacteristic but overwhelming feeling of fear and indecision began to tug at her. What the hell was she going to do about this? Had she misinterpreted her own feelings all this time? Could she have stopped what happened last night? Could she now walk away? Alix didn't know what to think or what to do. Perhaps her subconscious knew what was going on, but at this moment, that was of no assistance to her.

After she finished her cigarette, she slipped back under the sheet and curled herself around Tansie. Alix lay still, feeling the warmth exuding from Tansie's body. Her thoughts where Tansie was concerned were still unclear but what suddenly became very clear were thoughts of the children. What if one of them walked in, right now, and found her in an embrace with another woman? She felt sick and gasped involuntarily. How could she have just forgotten their existence? How would they feel and react if they knew? Could she keep such a liaison hidden from them?

She had no immediate answers. Her eyes filled with tears and her body trembled with each new sob that tore from her chest. How could she have done such a thing?

"What's wrong?" Tansie asked softly, still half asleep but conscious of Alix's distress.

"The children," Alix managed to mutter. "What about the children?"

Tansie did not have a ready answer either. She had never been in this position before. None of her former female lovers had had children to worry about. Preoccupied with her own desires and wants, she had never given Alix's children a single thought. Holding Alix tightly in her arms, she said soothingly, "We'll find a way, you'll see. They'll never have to know."

Out of sheer exhaustion, Alix eventually went to sleep. It was the heat of yet another scorching day which woke them later that morning. As a sudden warm breeze began to caress her body and billow the curtains, bringing with it the familiar smell of seaweed and wet sand, Alix knew that she would never again smell those scents and feel that breeze without remembering the night Tansie and she had made love.

Tansie put her chin in her cupped hand in order to gaze at Alix. She noticed an expression of bewilderment in Alix's eyes. Had she overstepped the mark or maybe blown it altogether, Tansie wondered?

Stroking Alix's cheek with the back of her hand, Tansie said, "Don't think badly of me, please."

Alix nodded but didn't reply. What was there to say when her mind was still in such turmoil? For want of anything else to say, she murmured, "I'll go and get some coffee."

Moments later when she padded across the sitting room, she burst out laughing. How could she think of anything as mundane as making coffee? Had she lost the plot totally?

Still deep in thought, she didn't look where she was going. She fell over Mitterand and stepped on his floppy ear when she walked into the kitchen. He yelped and gave her a sorrowful look. Alix quickly patted him.

"Hi, Mum," Drew greeted her. He noticed a sudden cloud cross her face. "Are you okay? You don't look so good." When she failed to reply, he grinned, trying to make light of the situation although he had no idea of the cause. "You could have killed the dog . . . but you didn't . . . so, cheer up."

Finally, she laughed and sighed at the same time. "You're right, I didn't kill him," she said, wondering whether her son could really detect that something was amiss. Did she look any different? That thought made her laugh even more as she told herself silently that she was being positively absurd. Ruffling her son's hair, she added, "I'm fine . . . I just need some coffee."

Drew seemed content with her reaction, and after grabbing another bread roll, made a dash for the door. "I've got to go . . . Felix is waiting in the boat, we're going fishing," he said over his shoulder, blew her a kiss and left. Just before the door slammed behind him, he shouted, "Felix packed a picnic dinner, so don't expect us back until later this evening. Okay, Mum?"

"Okay," Alix replied and sighed with relief.

Over the next couple of weeks, the breathless newness of their discovery of each other took on a less frantic pace and their comfort with each other grew from day to day.

Initially, Tansie felt as though she was still skating on very thin ice. She knew that she loved Alix but she didn't know how Alix felt.

Alix was preoccupied and said very little. After each new experience discovering the physical joys of being in bed with another woman, Alix invariably became ecstatic, yet unsettled. Her mind could not come to terms with what her heart and body wanted. Although she did not normally need other people to help her make decisions, she felt incapable of even forming a tentative conclusion. She felt isolated and confused.

Until now, her lovers had always been men. Why did she now desire a woman? At her age? Had she been deluding herself all of her adult life?

And, she was worried about the children and the possible repercussions it could have on their emotional welfare if they were to find out. Often, she found herself wanting to reach out to Tansie, touch her and kiss her but, fearful that some child might turn up unexpectedly, she didn't.

The day came when she could no longer stand the feelings of uncertainty and confusion. She had to admit, even if only to herself at this point, that she was in love. In love with another woman. Accepting that fact, was a separate struggle all of its own. Maybe she would never really come to terms with it. But then she wasn't even sure whether she wanted to continue this relationship, either in the short term or the long term. There was only one thing she was quite clear about: that she had loved men in the past. And now, she was in love with a woman. In a strange way, that thought gave her some comfort.

Planting a firm kiss on Alix's lips one afternoon as they were sunbaking at the swimming pool, Tansie murmured, "Can I talk to you?"

"You're going to tell me you're pregnant," Alix stated with a mischievous twinkle in her eyes.

"If I believed in the Virgin Mary I might," Tansie giggled. More solemnly, she added, "Please, can you be serious for a moment?"

"I'll try."

"What happened between us was as much of a shock to me as it no doubt was to you," Tansie said quietly. "But I do know that I love you." she added. In her mind she had wanted Alix almost from the moment they'd met, and then she had been guided only by lust. Now it was love that guided her and she had most certainly not planned on that.

Alix wiped a few tears from Tansie's cheek. "We both know that women have relationships with other women. I never expected it to happen to me," Alix replied. "I'll either have to come to terms with it or . . . walk away."

Tansie cringed inside. "I wouldn't ever want to hurt you." Tansie took a deep breath. "I'm as confused as you must be," she added with a tremble in her voice, "Can it last . . . us, I mean . . . or is this just a wild fling?"

"I don't know," Alix replied honestly. "I don't think I want this to be a fling. But can we withstand the social pressures . . . the children?" The latter part she added with such a groan it sounded as though she was in pain.

"We'll be careful, I promise," Tansie replied. At this point she was prepared to go to any length to protect the happiness she no longer had to yearn for. Except, Alix had not yet said that she loved her too and that worried her. Every time Tansie had said those very words to Alix, she had felt some ambivalence in Alix's responses. It was then that she decided that she would go home ahead of Alix. Her departure, she hoped, would make Alix miss her enough to tell her that she loved her. She needed the security of Alix saying those words, loudly and clearly.

As they lay in bed one evening towards the end of January, Tansie said softly, "I'm going to go home tomorrow, Alix."

"Why?" Alix asked.

"We're leaving for Europe in a few days," Tansie chuckled. "I've got a few things to organise, you know, pay some bills, that sort of stuff. Otherwise I might not have a place to live when I come back."

"I suppose that's fair enough," Alix replied. She didn't like the idea much. But she reminded herself that although she had other people to take care of such things, Tansie didn't.

On their last evening together at the beach house, Tansie drew Alix into her arms. "I love you," she murmured as she lowered her lips to Alix's.

Alix's response was immediate, although not in words. But she certainly made up for it when she slowly rolled Tansie on to her back and leisurely let her tongue caress the side of her neck, before moving further down to her breasts.

Alix felt as though, in finding Tansie, she had found a part of herself. Although she was well aware that from now on her whole life would change, she could not quite bring herself to tell Tansie that she loved her too. Somewhere deep inside, different parts of her were still warring with each other. She didn't like the conflict.

Afterwards when they curled into each other's arms, Alix felt closer to Tansie than she ever had before. Ever since their weekend at her country retreat, Alix had waited till the time was right to tell Tansie about her own child-hood. Now was such a time. The deep emotions Tansie had evoked in her suddenly made it easier to brush away the pain of losing her father and to talk about him.

With a glow on her face, Alix recalled the early years she had spent in different countries around the world where her father had served as a diplomat. She spoke of the extravagant parties at the embassy and of her wilful pranks with her brother Tom. She described the love she had had for her father and the love he returned in equal measure. She shuddered as she remembered her mother who had never shown even the slightest interest in her children or their welfare.

When Alix suddenly stopped, Tansie drew her closer into her arms. Instinctively she knew that something terrible must have happened at the end of all those wonderful years Alix had just described.

"How come you ended up at boarding school in Switzerland?" Tansie asked softly.

Alix took a deep breath. "My parents were killed . . . murdered . . . by a gang of extremists in South America." After a short pause, she added, "I was just eleven years old . . . and, had it not been for one of the guards, I too would have died . . . I saw it, I was there!"

"Oh, no! That's horrible. I'm so sorry," Tansie gasped. She felt for Alix, as Alix had felt for her, but she could not quite comprehend the real horror. This was the sort of thing you read about in the newspapers. Such things didn't happen to people you knew. "It's over now," Tansie finally said for lack of anything else to say. "And, for what it's worth, I love you . . . very much."

The following morning, Tansie returned to town. The telephone rang the moment she walked into her house.

Picking it up, she said cheerfully, "Are you checking up on me?"

"How did you know it was me?" Alix asked.

"Just a guess," she laughed. Although she had expected Alix to ring her, she had not expected a call quite so soon. She smiled to herself. Just as she had hoped she would, Alix was missing her. A few more days could only do wonders, she thought.

On the one hand, Alix welcomed the few days on her own in order to finish some work but she also had to admit that she missed Tansie terribly. She hated to wake up without her and hated even more to go to sleep without her. Her whole existence had been turned upside down.

Feeling passion was not new to Alix and it wasn't just the relationship with another woman which now caused her distress. The thought of a deep involvement with another human being made Alix's heart twist. She only too clearly remembered the pain of the love she had felt for Haig and Michael and for other men from time to time.

She was also quite aware that each one of them had abandoned or betrayed her in one way or another. Would only a man do that to her or was Tansie capable of doing the same?

After Michael's death, she had vowed never to love again.

She never again wanted to be in a position where someone else could inflict such devastating suffering upon her. However, she was also well aware of her fierce loyalties; once she had made a commitment, she found it almost impossible to extract herself no matter how difficult the situation might be.

Even if she did come to accept a relationship between two women, could she trust Tansie to fulfil her needs and wants? She had no way of judging. She would have to take the plunge if she was ever to find out.

Chapter 9

At the beginning of February, Alix settled the children back into school for the start of their new year. Together with Tansie, she left for her concert and the holiday in Europe two days later. As soon as the plane taxied towards the terminal buildings in Zürich, Alix was out of her seat and opened the overhead locker. She was on home soil or at least the only real home soil she had ever known.

"We're here . . . let's go," she said excitedly, moving towards the exit with considerable impatience.

Alix spotted her brother Tom in the arrival hall and flew into his arms. "Welcome home," he greeted her. Looking her over, he noticed her clear sparkling eyes and a vibrancy in her whole being he had not seen in recent times. "You look well . . . Life, whatever it is, must be agreeing with you," he added.

"It is indeed," Alix replied and gave him a kiss on his clean-shaven cheek. She would have liked to tell him just how happy she was but thought that now was neither the place nor the time. Instead she introduced Tansie to him.

As Tom gave her a courteous, "Hello," Tansie drawled, "Hello to you too." Following the siblings to Tom's car, she whispered into Alix's ear, "Why didn't you tell me how gorgeous he is?"

"He is, isn't he? He is also very much married." Alix responded and took her first real breath of crisp fresh air. There was a distinct clean smell about it. This was Switzerland.

Tom was as vibrantly energetic and impatient as his sister. Where Alix on her own tired her out, the two of them together would surely exhaust her, Tansie thought with a smile.

Tom dropped the two women off at the Baur Au Lac Hotel and, after a quick cup of coffee, returned to his chambers. He promised to take them both to dinner after Alix's concert at the end of the week.

The women were shown to their room on the second floor. Although it was bitterly cold, Alix opened the doors to the small balcony and stepped outside. Tansie came up behind her and put her arms around her. Neither spoke for some time as they snuggled together for warmth. They remained in their embrace and absorbed the scenery in front of them.

The lawn in the hotel's front garden was covered with a thick blanket of snow. A new snowfall a day or so earlier had seen to that. The garden stretched all the way down to the road and the footpath and the lake beyond. There were no strollers on the promenade and only a few lonely swans bobbed up and down on the still water. A soft mist hung over the lake and the surrounding mountains. The rising sun tried to break through but couldn't quite manage it yet.

"I have never seen anything quite as beautiful as this," Tansie finally said in awe. "How could you have ever left this behind?"

"Had I not left, I would never have found you," Alix responded and kissed Tansie on the lips.

"Then I'm glad you did," Tansie murmured.

Rocking together in a gentle sway, Alix's heart filled with joy. They had five whole weeks in front of them. She had not been this happy since falling in love with Haig twenty years earlier.

As she looked across the lake, she thought of Haig and the other men she had loved. She was overwhelmed with doubt about her present situation. Had she made the right decision in continuing this relationship on a physical level? Did she need to be nurtured by a woman as a substitute for the love she had never received from her mother? Or had she simply been ready for a romance and Tansie happened to come along at that time? Yes she had Haig, she rationalised but he was rarely there. With a smile she acknowledged that she had missed romance: long evenings curled up on the couch in front of an open fire with a lover and time to spare; or a walk in the park with only the moonlight to witness the kisses and caresses on the way. Alix had been ready for a romance but was she really ready for an enduring relationship with another woman?

Invariably such thoughts led to one question: could she now walk away from Tansie as though nothing had happened between them? She knew she couldn't. Not now! And, if ever, it would be with such pain she preferred not to think about the possibility.

On the first morning after their arrival, Alix was sorry when she had to leave Tansie. Blowing her another kiss from the doorway, Alix said, "I'll be back as soon as the rehearsal is over and Boris let's me go."

"I'll be right here," Tansie giggled and dived back under the covers.

For the next three days Tansie explored every shop on Bahnhofstrasse while Alix dashed off to rehearsals. Alix invariably returned to the hotel excited and full of news about the forthcoming concert. Tansie in turn showed her all the things she had bought with great delight. The only thing she didn't show Alix were the two identical rings she had bought. Tansie wanted to wait for the right moment before she gave Alix one of them.

"I haven't had so much fun in years," Tansie said and all but fell into Alix's arms. "The shops here are just amazing."

"I told you," Alix muttered lazily as she let her lips run down Tansie's cheeks and took in the familiar scent of her perfume.

Tansie in turn began to gently caress her breasts as she whispered into her ear, "I love you."

Alix could not remember another time when such a simple gesture had filled her with such excitement. It only took a few seconds and together they rolled on to the bed and into each other's arms. Even while taking off each other's clothes, they never stopped kissing and fondling. Their passion and desire for one another was overwhelming and making love became the only thing either of them wanted to think about.

On the evening of Alix's concert, Alix slipped into the new dress she had finally had time to go and buy. It was long, sleek and black with a gathered green silk belt that accentuated her narrow waist. The slit up one side gave her the room to move which she needed when playing the piano.

When she studied her mirror image for a moment, she was very pleased with what she saw. She looked radiant, even she had to admit that.

Alix had declined all offers to be escorted to the concert hall. She wanted to go with Tansie. As the two women stepped from the taxi outside the concert hall, many heads turned in their direction. Some recognised Alix and she heard whispers such as, "Isn't that Alix Clemenger?" Others asked, "Who is that beautiful woman with her?" Alix paid no attention to any of them other than giving them a wide smile as she passed and led Tansie into the foyer. Although the performers normally gained access through the stage door, Alix had found a way to get there from the main lobby.

Kissing Alix lightly on the cheek, Tansie murmured, "Good luck," and went to mingle with the other concert-goers.

Alix watched her disappear before she slipped through the nearby side door that would lead her to her dressing room where Boris was waiting for her.

Boris drew her into his arms and gave her a hug. "Are you ready?" he asked softly.

"Yes," she confirmed, and as she heard the orchestra tuning their instruments, she added with a smile, "you're on, maestro. Good luck!"

When it was time for Alix to go on stage, she walked just ahead of Boris to the enthusiastic applause from the audience. She gave them a dazzling smile, lightly bowed to Tansie, her brother, his wife Eva and her Aunt Hanna who had come up from Geneva that afternoon, and then took her seat at the piano. Although she had not performed on a concert stage for some time, neither her stride nor her smile showed any hesitation. There simply wasn't any. Alix was ready.

During the few seconds it took the concert master to lift his violin to his chin and to nod to the conductor, and for Alix to collect herself before she too lifted her eyes to Boris and nodded, she felt that same magic she had felt the very first time she had given a concert. Then Boris lifted his baton, the orchestra struck the first note of Beethoven's Piano Concerto No. 5 and Alix's entrance followed immediately afterwards. As that first note rang around the concert hall, nothing else mattered to Alix but her performance.

Alix moved through the roulades, from one end of the

keyboard to the other, the busy passagework and a frenzy of activity, with the delicacy and flexibility the composer had intended for the solo parts. But it was in the final movement where she excelled like never before. As the concerto neared its end, Alix flew through the double thrills, the fast scale-work and the long leaps with such ease it left the audience momentarily breathless.

And then came the applause that left both Boris and Alix not just breathless but so exhilarated they could barely contain their pleasure at such an exquisite performance. They laughed, looked at each other and shook their heads as though they couldn't quite believe it themselves.

Later over dinner, Boris shook his head again. "Alix, I do not understand," he cried. "You must continue to perform! How could you . . ."

Alix put her finger on his lips to hush him. "No, Boris," she said softly. "I said one concert and that's the way it will stay. As of right now, I'm on holidays." But it was with a wicked smile she added later, "In weeks to come, I might think differently."

The evening after the concert, Alix and Tansie took the night train to Vienna where they checked into the Imperial Hotel. Alix condensed the work she had to do with the Phil-harmonic Orchestra into two days. She couldn't bear to be away from Tansie for even the shortest period of time. She had already given up a few days in Zürich and was not pre-pared to give up any more. Now it was hers and Tansie's time.

Vienna was bitterly cold and, like many other European cities, had been inundated with a late snowfall. In Alix's view that only enhanced the city's charm. Fresh snow made everything look so bright and clean, she thought. They spent entire days exploring the city. Alix wanted to show her lover all the places she had frequented when she lived there. She took great delight in introducing Tansie to the city's wonders and in telling her all the little stories she remembered from the days gone by when she had studied with Randolf von Habkern.

They took long walks through the Stadtpark and admired the old master composers' monuments, and they sat in small restaurants where they quite openly held hands across the table, engrossed in intimate conversation. Even at the Staatsoper and the Musikverein where Herbert von Karajan gave one of his rare performances, they reached for each other. Where Tansie's gestures of intimacy were playfully seductive, Alix's were affectionately romantic. But whatever they were, each found the other's charming and compelling. Despite their vastly different backgrounds, they complemented one another well.

Tansie, who had travelled to England and the United States only twice when still living with Alan, was mesmerised by everything she now saw and did. She took it all in with childlike enthusiasm. She began to see it through Alix's eyes and saw the charming and quaint variety the Continent offered. She loved to listen to the different languages and to watch the people as they hurried about their business. She started to feel as Alix did, free and enchanted like she had never felt before.

This in turn so delighted Alix that she was quite oblivious to the numerous questions posed by Tansie. She answered them at great length and with great patience, a trait she did not often display. But then, she reflected with a smile, she had been more patient with Tansie right from the beginning. Was this a side-effect of being in love, she wondered? It had to be, she decided.

From Vienna they flew to Paris, the city of true love and romance.

Shortly before the plane landed, Tansie suddenly fell silent. She cast her glance downward, removed one of the two identical rings she had bought in Zürich from the middle finger of her right hand and slipped it on to Alix's.

Alix blushed. She was deeply moved by the gesture. Although until now she continued to respond passionately to Tansie's gestures of playful seduction, something inside her had still seemed to hold her back. It was as though she had to understand where her feelings led her before she could give her entire being, not just her body. Only when she accepted that she was deeply in love with Tansie could she surrender all of her freedom.

Finally the words she had wanted to speak for some time but could not, were uttered. "I love you, Tansie." Alix leant across the armrest in the first-class seat and quite leisurely kissed her on the lips.

She loved her for what she was: exotically beautiful, irresistibly seductive, charmingly vulnerable and naturally intelligent. And she loved her for what she gave her: a new way of life, a path she had never dreamed she'd ever walk. Her understanding of what Tansie gave her had taken time to develop. It had taken even more time to accept it. There was no going back now.

From the airport they took a taxi to the Hotel Crillon. Alix's passion for old worldy, elegant hotels was as great as any other. However, this particular hotel appealed to her mostly because of its magnificent Louis XV style architecture, its feeling of romance and the luxury of times long gone by.

Not quite used to such lavishness, Tansie was speechless when they entered their suite. She was overwhelmed by the opulence of the decor: the silk wall panels and drapes, the antique furniture, the gold fittings, the marble floors and walls in the bathroom and the thick plush carpet in the other rooms. Even the view from the balcony, over the Tuileries and the Place de la Concorde was breathtaking.

"A king-size bed!" Tansie gushed, a tone of disbelief in her voice. Both in Zürich and Vienna they had two single beds pushed together as was the custom in most old hotels in Europe.

"If you're not happy with the arrangement, I'll ring the desk. I'm sure they'll be happy to give us a suite with a French bed," Alix replied.

"Can I assume that a French bed is half the size of this one? And presumably for the both of us!"

"It is . . . but just think of the fun we could have!"

"You have a one-track mind," Tansie teased and, giving Alix a slight push, they both tumbled on to the bed.

It was not long before their coats, jeans, shirts and underwear were strewn all over the floor. Alix wondered for a moment or two whether she would ever be this happy again as she abandoned herself to a feast of physical pleasures.

Alix was as much in love with Paris as she was with Tansie. She still thought of Paris as the most exhilarating city in the world. The fascination it held for her the first time she visited it had not waned. Later, while studying with Jean-Jacques Dubois, she had grown to love it as much as the true Parisians did. She revelled in its architecture, its beauty, its culture, its wine and its food; she even revelled in the Parisians themselves with their brash arrogance. She adored the city's artistic atmosphere and its feeling of freedom and liberty.

Over the years, Alix had been in Paris with other lovers but never had she enjoyed Paris as much as she did now with Tansie. Alix abandoned all caution with her physical affections towards Tansie and, with her money, she gave and spent both freely and with lavish extravagance. Tansie occasionally tried to slow her down but Alix happily ignored her.

During the day they indulged themselves by frequenting the best restaurants, La Coupole and many others equally famous, or by walking in the many gardens or crooked narrow streets or by returning to the Crillon for the sole purpose of making love.

Quite by accident, Alix learnt about a concert being given by her friend and former teacher Jean-Jacques Dubois. He was to be both concert master and conductor, playing music from some of her favourite composers. Alix could not resist the program. At the last minute, and with the help of the concierge, she had acquired two tickets. She could have easily rung Jean-Jacques but chose not to do so.

Looking through the wardrobe to find something suitable to wear, both women were momentarily undecided. Alix chose a new dark grey skirt and pale grey silk shirt with gold buttons. Around her slim neck she fastened a gold choker chain studded with square-cut emeralds. Over it she wore a navy cashmere overcoat and a dark green scarf. Tansie chose a light blue shirt and navy fine-wool slacks.

When they took their seats in the concert hall, only moments before the lights went out, Tansie suddenly asked in a whisper, "Why is this concert so important to you?" She had picked up an excited restlessness in Alix as they rode in the taxi.

"Because Jean-Jacques is an old friend and I haven't seen him for some years."

Before Tansie could ask anything more, the orchestra members appeared on stage. Jean-Jacques came moments later.

Alix was instantly carried away and became oblivious to

everything other than the music. She closed her eyes and silently hummed every note of Mozart's Sinfonia Concertante and later Beethoven's only violin concerto. Although Mozart's tunes were a trifle fluffy in Alix's view, when they were played by a master of Jean-Jacques' calibre, they were enchanting. The music very much suited her carefree frivolous mood.

Tansie's mood, however, was not light. Not that she didn't like Mozart. She had in fact come to like his music a great deal. Her uneasiness stemmed from Alix's earlier excitement.

Alix was mostly vague about the relationships she had had in the past. But an inner feeling told Tansie that Jean-Jacques had assumed a more important role in Alix's life than Alix now wanted her to believe.

Was Alix still in love with him, Tansie wondered as she cast a sideways glance at her companion. She felt an immediate tug of jealousy pull at her heart. Looking for reassurance, Tansie slipped her hand into Alix's. Tansie wanted her to know that she was here now.

When interval came and they strolled towards the foyer, Alix invited Tansie to come with her to meet Jean-Jacques. Tansie declined, muttering that she wanted to have a look around. As she watched Alix walk across the foyer, Tansie noted that Alix periodically stopped to chat to people she obviously knew or who knew her. She wondered who all those people were. Her security was instantly threatened; not because there was an intimacy between those people and Alix but rather because she felt they belonged to Alix's past, a past she would never be able to influence no matter what control she had over the present. Tansie was jealous of that past. That there was quite a simple explanation – Alix was, after all, well-known in most parts of the world either for her compositions or her performances on the concert stages – never crossed her mind.

Alix, oblivious to Tansie's distress, eventually found Jean-Jacques in the conductor's room. He was engaged in an animated conversation with a young female admirer. She smiled, remembering herself many years ago in a similar situation.

Although he had his back to her, he seemed to know that someone was at the door observing him. His eyes lit up the moment he turned in Alix's direction and, rushing towards her, he embraced her.

"Alix," he gushed, "What a wonderful surprise . . . I have not seen you in so many years."

While he continued to talk to her in rapid French, Alix thought how little he had changed since their last meeting. His deeply tanned face was still surrounded by thick silver-grey hair and the flashing green eyes, much like her own, were as alert and intense as they used to be. His cheeks were perhaps a little paunchier but he was still a very attractive man.

Alix listened with some amusement as he tried to persuade her to have dinner with him after the concert. His voice was seductive and his words subtle. Nothing has changed, Alix reflected. Except she was no longer interested. She graciously declined the offer and gave him a disarming smile.

"I should never have let you slip away all those years ago," he said somewhat ruefully.

"You had a wife and three small children," she reminded him. Alix had in fact ended the liaison when she found out that he was married.

"Ahh . . . yes, I know," he agreed with a nonchalant shrug of his shoulders and added, "by the way, congratulations.

The music you composed for Pierre's movie *Toujours Et Jamais* was extraordinary." He turned, his fine silk and wool tails flapping around his legs, and walked away.

During the second part of the concert, Alix had trouble concentrating on the music. Instead she kept looking from the beautiful woman who was now her lover to the very debonair and talented man who once took that place in her life. The fond memories of him reminded her just how she had loved some of the men who had crossed her path in the past. What has happened to you, Alix, in a matter of a few short months, she asked herself once again.

When thunderous applause erupted all around her, Alix was pulled back to reality.

The two women were barely outside when Tansie burst out, "What took you so long with Jean-Jacques? You were there for the whole of interval!"

"I'm sorry," Alix apologised, adding, "We talked about old times and he asked me to have dinner with him after the concert."

"Would you have gone with him had I not been here?"

"I doubt it," Alix responded. If asked whether she was still attracted to him, she would not have denied it. But, Jean-Jacques belonged to another world, another life and another time.

"I couldn't bear it if you left me," Tansie murmured.

On impulse, Alix drew her into her arms and kissed her lightly on the cheek. Even though they were in the midst of all the other concert-goers, Alix didn't give them a single thought. Her only concern was for Tansie.

Chapter 10

When their days in Paris came to an end, they both felt a little sad. They knew that their holiday was rapidly coming to a close, with one last week of skiing ahead of them.

After they had dinner with Aunt Hanna at her house outside Geneva, the two women went upstairs to their room to pack. They wanted to leave for St Moritz early the following morning.

Standing in front of her chaotic suitcase, Tansie asked, "What clothes do we need for the Palace Hotel?"

"Everything we've got," Alix responded, not in the least ruffled by the prospect.

Once the packing was completed, Tansie decided to call it a day and went to bed. Alix kissed her a leisurely goodnight, promised to return soon and went downstairs to look for her aunt. It would be the last opportunity she had to talk to Hanna.

Alix found Hanna in her study. "Am I disturbing you?" Alix asked and approached the small antique writing desk Hanna was sitting at.

"Of course not, darling," Hanna replied, pleased that Alix had come to see her. "Go and sit on the couch near the fire. I'll pour us a cognac."

For some time they talked about Alix's concert in Zürich, her work and the children. Eventually Hanna said with a smile, "Now that we've discussed everything else but you . . . how are you? You look happier than I have seen you in a long time."

"I am very happy, Hanna," Alix replied, the sparkle in her eyes confirming her words. Without giving it another thought, she added, "I'm in love . . . with Tansie."

As soon as Alix had made that single statement, there was no holding her back. She told Hanna everything. She described the unconditional love they shared and Alix's hopes for the future. But she also told her of the fears and doubts this relationship still held for her especially where the children were concerned. It was preferable to keep this liaison secret from them but that may well cause both Tansie and herself difficulties.

"Can this happiness last, Hanna?" Alix concluded.

"It can," Hanna confirmed softly, delighted to see her niece so happy. "Love knows no boundaries if we allow it to blossom to its full potential," she added.

Alix threw her arms around her aunt. She was still one of the most beautiful women Alix had ever known despite her advancing years. But then, her beauty wasn't just on the surface but rather inside her. "Hanna, you don't know how happy this makes me," she said. After a moment's pause, she added more seriously, "How do you think the rest of the world would take it if they knew?"

"Darling, I doubt that it would make any difference," Hanna responded. "You have made your name in the music world . . . whatever else you may or may not do is of no concern to anyone other than to you and your partner." When Alix remained silent, she added, "I've known many people who've had similar relationships. Some were public, others weren't. In the long run, it didn't matter. They were accepted for their talents and compassion and not their choice of bed partner."

"Anybody I know?"

"Yes," Hanna smiled.

115

Alix thought about it for a moment. She laughed when a picture of Hanna's friend Carlotta came to her mind. Retired now from the world's opera stages, Carlotta had often been a guest in Hanna's house. And so had her friend Carolina.

"How are Carlotta and Carolina?" Alix asked.

"Getting on in years, but otherwise, very well."

"You know, whenever I looked at them, all I ever saw were two women together, not always harmoniously, but very happy just the same," Alix said with a smile, remembering some volatile temper tantrums between the two prima donnas.

"If such relationships were possible fifty years ago, it should be a lot easier now. Thank God the world has become more tolerant."

When Alix finally went to bed, she felt at peace. Drawing Tansie into her arms, she murmured, "I love you."

The train slowly made its way towards St Moritz, over narrow and fragile-looking bridges, with the river below in the valley gushing its way over rocks and broken tree trunks. The massive fir-trees alongside the railroad tracks were laden with fresh snow and, because of their load, barely swayed in the cold mid-afternoon breeze. As they neared St Moritz, Alix let her gaze wander to the left and into the Inn Valley towards La Punt and Zuoz. It had been here where she had gone to boarding school. She had many fond memories of those years and treasured them. But, she reflected, they were also the years she had to come to terms with her parents' death. Even after more than twenty years, she still felt a painful twist in her heart whenever she thought of her father or the circumstances of his last moments.

Glancing sideways at her lover, she smiled and took her hand. This part of the world may have some painful memories, she thought, but it also had some good ones, and now that she was here with Tansie, the good ones would predominate.

The two women were met at the station by the hotel porter who took charge of their luggage before motoring them to the village and the Palace Hotel.

The Palace was exactly as Alix remembered it. Some of her fellow students had often caught a train into St Moritz for the sole purpose of eating chocolate cake at the Palace. Its grandeur and understated elegance was unequalled anywhere in the world. The hotel staff, immaculately uniformed, moved about noiselessly in response to the constant comings and goings of its wealthy and often famous guests. All of this gave it an air of subdued excitement.

Since it was too late in the afternoon to go skiing, Alix and Tansie decided to take a stroll instead. They linked arms and made their way along the narrow path, on the hard-packed snow, to the lake. As they walked, they watched adults and children alike skating over the smooth frozen surface. Soft music drifted from the clubhouse across the ice expanse. People walked or skated and the rustling of the tree tops gave an impression of a romantic dreamland rather than reality.

While Alix was preoccupied with the scenery, Tansie paid more attention to their fellow strollers. Most of them were clad in heavy expensive furs, with the odd piece of ostentatious jewellery protruding from an open neck coat or dangling from bare earlobes.

In disbelief, Tansie gushed, "I have never seen so many mink coats in all my life! This place reeks of money! I must look like someone's poor cousin!"

Alix gave her a quick kiss on the cheek. "You're a beautiful woman without a mink coat," she said, adding with a twinkle in her eyes, "when I think about it, I couldn't bear it if I had to peel you out of a mink coat every time I wanted to touch you."

Tansie chuckled, squeezing Alix's arm. "I love your impatience," she said flirtatiously.

They made an elegant couple when they strolled into the restaurant later that evening. They had both chosen semi-formal evening gowns, bought in Paris the week before.

Bowing a little, the maître d' asked them to follow him. He lead them down the middle of the room to a small table in the window. Having made themselves comfortable, Alix reached into her small evening bag and took out the gold cigarette case with the matching cigarette holder she had also bought in Paris. When she noticed Tansie staring at her, she asked, "What's wrong?"

"I still feel intimidated by all this luxury," Tansie replied, looking around. "Although Alan could have afforded such hotels when we travelled, he always found something cheap. He was not as extravagant as you."

"Then I'm glad I can make up for his shortcomings!"

After a short pause, Tansie said, "It's just me being stuffy and worrying about what other people might think." With a smile now, Tansie reached across the table and squeezed Alix's hand.

Alix scanned the room and its occupants and said, "You should be worried. After all, it wouldn't do for the Edward Kennedys, or any of the other guests, to go home and tell your mutual friends that they saw you flirting, not just at the Palace and not just with another woman, but with the one and only Alix Clemenger!"

"It wouldn't, would it?" Tansie grinned.

Two days into the ski holiday, Barbara, Alix's friend from her early days in Washington and later from her boarding school days, rang from the neighbouring Carlton Hotel. They arranged to meet for lunch at the restaurant on top of Corviglia. Casting a searching eye around the bustling room, Alix spotted Barbara and her husband, Josef, at the far end and proceeded across the tiled floor.

Tansie, who followed a step behind, watched with dismay as the two women embraced. Although Tansie knew that Alix and Barbara had been friends for over thirty years and that they hadn't seen each other for some months, she didn't like what she saw. The jealousy she felt was not so much physical as emotional. She was jealous of the memories they shared and the closeness such memories brought with them. Coughing discreetly, she made Alix aware that she was there too.

Alix introduced Tansie and then took off her cap, gloves and jacket. "I keep forgetting how cold this country is," she moaned. "I need a schnapps to pick me up . . . will you have one, Tansie?"

Tansie still stood there, shivering and rubbing her hands together. "I don't think so. My knees are weak enough just looking at the mountains!"

"I thought something else gave you weak knees!" Alix whispered into Tansie's ear. Her eyes looked innocent enough, but her lips drew upwards into a lazy grin.

The comment wasn't lost on Tansie, but she ignored it except for a half-hearted smile. She still had trouble coming to grips with Alix's often nonchalant attitude. Tansie loved her for that as much as for anything else. Yet she couldn't bring herself to abandon the strictures that had been beaten into her as a child. She often showed ambivalence when in public.

They could not have hoped for more glorious weather conditions during their week in St Moritz. They skied every

119

day with Barbara and Josef until early afternoon and then returned to the hotel for a nap or to make love. Later they dressed to have dinner at one of the smaller local restaurants where Alix was less likely to be recognised and where they could chat more comfortably with Barbara and Josef who often joined them.

For Alix's and Tansie's last evening in St Moritz, Barbara and Josef joined the two women for dinner at the Palace. Retiring to the lounge for a nightcap afterwards, Alix's mood became pensive. She hated farewells. Tonight was no exception.

After Michael's death, Alix had considered returning to Europe with the children. As much as her three offspring loved to travel, they had made it quite clear that their home was Australia. They had no desire to be moved half way around the world on a permanent basis. For their sake, she had abandoned the idea.

Having picked up the change in Alix, Barbara leant over and said, "I don't know why you keep going back to that God-forsaken country. Why don't you come and live here again?"

"I can't," Alix replied. "The children belong there, it's their country. I couldn't ever deprive Michael's father of his grandchildren or them of their extended family. They need that stability and the security of knowing that they belong somewhere." After a short pause, she added softly, "A stability I never had."

"You had me, remember?" Barbara's dark-brown eyes lit up and she drew her lips into a smile.

Alix too smiled as she gave her friend a closer look. Her hair was black and tied into a jewelled clasp at the nape of her neck. The cream silk shirt was undone to the second button and the large aquamarine heart which hung from a gold chain down to the cleavage was just visible. Her features were well-balanced and gave the impression of calmness. Because she was comfortable within herself, she made others feel the same.

"I did but that wasn't quite what I meant," Alix said.

"I know," Barbara said. Giving her husband and Tansie a brief glance and noting that they were engrossed in a conversation of their own, she continued, "I'm so pleased to see you happy, Alix. Tansie is a very beautiful woman. There is something about her I too find very appealing."

As the full meaning of her friend's words sank in, Alix almost fell off the chair. "Is it that obvious?"

"To me it is. It's wonderful, Alix," Barbara confirmed. After a short pause, she added, "I admire you for doing what maybe many more women should do . . . we might well have a happier world."

"You mean you've thought about having a relationship with a woman?"

"I haven't just thought about it, I had one . . . many years ago," Barbara replied, a tone of sadness in her voice.

"What happened?" Alix asked, not out of simple curiosity but with genuine concern. It also revealed a side of her friend she had not previously known.

"I was a coward. I couldn't live with it. I left her," she said. "And yet, the few months we were together were probably the happiest in my life."

"Do you regret your decision?"

"I have my moments," Barbara mused. "Mostly because of the pain I inflicted on her and, in many ways, on myself. Marianne was a beautiful woman in every sense of the word . . . and still is. Although Josef is a good husband and an excellent father, I don't get the emotional support from him that I did from her."

"Do you still see her?"

"Yes, from time to time, and, I'm pleased to say, she's very happy with another woman and has been for many years."

Alix looked thoughtful as she momentarily watched the smoke from her cigarette curl towards the ceiling. "It was not an easy decision to make," she said. "I love her, I can't do anything about that, but whether I'll ever be strong enough to make it public is another matter."

"What's there to make public?" Barbara asked. "That you share the same bed with another woman? Or how wonderful such a relationship can be? Surely we're all entitled to keep some things private, don't you think?"

"I agree, as you well know," Alix smiled. "But, thanks for that. It means a lot to me."

Despite appearing to be immersed in conversation with Josef, Tansie said abruptly, "I've got to go to bed, I'm beat." Secretly, she was glad their holiday in St Moritz had come to an end. Barbara had taken far too much of Alix's time and attention.

Still in a pensive mood when they got back to their room, Alix undressed and slipped into bed and into Tansie's arms. Tonight, in particular, she had to be close to Tansie, to feel the soothing warmth between them. Despite her often breezy smile, she craved love, affection and harmony like most other people. It was that part of her which now needed to be nurtured.

Early the following morning, the Palace limousine drove them to the nearby airport in Samedan. As their luggage was loaded on to the plane, the two women stood in silence and surveyed the peaceful scene one more time. The lake in the distance was still deserted and the village was asleep, not quite ready for yet another bustling day. With the sun just making an appearance over their tops, the mountains looked even more gigantic in the pale morning light.

Tansie gave Alix a warm smile. "Thank you for a great holiday. I won't ever forget it."

"Well, we laughed a lot and we cried a little. But, I think we'll always look back with fond memories," Alix replied and returned Tansie's gaze.

During the long flight home, Alix wondered where they would go from here. Alix was well aware that since they had become lovers, they had lived in a dream world. First at the beach house over the summer holidays and then in Europe. What sort of strain would every day life put on their relationship? Could they sustain it given the society they moved in, the children and their respective professions?

Tansie gave Alix a sideways glance when she sighed. "Are you all right?" she asked.

"Yeah . . ." Alix mused. "What's going to happen to us when we get home?"

"Nothing is going to happen," Tansie said. "We love each other but nobody needs to know, if that's what you're worried about."

"No, I'm not worried about what other people might think," Alix replied. She was rarely pessimistic, yet something she could not identify weighed in the back of her mind. With a smile, she added, "Maybe I just don't want to go home and, were it not for the children, I'd stay right here with you."

"What a wonderful thought, but you're such a dreamer, my love," Tansie murmured affectionately, dropping her head on to Alix's shoulders.

Chapter 11

Soon after their return, the hot days of summer turned into autumn, and before long, an early winter. Leaves were swept off the trees overnight, leaving them bare and vulnerable.

When the Oscars were announced that autumn, Alix and John were ecstatic. Ralph Schönberg's movie *Let Yesterday Be* won the Oscar for Best Director and Best Music Score. Although the album had sold well before the announcement, afterwards its success soared to heights even Alix and John found incredible.

But regardless of her newest success, Alix was still totally consumed with her lover. While she and Tansie had discovered and explored their love during summer and autumn, that winter it came to maturity. Both Alix and Tansie were creative people and it was through their work that each expressed just how much she meant to the other. Every one of Alix's new compositions came to her with ease and overflowing inspiration; they were extravagantly cheerful. Tansie attacked her work with an enthusiasm she didn't know she had and her art pieces exuded a charm all of their own. She was delighted with every sculpture she created and now, she rarely destroyed one. She knew that Alix loved her unconditionally and passionately.

Weeks turned into months and Tansie and Alix shared many happy and intimate moments.

Since both Felix and Michael's father regularly took the children away for weekends, they had more uninterrupted time together. Alix had always liked her father-in-law, Joe

Clemenger, and, even after Michael's death, she had maintained a reasonably close relationship with him both in private and on the Board of Directors of the family company. Joe was the only one Alix could trust within Clemenger Pharmaceuticals, and only he knew that she had started to buy up as much stock as became available on the stock exchange.

Alix's beach house and her country retreat became peaceful havens and places of tranquil seclusion. Tansie worked on her sculptures and Alix on her compositions.

In the past, Alix had often encouraged crowds of people around her. During her marriage to Michael in particular, she had experienced an inner sense of emptiness, an emotional void. It wasn't until after his death that she realised that she really did not need lots of other people. With Tansie, who was both stimulating and calming, she felt whole and deeply contented. Alix constantly discovered new things in Tansie's varied personality which she found interesting as well as deeply touching.

Tansie in turn thrived on Alix's love. She found an inner security she had never felt before. Although not consciously aware of it, she had found her true self for the first time in her life and had allowed it to blossom. Although she experienced moments of jealousy, mostly she felt loved and secure. It did not occur to her that her profound insecurity would surface again sooner or later.

Twice, when Alix had to go overseas to New York and Munich, Tansie didn't like it much, but declined the invitation to go with her. Despite the love and care Alix showered upon her, Tansie had moments of restlessness and was not content with the love of just one person. Alix's absences allowed Tansie the time to resume having affairs with both men and women. They were mostly two- or three-night stands which, in Tansie's opinion, meant nothing. It was simply something she had always done, and anyway, Alix would never know.

What Tansie didn't know was that her need to be loved and nurtured was so great, she forever confused love with sex. There had been other people before Alix who had genuinely loved her, and yet, she continued to search for more. Her profound belief that she was unlovable prevented her from behaving in any other way.

For many weeks, Tansie was on cloud nine: at least until Alan told her he was starting formal divorce proceedings. He had moved in with his girlfriend and wanted to be free of all emotional and financial commitments to his first wife. Alan was prepared to make a substantial settlement so that Tansie would never want for anything, but that would be his final contribution. After that, Tansie would be on her own.

When Tansie heard the news from the lawyer Alan had demanded she hire, she stormed around the house in a rage.

"You bastard," she shouted over and over. Although initially she had not wanted a permanent separation, in more recent times she had come to change her mind and had, in fact, believed that she had accepted an imminent divorce. But the finality of this new turn of events brought out the worst in her. Not least of all, because Alan had started divorce proceedings. If anything, that should have been her prerogative, she thought.

After the initial outburst, Tansie's moods alternated between uncontrollable rages and bouts of deep depression. She took the rage out on Alix simply because she was close by. Later, she'd curl into Alix's comforting arms, apologise and weep at the same time.

Alix would never forget the very first temper tantrum

thrown by Tansie the day she received the news. They had returned from dinner when Tansie opened her mail. The moment she read the solicitor's letter she flew into a rage. At the same time, a bout of lightning lit up the black sky and thunder broke in the distance. An incredible storm unleashed, uprooting the evergreen alder tree in the front garden.

Alix cringed and shuddered, not sure whether to take cover from the elements outside or from Tansie who hurled objects at random across the room.

In the darkness and surrounded by a strange foreboding, they both lost their balance and tumbled on to the couch. For a while Tansie kicked and shrieked underneath Alix. Then her whole body seemed to go limp and she lay there, quietly weeping into Alix's shoulder and murmuring, "Why don't you just let me die . . ."

Alix sighed and held her lover. She was still stunned and didn't know what had struck her. She was flabbergasted by Tansie's outburst and deeply alarmed by her words. Tansie had had short bouts of depression which seemed to come upon her without warning. Alix thought she might suggest to Tansie that she seek outside help. But, Tansie's tantrum disappeared as quickly as it had appeared and she was her old self again. Alix rationalised that Tansie was simply stressed out over the impending divorce and that in due course all would be well again.

Alix could not know that Tansie's instability was so profound that it would need much more than a new house and a caring lover to stabilise her. At one stage when she was near despair with Tansie's behaviour, she suggested Tansie come and live with her.

"Oh, Alix, my love," Tansie sighed and kissed her. "I love you dearly for that offer but it wouldn't be fair to the children. And, I wouldn't want to hurt them . . . what if they realised that we're more than just friends? I don't think it'd be long before they started to ask questions," she pointed out.

"So far they have never said anything when you've stayed at my house overnight," Alix replied, confident that they would have told her had they thought it in any way unusual. Thoughtfully, she added, "They seemed to have accepted you as part of the family and . . ."

"Maybe you're right but let's not complicate our lives, shall we?" Tansie interrupted with a convincing smile. Only she knew that this was less than truthful. In her mind, cohabitation would make her relationship with Alix more important than what she, in a way, wanted it to be. And, to live with Alix would considerably curb her other activities. She could not run the risk of Alix finding out that she had other lovers. Even if in her mind they meant nothing, she felt that even Alix's patience and tolerance might be stretched to unacceptable levels.

Alix eventually accepted Tansie's argument. She wanted to believe her and she most certainly trusted her. She had no reason not to.

Since Alan had given Tansie a most generous settlement, as he had said he would, in Alix's mind there seemed to be no need to delay the purchase of a house. Over several weeks and through her real estate agent, Alix suggested numerous houses but Tansie found something wrong with each one. Tansie explained her reluctance by saying that she was going through a grieving period over her failed marriage. Alix believed her. It wasn't until Tansie felt that she had tried Alix's patience to the limit that she decided on a house not far from Alix's.

As soon as the contracts were signed, Alix took the

children skiing for the first week of the spring holidays. Tansie had at first accepted Alix's invitation to join them, but later cancelled. She was in a creative mood and didn't want to be interrupted, she explained. Given the work she herself did, Alix understood what it was like when a creative mood struck. It had to be explored before it passed. Although she was disappointed, in the end Alix looked forward to spending some time with the children on her own. She knew she wouldn't get another chance until Christmas when she planned on taking them overseas.

As had become her habit whether Alix was in or out of town, Tansie rang every evening. She talked about her day's sculpting and her social life with one or the other friend. The outings were mentioned casually and the implication was that none of them were of any importance. Only Tansie knew that her description was less than honest.

Alix had just replaced the receiver after one such telephone call when a sudden sharp knock on the front door jolted her. Before she managed to answer it, the door flew open. Haig walked in, followed by a gust of freezing cold air from the open staircase.

"Haig!" she cried and flung herself into his arms. She hadn't seen him since the day after Christmas and this was September. Burying her head on his broad chest, she rubbed her cheek against the soft damp fabric of his cashmere overcoat. He tilted her head backwards, bent down and kissed her.

"What're you doing here?" her voice did not betray her surprise. He despised winter and everything it brought with it.

Kicking off his soaked Bally shoes, he laughed. "A home visit without seeing you just wouldn't be the same. I missed you," he said with a broad smile.

Alix returned his smile. Had he said that twenty years ago, she probably would never have left him. How different her life would have been, she reflected.

While Alix prepared him a stiff scotch on the rocks, they chatted and caught up on their news. Although they often spoke to each other on the telephone, there wasn't always time for everything.

Afterwards Alix lay down on the couch, her head resting in his lap and a feeling of contentment within her. Her earlier loneliness at not having Tansie there dissipated. When he pushed his hand underneath her sweater and began to caress her bare breasts, she froze.

I can't do this, she thought in a panic and broke into a cold sweat. Alix hadn't seen Haig since she and Tansie had become lovers. She had never thought about how she might feel or what she would do if she and Haig were alone together.

Now that he was here, she had to think fast. Body and mind were torn in two different directions, adding to her dilemma. She abhorred the idea of cheating on Tansie, but didn't know how to explain to Haig that she couldn't make love to him. How could she tell him that she was in love with a woman?

Seemingly oblivious to her problem, he continued his teasing manipulations and her body reacted to it as it had for nearly twenty years. Her physical desire mounted so rapidly, she could not fight it even if she wanted to. She capitulated when he carried her into the bedroom.

Later when they sat up in bed, smoking a cigarette and sipping champagne, Haig asked softly, "You're in love with Tansie, aren't you?"

Alix gulped. "Yes," she murmured.

"Why didn't you tell me?" he implored with compassion

and took her into his arms. Although rationally he knew he shouldn't feel like this, emotionally he still felt some jealousy.

"I couldn't tell you!" she cried and leant her head against his chest.

"Because it's a woman you're in love with?" he asked.

"That too," she replied and lifted her eyes to meet his. "I despise cheating but that isn't all. I'm confused, Haig. I love her and yet . . ." She let her voice trail off momentarily and then smiled. "It's not in very good taste to discuss one lover with another one," she said.

"At my age, I can cope with that," he assured her.

Alix sighed and then started to say what was on her mind. "Since Tansie and I have become lovers, I have not had the slightest desire to go to bed with a man. But when you turned up, it wasn't my mind but my body that betrayed me."

"I'm sorry that it was me who caused that confusion."

"Don't be sorry. Sooner or later it had to happen. I have to find out what I really want."

"Possibly," he mused, and lighting another two cigarettes, he handed her one. "Are you happy?"

"Very happy," Alix exclaimed, adding softly, "I'm sorry if I hurt you but once you asked, I couldn't lie to you."

"No more than I could lie to you," he replied, thinking that he would never insult her intelligence or her pride in being anything less than honest. After a short silence, he said, "Right now I'm not sure what I feel but I would lie if I said that this turn in our relationship evokes no emotions. Although I suppose, deep down, I have always known that you were far too sensual not to have other lovers, the reality does cause a twinge in my heart. But, if you've found happiness with Tansie then my own feelings are of little

131

importance, particularly given the way I have floated in and out of your life without ever really making a commitment."

"Your commitment was to a friendship and I don't expect anything will change on that score. Nobody can ever take that away from us," Alix replied and briefly ruffled his hair. When he didn't reply, she continued. "At first I was surprised, shocked even, I was not prepared for something like that to happen to me. But I couldn't stop myself from falling in love with Tansie."

"Love knows no boundaries and often it comes when we least expect it."

"That's what Hanna said too."

"I always knew she was a smart lady," Haig grinned.

"Or you're getting wise and old like her," Alix laughed.

"That's a possibility of course." After a while he added, "For what it's worth, you'll always have a very special place in my life, and, I admire you for following your heart. And as you said, we'll always be friends."

"Thank you, Haig," Alix replied and curled into his protective arm. When he left the next day, Alix kissed him, sure that they would always be friends.

When the weather changed into sleet and rain, Alix decided to go home a couple of days early. She still had a lot to do for Tansie's birthday party the following Tuesday. She dropped the children off at home and went straight over to Tansie's place.

After a week's absence, they flew into each other's arms and, temporarily, the rest of the world ceased to exist. When they made love, Alix's thoughts wandered to Haig and to the fact that she had been unfaithful to Tansie. This knowledge still did not sit comfortably with her. But having determined that it would not happen again, she felt a little easier. She was glad she had seen Haig and told him about Tansie. Now she could enjoy what her female lover offered her.

Alix was running late on the evening of Tansie's birthday party and came flying into the kitchen just before seven o'clock. "I'm sorry, Felix," she apologised. "I tried to get home early but it didn't work out that way."

"It's all under control," Felix assured her, pushing a tray laden with little delicacies into the oven.

"Thanks, Felix. I wouldn't know what to do without you," she muttered and disappeared.

She showered and then dressed in a slinky, soft yellow silk outfit and high-heel shoes. As she walked past the large mirror in the hall, she gave her image one last glance. She sighed and pulled a few stray curls back into place.

Alix had often entertained the idea of changing her hairstyle; let it grow and put it up into a French plait or something. But she knew it would drive her crazy if she had to spend more than a minute or so every morning doing her hair. Alternatively, she could cut it very short, down to an inch or so as she had after she saw the French movie *Breathless* for the first time.

Returning to the present, she gave herself one last glance in the mirror. What she saw was a very happy woman and this pleased her.

Alix was just coming down the stairs when she heard Felix open the front door and welcome James. She had baulked at the idea of inviting a male partner for the formal sit-down dinner. In her view there was not a single reason why she should do so. Least of all in her own house. But Tansie had been so adamant that they both have a partner for the night, Alix had relented. She hated arguing, particularly with a lover. Later, she decided that it really didn't matter a great deal anyway. They both knew to whom their hearts belonged.

Alix had chosen to invite James because he was easy to be with. They had met some years earlier at an AFI award evening. Afterwards they had dated for a while but when they both realised that the chemistry was not right between them, they were happy to settle for a friendship. Now they dined together from time to time, and on rarer occasions, escorted each other to a function when a partner was necessary. The solid friendship they had suited them both.

Alix helped Felix put the finishing touches to his preparations as James sat on the kitchen bench and chatted about his work at one of the major TV networks. He was a producer rather than an actor, but he kept her amused by mimicking some well-known actors he had to deal with.

After a sumptuous meal, Alix invited her guests to return to the sitting room for coffee and cognac.

Lingering, Tansie moved towards Alix and casually put her arm around her waist. "What a shame we can't just disappear upstairs for a while," she whispered into Alix's ear.

"Why not?" Alix smiled nonplussed.

"God, I love you," Tansie exclaimed, ruffled her lover's hair and followed the other guests.

Given that it was a week night, most guests left before midnight. The two women were finally on their own.

Wandering upstairs, Tansie stopped half-way up. "Do you sleep with James when I'm not around?" she asked timidly.

"Most certainly not!" Alix protested, a little hurt that Tansie would assume that.

It was almost dawn by the time they had exhausted themselves. Snuggling into Alix's embrace, Tansie muttered, "You were right, we shouldn't have invited partners for us . . . I'm sorry."

"It doesn't matter now. But, I want you to know that I'm not ashamed of what we do," Alix replied and gently stroked Tansie's cheek.

"I know," Tansie mused. After a short pause, she added, "I just feel uncomfortable sometimes. You see, you have money, power and a high professional profile, it wouldn't matter what you did. But for me, it's different. I'm just an ordinary, everyday woman who has to protect her integrity. Especially now that I'm divorced."

"I'm sorry you feel that way," Alix replied and, leisurely kissing Tansie's lips, continued, "do you regret having. . ."

"How could I, my love?" Tansie cried and let her hand wander from Alix's neck down to her thighs. "I don't ever want this relationship to stop," she added just before she lowered her lips on to Alix's.

"At this rate, we won't sleep at all," Alix murmured with pleasure. The thought of ever feeling less excited when making love with Tansie in times to come, brought a smile to her face. Alix could not imagine it.

It wasn't until much later that Alix wondered whether there was some truth in Tansie's statement. Did she have more freedom to do as she chose because of her high profile? It was possible, Alix decided. But, she also had to admit that she had no idea how other women in similar relationships coped and how they dealt with them. She had never made a conscious choice not to mix with lesbians. That was just the way it was. With a wry smile she acknowledged that she had never actually contemplated what their lives must really be like.

Chapter 12

The first blossoms of spring were out when Tansie was getting ready to move into her new house. Alix would have liked to help her but was called to Los Angeles to discuss a new movie score with Ralph Schönberg. Afterwards, she would go to New York to meet with Rita Stone, hers and John's American music publisher. Neither Alix nor Tansie were happy with the arrangement, but Alix had no alternative.

Alix returned from overseas just in time to collect some music sheets from her studio, before going to rehearsal at the concert hall. But, as she was leaving, her brother-in-law Jason stormed in.

He was hot and could feel himself starting to sweat. He hated his dead brother for having put him in this awkward position. And, he despised Alix because she had turned him down when, after Michael's death, he had suggested a relationship.

"We want you out of Clemenger Pharmaceuticals," he said.

"Why should I get out?" Alix asked hotly. "You boys had fair warning that I would get rid of you if you didn't lift your game. You've run out of time and I've run out of patience. I will never compromise my integrity!"

"Really?" He smirked. "I hear you've got a new friend. What's her name again, the dark skinny broad?"

Alix despised violence and yet, her hand flew out and hit him squarely on his jaw. His head snapped backwards on impact. Stunned he rubbed the side of his face.

"Get out, Jason!" Alix opened the door and stood to one side. When he didn't move, she gave him a sharp push and repeated, "Out, Jason!" The door slammed in his face.

Later she acknowledged that it was because of people like him that she was reluctant to make her true relationship with Tansie known. Alix now wondered whether it was even possible that, because of men like Jason, women chose other women as partners.

Alix was still furious when she arrived at the concert hall. Without being aware of what she was doing, she opened the piano lid with a bang and slapped the music sheets on to the stand.

"Are you all right?" Boris asked, giving her a curious glance from the conductor's platform.

Alix nodded and smiled. "Yeah."

"Okay," he muttered and lifted his baton. "Second movement, violins and piano only, please . . . pianissimo."

When she and John had decided to record a new movie score with the MSO under Boris' direction, Alix had also decided to play the piano solo parts herself. It wasn't something she did often, although when she did do it, she enjoyed it immensely. She particularly enjoyed working with Boris. Between them they had an inner understanding not just of music in general, but also of each other's personality.

Hours later when Boris put down his baton and left the stage, Alix flew to her feet.

"You are in a hurry?" Boris observed.

"Yes, I'm sorry . . . I've got to run." She had not seen Tansie for ten days and now could not wait. Letting herself into Tansie's house a short while later, she called out, "Where are you?"

When no response came, she wandered down the passage

to the sitting room at the back of the house. Tansie was crouched in front of the open fire and, as she rocked back and forth on her buttocks, she wept quietly. Alarmed, Alix rushed to her side.

"What's wrong?" Alix asked.

Tansie looked up. Her eyes were red and puffy. "I'm pregnant!"

"You're what?"

"I'm having a baby!" Tansie shouted.

"I thought that's what you said," Alix muttered as though in shock. Before she could stop herself, she asked, "Are you sure . . . whose is it?"

"I don't know," Tansie cried. "Maybe Graham's . . . maybe Peter's!" Or maybe someone else's she couldn't even remember, she thought. She had spent most of her life trying to forget things. Her mind was cluttered enough without the extra baggage of the various disasters she had experienced.

A wave of nausea hit the pit of Alix's stomach. She scrambled to her feet and made a dash for the bathroom. It seemed an eternity until her body stopped heaving. She turned the tap on and splashed cold water over her pale, distraught face. She tried to tell herself that this was a nightmare but to no avail. Instead, pictures of Tansie with Graham and Peter, and maybe others, began to flash through her head. She respected other people's independence, even a lover's, but she did not think this was playing it fair. It was not that she had never been unfaithful, she was well aware of that. However, if or when such occasions arose, she would never tell her partner. She knew only too well what pain such a revelation caused.

Alix had met both men, Peter and Graham, but had never given either of them much thought. She now recalled the sweet stale smell of hashish which had hung in the air in Tansie's bedroom on a few occasions. Peter was the only person Alix had seen smoke the stuff in recent times.

"What am I going to do?" Tansie asked.

Alix took a deep breath. She wanted to reach out to Tansie but couldn't. She was glad that her friend and family GP, Douglas Hamilton, was by coincidence also Tansie's GP. "Firstly, you'll see Douglas and have it confirmed. Then, depending on the result, we'll think of something."

"I want to keep it!"

"You told me you never wanted children," Alix gasped.

"I didn't mean it. That's all I ever wanted. You'll help me, won't you? What do I know about babies," Tansie cried and flung herself into Alix's arms. "Will you leave me if I keep the baby?" The bombardment continued.

Alix was more than just a little confused by that statement, but now was not the time to question Tansie further. Right now, Alix had more pressing things to deal with. "No," Alix replied with a heavy heart and prayed that the suspected pregnancy was just that, suspected only.

She couldn't bear the thought of Tansie having a baby and realising later that she didn't want it. Alix feared that the novelty of a baby in the house would be very temporary.

After a moment's silence, Tansie stood up and pulled Alix with her. "I never wanted you to know about Graham or Peter because it really didn't mean anything," she murmured.

Alix only nodded and held back the tears which stung her eyes. She felt betrayed and couldn't bring herself to ask about the lies she had been told in the past. She had no desire to cause herself any more distress. Right now, all she wanted to do was go home and crawl into bed, preferably by herself.

But Tansie had other plans. "Will you come and tuck me

into bed?" she asked timidly.

"Okay." Regardless of how she felt, Alix could never desert Tansie. Certainly not at a time like this. Alix followed Tansie down the hall to her bedroom with a heavy heart. Although she had no clear idea how she was going to do it, one way or another she would have to weather this storm.

Tansie undressed and slipped under the covers. Alix sat down on the bed and drew her into her arms.

"I wish I could tell you why I do those things, but I can't," Tansie began. Only she knew that this was less than honest. Now that she was divorced, she would have to keep her options open again. Staying single was not one of them. Nightmares of her childhood, of being a nobody without a name and of being ignored, had started to plague her again. "There is no excuse for what I did and for the pain I caused you, but I can't undo it. All I can do is tell you that I'm sorry."

Alix remained silent and Tansie continued.

"Maybe it's just easier to say 'yes' to those guys than it is to say 'no'. At least that way you get it over and done with as quickly as possible. You know what it's like!" Tansie said.

"No, I don't know what it's like. If I don't want to sleep with someone, then I don't! And nobody could ever change my mind about that!" Alix replied sharper than she had intended. Although she had had one indiscretion with Haig, she knew it would never happen again. Not with him or anyone else.

Now it was Tansie's turn to remain sullenly silent and Alix continued. "I can't pretend that what you have done hasn't hurt me. But, since Michael did enough of that, I don't want to go through it again. I don't want to share you with other lovers."

140

"What are you saying?" Tansie gasped.

"What am I saying?" Alix mused. "It might be better if we went back to being friends again rather than lovers."

"You can't mean that?" Tansie cried with horror and clung on to Alix. "I love you, you know that! And, how could I ever give up anything as special as what we've got . . . life wouldn't be worth living without you," she barely whispered.

"Taking your own life is not the answer," Alix replied.

"I know . . . I won't, but don't leave me, please."

"I'm not going to leave you," Alix reassured her. After a short pause, she added, "If it's a baby you want so desperately, then let's talk about it. There are ways we can have one together and. . ." At least if they had a baby together she would have some input into its future welfare, she rationalised.

"That's the nicest thing anybody has ever said to me," Tansie murmured. "I won't see any of those men again, I promise." After a short silence, Tansie asked, "How do you like the house?"

Glad that Tansie had changed the subject, Alix gave her a semblance of a smile. "I like it a lot," she said, "Although I haven't really had a chance to take a good look around, it already looks very much like you – chaotic!"

Tansie chuckled, unperturbed by her untidiness. "I'll be very happy here," Tansie exclaimed, adding, "I'd like you to come shopping with me. I want to get rid of all the furniture I took from Alan's house. I want to be free of him . . . to start again."

"I will and that's great," Alix replied. She was delighted and welcomed the idea, believing that Tansie had now fully accepted her status as a single woman. And although Tansie did not want to live with Alix, for reasons she had accepted but not fully understood, Alix felt that Tansie was now making some sort of commitment to their relationship.

As Tansie reached for Alix's shirt buttons, she lifted her head and gazed into Alix's eyes. That simple gaze melted Alix's heart in an instant. She tilted her head sideways a little and lowered her lips to Tansie's. They felt warm and moist and enthusiastically responded to Alix's pressure. When Alix felt Tansie's hand gently cupping one breast after the other, she knew she could never resist her. Her desire for Tansie was as great as it had been at the beginning of their relationship.

By Friday, Tansie told Alix that the pregnancy had been a false alarm. Alix sighed with relief. She could now put Tansie's male lovers out of her mind. And if or when Tansie mentioned a baby again, Alix would deal with it, although she had no idea just how she would go about it.

As she had promised, Alix went shopping with Tansie early the following week.

Wanting to keep the furniture in the style of the house, which was modern with clean straight lines and white-washed walls, Tansie chose large square couches which were upholstered in a striped cream, burgundy and green linen fabric. The coffee and lamp tables were made of thick glass plates over travertine pedestals, as was the dining table. By the time the furniture had been arranged, the numerous books shelved into the wall unit, the paintings that Tansie had collected over the years hung on the walls and her own sculptures and other personal nick-nacks tastefully displayed, the house had an air of elegant comfort about it. It even had an acceptable amount of untidiness, Alix thought with a smile.

Wandering from room to room when it was all finished, Tansie draped her arm around Alix's shoulders and gushed excitedly, "I love it . . . I just love it . . . don't you think we did a wonderful job?"

"We did," Alix confirmed with a smile, enjoying Tansie's childlike joy. Alix felt very much at home in Tansie's house and had every intention of visiting as often as possible. She was still nervous about the children walking in on them whenever Tansie stayed over. They would have more privacy here.

At the beginning of December, the two women began to make plans for a short holiday in Tahiti, before going to Aspen with the children for their Christmas vacation. Although they saw each other daily, they had less real time together than they used to have, mainly because of Alix's workload.

Shortly before their departure, Alix was working late one evening when Tansie rang her. She wasn't feeling well, she said, would Alix come over.

"I'll be right there," Alix said and slammed down the phone. Something in Tansie's voice had sounded odd, Alix thought and she flew from the house.

When she walked into Tansie's house five minutes later, Tansie was sprawled out on the floor, seemingly unconscious.

Alix paled and gasped. The lower part of Tansie's white dressing gown was soaked in blood. She was haemorrhaging so badly Alix thought she'd bleed to death before she had a chance to do anything.

Panic-stricken she called an ambulance and then Douglas. He promised to meet her at the hospital. Holding Tansie's wrist and continuously checking for a pulse, Alix anxiously awaited the arrival of the paramedics.

During the short ride to the hospital, Alix felt totally numb. She was gripped by such fear of losing Tansie she thought her heart too would cease to function at any moment. Holding Tansie's cold hand in her own and rubbing it gently, she muttered, "Don't you die on me . . . I love you, Tansie."

When the ambulance pulled up at the emergency entrance at the hospital, Tansie was immediately wheeled off down the corridor with two doctors shouting instructions to a couple of nurses.

Later, Douglas told Alix that Tansie had suffered a miscarriage. When Alix looked at him aghast, he asked softly, "Didn't you know she was three months pregnant?"

Alix shook her head as tears began to fill her eyes. "A few weeks ago she told me that she thought she was. Later she said it had been a false alarm."

"I'm sorry," Douglas said.

"Does Tansie know she lost the baby?"

"Yes," Douglas confirmed. "If you want to wait, you can go and see her in a little while."

"I'll wait outside," Alix said. Alix went to stand underneath the canopy at the main entrance and lit a Davidoff. It was raining heavily, and although she felt water splash around her feet, she ignored it. She sighed and drew up her narrow shoulders. She felt chilled right to her bones.

Suddenly she knew that she could not go and see Tansie right away. Alix dropped the unfinished cigarette into the ashtray and went home.

For the next few days, Alix sat at Tansie's bedside. Not convinced that Tansie was all right, she stayed with her virtually around the clock. What if she died anyway? Alix could not help but ask herself over and over.

Tansie slept most of the time. Periodically when she opened her eyes and saw Alix, she smiled weakly and went back to sleep. Surely if Alix hadn't forgiven her for having lied to her about the baby, she would not be with her now.

She was comforted by that thought.

During the ensuing days while sitting with Tansie, Alix did a lot of soul-searching. Was she prepared to continue this relationship given that Tansie was probably unlikely to ever stop having male lovers or for that matter stop lying to her? At the same time, she didn't believe that any man could ever be a threat to their relationship. After all, Tansie had said on more than one occasion that she didn't particularly like men. Alix believed her because she wanted to believe her.

But Alix also acknowledged Tansie's vulnerability and accepted her emotional frailty. Knowing how susceptible Tansie was to any offering of love, in the end she decided that she had come too close to losing her and little else now mattered.

"How are you?" Alix asked when she returned to Tansie's bedside late one afternoon. She smiled as she bent down to kiss Tansie and brushed a stray wisp of hair off her forehead. Tansie looked so frail and vulnerable, all she wanted to do was draw her into her arms and tell her that she loved her. She did.

Drawing away a little, Alix said, "You look much better."

"I am much better," Tansie confirmed, and although her cheeks seemed terribly hollow, at least they had a little bit of colour. Her eyes too seemed less opaque. "Douglas said I can go home at the weekend."

"That's wonderful news," Alix said. Suddenly she felt very tired and looked forward to a good night's sleep. Drawing the straight-backed chair closer to the bed, Alix sat down and reached for Tansie's hand.

Holding tight on to Alix's hand, Tansie let her gaze wander to the window and said, "Please, don't be angry with me for not having told you that I was pregnant."

When Alix didn't reply, she slowly turned her head to look at Alix. Her eyes were vacant and her voice flat and emotionless when she continued. "I'm glad I lost it," she said. "Our love is more important than any baby could ever be." Not a single tear fell from her eyes because she had none to cry. Peter and Graham had both told her to have an abortion. Neither was prepared to marry her or to give her and the baby a name. Without that, she didn't want a child. Luck had been on her side when she miscarried.

Alix was momentarily caught off guard. She had expected some sort of reaction but not this seeming indifference. She didn't know what to make of it.

Before Alix could say anything, Tansie continued. "Please, just take me home so that I can forget this ever happened."

"I'll pick you up tomorrow morning," Alix promised.

Chapter 13

After long and serious deliberations, Alix finally decided not to spoil the children's ski holiday in America. She was torn between staying home with Tansie who was not yet well enough to travel and to go with the children. She hated to make such decisions, but having spent considerable time with Tansie during her illness and subsequent recovery, she felt she had neglected the children long enough. When she discussed it with Tansie, Tansie assured her that she would be fine.

"Stop worrying about me," Tansie said and kissed Alix languidly on the lips.

"Maybe we can take the holiday in Tahiti after the summer concert season is over," Alix said. "I promised Boris that I would give a couple of concerts with the MSO but, once they're over, I'll be free again."

"I'm very flattered," Tansie chuckled, peeling off Alix's silk shirt and rubbing her cheek against the smooth skin of her bare breasts. "Not everyone gets to go to bed with a famous pianist."

"You're the only one with that privilege," Alix said. "At least with this particular pianist."

On Christmas Eve, Alix gave a lavish party which was, as usual, a great success. The whole house was alive with vibrant energy, the dining table was festive with its delicate decorations of soft-pink, dark-green and gold ornaments and the Christmas tree glittered with light pink hearts, gold cherubs, white bows and doves. Alix smiled to herself as she made a last inspection. She had noted Felix's slightly raised eyebrows when he first saw the Christmas tree. Of course he was far too polite to comment on its unusual decorations.

As a special treat for her guests that evening, she played her latest composition, a piece for solo piano. She had named it Fantasy in C major, a tribute to Tansie. She had packed a variety of moods and a striking diversity of ideas into this music, much like the way she saw her relationship with Tansie. Its variations were magnificent with incredible leaps, moving from one end of the keyboard to the other. But it was in its final fortissimo trills, like the sounds of a nightingale, that her personal joy with her lover could be heard.

When she finished and the applause had died down, Kate ambled over to the piano.

"That's some piece of music," she said, adding with a wide knowing smile, "Do I have to fall in love with you before you dedicate one of your compositions to me?"

"Since that's not likely to happen," Alix smiled, "I'll compose something for your fiftieth birthday!"

"I'll never turn fifty!" Kate scoffed mildly and ambled off again.

Alix presented Tansie with a recording of the Fantasy in C major for their first anniversary as lovers. Tansie was so enchanted and deeply moved by the gesture, she wept and laughed at the same time.

The day after their anniversary, Felix drove Alix and the children to the airport. They stopped in Los Angeles for three days so that Alix could attend meetings with Ralph Schönberg.

After one week skiing in Aspen, they flew to Canada. Felix met them at the airport in Vancouver, and when at the end of the two weeks in Banff Alix returned home, he took the children to Hawai'i for a few days.

Although the two women had spoken to each other every day on the telephone, they raced into each other's arms when Alix arrived home. "You have no idea how much I missed you," Tansie cried, wrapping herself around Alix.

Later, Alix was delighted when Tansie showed her several new sculptures she had produced during Alix's absence.

"Please, Tansie," Alix said, replacing one of the sculptures on the workbench. "Let me organise an exhibition for you. You've met Marlow, she owns the gallery On High and. . ."

"Give me a little bit more time, maybe until the end of the year or even early next year," Tansie replied, unsure.

Alix didn't understand why Tansie was so reluctant to have a solo exhibition. But, she respected her wishes and dropped the idea for the moment.

After her month overseas, Alix threw herself into a composition for Ralph Schönberg's movie, *Broken Promises*, a dramatic story about wife and child bashing. Her music was equally dramatic, emphasising the tragedy of compulsive male brutality. She deplored violence of any kind and felt pleased that the music was for a film designed to make people more aware of domestic violence.

Alix also prepared for the MSO concerts in March. Boris was unrelenting during rehearsals and drove the members of the orchestra and Alix to near exhaustion.

This gruelling schedule left her little time to spend with Tansie but, no matter how busy she was, not a day went by when they didn't see each other even if only for half an hour.

Tansie had fully recovered from her pre-Christmas ordeal and her creative energy seemed endless. She could not remember another time when she had been this happy with her work and her lover.

On the evening of the first MSO concert, Tansie sat in the front row at the Myer Music Bowl together with the children and numerous friends. Although Tansie often heard Alix play the piano, to hear her performing in a real concert was much more exciting. Tansie listened in awe, mesmerised by Alix's talent and by the woman herself. With an inward smile, she wondered how she had ever managed to find someone like Alix.

At the end, Alix was called back on stage several times before she gave the audience a dazzling smile and prepared for an encore. She played the Fantasy in C major. Tansie was flattered and tears came to her eyes when she read the review the next day which described the piece as 'simply brilliant'.

One evening towards the end of March after a gruelling day's work, Alix stood up and arched her aching back. "That's enough for today," she said to John and reached for the packet of Davidoffs.

Lighting it for her, he asked, "You got a date tonight?"

"No . . . not really." Much to Alix's chagrin, Tansie had cancelled their evening together.

"I'll shout you a couple of beers at the local pub and, if you're good, I might even stretch it to dinner."

"Let's go," Alix welcomed the idea. With the heavy work-load and her time away in the United States, they hadn't had any real opportunities to just sit and talk in recent times.

Over drinks and dinner they chatted about work, their respective families and John's disastrous love affair with the opera diva. It had come to an end when she left him for an Italian tenor who, unlike John, was unattached.

Suddenly John flicked his finger as though he remembered something he should never have forgotten in the first place.

Deep furrows appeared at the top of his nose and between his eyes.

"What have you forgotten to tell me?" Alix asked.

"Your mate Pierre rang from Paris while you were in LA," John smirked.

"How could you, John," Alix gasped. "That was nearly three months ago!"

"Yeah, I know," he sighed, although showing little concern at his forgetfulness. "He asked how you were and sent you his love. By the way, his English isn't getting any better either," he informed her with deliberate slowness.

"How's your French these days? Is it improving?" He was trying her patience, but she wasn't about to take the bait.

"Okay, okay," he grinned. "He thinks we have an excellent chance of winning some of the awards at Cannes for the movie *Patrick*.

"And you forgot to tell me!" Alix cried incredulously. She shouldn't have been really surprised. He always forgot to tell her things.

"Sorry, love, it slipped my mind," John apologised. "He's also negotiating another movie and wants us to write the music. Are we interested?"

"Interested?" She shook her head in exasperation. "How could we not be?"

He balanced his chair on its back legs and gave her a smirk. "Ohhh . . . I don't know," he mused, adding slowly, "are you sure you don't have an ulterior motive for wanting this particular score? After all, if we get a local one, it would save you travelling half-way around the world for meetings."

Alix smiled. She knew what was going through his mind but wasn't about to spell it out. "When does he want to talk to us?"

"Around May or June, just the right time for you to spend a few days in Paris. I believe it's quite lovely at that time of the year, especially for lovers!"

"It is! Would you like to go?"

"I don't speak French, remember?"

"Your activities don't require any talking, do they?"

John roared with laughter. "Touché!" Taking a sip of beer, he glanced at her over the narrow gold frame of his glasses. "Why don't you take Tansie with you?" He asked, adding, "as I said before, Paris is quite lovely . . ."

"Especially for lovers," Alix smiled, finishing the sentence for him. "How long have you known?"

"Quite a while."

"And you never said anything?"

"What was there to say, Alix?"

"You're right," Alix confirmed.

"Go for it, love," he said, adding with a wide grin, "Just give me some warning before you go walkabout with a placard around your neck next time the gay community takes to the streets!"

"Whatever for?" Alix laughed.

"Someone will have to take care of the broken-hearted men you've ditched!"

"I'll keep it in mind."

When John dropped her home, Alix went straight upstairs to her bedroom. However, unable to sleep, she found herself in her studio long before dawn.

Playing a short étude, she allowed her thoughts to wander to her conversation with John. If John had known about her relationship with Tansie, everyone else must know too, she decided. With a smile she reflected on the many nights the two of them had spent with Alix's friends. For some time now, her friends had invited them out together, and although she had never given it any thought, she concluded that they had simply accepted them as a couple. As she started to play a round of scales, she decided that the time had come to talk to Kate about it. Kate was after all one of her oldest and best friends. Alix would talk to her about it at the first opportunity.

The moment for that intimate chat came about rather sooner than Alix had expected.

She was about to leave Kate's house after a party the following week, when Kate drew her aside. "Why don't you come over tomorrow afternoon? Richard's taking the kids to see his mother, so we can have a good old chin-wag and drink a bottle or two of his French champagne. We haven't done that for a while, you know."

"No, we haven't. Expect me straight after lunch," Alix agreed. She kissed Kate and then wandered out on to the back terrace to collect Tansie.

As soon as she realised that Alix was standing right next to her, Tansie asked, "Are we ready to go?" Without waiting for an answer, she steered Alix towards the front door.

"What's up?" Alix laughed. "Why are you in such a hurry to leave?"

"Do you know that guy I was talking to?"

"Herb Mullins?" Alix responded, adding, "he's David's father . . . you know, the short skinny boy, Drew's friend."

"He's a cretin! I'm surprised Kate has him in the house," Tansie said.

Alix laughed. "I expect when she made up the guest list, she felt in a charitable mood."

"Thank God," Tansie giggled. "His table manners were atrocious. Let's get out of here before Mullins realises I'm still here. He followed me around all bloody night!" What she failed to tell Alix was that she had given him her telephone number when he had asked for it.

Although it was already autumn, it was one of those rare beautiful days with a clear blue sky. Kate was stretched out on a sun lounge in a skimpy pair of white bikini bottoms when Alix arrived at her house. Her perfect heavily oiled body glistened in the sun and she reached for the bottle of champagne which stood in an ice bucket next to her.

"Have a drink, pet," she invited her friend and handed her a glass.

"Why not?" Alix replied and took a sip of the icy cold champagne. Over the years, Alix had gotten used to being called pet by Kate. She got away with it, nobody else would.

Never having been one to beat about the bush, Kate continued, "I've been meaning to talk to you for some time. You and Tansie . . . you're in love with each other, aren't you?"

"I suppose that's what most people would call it!" Alix smiled as she too stripped down to a pair of bikini pants. "How did you know?"

"I've known you for many years and I see more than most other people." What she omitted to add was that she had also seen Tansie flirting with a couple of the single men including Herb Mullins at the party. If Alix hadn't seen it, then it was better not to say anything.

When Alix finished telling her everything there was to know, she asked with a wide smile, "Now it's your turn and, although I don't care much for gossip, if there has been any floating around you might as well tell me now."

"I wouldn't call it gossip," Kate mused. "But yes, the question has been raised on a couple of occasions amongst our friends. But once we decided that there was a fair possibility that you and Tansie were having a relationship, it has never come up again."

"What gave us away?" Alix asked with curiosity.

"Your happiness," Kate said. "It was obvious a long time ago that your relationship was special. But tell me, who made the first move?"

A brief curve of Alix's lips indicated amusement. "You always tell me how square I am, so, it couldn't have been me. In the end, it doesn't matter. I chose to continue."

"I don't think you could have done anything else," Kate commented dryly. "Not even you can stop yourself from falling in love."

"You're full of wisdom today."

"No need to be smug about it," Kate scolded lightly and went inside to fetch another bottle of champagne. When she came back, Kate asked, "How do you feel about it?" filling the glasses.

"My happiness is more important than anything else," Alix replied. "Tansie has given me great joy and when we go through rough times, I'm sure it has to do with Tansie's personality rather than the fact that we are both women."

"I love Richard dearly but it must seem like bliss not to have to pander to a man's fragile ego," Kate laughed.

"That's a point."

After a considerable pause, Kate asked, "What do you think her plans are for the future . . . I mean, a future for the two of you?"

"I don't know," Alix replied. "She says many things and yet . . ." Her voice trailed off.

Alix often thought about their future but had little idea of what it would eventually be. All Alix knew was that she could not imagine a life without Tansie. Tansie often said the same about Alix.

When Alix remained silent, Kate said, "I'm sure your highly developed romantic ideals would have you believe that your relationship will last forever."

"Something like that."

"By the way, does anybody else know about you and Tansie?" Kate asked after a lengthy pause.

"I've told Hanna and Barbara, John and Haig."

"How did they take it?"

"Much to my amazement, both men took it extremely well, as did the women of course," Alix replied.

"I'm pleased to hear it," Kate said and refilled the glasses.

A few bottles of champagne later, Alix only vaguely remembered catching a cab home, speaking to Tansie and then falling asleep.

Tansie woke up the following morning earlier than was her normal habit and her first thought was of Alix. Why had Alix been so drunk the night before, she kept asking herself. Alix never drank a great deal. With a sickening, guilty feeling, Tansie wondered whether Alix had seen her flirting with a couple of guests at Kate's party. Or maybe Kate had told her.

No matter how tolerant Alix pretended to be, Tansie knew that Alix too had a breaking point. After all, Alix had warned her in the past that she did not like the idea of sharing her lover with others. In Tansie's mind such flirtations meant nothing, but she would have to be more careful in the future when Alix was around. She certainly never intended to deliberately hurt Alix.

Within half an hour, she arrived at Alix's house and was told by John that Alix was unwell and hadn't come to work yet. Tansie used the private door which led from the studio into the main house and went upstairs to the master bedroom. She found Alix sprawled out sideways on the king-size bed and in a near comatose state.

"Alix, wake up," she said and stroked her cold clammy forehead.

"Leave me alone!" Alix groaned. She could not remember another time when she had felt so sick.

"You've got a hangover, that's all," Tansie stated. "I'll get you some aspro."

When Tansie returned, she sat down on the bed and lifted Alix's head into her arm. Sip by sip, Tansie poured the milky liquid into Alix's mouth.

Alix moaned, spluttered and fought as much as her fragile body would allow. Then she sank back on to the pillows.

"You'll feel better soon," Tansie comforted her. "Why did you drink so much last night?"

Half opening her eyelids, Alix stared at her with unfocused eyes. "It was Moët et Chandon and it was free!"

"You can afford to bathe in the stuff. What does free have to do with it?" Tansie replied.

"What does it matter?" Alix groaned. In her view, it didn't matter. She had obviously misjudged her intake, a mistake she was not likely to repeat in a hurry given how awful she felt now.

By the time Alix was able to get out of bed later in the day, Tansie had extracted the promise that they would finally go on the holiday they had planned before her miscarriage. The morning of their departure, Alix stood in her walk-in wardrobe trying to decide what clothing she should take. In the end, she chose a couple of light cotton summer skirts and tops and several pairs of shorts and T-shirts. Their colours were bright and sunny just like she wanted the holiday to be. Two days later, they were on a flight to Tahiti.

Strolling back to their hut one evening after dinner, Tansie hooked her arm underneath Alix's. They walked in silence along the deserted beach until they came to their own private stretch outside their bungalow.

"Let's stay here for a moment," Tansie said and drew Alix down on to the warm dry sand.

Alix smiled, remembering the very first time they had made love. Then too it had been a moonlit, warm, balmy night on the beach. She had come a long way since then, she reflected. "Are you going to seduce me again?" she asked softly, sweeping Tansie into her arms.

"Now why didn't I think of that," Tansie chortled and carefully undid the knot in Alix's sarong.

Where Tansie was more experienced in her love making, Alix was passionate. She was no longer afraid and hesitant.

Tansie was the first to catch her breath. Quite out of the blue, she asked, "Do you miss not making love to men?"

If Alix was surprised by the question, she didn't show it. Her reply was simple. "No."

"What about that gorgeous-looking hunk at Kate's party the other night?" Tansie pressed. "I wasn't introduced to him because that Mullins bloke hung around me all night."

Alix smiled sardonically. "Anthony . . . he's an old friend of both Kate's and mine. He's a cellist with the . . ."

"Do you make other music together as well?"

"Never have and never will," Alix laughed. What she could have added, but didn't, was that Anthony was very happily ensconced with Luciano, his equally beautiful Italian male lover.

"The thought that I might lose you one day to some man nearly drives me crazy. I'd die if I lost you or you stopped loving me."

"That's not likely to happen," Alix replied gently but confidently.

"Oh, Alix, I haven't been this happy in years. You're my love, my inspiration and my most precious possession,"

Tansie gurgled and curved her body into Alix's.

"And, you'll never find another me!"

"Modesty is not one of your virtues," Tansie chortled.

"I never claimed it was."

After a short silence during which they continued to playfully stroke and caress one another, Alix asked, "It's your birthday soon, and since it's your fortieth, I thought I might give a party."

"No! Don't do that!" Tansie cried. "I hate the thought of turning forty, it makes me feel old! Can't we just have dinner together?"

"We can, if that is what you want," Alix agreed.

"Well, then that is exactly what we'll do," Tansie said and drew Alix closer into her arms. "How I love your body," she moaned moments later, and burying her face in Alix's curls, she took in the fragrance of the frangipani shampoo Alix had used earlier that evening.

Chapter 14

After their holiday in Tahiti, Alix threw herself into her work with renewed vigour. The score for a new symphony came to her with overflowing inspiration. It was to be called the Rostoff Symphony.

The slow *adagio* in the opening movement, with the dull rolling of the drums and the melancholic sounds of the string instruments, expressed the Russian people's hardship under the communist regime. It was interspersed with an occasional *fortissimo* as the whips of the overseers cracked through the air. The trumpet solo in the second movement was magic and had the same dynamic force as Boris, the maestro Alix had composed it for. The metallic sound of the xylophone was much like the biting icy wind which swept through the Siberian desert in winter. The final movement was a flourishing *allegro* with the violins leaping from one crescendo to the next. They were the sounds of freedom.

When Alix played part of it for Boris he was delighted and couldn't wait to rehearse it with the whole orchestra. At the end of the first uninterrupted performance, Boris turned to her. Remembering that he had grown up in a small village under horrendous conditions before escaping to the West, tears glistened in his eyes.

"Alix, you are a genius. This is a true masterpiece," Boris cried. Later, shaking his head, he argued, "Why do you keep wasting your time with film music when you can compose such masterpieces?"

Alix smiled. "Composing music for movies keeps me in

five star hotels. I'm too old to go camping."

Tansie too thrived on her own creative work and produced some superb sculptures. With Alix's support, she began to believe in herself and her talent. The thought of showing her work publicly was not nearly as daunting to her as it used to be. She had not yet told Alix but she was now more seriously considering having an exhibition before the year was out.

When Alix had to go to Paris towards the end of autumn to discuss yet another movie score with Pierre, she asked Tansie to accompany her but Tansie protested that she couldn't. She had promised Julie and Margret that she would help them move house, she explained.

Alix was glad to get out of the cold wet Melbourne weather and, when she arrived in Paris, she smiled. It was late spring and the whole city seemed to bloom after its long winter sleep. Because Pierre wanted to get down to Cannes for the Film Festival, which was due to start the following week, they worked at a frantic pace. She thrived on the bustle the film set provided. At the end of each day, she joined Pierre and some of the actors for dinner at a small inconspicuous bistro on the Left Bank.

When Pierre was ready to leave for Cannes, he invited Alix to accompany him but she declined. She had attended the Festival in the past and, although she had enjoyed it, she felt a few days rest on Boris' yacht would be preferable. She would hear soon enough if their movie *Patrick* won any awards.

At the end of the week, Alix rang Boris and informed him that she would arrive in Monte Carlo the following day. She had not yet had time to buy Tansie a present and decided to do so before leaving Paris. Convinced that Cartier would have a suitable trinket, she headed down

Rue de Rivoli. For herself, she bought a few summer outfits in the shades of green which suited her olive skin and highlighted the colour of her eyes.

When she returned to the Hotel George V after her shopping spree, the concierge handed her a fax. Reading it, she paled instantly and flew across the lobby to the lift.

She flung herself across the bed and dialled Tansie's number. As soon as she heard it ring at the other end, she muttered, "Damn you, Tansie, answer the phone!" When she finally picked up the receiver, Alix almost shouted, "What's going on, Tansie? Are you all right?"

"No, I'm not," Tansie replied, her voice vague. "I don't want to live any more."

"Tansie, please . . . I'll fly straight home," Alix cried in panic.

"You don't have to do that," Tansie said. "I just feel so awful without you and I can't bear the idea of you sleeping with other people."

Alix was flabbergasted. What on earth had brought this on, she wondered. Why was Tansie still so insecure? Alix could not think of a single reason. There was a distinct tone of exasperation in her voice when she said, "Tansie, listen to me. I don't sleep with anybody else, you know that, don't you?"

"I don't know," she replied faintly.

Their conversation lasted for nearly an hour. Alix was reluctant to hang up until she was quite sure that Tansie was okay. With a heavy heart, Alix eventually let herself be talked into taking the few days with Boris as planned. Before hanging up, she suggested again that Tansie come and join her, but Tansie declined saying she was in the middle of supervising the casting of some bronze sculptures.

Boris, dressed in a pair of white shorts and a captain's

hat pulled down over his blond hair, waved from the deck when the taxi drew up alongside the *Svetlana*.

He kissed Alix on both cheeks and exclaimed, "You arrived just in time. Another night at the casino and I wouldn't have had a boat to take you sailing on! We will play some bridge on board. That will be much safer for me."

"If your yacht is the stakes, then I will," Alix smiled.

"What do you want my boat for? You could buy half a dozen of them and still have cash in your pocket," Boris replied boisterously and led her to her cabin.

As soon as the highly polished mahogany door had closed behind her, Alix burst out laughing. She found herself in a stateroom full of gold ornaments, marble statues and a miscellaneous variety of kitsch. Huge, bright-pink silk cushions were scattered desultorily on the bed and over the floor, and a frilly canopy hung above it. Elaborate Russian icons consumed every bit of wall space.

"I'll have nightmares sleeping in here," Alix gasped aloud. Moments later though, she was sorry that Tansie wasn't with her. Despite the kitsch, it appealed to Alix's romantic nature and she could imagine herself having a very nice time indeed if her lover was with her.

As it turned out, Alix did have nightmares. Waking from each one, she sat up in bed, smoked and wondered whether Tansie would ever do as she had threatened to do: take her own life.

On the third day when she couldn't bear it any longer, Alix asked Boris to take her to the nearest port. While she accepted that mobile telephones were a necessity, she didn't like them. Mostly because she believed that there came a time when she didn't want to be found. But now, for the first time, she regretted not having brought hers so as to stay in touch with Tansie. She was reluctant to use the phone on the boat. Her conversations with Tansie were too private to be made from the captain's deck.

"What's wrong, Alix?" Boris asked with concern. "You are not having a good time?"

"No, that's not it. I'm worried about Tansie," she said.

For a brief moment he looked at her as though he didn't understand. Eventually he did. He gave her a hug and said, "Then you must go home immediately. We should get to Sardinia by tomorrow morning. I'll wire ahead to book a flight for you."

Just before boarding the Swissair flight in Zürich, where Alix had arrived the evening before, she was finally able to get through to Tansie.

"I'll be home within twenty-four hours. Will you pick me up?" Alix asked.

Tansie promised to do so and Alix slept fitfully in her first-class seat for most of the trip. Racing down the corridor to the customs hall, Alix had trouble stopping and ran straight into a man carrying a violin.

"Jean-Jacques!" she exclaimed, delighted to see him.

After considerable commotion they finally passed through customs.

Both Tansie and Felix were waiting for her. Giving Felix a friendly nod, she embraced Tansie.

"I missed you," Alix whispered and kissed the side of her neck.

Tansie all but pushed Alix away. "What's Jean-Jacques doing here? Have you been spending time with him?" Tansie hissed. She couldn't ignore Jean-Jacques' presence no matter what Alix had told her only a few days ago.

"No!" Alix cried, flabbergasted at her lover's accusation. "He's just flown in from New Zealand and . . . you know I was on Boris' yacht!"

"Don't lie to me," Tansie accused, adding, "I'll catch a cab home. You go with him!"

Tansie disappeared in the crowd before Alix could say anything else. She followed her lover with her eyes, hurt and dumbfounded.

Without a word, Felix took Alix's bags but grimaced seconds later. "I should have brought a bus," he said as he pointed at the group of people who stood behind Jean-Jacques carrying a variety of instruments.

"Only Jean-Jacques is coming with us. The Windsor Hotel bus will take the others," Alix replied absentmindedly. She wondered what could possibly have made Tansie behave in such an irrational manner, particularly after their recent conversation.

"I knew you were coming for a concert tour, Jean-Jacques, but you're here ahead of schedule," Alix said as soon as they were in the car. "Where is the spunky pianist who was to accompany you?" she added with a wide smile.

"She broke her leg in New Zealand and has returned to Paris," Jean-Jacques sighed.

No wonder he looks so harassed, Alix thought and patted his arm. "Can you change the program and do without a pianist?" Alix asked.

"I could, but I do not want to," he retorted. By the time Felix pulled up at the Windsor, Alix had agreed to the concert and would play Mozart's Piano Concerto No. 15.

As soon as she arrived at her house, John greeted her with the news that the film *Patrick* had indeed won several awards in Cannes. Due to the reception Tansie had given Alix at the airport, Alix was too preoccupied to take the news with enthusiasm but promised John that they would share a bottle of 'Dom' later in the day. She told him about the concert she would give with Jean-Jacques and then left to visit Tansie.

Ten minutes later, she walked around the back of Tansie's house. "Tansie, where are you?" she called.

Tansie was ambling down the passage towards her. She was in her dressing gown with her hair falling bedraggled around her face. Her steps seemed slower than usual and her shoulders were stooped, and yet, she looked most unfriendly. "Hi," she said with cold aloofness. "You want some coffee?"

Given the way the question was asked, Alix declined. Instead she stuck her hands into her pockets and came to the point of her visit. "I didn't like your allegation at the airport and . . ."

"I bet you didn't . . . the truth is never pleasant!" Tansie snapped. She could no longer control her jealousy no matter how unsubstantiated it was.

The tirade of abuse which followed left Alix momentarily speechless. She let her gaze wander to the windows, hoping to control her welling anger.

Turning back to face Tansie, she asked, "Tansie, what do you want from me?"

"Nothing!" Tansie bellowed. "Don't you know that the only times I wanted to make love to you were when I was drunk?"

Alix began to walk away, past Tansie and down the hallway. She was not going to continue this one-sided, insane conversation. Tansie followed her. She was still yelling when Alix reached the front steps.

"I'll take an overdose instead . . . much quicker and cleaner. I hope you can live with that, if you really care," Tansie raved. "You didn't come back from Europe when I was close to taking my life . . . why should you . . ."

Alix didn't hear the rest. She simply walked out. Moments

later, she collapsed behind the steering wheel. As she wept, she wondered what it was that Tansie was really trying to say. Her first thoughts were that perhaps she should have flown back from Europe immediately. Or was Tansie simply uncomfortable with their relationship and this was her way of saying, "I want out"? Alix had no idea what had caused this outburst.

Alix was so distressed she had no recollection later of actually leaving Tansie's house or driving home.

She hated such confrontations. Not just because they served no purpose but because they reminded her of her volatile relationship with Michael. Alix hadn't liked it then and she didn't like it now.

After a restless night, Alix arrived at the concert hall long before anyone else and was already at the piano when Jean-Jacques strolled in.

Introductions were made and they all settled down to work. At first, Alix's mind kept wandering to Tansie. She had tried to ring her just before she left for rehearsal, but there had been no answer. During their short lunch break, she tried again. Still Tansie wasn't there.

Rejoining the orchestra, Jean-Jacques whispered so that only she would hear, "You look worried?"

Alix shook her head and gave him a weak smile. "I'm fine."

Half-way through the afternoon, when Jean-Jacques let them go, she made a dash for her car. She dialled Tansie's number on the mobile phone at the same time as she reversed the car out of its allotted space. There was still no answer. In a state of panic now, she saw pictures of Tansie sprawled out on the floor somewhere in a coma or, worse, dead. Her words, "I'll take an overdose, much quicker and cleaner," began to haunt her. Am I too late, she wondered.

Should I have gone back last night?

"Tansie?" she called out as she walked from room to room. Her knees became weaker and the knot in her stomach tighter, fearing what she might find behind the next closed door. The house was empty.

The car, Alix thought and raced out to the garage, as her stomach now turned violently. The car was there but no Tansie. What is this, Tansie, some sort of a sick joke? Alix began to tremble.

She went back inside and made yet another check of the house. What had she missed? Then it came to her. All Tansie's toiletries were gone and, on further investigation, so was all of her ski wear. Relief and anger fought one another for first place.

Anger, such as she had never experienced before, finally won. In a sheer fit of temper she hit out at the sculpture which was nearest to her: a huge modern construction of welded and interwoven steel plates and rods. Her left wrist caught one of the sharply protruding pieces of steel.

"Damn you, Tansie Landon!" she shouted as her wrist was torn open on impact. The pain was so excruciating her legs buckled beneath her and she crumbled into a heap on the floor. Holding on to her wrist with her right hand and trying to stop the blood flow, she dropped her head between her knees and wept. Blood and tears soon mingled on her jeans, leaving wet red patches.

Alix was still in the same position when Kate strolled through the open front door moments later.

"I saw your car outside and I thought I'd come in and have a coffee with you girls. Where's Tansie?" she asked but stopped when she saw the bright-red blood gushing from Alix's wrist. "What happened?" Kate gasped and went to fetch a couple of towels. Looking at the gaping wound, she added, "Next time you want to throw a wobbly, pick on something a little softer and rounder!"

"Thanks for the advice, I'll try and remember it next time," Alix replied between gritted teeth. She proceeded to tell Kate about the mindless row they'd had the day before, Tansie's suicide threat and then her sudden, silent disappearance. Concluding, she said, "I was so angry, I didn't even think what I was doing."

"I'd say, judging by the damage you've done to yourself, angry is putting it mildly," Kate stated and helped Alix to her feet. "You know, I hadn't heard from Tansie for months, until a day or so ago. She rang to tell me that she was thinking about going skiing for a few days with a friend called Penny and . . ."

"Penny who?" Alix asked bewildered.

"I don't know . . . I thought you'd know."

"I've never heard of her," Alix said. She cringed and swore under her breath when Kate wrapped the towel around her wrist. "That hurts," Alix grumbled and again clenched her jaw with the pain.

"So does having children . . . you had four!" Kate pointed out with a smile. Just before leaving the house, Kate checked that there was no blood on the carpet.

"Let's get you to a doctor before you faint on me . . . you do look a trifle pale around the lips," Kate said and led her friend to the car.

Despite everything, Alix let out a hoarse chuckle and slipped into the passenger seat.

By the time they arrived at Douglas' surgery, the towel was soaked through. Caroline, his nurse, asked Alix to come straight into the small operating room. Kate followed them, and while she sat down on the chair, Alix perched herself up on the narrow examination table.

"It's always a pleasure to see you ladies," Douglas greeted them and wasted no time in anaesthetising Alix's hand. After making sure that there was no muscle damage, he prepared to sew up the gash. "What happened?" he asked. "Did you try to slit your wrist?"

"No."

"I didn't think so," he replied.

Alix related the events which led to her injury, adding, "I know . . . it was a dumb thing to do, so don't remind me."

Working steadily, he listened until she'd finished, then said, "Has Tansie threatened suicide before?"

"Yes," Alix admitted miserably, hating to betray her lover.

"Don't you think as her doctor I should know about these things?" he asked without reproach.

"I suppose so."

"She is emotionally blackmailing you, you know that? Look, I don't know what her ulterior motives are, I don't even want to guess but, if she does it again, I want you to tell me, okay?" Douglas continued.

"Okay," Alix agreed lamely, adding, "what if she does take an overdose? I couldn't ever live with that, thinking maybe, just maybe, I could have done something to prevent it."

"You'll just have to learn to let your head rule your heart and not the other way around," he reminded her. "I wish I could put your mind at rest and tell you that she won't ever try to take her own life. But I can't." He tied the last bit of bandage securely around her wrist. "Have you ever discussed the possibility of her seeing a psychiatrist?"

"It has crossed my mind once or twice but I haven't said anything." Seconds later she wailed, "How can I play the piano?" She held her boxing glove-like hand in front of his eyes.

"Try using your toes!"

"Very funny," she said. "I'm supposed to give a concert in less than three weeks . . . Mozart's . . ."

"Mozart?" he grinned, "a piece of cake!"

She gave him a weak smile. "Are you going to supply the morphine for the pain?"

"I might have to but see how you feel tomorrow," he replied, "You will have limited use of your hand because of the swelling, the stitches and the pain." He thought about it for a moment and then added, "We'll leave the bandage as it is until tomorrow morning, then we'll have another look at it."

"Is that the best you can do?"

"I'm afraid so!" Douglas said and got up from the small stool he had been perched on. "By the way, I'm going on leave tomorrow but one of my colleagues will look after you and . . ."

"How can you do this to me?" Alix wailed in jest. "What if he's tall, blond and good-looking? I must look an absolute fright, blood-spattered and all!"

"You can always take your clothes off before the gentleman comes in." Kate was being helpful.

"Jesse? Have you got a minute?" Douglas called as he opened the door. "You'll soon see for yourself," he added.

Moments later, a beautiful woman strolled in, the long white coat flapping around a pair of shapely legs which were highly visible from underneath a short skirt.

"Up to your expectations?" Douglas grinned, adding, "Jesse, this is Alix Clemenger, your new patient and her friend Kate Hilton."

Alix laughed. "Despite a minor difference in the anatomy,

very much up to my expectations!"

Looking from Alix to Douglas, Jesse asked, "Am I going to be let into the secret?"

"Alix wanted to know whether my new partner, was tall, blond and good-looking," Douglas responded.

"Thank you for the compliment, Alix," Jesse said, allowing a soft smile to cross her face.

"You're most welcome," Alix replied in her nonchalant manner. Moving towards the door, Alix gave Douglas a peck on the cheek and took Kate's arm. "I'm sure Jesse and I will get along just fine. Have a nice holiday, Douglas." The swing door closed behind the two women before either of the doctors could reply.

"It makes a nice change to see such an elegant fashion-conscious lady doctor," Kate quipped.

"Only you would notice such things," Alix laughed.

"Is there anything else in life but fashion?" Kate joked. "However, if she's also good at her job, we've got ourselves a real winner."

Alix smiled. "She's very attractive."

After a quick cup of coffee, Kate left together with Felix who was going to pick up Alix's car. Alix disappeared into her studio. Although she couldn't play the piano, she could at least scan a music score John had finished only days earlier.

When John walked in moments later, he said, "What happened to you? I'd hate to see the poor bastard's eye. Did he lose it?" Jenny had warned him that Alix looked less than glamorous with her left hand swaddled in bandages.

"No, he got lucky!" she grimaced.

"What about the concert? Can you play?"

"I hope so."

"Just behave like a real prima donna and . . ."

"Pianists are not prima donnas!"

"What's the difference? A stage is a stage and a woman is a woman, right?"

"Only a chauvinist male could make such a comment," Alix scoffed.

The next morning Alix returned to Douglas' surgery to have her bandages changed.

"How is your hand?" Jesse asked with concern.

"Painful, to say the least, but I'm sure I'll live."

"Let me have a look," Jesse replied and motioned for Alix to sit down. Her deft fingers swiftly removed the bandage and then gently traced contours over Alix's hand and wrist. Lifting her gaze to meet Alix's, Jesse's blue eyes sparkled when she asked, "By the way, did you break his nose?"

"Unfortunately my encounter was with a steel sculpture . . . needless to say, I drew the short straw!"

"Maybe you should stick to composing and playing the piano," Jesse replied, arching her slim beautifully curved eyebrows and studying her patient. Jesse had noticed a slight catch in Alix's voice and now wondered what lay below the smooth surface.

"I will, believe me," Alix said.

As she watched Jesse tie the new bandage around her hand, Alix smiled to herself thinking that Jesse was indeed a very beautiful woman.

Alix guessed her to be much the same age as herself. Her short blonde hair curled just over the collar of her white coat, leaving most of her slender neck exposed. Alix noticed the way Jesse held her head, slightly askew but so very dignified. Alix also noted that Jesse wore no jewellery at all and wondered vaguely if that meant that Jesse was not married. Since she had become involved with Tansie,

Alix no longer assumed anything about what kind of life a woman might have.

Working away efficiently, Jesse said, "You're a wonderful pianist, you know. I attended all the concerts you gave earlier this year at the Myer Music Bowl." Not giving Alix a chance to reply, she added, "I also heard you play many years ago in New York, Chopin's Piano Concerto No. 1. I thought your performance was superb. Even on a shoestring budget, as I was in those days, I rushed out and bought a tape."

"Thank you," Alix replied, accepting the compliment gracefully. "I'm playing with the Jean-Jacques Dubois orchestra in just over two weeks, would you like a couple of tickets?"

"You're assuming I can fix you up by then!"

"I am," Alix said, thinking what an unusual beautiful colour Jesse's eyes were. They not only reminded her of hyacinths but also of a deep blue winter sky.

Smiling, her gaze met Alix's and she said, "I'd love to come. One ticket will be fine though, thank you."

When Jesse finished, she reluctantly gave Alix a couple of strong pain killers. Alix swallowed one without hesitation and by the time she arrived at the concert hall, the pain was gone.

"What is this?" Jean-Jacques asked incredulously and pointed at her hand.

"I got into a fight!" She gave him a sardonic grin and took her seat at the piano. She wasn't going to let this small mishap interfere with her performance. At least now that she knew where Tansie was she didn't have to worry about her any more. Not that it really mattered but Alix was curious as to who Penny was. She could not place her.

As Alix started to play, she quickly realised that her left

hand was not much good at the moment. Although there was no pain, her wrist felt stiff and her fingers were not as flexible as they needed to be. But she persevered. She couldn't let Jean-Jacques down. When rehearsal was over for the day, Jean-Jacques and Alix left together.

"Will you have dinner with me?" he asked. "Where do we go for some real French food?"

"Yes I will, thank you," Alix replied, and remembering the numerous dinners they had had together in Paris many years ago, she added with a smile, "there's an excellent restaurant not far from here. Both the owner and the chef are from Paris."

Later over dinner, Jean-Jacques said, "Alix, would you consider finishing the concert tour with us?"

"Maybe," she responded slowly. Although she had not gone on tour now for several years, the idea started to appeal to her. For Jean-Jacques she might just make an exception. "Where will you go from here?"

"Around Australia and then to Hong Kong and Singapore," he replied.

"Can I let you know in a day or so?"

"Of course," he agreed.

After consulting with John, Alix told Jean-Jacques the following morning that she would accompany him.

Each evening, Alix fell into bed exhausted, but she was awake instantly when the telephone rang around midnight one night.

"Hello?" she said, but all she heard was heartbreaking sobs at the other end. "Tansie, calm down," she added, not so much with impatience but with decisiveness.

"Alix, come and pick me up, please," Tansie wailed.

It had taken Tansie nearly a week to realise that what she had done was outrageous. At first she had justified her behaviour by blaming Alix for the row they had had. But the more she thought about it, the more she came to the reluctant conclusion that she had acted foolishly. Alix would have gone looking for her and, when she couldn't find her, she would have been devastated. Tansie knew that and would now have to put things right.

Noticing that Alix's voice was brittle, unforgiving even, Tansie curbed her weeping. "Are you angry with me?" Tansie asked meekly. "I didn't mean it. I'm sorry."

"What you did was unacceptable, if not unforgivable," Alix replied belligerently. She was determined that she wasn't going to be swayed into accepting Tansie's apology quite that easily. "If you don't mean what you say, then don't say it at all. Have you any idea what anguish I went through when I couldn't find you?"

"I'm so sorry, Alix. I just didn't think," Tansie apologised. "Can you forgive me?"

"I don't know."

"Alix, I love you . . . it breaks my heart to hear you say this. Please, come and get me so we can sort this whole mess out, I beg you."

"I can't, Tansie. I have rehearsals every day. It's . . ."

"What for?" Tansie asked.

"I'm giving a concert at the end of next week."

"I'll find someone to give me a lift down the mountain, I'll even walk if I have to! I'll ring you as soon as I get home."

Tansie hung up and packed her bags. At first light the next morning, she was at the village bus stop. It only took her a few seconds to find a single man. Without hesitation she walked over to him and asked him for a lift.

Once back in town, she waited for two days to ring Alix. She believed that the longer she left it, the more likely it was that Alix was going to be in a more forgiving mood. Then she invited her over for dinner, promising to cook something extra special.

As soon as Alix wandered through the backdoor that evening, Tansie took little tentative steps towards her. She was just about to put her arms out, but then changed her mind. Her stare fixed to the ground, she murmured, "I'm sorry, Alix. It'll never happen again."

"I don't know what makes you behave like that but it deeply distresses me," Alix replied slowly. Deciding that now was as good a time as any to say what she had to say, she added, "How would you feel about seeing a psychiatrist? Maybe he can help you, it's . . ."

"I'm not crazy!" Tansie exclaimed. "I saw one years ago when I had problems with Alan but all she did was harp on about my childhood. It was a waste of time."

"Why don't you discuss it with Douglas?" Alix suggested.

"If it makes you happy . . . okay, I'll talk to him," Tansie reluctantly agreed.

Reaching for Alix's hand, she noticed the bandage. "What have you done to yourself?" she exclaimed, staring at what was visible of Alix's discoloured fingers. "Why the bandage?"

It didn't take Alix long to decide what to tell her. "When I realised that you had left town without telling me about it, especially after you said you were going to take an overdose, I was very angry. I was stupid enough to think that if I lashed out at one of your sculptures I'd feel better."

"Aren't I supposed to be the one who does dumb things like that?" Tansie giggled and, enfolding her lover into her arms, she added with a mere whisper, "that was a sick joke. I'm sorry."

With some difficulty, Alix convinced herself that this

was simply the way Tansie was: unpredictable and erratic but never boring.

Ambling into the kitchen, Tansie called over her shoulder, "Which sculpture did you lash out at? Did you kill it?"

"It was the monstrosity in the hallway, and no, I didn't kill it," Alix replied.

Over dinner, the two women chatted more or less in an easy manner. When Alix asked who Penny was, Tansie looked surprised.

"She's one of my oldest and dearest friends. I just haven't seen her for a while," Tansie said. "She's got a place at Buller. Surely I've told you about her."

"No," Alix shook her head.

"Oh well, now I have," Tansie stated and went on to talk about something else.

Alix was not sufficiently curious to ask any further questions. She had seen other people arrive in Tansie's life seemingly from nowhere only to disappear again. That was just another one of her idiosyncrasies.

Tansie didn't ask Alix to stay the night, feeling that Alix probably hadn't quite forgiven her. She didn't even object when Alix said as she was leaving that she probably wouldn't have much time to see her again before the concert.

"I love you, Alix," Tansie muttered and kissed Alix on the lips. More timidly, she added, "It's my birthday on Saturday, are you still planning on taking me out for dinner?"

"Of course," Alix replied, feeling suddenly very fragile. Given different circumstances, she would have liked nothing more than to fall into bed with Tansie, to be held, caressed and comforted. She didn't. "I've made a reservation at Max's, so I'll pick you up at seven-thirty."

Chapter 15

During Douglas' absence, Tansie reluctantly saw one of his colleagues for a referral to a psychiatrist. He recommended Dr Jim Callahan and made an appointment for her.

Dr Callahan opened the front door when she arrived at his house the next day.

Tansie gave him a hostile glare. "Now that I'm here, what do we do? It's a while since I saw a shrink . . . maybe I shouldn't call you that but . . ."

The older man smiled. "I don't mind, say whatever you're comfortable with. Why don't you tell me a little bit about yourself. What you do, that sort of thing," he invited her.

Tansie proceeded to tell him that her reason for seeing him was because she had a drinking problem or so her lover Alix Clemenger thought. "Have you heard of Alix?" she asked. "She's a well-known pianist and composer."

"I have," Dr Callahan confirmed. What he didn't say was that he knew Alix quite well. They were both on the Board of Directors of the Melbourne Symphony.

"Are you shocked that I have a female lover?" she blurted out.

"If you're asking me whether I'm going to make a moral judgement, the answer is no," he replied. "How do you feel about it?"

"It's fine with me," Tansie said. "Well, it sort of happened, I mean, Alix made it happen, although I have plenty of boyfriends as well. I'm perfectly normal, you know. But in any event, I don't have any hang-ups about women lovers and certainly don't think it's an issue for discussion."

"Then we won't talk about it." Dr Callahan made a few more notes. Something didn't ring true but, with what little information he had, he could not form a clear picture. They went on to discuss the possibility of Tansie taking some sort of art classes to give her life some regularity and a disciplined structure. When the session came to an end, he asked, "Would you like an appointment for next week?"

"I might as well, although I'm really only doing this to make Alix happy," she responded and headed for the door.

Alix did believe that Tansie loved her regardless of her behaviour and that her love was not the cause of her periodical distress. No matter what Tansie said, Alix could never be quite sure that she would not execute her threat of committing suicide. The mere thought of it made her shudder. More and more often, Alix began to wake up from nightmares. She saw Tansie as clearly as anything, in a pool of blood, dead on the bathroom floor or floating in a river.

However, now that Tansie had agreed to see a psychiatrist Alix felt a little easier. After her first visit to him Alix asked her about it. Tansie had not been forthcoming with what they had discussed and only said that he wanted her to start a new art course.

"He thinks all I need is some structure in my life," Tansie had told her. "Particularly since you're so busy and don't always have time for me." The latter part she had added with an accusatory undertone.

Had she neglected Tansie, Alix wondered afterwards. Obviously Tansie thought so. Alix decided to chat to Jesse at her next check-up. She too needed to speak to someone and Jesse seemed as good a choice as any. The impression Alix had of her was that of a caring, trustworthy and compassionate woman.

As Jesse began to remove the bandage, Alix said, "Do you have a minute to talk to me?"

"Of course," Jesse replied warmly. "I have more than a minute if need be."

"Thanks," Alix responded with a weak smile and proceeded to tell her about her relationship with Tansie and the distress Tansie's erratic behaviour was causing her.

"Judging by what you've told me, Tansie seems to be a little unbalanced. And, you must know as well as I do that there is no quick or easy solution," Jesse said with compassion. "Her behaviour could have many reasons. The simplest, of course, is that she can't cope with having a relationship with another woman."

"That has crossed my mind," Alix said. "I'm not sure, but I think she's had at least one such relationship before . . . maybe several . . . I don't know."

"Just because she wants it and has had it, doesn't mean she can live with it," Jesse pointed out. After a momentary pause, she continued. "Or it could be fear of intimacy or fear of commitment or a highly developed sense of inferiority and insecurity. I don't know, Alix."

"What do I do?" Alix asked. "I'm frightened that one day she'll really freak out and do something irrevocable."

"That's always a possibility," Jesse confirmed although she hated to say it. "The best advice I can give you is to be a little more wary. Don't take everything she says at face value and hope that Dr Callahan will get to the bottom of it."

When Alix remained silent, Jesse added, "I'm sorry I couldn't be more helpful. But, if it's the relationship with another woman that's causing at least some of the problems, then I'll be able to help you more." She smiled. "That I do understand without being a psychiatrist."

When Alix only gave her a puzzled stare, Jesse said, "I

haven't surprised you, have I?"

"Just a little," Alix laughed. As the two women walked towards the door, Alix said with a warm smile, "You know, I had no idea about you . . . and yet, I had no qualms about talking to you as frankly as I did. I don't normally do that, least of all with strangers."

"I'm glad I inspired your confidence," Jesse responded. "Now you take care of that hand of yours, I'll expect a perfect performance next week."

"I will, and . . . thanks."

The evening of the concert arrived, and leaving the children for Felix to bring, Alix went to pick up Tansie. Kissing her leisurely on the lips, Alix said, "You look lovely, that amber colour suits you." When Alix had seen the dress, with its wide shoulders tapering down to the knees, in a shop window in Paris, she had thought of Tansie and bought it for her.

"Sometimes I think you know me better than I know myself," Tansie smiled. "The dress is perfect for me."

"Good luck," Tansie murmured when it was time for Alix to go backstage and gave her a warm hug.

Just as the two women drew apart, a soft voice behind them said, "Good evening."

Alix turned and, leaving her hand on Tansie's arm, smiled. "I'm so glad you came, Jesse. This is Tansie."

"Hi," Tansie said curtly and strolled off towards the main entrance.

"How is your hand?" Jesse asked with concern, casting a scrutinising glance over Alix's face. She was pleased when she noticed that Alix looked less harassed than when she had first met her in the surgery.

"You did a wonderful job," Alix replied. "By the way, I've got the orchestra and a few friends coming to my house after the concert for a little gathering. Why don't you join us?"

"I'd love to," Jesse said and, turning to leave, added, "good luck, Alix."

As Jesse began to walk in the direction in which Tansie had just disappeared, Alix stood and watched her go. Jesse seemed so unselfconscious, so warm and natural and yet so elegant. Tonight she wore a simple dark-red, fine-wool dress with a strand of pearls wound around her neck. An overcoat was casually draped over her shoulders. Alix wondered whether to be on her own was of her own choosing.

"Are you ready?" Jean-Jacques asked when Alix came through the stage door.

She held up her hand which was still bruised but now only sported a narrow bandage on the cut. "As ready as I'll ever be," she replied.

"Don't worry, cherie, we'll show those 'colonials' what real music is all about," he said with confidence.

Alix had to laugh at his expression. Someone like Kate would hate to be called a colonial, she thought.

While the orchestra played Bach's Orchestral Suite No. 3, Alix stayed backstage and went over the score for her solo part. She knew she'd memorised every aspect of it but, quite unexpectedly, she felt an attack of nerves turn her stomach inside out. She rarely suffered such attacks and could not now explain even to herself why she felt like this. Her emotions seemed unnaturally torn between apprehension and excitement. Stretching her fingers and flexing them she felt a slight tinge of pain and decided that it was probably the injury which gave her those unsettled feelings.

When Jean-Jacques came to get her, she stood up and walked ahead of him on to the stage. The emerald-green evening dress she had chosen for the occasion glittered in the bright spotlight, much like the ocean would on a sunny day. She didn't just look stunning but also perfectly at ease when she gave the audience a dazzling smile. Spotting her children and her friends together with Tansie and Jesse in the first row, she gave them an extra bow.

Alix took her seat at the piano. After she had arranged her dress so that it would not hinder her legs in any way and after a moment's concentrated silence, she gave Jean-Jacques a nod. She was ready. As soon as he lifted his baton and the orchestra played the first few bars, Alix was instantly engrossed in the music.

Throughout the concert, her concentration never wavered and she played as perfectly and skilfully as was possible. She played each note with the utmost ease and without restraint. But then the restless modulation and busy passage-work suited her current frame of mind. Her performance was absolutely flawless and she played with heart-rending passion. It was Mozart, after all, and it should never be played in any other way.

The last note echoed around the concert hall, but for just a split second nobody in the audience moved. Then a thunderous applause broke out. Jean-Jacques stepped down from the conductor's platform and escorted Alix from the piano stool.

He kissed her on both cheeks while the orchestra members tapped their bows on the music stands. The enthusiasm from the audience and her fellow musicians was over-whelming. He took her hand, lifted it high above their heads and gave her a wide smile.

Leaving the stage, he kept muttering, "What a waste . . . what a waste . . . extraordinary! I will never understand why you do not travel the world!"

After two calls, Jean-Jacques whispered to Alix, "Time

for an encore".

Now that it was all over, she could afford to give the audience an insouciant smile. For a passing moment she thought of Jean-Jacques' words. She could indeed have audiences like this one anywhere in the world. But, she also knew that she didn't need to have her ego fed by performing on a concert stage more often than she did. She knew that her talents were unique without it. And she still preferred her freedom to the more restricted regime of a rigorous concert schedule. As for spending more time away from her children and her lover, this was even less appealing.

For the encore she chose Chopin's Barcarolle in F-sharp major. She was applauded back on to the stage three more times. For the next encores she chose short works by Schumann, Chopin and Liszt – pieces she felt best suited the mood of the evening: they were all charmingly light yet they had an enchanting, dashing quality about them. She finished her concert to a standing ovation lasting several minutes.

The whole orchestra, as well as numerous friends, returned to Alix's house to celebrate. Still very much on a high, Alix wandered around as though in a daze. The knowledge that this had been one of her finest performances, gave her a deep sense of achievement.

When she spotted Jesse who had arrived a little after the others, she sauntered over to meet her.

"What a performance, Alix," Jesse exclaimed and kissed her on both cheeks. "I don't know why you lock yourself up in a studio most of the time when you could have the world at your feet."

Alix laughed. "Jean-Jacques said the same!" With a wicked glint in her eyes, she added, "Maybe I don't like to be told what to do all the time! Take my word for it, most conductors can be regular beasts if you don't toe the line. A concert stage can only ever have one master and it's usually the gentleman on the platform."

"I'm sure you'd get around the best of them," Jesse responded smartly.

"Thanks for the compliment," Alix said, and taking Jesse's arm, added, "come and meet some of my friends."

When Jesse easily fell into a lively conversation with Alain, the first violinist, Alix noted with as much surprise as pleasure that Jesse spoke fluent French. Satisfied that Jesse needed no further looking after, Alix joined another group at the far end of the sitting room. Before the evening was over, a delighted Jean-Jacques finally announced that Alix was to accompany him for the remainder of the tour.

As the first guests started to leave, Jesse went to look for Alix. When she found her, she said, "Thanks for a lovely evening, Alix." As their eyes met, Jesse added, "Maybe I can return the invitation some time."

"I'd like that very much," Alix said with genuine pleasure. "Can I ring you when I come back from the concert tour?"

"I can do better than that," Jesse replied. "How about dinner at the Peninsula Hotel in Hong Kong? Say on the twenty-second of next month?"

"You mean you're going to be there at the same time?"

"I am indeed," Jesse confirmed with a wide smile. "I was invited to give a paper on women's health at the International Women's Medical Conference."

Alix looked mildly surprised. She didn't know about this part of Jesse's profession. "A date it is then, Jesse."

After everyone else had left, only Tansie stayed behind. The two women embraced, although Alix remained aloof and wary. She could not forget the recent trauma that quickly. Clearing her throat, Alix drew away and stroked

Tansie's cheek.

"I'm leaving with Jean-Jacques tomorrow and . . ." Alix started but Tansie put her finger over Alix's half-open lips.

"So he said," Tansie interrupted. "You really want to go on this concert tour, don't you? I thought you didn't like concert tours much. What made you change your mind?"

"Yes, I very much want to go," Alix replied. In her heart she knew that this offer couldn't have come at a more opportune time. A short break from her lover couldn't do either of them any harm. "As for changing my mind," she joked, "maybe I need my ego stroked just a little."

"I'll stroke more than your ego," Tansie giggled and promptly slid her hand inside Alix's dress, gently caressing her back. As she drew Alix into her arms, Tansie murmured, "I've missed you. Please let me stay here tonight."

Half-way up the stairs, Tansie stopped and gave Alix a sudden disconcerting stare. "That woman you introduced me to at the concert, who was she?" Tansie asked tightly.

"Dr Jesse Carrington."

"You're driving me crazy with your short answers," Tansie growled. "What else do you know about her?"

"She's Douglas' new partner," Alix said with some impatience. "Why all the questions?"

"Forget I mentioned it!" Tansie muttered and drew Alix up the last few steps. Although there was nothing overt about Jesse, if Alix hadn't worked out that she was gay then Tansie would not be the one to tell her. She most certainly didn't want Alix to get any ideas about a potential new lover. Least of all, one of Jesse's calibre. It had not escaped her that Jesse was not just very beautiful but also very bright and dignified. She was just what she had come to learn Alix looked for in her friends.

Alix left early the following morning. Throughout

Australia, the concert tour was more successful than she could have hoped. No matter what concert hall they appeared in, the audience was delighted and gave them standing ovations. Hong Kong was no different. But there, Alix had the extra pleasure of meeting up with Jesse.

In the afternoons when Alix didn't have rehearsals, she went with Jesse to explore the city. It was not one of her favourite cities but she enjoyed its bustle. As they wandered down yet another busy street, Alix remembered the wonderful times she and Tansie had shared overseas. Alix enjoyed Jesse's company and yet her thoughts often wandered to Tansie. She missed her.

When Jesse noticed that Alix had suddenly gone quiet, she asked, "Are you all right?"

"Yeah," Alix replied pensively. For a brief moment she contemplated telling Jesse what was going through her mind. In the end, she decided against it. Instead, she said lightly, "Let's stop for a coffee and you can tell me more about the paper you gave this morning."

They sat in the Peninsula foyer for well over two hours talking about Jesse's interest in women's health and other women's issues and about Alix's work.

Eventually Jesse asked, "I think I read somewhere that you don't often go on concert tours, is that right?"

"Quite right," Alix smiled. "However, ever since I started this one, I have also started to think that I might do them more often. When I told Boris about the tour with Jean-Jacques, he immediately invited me to go on a Pacific tour with him next year."

"Are you going to accept?"

"I'm seriously thinking about it," Alix replied. "During this tour I have actually enjoyed myself more than I antici-pated." For a moment Alix let her gaze wander over the many guests who mingled in the foyer. Then she smiled and looked at Jesse. "This tour has given me quite a buzz and I like the attention I'm getting."

"Then accept Boris' invitation," Jesse said.

Having enormously enjoyed the three days they'd had in Hong Kong, Alix spontaneously invited Jesse to come to Singapore for their final concert. She was delighted when Jesse accepted, saying that she was in no great rush to go home. Alix found Jesse's conversation most scintillating and her sense of humour enchanting. But it was the aura of dignity and soothing calmness Alix was especially drawn to.

During Alix's absence, Tansie had been as good as her word, or so it appeared. Every day or evening, whenever Alix rang her at random hours, she had without fail been at home to receive Alix's phone calls. Tansie wasn't going to risk losing Alix perhaps for good this time. She stayed at home for nearly the entire three weeks Alix was gone. She worked on her sculptures, attended classes at college and saw Dr Callahan as promised.

What she did not convey to Alix was that she had also seen Herb Mullins a few times. After the party at Kate's house he had rung her and invited her out. She had accepted despite the fact that she didn't particularly like him.

Alix returned in time for the children's September holidays, and together with Felix and Tansie, they all went to the beach house.

Allowing herself the luxury of staying in bed one morning and reading the newspaper, Alix was still there when Drew came looking for her.

Although still only in his teens, Drew was now taller than his mother. His body had filled out and he'd become an extremely handsome young man. Flicking his long blond hair off his face, he asked, "Can David come and stay for a few days? He's got hassles with his old man again."

"Of course he can," Alix replied.

She had no time for the boy's father, Herb Mullins, but liked David and had always made him welcome in her house. He was a frequent visitor. She had felt sorry for the three boys when their mother had left them, although she often wondered what had made her marry Mullins in the first place.

"Herb is going to bring him down this afternoon," Drew said, leaving no illusions that he wasn't fond of his friend's father either. "Thanks, Mum," he grinned and leapt from the room, causing the floorboards to creak beneath his step.

Soon after lunch, Kate and Jackie arrived to make up a tennis foursome. They had just started on their third and deciding set, when Herb arrived with his three sons, Ben, David and Jack.

"Hi, Mrs. C. Hi, Mrs. H," David called out, gave them a broad grin and, followed by his brothers, disappeared inside the house. Herb barely waved to the women on the tennis court.

"Make yourself comfortable on the terrace, Herb. We shouldn't be long," Alix said just as she prepared to serve another one of her lethal aces down the centre line.

Within half an hour the game was over. When the four women walked off the court, Herb hadn't moved. Nor did he now make any attempt to get to his feet to greet them.

Tansie was the only one who gave Herb a wide smile. "It's nice to see you again, Herb," she said casually. "Are we having drinks inside?" she called after Alix.

"Yes," Alix replied.

Alix fetched the drinks from the kitchen and then joined her guests in the sitting room. While the women chatted,

Mullins sat slouched deeply into the leather couch. The only time he spoke was when he refused a glass, saying that he preferred to drink beer straight from the can.

In Alix's view, his manners were insufferable, and given different circumstances, she would never have a man like him in the house. But for her son's sake, she tolerated him.

When Jackie left, Alix and Kate retreated to the kitchen to help Felix with the dinner for the children.

The two women were setting the large table in the conservatory when Tansie strolled in. "By the way, I've invited Herb for dinner," Tansie informed them.

"You what?" Alix and Kate gasped simultaneously.

"Oh, come on, don't be like that," Tansie reprimanded them. "Show some of the wonderful hospitality you always pride yourself on!"

"I don't want him at my dinner table!" Alix exclaimed.

"You're lucky I only invited him for dinner and not for the night!" Tansie grinned and disappeared again.

For a while, Alix and Kate tried to include Herb in their dinner conversation, but, despite their efforts, Herb replied in monosyllables. Eventually they gave up and ignored him. However, much to the women's chagrin, his oldest son's mouth never closed. Whatever was said, Ben knew it all better.

When Kate's impatience began to boil over, she raised Ben from his chair. "You come with me, kiddo," she said and marched him out of the room. Shoving him into the children's playroom, she said, "You're still a head shorter than me and, until you've grown some more, you play with the kiddies. Understood?"

Only Tansie seemed to take some sort of liking to the Mullins family. "You shouldn't be so hard on the poor boy," Tansie remarked when Kate returned. "I'm sure all he needs is a mother . . ."

"There's your chance, love! He's all yours," Kate replied and turning to Alix, she added, "anyway, I'd better run along. Thanks for dinner, pet. I'll catch up with you tomorrow."

Half an hour later when Herb had also left, Tansie joined Alix in her room and sensuously curved her body into her lover's.

Lying in each other's arms, Tansie suddenly laughed. "I wonder how Herbie performs in bed?"

"Ask him!"

"Oh, I couldn't do that!" Tansie replied, shocked at the thought. "Didn't you see how tight his jeans were?"

"No! His endowments are of no interest to me!"

After a short pause, Tansie continued. "I do feel sorry for him, you know. It wouldn't be easy to keep those boys in line, especially Ben."

"I wouldn't worry about it," Alix responded laconically. "He'll find another wife in due course . . . most men do, even the least desirable ones."

"Just as well we're not looking for new husbands. If that's the best there is, I don't want to know," Tansie giggled and proceeded to let her hand wander over Alix's thighs and further up over her flat stomach.

For a brief moment, Alix thought about Tansie's remark. It was just a little strange in her view. But as Tansie continued to caress her, Alix soon forgot about him.

Chapter 16

Half-way through spring, Tansie broached the subject of Alix's forthcoming fortieth birthday.

"Have you given it any thought?" Tansie asked.

"What makes you think I want to do anything?" Alix laughed. "You didn't want a party for your fortieth."

"That was different," Tansie grumbled. "With two teenage children, you can afford to be that old!"

Alix raised her eyebrows but the gesture went unnoticed. "Actually, when you were away skiing, I booked Sergio's. They have an in-house band and the food's fantastic too."

"I thought with your resources you'd at least fly your mates to Paris for a weekend," Tansie replied, a touch of envy in her voice.

Alix smiled. "Talking about Paris, have you thought about coming to Europe with me at Christmas?"

"I'm still thinking about it," Tansie said, adding, "Getting back to your party, who're you taking?"

"You, of course," Alix replied.

Tansie shrugged her shoulders but didn't reply. As soon as Alix left, Tansie reached for the telephone. Moments later Herb Mullins answered and she invited him over for dinner.

Herb arrived an hour late for their date and, somewhat flustered, he followed Tansie down the hall. "I'm sorry about this, but the boys were out of control, I couldn't leave."

"Send them to boarding school!" she growled.

"I couldn't ever afford that!"

Tansie gave him a condescending look. Her manner was haughty and her lips were drawn into a thin sulky line. "If you're that poor, let's not worry about dinner." She drew him along the passage to her bedroom. Now was as good a time as any to try him out.

Discarding her clothes, she fell on to the bed. She stretched out and, reaching for his hand, pulled him down. Tansie fumbled with the zip on his jeans and slid her hand inside his shorts. Feeling him, she only just managed to suppress a laugh. He was diminutive. What had she let herself in for, she wondered, but quickly reminded herself that she was not in this for the pleasure of it.

Herb, in a frenzied haste, pulled down his pants and boxer shorts to his ankles. He had wanted her from the moment he'd met her. Now he was actually going to have her. Having come this far, his confidence was boosted rapidly and he already knew that he would ask her to marry him.

When she felt him pushing himself inside her, Tansie turned her head into the pillow. Although she continued to take men to bed, she didn't like their fumbled, unsatisfactory attempts at making love. In order to tolerate it though, she thought of Alix and other women before her. She used her own hands to caress her breasts just the way she liked it. She could now make herself believe that they were actually Alix's hands.

It was all over before it had really started. She was tired, she said and told him to go home. She couldn't bear to look at his head of thin red hair and his lily-white, freckled flabby body any longer. But then, in her view, men served only one purpose: to marry her and make her respectable. For that he might do well enough in due course. The fact that he was neither well-endowed nor well-off, didn't bother

194

her. Her own money would be enough to keep her independent and allow her whatever luxuries she wanted.

When Tansie arrived for her next session with Dr Callahan she informed him that she felt wonderful and wouldn't be needing him any more. She had seen him now for several weeks she rationalised and even Alix should be satisfied with that. He wished her well and let her go.

An hour later, she sauntered into the restaurant where she and Alix had arranged to meet. She felt good about the world. She would no longer need to chat to the shrink. Her visits to him had become quite tiresome, mostly because she had to try and remember what she'd told him during the previous visits.

But, she was also pleased that she could still attract a man even if it was only Herb Mullins. She had not had a man around now for some time. Each one of her former lovers had ultimately left either of their own accord or had been asked to leave.

Blowing Alix a breezy kiss, Tansie took the seat opposite her. She brushed her fringe off her forehead, a gesture Alix particularly liked.

"You look very chirpy this evening," Alix commented with delight. She too felt good, happy to be in her favourite restaurant with her lover. Ever since Le Petit Trianon had opened some three years ago, she had been a regular customer. Its decor and bustle reminded her of the restaurants she used to frequent in Paris.

"I feel just fantastic, Alix. Dr Callahan told me that he didn't want to see me any more. He thinks I'm in excellent shape," Tansie chortled in response.

"That is good news," Alix replied, reflecting that Tansie looked much like the day they had met. Shy, yet seductively childlike.

"And, because I feel so terrific, I've decided to do something really charitable. I've invited Herb to come to your birthday party."

Alix gave her a flabbergasted stare and started to choke on a piece of meat. Reaching for a glass of water, her voice was still hoarse when she said, "You will do nothing of the sort, Tansie!"

"Please, Alix, you know how uncomfortable I am about attending such functions without a man," Tansie pleaded.

"There'll be plenty of other single women as well as men if that's what you're worried about."

"Where do you find all those guys?" Tansie asked with curiosity. "Are they all rich and good-looking?"

"Would I invite anyone else?" Alix was flippant but inside she was hurt. The sudden curiosity in Tansie's voice had not escaped her. "However, let's not change the subject. Mullins is not coming and that is all there is to it."

"Please Alix, don't put me in that position," Tansie exclaimed aghast.

After a short pause, Alix said, "Look, if it makes you feel better then bring someone but not Mullins." She didn't like the idea much but didn't think it important enough to start an argument.

"I don't know how I'm going to tell Mullins, but thanks, Alix, I'll bring someone else," Tansie gushed, adding with a giggle, "you know, you're the most infuriatingly stubborn woman I've ever met, and yet, that's one of the things I love about you."

Alix had hoped that she and Tansie would dine together the evening before her birthday, but Tansie informed her that she had made other plans. Alix was disappointed but in turn accepted a last minute dinner invitation from Jesse.

When Alix arrived at Jesse's house at the appointed time,

four other women were already assembled in the sitting room sipping champagne. Alix was not surprised when she noted that they were all well-known and successful in their professions.

Carol was an architect in her own practice; Kelly was a paediatric surgeon; Kris a partner in a stockbroking firm and Maxine a Member of State Parliament.

By the time Jesse asked her guests to take their seats in the dining room, Alix had made her assessment of the women. She liked them and very much enjoyed their company. As the evening progressed, Alix felt more and more at home, as though she had known her fellow diners for a long time.

Needing far less sleep than most other people and still feeling rather stimulated, Alix found herself alone with Jesse. The two women had barely settled into the comfortable couches when Alix looked across at the clock on the mantelpiece and flew to her feet.

"I had no idea it was this late," she said, fidgeting with the narrow wedding band she had never bothered to take off.

"Relax," Jesse replied, inviting her to sit down again.

Alix sat down and took a sip of cognac. She smiled when she asked, "By the way, did you buy that new dress you were telling me about?"

"Would you like to see it?" Jesse asked.

"I would."

Jesse sauntered off and returned moments later carrying a shiny white Laura Machiavelli bag. Removing the hyacinth-blue, soft jersey dress and holding it up, she smiled. "Is it slinky and sexy enough for you?"

Alix laughed but blushed just a little, remembering that she had suggested that Jesse buy such a garment. At the time she had made the comment in passing and without much thought. Now she realised that it had probably neither been made nor received quite as casually as she had thought. "As I said once before, you've got great legs, show them . . . and yes . . . it is very sexy indeed. The colour looks stunning on you. Any man would take a second look!"

"They're welcome to look but that's all they're going to get," Jesse replied with aplomb and draped the garment over the back of the couch. Taking her seat next to Alix again, she added more seriously, "I'm glad you came, Alix."

"The pleasure was all mine. I had a wonderful time," Alix smiled. After a short pause and another sip of cognac, she continued, "You know, I'd almost forgotten what it was like to just sit and talk, particularly to such interesting women."

"I used to have such gatherings at least once a week. In more recent times, I haven't quite felt up to it," Jesse said slowly.

"You haven't been ill, have you?" Alix asked, alarmed that she was keeping Jesse up even later.

Jesse shook her head. Her eyes took on a momentary troubled look as a gentle smile started to crinkle the corners of her lips. "No, I'm perfectly healthy. My problems are of a romantic nature and not quite as easily fixed as a sore throat or appendicitis."

"They never are," Alix mused. Although they had seen each other socially a few times since their return from Hong Kong, Alix was in two minds about probing into her private life.

"Just over six months ago, my lover of eight years left me," Jesse said. "Maxine left me for Kelly."

It was on the tip of Alix's tongue to say, "How could she

leave someone as lovely as you." She decided however that this comment was not appropriate at this time despite the fact that she was actually curious as to why.

Suddenly the image of Tansie with another woman flashed through Alix's mind. She felt sick and did not think she could cope if Tansie now had other female lovers.

Meeting Jesse's gaze, she shrugged her shoulders in a helpless gesture. "What can I say . . . other than how deeply sorry I feel for you," Alix said.

"There isn't much to say." Jesse smiled. "I know this may sound strange to you but having you here this evening has made all the difference. Thank you."

Still lost for words, Alix replied simply, "I'm glad I could help. And, as I said, I've very much enjoyed being here."

After a brief pause, Alix broke the silence. "Jesse . . . can I ask you something a little more personal?"

"Of course."

"How do you feel about being a lesbian?"

Jesse smiled and said softly, "Very happy."

"After what happened with Maxine would you consider a man as a partner?"

"Good grief, no! That would be the furthest thing from my mind," Jesse laughed, adding, "I wouldn't even know how to make a pass at a man let alone what to do with him afterwards."

Alix wondered whether she too would one day be so unequivocal. Or would she be torn forever between choosing a male or a female partner. All she knew was that she could not presently imagine herself with anyone else but Tansie.

"Would you?" Jesse asked, as though she had read Alix's thoughts.

Alix's eyes twinkled with amusement and she smiled. "I don't know." After a short silence, she added quietly, "I hope that I'll never have to look for a new partner and make that decision."

"You're so wonderfully romantic," Jesse said, adding, "don't ever lose that."

Two hours later, Alix finally got up to leave. She had many more questions she wanted to ask Jesse, but they could wait. Now that their friendship had reached a much more personal level, she was confident that there would be other times to talk.

Alix fell into bed as soon as she got home and was asleep the moment her head hit the pillow. When the phone rang, she reached for it with a groan, feeling as though she hadn't slept at all.

"Oh, you are home!" Tansie said.

"Where else would I be?"

"I tried to ring you half the night, but you weren't there." When Alix failed to respond, she added, "Happy birthday . . . how does it feel to be forty?"

"No different from yesterday when I was still thirty-nine," Alix replied. "Anyway, why aren't you here with me?"

Tansie gave a brief chortle but otherwise ignored the question. "Guess what? Herbie has asked me to marry him."

Alix awoke instantly and gasped. "Are you going to?"

"Are you mad or something?" Tansie cried. "He's a peasant, you know that!"

"So, why tell me about it?"

"One doesn't get an offer of marriage every day of the week. I thought it was important."

"In his case, it's an insult."

"No one's proposed to you lately!"

"Times are tough!" Alix laughed good-naturedly. "Anyway, how come he proposed? Have you been seeing him?"

"Just a couple of times," Tansie admitted. "I feel sorry for him, that's all."

Once they finished their conversation, Alix felt a little disturbed by Tansie's revelation. She wondered briefly whether Tansie was having an affair with Herb. But the thought of any woman in bed with him made her laugh. Surely nobody could be that desperate!

After she had tossed and turned for a while with sleep eluding her, she decided to get up and work. But still, she could not get Tansie out of her mind. She wondered, yet again, why Dr Callahan had given Tansie the book, *Why Do I Think I'm Nothing Without A Man?*

"I don't need that crap!" Tansie had said at the time and tossed it into the fireplace. "I don't even particularly like men."

Alix would have liked to ask her, why then was she forever chasing them. Not knowing what Tansie had told Dr Callahan, Alix could now only assume that the substance of his conversations with her had revolved around Tansie not being able to come to terms with her sexual preference. She very much hoped that he had addressed that problem, although there were others that needed to be looked at as well.

Before leaving home, Alix gave herself a scrutinising stare in the mirror, looking for new wrinkles. She found none and smiled. She didn't look a day older than forty, she decided.

Alix collected Jesse on the way to Sergio's. Tansie was to make her own way, together with her escort, she had told Alix without disclosing his identity.

Alix wore an off-the-shoulder outfit, with a slit up one side, showing as much of her long slim legs as was decent. The brilliant white of the dress set off her olive skin and the emerald necklace reflected in her eyes.

Jesse wore the dress she had shown Alix the night before. With a smile, Alix noted that Jesse indeed looked lovely and sexy. The neckline plunged to where the roundness of her breasts started, showing enough cleavage to stir people's interest. The back plunged to just below her narrow waist. As Alix had predicted, many male guests could not keep their eyes off Jesse. She wondered whether any of them knew that she was lost to them forever. That thought brought an amused smile to her lips.

"What's so funny?" Kate asked. She had appeared at Alix's side moments earlier.

"Never mind," Alix laughed.

"Nobody else would get away with that answer, pet," Kate grinned. "By the way, our friendly lady doctor looks quite stunning. I wonder why no knight in shining armour has whipped her off her feet."

"She does indeed," Alix confirmed, ignoring Kate's second statement.

Observing Jesse, who had just emerged from the powder room and was walking across the foyer towards the two women, Kate continued, "It's amazing, Alix, how remarkably alike you two look. You know, I hadn't noticed it before but you could quite easily pass for sisters."

"It's taken you an awfully long time to appreciate how stunning and sexy I am," Alix replied nonplussed, thinking how right Kate was.

Kate and Alix were still exchanging pleasantries when Kate suddenly breathed, "Good grief! What's he doing here?"

As Alix saw Herb come through the front door, the smile froze on her face. "What is he doing here?" Alix gasped the moment Tansie gave her a breezy kiss on the cheek.

"When you said you had invited Jesse, I saw no reason to arrive by myself," Tansie replied defiantly.

Alix swallowed hard. This was not what had happened. They both knew it. For the first time, Alix felt anger well inside her and she was about to say something but thought better of it. It could wait.

"Hi," Alix acknowledged Mullins' presence, adding when Jesse appeared at her side, "Jesse, you haven't met . . ." She stopped just before she let 'Mullins' slip and smiled sweetly. "Herb Mullins . . . Dr Jesse Carrington."

Jesse offered him her hand, but Herb either deliberately ignored it or didn't know how to respond. His hands remained buried in the pockets of his baggy pants. She was about to turn her back on Herb, she had no time for ill-mannered people, when she noticed a mixed glimmer of disappointment, anger and hurt in Alix's eyes. Jesse would have liked to put her arms around Alix and comfort her. But this was neither the place nor the time.

"I'll see you in the restaurant," Jesse murmured into Alix's ear and headed for the double glass doors which led into the actual restaurant.

Tansie looked sophisticated in a royal blue taffeta dress. Alfredo had styled her hair that afternoon and added a slight touch of red. Her fringe was swept off her face and was pulled together into a French knot, making her eyes seem even larger and more luminous. Alix also saw the vulnerable child she had encountered when they had first met. At the same time, she realised just how much she loved her. To now have to watch her with such a crass individual made her cringe inside.

With other guests arriving and the party getting under-way, Alix had to put Tansie to the back of her mind. She had to consider nearly a hundred other people.

When Alix eventually found her own seat in the restaurant, she noted with a smile just how comfortable Jesse seemed amongst a group of virtual strangers. Alix was pleased to see that she appeared as relaxed in male company as she was in the company of women. Very much how she herself felt, Alix thought.

From time to time, Alix cast a glance towards Tansie to see that she was all right. She seemed perfectly content and appeared to be having a good time chatting to many of the guests. She paid no attention to her escort.

Alix remained blissfully unaware of an encounter Tansie had had with Jesse when they met in the entrance hall during the evening. Kate had seen it though and wondered what Tansie was up to now. Although she could not hear the conversation between the two women, it very much appeared as though Tansie was making a pass at Jesse and Jesse was turning her down. Kate was glad that Alix had not seen this exchange. In time, she would tell Tansie what she thought of her behaviour.

Even before the evening came to an end, Tansie ambled over to Alix. "I'm going home," she said truculently.

"Why?" Alix asked.

"I'm tired." Tansie kissed Alix lightly on the cheek and left. Herb followed two steps behind her.

As Alix watched them leave, she couldn't help but smile. As a pair, Tansie and Herb looked positively comical. How could she even have entertained the idea of Tansie having an affair with Herb! Moments later she frowned. She was just a little hurt that Tansie had left before the night was out. Then she sighed, remembering that she would have to talk to Tansie about having brought Herb to the party. Although she was angry about it, she didn't look forward to talking to Tansie.

When the evening finally drew to an end, a small group of party-goers arranged to meet at Monsoon Disco where they danced until morning. As they all danced individually to the heavy rock music, Alix wondered what it would be like to dance a Vienna waltz or a tango with her lover. She smiled and decided that it would probably be a very sensuous experience to hold Tansie in her arms and sweep her across a dance floor.

After an early breakfast of bacon and eggs at Kate's house, Alix drove Jesse home just before four o'clock.

"Thank you for a lovely evening," Jesse said and kissed Alix on the cheek.

Suddenly Alix became very aware of Jesse's presence, her sensuality and, at the same time, she felt immensely alone. This is all wrong, she thought. Tansie should be here. Alix hated the idea of having to crawl into bed on her own.

Watching her friend, Jesse put her hand on Alix's arm. "If there is anything I can do to help, as a doctor or a friend, I'm always available. All you have to do is ask," she said softly.

Alix nodded, thanked her and drove home. She had just opened her front door, when Drew came flying down the stairs.

"Good morning, mother," he greeted her.

"Why're you up so early, it's Sunday?"

"Felix's taking us windsurfing . . . we thought you might need a quiet day after your two late nights," Drew chirped and gave his mother a kiss. "After all, you're no spring chooky any more."

"I'm not over the hill either," Alix laughed and went upstairs.

Tansie's last thought that night had been of Alix. Was she really angry with her for having brought Herb to the party she wondered? What if Alix had seen her with Jesse in the entrance hall? She knew Kate had seen her. For the first time in a long while, Tansie felt just a little uneasy.

When Alix arrived at Tansie's house late the following afternoon, Tansie drew her into her arms. "What a lovely surprise." When no response came from Alix, she asked, "Aren't you going to kiss me hello?"

Alix kissed her lightly on the cheek and then wandered down the passage to the sitting room.

"You're angry with me, aren't you?" Tansie murmured, her voice a little shaky now.

Studying Tansie, Alix replied, "Angry, hurt, disappointed, call it what you like. But, what I want to know is why you brought Mullins along when I specifically asked you not to! You let me believe that you'd bring someone else."

"If it was good enough for you to come with that . . . that . . . lesbian . . . it was good enough for me to bring Herb!" Tansie snapped. "Anyway, you were downright rude to him and . . ."

Alix stayed aloof and held Tansie's gaze. "That is not what happened and you know it," Alix replied, controlling her welling frustration.

"Where were you until early this morning if not with her? I tried to ring you many times," Tansie snapped.

"I went to Monsoon's with a whole lot of people," Alix replied. She hated to have to account for her whereabouts but she positively despised playing games.

Tansie ignored Alix's explanation and exclaimed angrily. "Who does Jesse think she is? Did you know she made a pass at me last night?"

"Give me a break, Tansie. You don't expect me to believe that, do you?" Alix said with exasperation. She most certainly did not believe Jesse would do such a thing. She wouldn't need to, anyway, Alix thought.

"All right, take her side," Tansie retorted, very much on the defensive now. "If you don't like what I do, then go!"

"Tansie, I love you and nothing will ever change that, but that doesn't mean . . ."

Tansie flung herself into Alix's arms. She hadn't missed the opening she was waiting for. "Alix, I love you and I never, ever meant to hurt you. You know men mean nothing to me." Tansie let her voice trail off, as a flood of real tears emerged from her eyes. "I'll get rid of Herb if that's what you want."

"Tansie, it's not what I want, it's what you want that counts. If you think Herb can make you happy and give you what you're after, then go for it," Alix replied quietly, although she could not imagine what Herb could possibly give Tansie.

"I want you, my love . . . nobody else," Tansie gushed.

After what seemed an eternity, Alix dropped her head on to Tansie's shoulder and mused, "Maybe there is no love without pain."

Later she wondered just what permanent damage Tansie's appalling childhood might have done to her. Was she so badly affected by it that she simply no longer knew right from wrong or good from bad? But if that were so, then surely Dr Callahan would have asked her to continue with the therapy, she rationalised. Not satisfied with her own silent dialogue, Alix made a mental note to ask Jesse for some literature about childhood trauma and its long-term effects. She loved Tansie and she would spare no effort to try and learn to understand her. She wanted to understand her.

When Alix left Tansie's house the following morning, she noticed Mullins' car parked across the road. He sat behind the wheel and pretended to read the newspaper. Alix wondered what he was doing in this neighbourhood and at this hour. For a fleeting moment it occurred to her that he might be checking up on Tansie, but she dismissed the thought. Not even a jerk like Mullins would lower himself to such a despicable level.

She retrieved a pair of binoculars from the boot of her car, boldly walked across the road and knocked on his window. When he opened it, she flung the binoculars into his lap.

"The real birds are in the park . . . two blocks down the road!" She caught a glimpse of his bright red face, but didn't wait for an answer.

Two weeks later, Alix and Tansie stood at the check-in counter at the airport, glancing at each other. Their looks said everything that could not be said aloud. When Alix had originally made the arrangements to take the children overseas for their Christmas vacation, Tansie had been vague about whether she would go with Alix or not. Much to Alix's distress, Tansie was still undecided.

As though it had only just come to her that Alix was going to be away for some weeks, Tansie said timidly, "Maybe I will come to Europe, if that's still okay with you."

"Of course it is," Alix replied and gave her a hug. "Just ring me and let me know when you're coming."

"I will," Tansie promised.

Chapter 17

After a two day stopover in Hong Kong, Alix arrived in Switzerland where she and the children installed themselves at her Aunt Hanna's house. Hanna had not seen the children for some time and was delighted to have them with her. With Christmas only ten days away, they went shopping most mornings and spent the afternoons on long walks across the snow-covered fields or ice-skating.

Although they spoke on the telephone every day, Alix missed Tansie and still waited to hear whether she was going to join her for Christmas. But, at the same time, Alix felt very much at peace in the tranquil surroundings. From Hanna's music room, where Alix often sat and played the piano, she had a wonderful view over the still water of Lake Geneva. The French Alps beyond were covered in a thick blanket of snow as were the vineyards which gently sloped away from the house towards the lake. The road which hugged the shoreline was sufficiently far away so that the traffic noise could not be heard in the house. From the same spot, Alix could also watch the children romp in the snow. Their squeals of delight filtered through the windows.

Sometimes Hanna joined Alix at the piano. As they played, they recalled the times they had performed together a long time ago.

After finishing one of Alix's sonatas one afternoon, Hanna lifted her hands from the keyboard and folded them in her lap.

She smiled at her niece and said, "You know Alix, I'm

glad you decided to become a composer rather than a full-time concert pianist. As much as I loved the glamour and the excitement of being an artist and travelling the world, it was also very lonely, particularly when Siggy and I performed in different parts of the world. I would not wish that life on anyone. You have the best of all possible worlds: the music and the success, the children and as normal a life as is possible with your busy schedule."

Alix put an arm around Hanna's fragile shoulders and let out a short chuckle. "I think so too, but I also remember sitting at this very piano and envying you the intimacy and the companionship you had with Siggy."

"Oh yes, we had all of that and more," Hanna mused, a soft smile creasing the corners of her alert blue eyes. Despite her advanced age, she was still a strikingly handsome woman. Her face, although lined now, was oval and finely chiselled. Her hair was still thick and curly like Alix's but a few shades darker with streaks of grey through it.

An expression of melancholy crossed Alix's face. "I was married and much lonelier than you think. By the time I realised just how lonely marriage can be, I had the children. Without them, I think I would eventually have chosen a full-time concert career."

"I know that, darling, but instead you've composed some very fine music, for which you'll be remembered long after you're gone." After a short pause, she added, "How are you and Tansie getting along? Are you still as happy as last time I saw you?"

"Yes, most of the time," Alix agreed.

The undercurrent in Alix's voice did not escape Hanna. Despite the fact that she was much smaller than Alix, Hanna took her into her arms and gently cradled her. She had always known that Alix was far too sensuous to be on her own for any length of time and when Tansie came into her life, Hanna had been very pleased. She hoped that the restlessness and loneliness Alix had experienced during her marriage would dissipate. Deep inside, she prayed that whatever difficulties Alix and Tansie were currently experiencing would be short-lived.

Alix had little time during the day to dwell on the fact that Tansie wasn't with her. But the nights were different. Lying in the bed in the large attic room the two women had shared during their previous visit, Alix missed her desperately. She often found herself automatically reaching out, expecting Tansie to be there. She conjured up Tansie's warm slim body and could almost feel her smooth skin which was so responsive to Alix's touch. The whole room seemed to be filled with everything that was Tansie: her easy laugh, the scent of the Nina Ricci perfume she always wore and even the chaos she created when unpacking her belongings.

Curled up in front of the fire one evening, Alix got up to answer the telephone. Hanna and the children had retired some time earlier. Alix, not yet ready to slip into the cold empty bed upstairs, had remained in the sitting room to read. She hoped that it was Tansie. Alix had tried to ring her earlier but there was no answer.

"Hello?" she announced in French.

"Alix? . . . It's Jesse."

"Where are you?" Alix asked, with obvious joy in her voice.

"I'm in London," Jesse replied. "How about joining me for a couple of days? Charles Dutoit is conducting the London Philharmonic . . . and Accardo is playing Paganini's Violin Concerto No. 6 the day after tomorrow. It'd be . . ."

Alix took less than a second to make a decision. "How could I refuse?" she cried, adding, "where're you staying?"

"The Ritz."

"You're a woman after my own heart! I'll be there some-time tomorrow," Alix responded. Slowly, she replaced the receiver as she wondered why Jesse had so suddenly popped up in London. She hadn't mentioned an overseas trip when Alix had had dinner with her shortly before her departure. In the end, she decided that Jesse probably wanted to surprise her. That would fit in well with her temperament, Alix thought.

Alix caught a flight out of Geneva the following day and arrived in London just after lunch. She walked into the lobby of the Ritz, just ahead of the porter, when Jesse stepped out of the lift. As usual, Jesse looked distinguished in a pair of dark grey fine-wool trousers, a casual white shirt of heavy silk and soft leather boots. A tartan scarf was carelessly draped around her slender neck and a cashmere overcoat flung over one arm. Alix smiled when she noticed that Jesse had also had a haircut, which Alix thought gave her an even more youthful and flamboyant appearance.

They greeted each other warmly and then strolled over to the reception desk for Alix to check in. Since Jesse was on her way to Harrods to do a spot of shopping, Alix accompanied her. Laden with parcels, they returned to the hotel in time to shower and change for dinner. Given the miserable London weather, neither could be bothered going out again and they decided to eat at the Louis XV restaurant at the hotel.

When Alix returned to the lobby and looked around to see whether Jesse had already come down, the concierge said, "Ms Clemenger, your sister is over there," pointing to a group of comfortable armchairs and small tables.

"Thank you," Alix said with a smile playing in her eyes. It amused her that he thought Jesse was her sister but she was not surprised. Kate too had seen it and pointed it out to her. She could see how easily such a mistake could be made even by a concierge of a busy hotel. They were both tall and willowy, had much the same coloured blonde curly hair and dressed in a similar fashion.

"What are you smiling about?" Jesse asked curiously, turning around as she felt Alix's warm hand lightly touching her shoulder.

"The concierge thought we were sisters," Alix said.

"I'm glad we're not," Jesse replied promptly and, standing up, casually wound her arm through Alix's, kissing her softly on the cheek. "I'm starving," she added.

Although Alix thought she knew what Jesse had implied, she decided not to react other than in a light-hearted manner. "I always missed not having a sister. My only brother is nearly six years older and, because of it, we didn't spend a lot of time together."

Jesse chuckled. "If it's a sister you want, I've got two . . . you're welcome to borrow them any time."

"I might take you up on that offer sometime." Alix kept her response light.

Independently, both women had changed into semi-formal evening dresses. They both looked striking and, although they were oblivious to it, many heads turned when they strolled into the restaurant.

Once they were comfortably seated at a table at the back of the restaurant, they sipped the champagne the waiter had poured and momentarily held each other's gaze.

"I'm so glad we finally have an evening to ourselves, particularly here where we're not likely to run into anyone we know!" Jesse eventually said.

"I promise I won't even say hello to the Queen!"

"I should have known you'd know her," Jesse responded.

She mockingly rolled her eyes just before she put on her narrow-framed tortoise-shell reading glasses to study the menu.

As Alix too started to study the menu, she asked, "What are you doing in London?"

"I was invited to give a paper at the International Conference for Women Doctors in Cambridge. I wasn't sure whether I could make it, hence my sudden appearance," Jesse replied, adding, "I think I've told you before that I'm very interested in helping women who don't wish to conceive children in the normal way. I'm giving a paper on self-insemination."

"Can I go with you?" Alix asked with a wide smile. "I promise I won't make any smart comments from the auditorium!"

"I might return the compliment," Jesse laughed.

"That could be a bit of a worry."

"Anyway, I'd very much like you to come," Jesse said. Studying her companion for a moment, a wide smile crossed her face and she continued, "You seem to be taking an interest in this subject. Is it for personal reasons?"

"Maybe."

Although Tansie had not mentioned her desire to have a baby again, Alix still thought about the possibility of their having a child together. Now was as good a time as any to find out more about it and she couldn't think of a better person to hear it from than Jesse.

The two women ordered dinner and chatted like old friends. Alix realised just how much they had in common. She was very interested in Jesse's work, the papers she gave around the world and the voluntary work she did for several women's refuges. Alix began to truly respect and admire her and her views on many issues.

"It's a shame there are not more women like you," Alix eventually said with a smile. "If there is anything I might be able to contribute, please let me know."

"Thank you." Jesse returned the smile and added, "How would you feel about giving a benefit concert?"

"Why haven't I thought of that?" Alix responded. "I'd be delighted. Just tell me when and where. I'll make sure all my friends are there too. We might as well raise as much money as possible."

"We might as well, and thank you, I really appreciate this," Jesse replied and gave Alix's hand a brief pat.

After a short silence in which the waiter cleared the dishes, Alix asked, "Jesse, what books can you recommend for me to read on childhood abuse. Has there been much written about?"

"There has indeed," Jesse said, adding, "I take it you want to know more about this because of Tansie?"

"Yes, I do," Alix confirmed. "It might just help me to understand her a little better. Quite frankly, I can't even imagine what sort of a life she must have had as a child."

"It's hard for anybody who hasn't suffered childhood abuse themselves to imagine what it is like," Jesse sighed. "I suggest you start with Alice Miller's publications. She has made a name for herself worldwide as an authority on such matters."

"I will, thank you."

Early the following morning, they were chauffeur-driven to Cambridge.

"Is Tansie coming over to join you?" Jesse asked, leaning into the Jaguar's soft leather seats.

"I don't know," Alix replied with a slight edge to her voice. "I'd very much like her to . . . but she still wasn't sure about her movements when I spoke to her a day or so ago."

"I would think she'd have missed you enough by now to want to come," Jesse comforted her.

"I very much hope so."

When they arrived at the conference centre, they were welcomed by Dr Jane MacCormick, the president of the conference. Since they had arrived a little later than planned, they were immediately ushered into the auditorium. Alix gave Jesse's hand a quick squeeze, smiled and then took a seat from where she could observe the audience as well as have a good view of Jesse.

Jesse followed Dr MacCormick on to the platform and, after the introduction, unfolded her notes. Slipping reading glasses on to the bridge of her nose, she commenced, "Good afternoon, ladies and . . ." she stopped a moment but continued with a smile when she spotted several men, "and gentlemen." Given the content of her speech and past experiences, she hadn't actually expected more than a couple of men. She was now pleasantly surprised to find a relatively large number.

Alix settled into the hard seat, and although she listened to Jesse's speech, she was also preoccupied with observing Jesse herself.

Jesse was dressed in an elegantly but conservatively cut light grey Max Mara suit over a delicate dusty pink Swiss cotton shirt. The whole outfit emphasised her trim figure and highlighted her smooth lightly tanned face. Her voice was strong yet mellow and deeply compassionate when she spoke. And, despite the seriousness of the subject, she managed to come out with some subtle and humorous comments which evoked chuckles from the audience.

Alix very much liked the way Jesse moved her hands from time to time to emphasise a certain point. Or the way she peered over the rim of her glasses, her hyacinth eyes sparkling with humour at times, or the way she crossed her feet at her slim ankles, draping one neatly over the other when standing.

Judging by some of the statistics Jesse quoted, self-insemination seemed to gain popularity year by year. Although this procedure was contrary to all conventional thought on reproduction, obviously the need was there even if only for a small proportion of the population.

Alix understood the logic and the need for women to take charge of their lives and the right to do so. She decided that conceiving and bringing up a child like this must be preferable to conceiving one in a loveless or even emotionally abusive and physically violent marriage.

When Jesse finished, the applause was overwhelming. But, with seemingly endless questions from the audience, it was another hour before they left and returned to London.

The concert that evening was everything Alix had expected. Through his brilliant delivery, superbly combining Paganini's wit with his boisterousness, Accardo irresistibly carried the audience with him. In Alix's view there was no greater composer of violin music than Paganini. Jesse did not agree; she liked Mahler, but enjoyed Alix's enthusiasm.

Alix returned to Switzerland where she learnt that Tansie was joining her just after Christmas. While in London, Alix had contemplated inviting Jesse for a few days skiing but had hesitated. What a disaster that could have turned out to be!

When Alix told her aunt about Tansie's arrival, Hanna embraced her and said, "I'm so happy for you, darling."

Without another thought, Hanna rang her friend Carlotta in Rome and informed her that she and the children would be arriving the day after Boxing Day.

"Hanna, you can't," Alix gasped, as soon as her aunt

was off the telephone.

"Please Alix, let me take them," Hanna responded quickly. "We might be old, but we're not past taking care of a few children. They'll love Carlotta's palazzo just as you did when you were younger. Anyway, it's good for young people to mix with others; Carlotta's grandchildren will all be there."

"Carlotta's grandchildren?"

Hanna laughed. "They're actually Carolina's. She was married to some count for a few years and had a couple of children. She left him though when she met Carlotta," Hanna said.

"You had me confused there for a minute."

Two days after Christmas, Alix put Hanna and the children on a flight to Rome and then waited for Tansie's flight from Singapore to arrive. The two women fell silently into each other's arms.

Tansie whispered, "Don't ever go away without me again. I nearly went out of my mind."

"It wasn't my idea," Alix reminded her gently.

"I know, but I was stupid," Tansie admitted and, hooking her arm underneath Alix's, continued, "where do we go from here?"

"We'll stay in Geneva for a couple of days and then we're off to Mexico, via a short stop in New York. I need to discuss a few things with my American publisher."

New York was freezing cold and it snowed every day. The uniformed doorman at the Hotel Pierre had barely time to tip his cap as the guests arrived and left. He was kept busy sweeping snow all day and keeping the entrance clear. Alix liked the Pierre because of its location on Fifth Avenue, its view over Central Park, its large elegant rooms and its refined yet unobtrusive service. It brought back

218

memories, good memories, from the days when she used to travel with her parents and reminded her of some of the embassies she had lived in.

As those memories surfaced, she became aware that Tansie had no such pleasant recollections. She will have in time to come, Alix thought with a smile, glad that she was able to make up for some of the things Tansie had missed out on in her youth. It would never compensate for her lack of childhood, but it would at least give her some pleasure now.

Both women were glad when the time came to venture further south and into the warm weather. After a short stop in Mexico City, they flew to Manzanillo. With its location on Mexico's Pacific coast, it made a perfect playground for the rich and the romantic at heart. Their suite was large, expensively furnished with white marble floors and, from the private balcony, they had sweeping views over the clear, dark blue water of the Pacific.

At the beginning of January, they celebrated their second anniversary as lovers. When Alix woke up that morning, she padded over to the wardrobes and retrieved a small package wrapped in shiny silver paper.

"Happy anniversary," she murmured into Tansie's ear and kissed the side of her neck.

Still half asleep, Tansie sensuously stretched her body underneath the satin sheet just moments before Alix whipped it away and dropped it on the floor. She wondered for a moment or two whether she would ever get tired of looking at Tansie: her long limbs, her small round breasts, the square angle of her shoulders and even the few fine lines at the corners of her large eyes.

Slowly Tansie opened her eyes and swept Alix into her arms. "Happy anniversary," she smiled and planted her lips firmly on Alix's.

When she eventually opened her present, Tansie was overwhelmed by its exquisite beauty, intricate design and no doubt extravagant price tag. It was a choker chain made from 22 carat white gold. A small square-cut topaz, matching Tansie's eyes, glistened on each link.

"I don't know what to say," Tansie finally muttered.

Gently tracing Tansie's lips with her forefinger, Alix said, "I love you . . . I'll always love you."

Tansie had a little surprise of her own. From her address book on the bedside table she withdrew three photographs and handed them to Alix. "I'm sorry I couldn't bring the real thing," she said.

Alix laughed as she studied the photographs. They were of a bronze sculpture of two women. The likeness to Alix and Tansie was so remarkable it left Alix breathless. The head of one woman was cocked sideways, gazing at the other in much the same way that Alix often looked at Tansie. One leg was straight, with the foot firmly planted on the ground. The other was loosely wound around the other's leg. Again, they were much like Alix's gestures. The second woman stood just slightly in front, her body sensuously curved into the first. One of her arms was draped around the waist and the other hand was cupped around her breast much like Tansie would do. The sculpture was so magnificent, Alix was simply speechless.

For the entire two weeks they were in Manzanillo, they sat in the sun and enjoyed each other's undivided attention. They dined in some of the small local restaurants, shopped for Mexican trinkets and made love impulsively and passion- ately. A simple touch of the other's hand or a moment's gaze was often enough to make them fall into each other's arms and kiss wildly. At times, the hunger for each other was so intense, it left them both breathless. Everything seemed perfect: the weather, the hotel, the food and each other.

After a particularly happy and intimate day, Alix reflected that whenever they were away from home, work and children, Tansie was quite different. She was more relaxed and carefree and was in fact a wonderful and loving companion. With a smile, she thought that the answer might well be for the two of them to simply abandon everything else and travel the world permanently. Alix decided that if it weren't for the children, she could be tempted to do just that.

By the time they returned to Geneva, whatever minor problems had hindered their love at times had now been relegated to the past. A chauffeur in a sleek limousine collected them at the airport to drive them to Gstaad.

Towards the end of the day, with darkness having already settled over the village, the two women were deposited in front of the chalet-style block of apartments.

Their own abode was the penthouse on the fourth floor, with a full-length balcony overlooking the alps. Although the ceilings were low and slanted under the roof, the main room was huge, yet unpretentious, with a stone fireplace as its centrepiece. The kitchen was tucked away into one corner with a dining alcove running alongside it. Bedrooms and bathrooms were off the entrance hall with another, smaller sitting room between the master suite and the children's bedrooms.

"This place is heavenly," Tansie cried and ambled from room to room. Finally she flopped down on the king-size bed in the master suite. She looked up at Alix who stood gazing down at her and smiled. Reaching for Alix's hand, she drew it to her lips and planted a kiss in its palm. How she loved Alix's hands and what exquisite feelings they evoked in her when they ran over her breasts or further down to her thighs. She would never get tired of making love with Alix.

"I often wonder what direction my path would have taken had I not met you," Tansie said slowly. "Until then, my life had been pretty mediocre and I certainly never could have imagined the sort of life you've shown me, the love you've given me, the intellectual stimulation and your endless encouragement to keep going with my sculptures." With a wide smile and sweeping gesture of her hands, she added, "Least of all such splendour."

"I had so much as a child, I want you to have some now," Alix replied simply.

"Thank you for inviting me. We'll have a wonderful time, I know."

"We will," Alix agreed, adding, "I'm starving. Let's dress up and go to the Palace for dinner . . . if we're lucky, we might even run into Roger Moore!"

A wicked grin played on Tansie's upturned, generous lips. "How can you think of anything as mundane as food when you can have me? Next, I suppose, you'll tell me that you've outworn and out-romanced yourself."

"Never," Alix replied softly. "However, no food, no energy," she added and pulled Tansie to her feet.

On their last evening before the children were due to arrive, Tansie slipped from the couch on to the floor to sit next to Alix. She folded her arms around Alix and drew her closer, nibbling at her neck and moving her hand underneath Alix's sweater. Alix's response was immediate and she dropped the newspaper she had been reading. She no longer questioned the why but simply gave herself to the pleasures Tansie provided.

They were both aware that this would be the last time

they could make love for a while without having to worry about children walking in on them. They were in no rush and playfully started to take off each other's clothes, nibbling and caressing each part of their bodies.

For a long time afterwards, they lay in each other's arms on the couch. It wasn't until they both started to get cold that they ambled into the bedroom. They were barely between the sheets when their bodies locked once more into a tight embrace.

The following morning they took their time getting up and getting dressed. Both knew that only too soon their privacy would be invaded by children once again. Later, they strolled into the village where they ate a hearty Swiss meal at one of the local inns and then walked the short distance to the railway station to pick up the children. As they waited on the bitterly cold platform, Tansie hopped from foot to foot to keep warm. Alix put her arms around Tansie and her breath soon began to warm Tansie's frozen cheeks.

They soon heard the Montreux Oberland Bahn rattle over the viaduct just above the village and watched it slowly wend its way around the last bend. It had barely come to a halt, its brakes squeaking, when the doors flew open and one child after another came tumbling out on to the platform. Hanna stood in the open doorway ready to hand out their luggage.

"How did it go, Hanna?" The question seemed superfluous. The children looked great, she thought as she gave each one a hug. They were indeed three beautiful children.

"We had a wonderful time, darling. Carlotta, Carolina and I haven't had so much fun in years," Hanna replied and, judging by her flushed face and twinkling eyes, she meant what she said.

"Thank you, Hanna," was all Alix had time to say before the station master blew his whistle to announce the train's departure for Lausanne and Geneva.

Throughout dinner, Alix listened to her children's excited chatter as they described their holiday with their great-aunt Hanna: Christian's love for Italian food, Drew's narration about the various museums they had visited and Sara's shopping spree on Via Veneto and her romantic encounter with Carolina's grandson, Paolino.

Periodically when Alix looked at her three fine children, she wondered whether Michael would feel the same or whether he would still treat them with indifference. Sadly she thought it would probably be the latter. She was glad that they would never have to find out.

"Aren't you a little young for such nonsense? Boys indeed!" Tansie suddenly interrupted Sara.

Taken aback by Tansie's terse comment, Alix was about to say something but thought better of it. Tansie was probably just overwhelmed by the fact that the children were back.

Later, when the children were in bed, Alix turned on the TV to watch an English movie and sighed. "Even I forget sometimes how boisterous children can be."

Tansie didn't reply in words but curved her eyebrows into an upside down 'V', indicating that she had some reservations. But Alix, still in a blissful state, didn't notice.

Chapter 18

They were into their second week of the ski holiday when Christian became quite ill. Alix thought at first that he was simply tired. After all, he was still only a small boy and had been dragged all over the world. Very little consideration had been given to his individual needs. Late one evening, he collapsed into his mother's arms weeping. She realised he was running a high fever. The village doctor confirmed that he had a middle-ear infection.

Over the next couple of days, Alix had no alternative but to nurse him. His sleep was restless and he woke almost hourly, crying with pain. Because it was easier to look after him on a twenty-four hour basis, Alix moved into his room.

"If I sleep in his room, I won't disturb you every time I have to get up," Alix explained to Tansie, adding, "I won't get much sleep but still . . ."

"Please yourself," Tansie interrupted less than graciously. She hated the idea of sleeping by herself and resented the extra time Alix had to spend with her young son.

In the meantime, Drew and Sara took themselves skiing and, later in the day, did the shopping and cooking. They invited Tansie to come along but she refused. She wasn't well either, she told them.

For three days Alix attended to her young son, barely able to sit down even for a few minutes at a time. Finally Christian fell into a peaceful sleep and the other two children retired to their room for the night straight after dinner. Alix poured herself a glass of wine and wandered over to the large windows. She tried to see outside but it was impossible. A blizzard was howling, dumping more and more snow on the terrace. Storms and disasters go hand in hand, she thought with a wry smile and wondered what disaster could possibly loom now. She turned to look at her lover.

Tansie sat on one of the leather couches, reading a book. She seemed calm and content. Alix noticed how beautiful she looked in the soft light of the lamp next to her. They had barely spoken for the last few days. Alix was aware that she had been neglectful of Tansie's needs but, now that her young son was on the mend, Alix was determined to rectify that situation. The setting for a peaceful evening was perfect, she thought.

Alix too went to sit on the couch. She took off her shoes and socks and curled her feet into the soft down cushions. "I'm sorry, I haven't been much company for the last couple of days but . . ." she started, but stopped when she noticed an icy aloof glare in Tansie's eyes when their gaze met.

"So you bloody should be," Tansie snapped. "I didn't fucking travel half-way around the world to be ignored!"

Alix was exhausted from the sleepless nights and her temper too was on a shorter fuse than normal, but she managed to remain calm. "I said I was sorry, although there wasn't much I could do about it."

"You mean, didn't want to do," Tansie yelled, her voice having risen several decibels within seconds. "Whatever they want they get. They're all spoilt rotten with no consideration for anyone but themselves! Let me tell you, a good daily belting is what they need. They'd soon toe the line and become better for it."

Alix tolerated many things but under no circumstances did she tolerate the abuse of children. She was flabbergasted by Tansie's statement, particularly because Tansie herself had suffered abuse and should know better than to want to inflict it on others.

"You know how I feel about abusing children whether or not they're mine!" Alix retorted, only just controlling her flaring temper. "However," she added, "leave the children out of this. Whatever the problem is, it's between us and we're going to discuss it."

"Why should I?" Tansie snapped, hysterical now and out of control. Her face contorted with anger, her lips were drawn back over her teeth and her voice became a snarl. "Nobody gives a fuck about how I feel . . . not even you! I might as well throw myself off the balcony now . . . it'll put me out of my misery for good," she continued as her whole body began to shake with rage.

Stunned, as though she didn't immediately understand Tansie's words, Alix looked at the woman she loved so passionately. What she now faced was a stranger with a voice that no longer whispered words of endearment, a face that no longer smiled and lips that no longer kissed. Had she done something to provoke this attack? Alix didn't know and shook her head as though this would make things clearer.

For a split second, Tansie became rigid. The abuse stopped. Then, she jumped to her feet and made a dash for the glass doors which led out on to the terrace. She pulled them open and kept running. Freezing cold air and snow instantly blew into the room, covering the light cream carpet.

Alix clamped her eyes shut and her stomach started to heave so violently it hurt. In the few seconds it had taken Tansie to run outside, Alix had also jumped to her feet and, in so doing, knocked over a glass. Almost losing her balance, she stumbled. The glass crushed underneath her bare foot. As though in a trance, she stared at the bloody patch on the carpet and the glass splinters which lay scattered around it.

Suddenly it registered that her cut foot wasn't at all important. Tansie? Where was she? For a fleeting moment Alix thought she was going to throw up. Her legs felt like rubber, ready to buckle beneath her at any moment as she hobbled out on to the balcony. She barely noticed the snow under her naked feet. Having reached the balustrade, she involuntarily shut her eyes. She didn't want to look down. It was with great difficulty that she forced them open and lowered them to the snow-covered pavement four stories below. The street light across the road cast a pale, eerie glow over it.

Alix thought she would choke, faint or go crazy. After Tansie's threat, it hadn't occurred to her that Tansie could be anywhere else but splattered on the street below. There was simply nowhere else for her to go. Fleetingly, she wondered whether other people ever felt like she did right now, teetering on the fine line between sanity and insanity.

She had just turned back towards the sitting room, when she caught a glimpse of Tansie. She was half-hidden behind a pillar, her white tracksuit just visible in the obscure moonlight. Alix froze and her face turned ashen.

Alix felt such anger well inside her, she stamped her foot into the snow until she felt the cold concrete underneath it. The force of it drove a glass splinter so deep into her foot that she cried out.

Alix had to make up her mind what to do first: take care of Tansie or look after her injury.

"How dare you do this to me?" she shouted, shaking with anger she could no longer control. "You deliberately hid to make me believe that you'd actually jumped off the balcony. Why don't you just get the hell out of my life and . . ."

Alix's voice broke and, turning her back, she scrambled inside and slammed the door. Hobbling into the bathroom, Alix could hear a tirade of the vilest verbal abuse emanating from the balcony. She was well past the stage of caring what happened to Tansie. Had the children not been there, she was sure she would have walked right out of the apartment and out of Tansie's life.

Alix sat down on the rim of the bathtub just as Tansie flew down the passage and disappeared into the bedroom. It wasn't long she emerged again. Dragging her suitcases behind her and banging the walls, she lurched towards the front door. She grabbed the handle but it wouldn't open.

Kicking it, Tansie shouted, "Give me the fucking key or I will throw myself off the balcony!"

"It's in my jacket pocket!"

Then the screaming stopped, the door slammed shut and silence settled over the household. Leaning against the bathroom door, Alix wondered how the children could have slept through such a racket. Since none of them appeared, she expected them to be still sound asleep. She sighed with relief. They did not need such memories to clutter their minds in years to come, she thought.

Alix's whole body was still shaking from the ordeal as her gaze fixed on the tiled bathroom wall. Had she had a bad dream? She couldn't have. The blood which was still dripping from her gash proved otherwise. Slowly she washed her foot as best she could under the running bath-tap and began to remove the glass splinters with a pair of tweezers. When she was satisfied that all was well, she reached for a bandage. Alix didn't hear Tansie when she returned to the apartment.

"Let me do that," Tansie said from the open doorway and timidly approached Alix.

"Get out!" Alix responded without looking up. She continued to wrap the bandage around the wound. "Don't push it . . . just leave me alone," Alix growled, unwilling to give Tansie even an inch. Moments later, she hobbled into the sitting room and poured herself a stiff cognac. Her hand trembled when she lifted the glass to her lips. She waited, tense and rigid, for Tansie to come hurtling down the corridor, start all over again and deliver another round of abuse. Nothing happened. The apartment was engulfed in deadly silence. Only the howling blizzard could be heard as it whistled around the corners and rattled the wooden shutters she had not yet closed for the night.

Alix poured a second cognac down her throat and felt it hit her stomach, warm and soothing. She placed the glass on the tray and ambled down the corridor to Christian's room.

She had barely undressed and crawled into the spare bed when her teeth began to chatter and her body began to convulse in uncontrollable shivers. There was nowhere for her to go for help. Whatever the nightmare and the emotional battering she was experiencing, she was alone with it. What if Tansie did start all over again? What if she did throw herself off the balcony, or under a train or thought of some other madness to punish Alix with? For what reason, Alix couldn't even begin to imagine, let alone figure out. Alix swallowed dry, hoping she would not be sick.

Slowly she calmed down but stayed on the alert, half-expecting another tantrum. No noise came from the master bedroom. Eventually she drifted into a restless sleep, her only comforting thought was that the children had been spared the trauma. She knew that if they'd been drawn into this, she couldn't forgive herself.

Alix had never waited for daylight to come as desperately as she did that night. Although she felt as though she had been through the wringer, she forced herself under the hot shower. She winced when the hot spray ran over her cut foot. But for the little comfort it gave her, Alix knew that the physical pain was only temporary. What she couldn't predict was the long-term effect the emotional trauma might have on her. She willed her mind into neutral. One way or another, she would have to safeguard her sanity and this was as good a way as any, she figured.

After drying herself, she padded into the kitchen and put on the kettle. She hoped that the coffee might at least clear her head. Waiting for the water to boil, she suddenly thought of Jesse. She could not remember another time when she had needed a friend as badly as she did now. Jesse would understand all of this, Alix thought, and allowed the tears she had controlled to burst forth.

Alix was glad that the children had not yet woken when Tansie appeared in the kitchen. For a moment or two, their eyes met but neither spoke.

"Alix," Tansie eventually said, "What can I do to make it up to you?"

Taking a deep breath, Alix replied, "I can't just sit back and watch you slowly destroy what we have shared. Nor can I risk the children ever being witnesses to such . . ." Alix stopped just before the word 'madness' fell from her lips. "Behaviour," she continued. "I don't want to take that risk. I can't take that risk." After a short pause, she added, "Right now, I think the best thing for you to do is to leave." Alix shivered. She had never thought that she might one day have to send her lover away. Everything inside her seemed to protest; her stomach heaved, her arms and legs shook and her heart beat erratically. Don't falter now, she told herself, because if you do, you'll end up hating your-

231

self and Tansie. You can't let that happen.

Lowering her eyes to the floor, Tansie asked, "Is that the end of us . . . our relationship?"

"I don't know, Tansie," Alix said, adding, "I don't want it to be over but you must understand once and for all that I cannot live like this."

"I understand," Tansie responded meekly and walked over to the telephone in the sitting room. Within an hour, she was packed and ready to leave. She was to catch a flight out of Geneva that same evening.

Despite her sore foot, Alix helped her take the suitcases downstairs and waited with her for the taxi. Glancing at her lover who seemed more vulnerable and fragile than ever, with her shoulders stooped forward and her gaze fixed somewhere in the distance, Alix wondered how this person could have launched such an all-out attack only a few hours earlier. A wave of guilt for sending Tansie away hit her with such force, she broke into a cold sweat and began to shiver. Had it not been for the cab which pulled up at that very moment, Alix wasn't sure whether she could have seen this through to the end. She thought that there was a fair possibility that she would have swept Tansie into her arms and asked her to stay.

"Don't ever hate me, please Alix. I love you," Tansie murmured as the cab driver loaded the luggage into the boot.

Alix didn't respond out of sheer fear that she would burst into tears if she spoke even a single word. She felt drained as though the ordeal had taken several years off her life. She brushed the back of her hand over Tansie's cheek and went back inside.

When the children got up later that morning and asked where Tansie was, Alix simply told them that she had decided to go home earlier than planned.

Drew gave his mother a scrutinising glance. "You two didn't have a fight, did you?"

With great willpower, Alix forced a smile on to her face. "I'm a little too old to fight with my friends, don't you think?" she asked lightly. Inside she felt sick at having to deceive her son like this.

"Probably," he grinned, adding nonplussed, "you weren't that much younger when you used to fight with Dad."

"No, I wasn't," she admitted readily and watched as the children bounced from the room. Although she felt some guilt, she sighed with relief that they had obviously accepted her explanation. Could she ever tell them what happened last night or what her real relationship with Tansie was? She decided that for the present she couldn't. Maybe she never could.

Four days later, Alix and the children returned to Geneva where one of Hanna's vineyard employees picked them up from the station and drove them to the house some sixty kilometres outside town. As soon as the children had gone to bed, Alix went to the music room.

Having picked up a tension in Alix when she first arrived, Hanna joined her soon afterwards. But instead of sitting next to her on the piano stool, Hanna pulled up a wing chair. She sat down and said softly, "Keep playing, darling."

After Alix had played a few scales and two short pieces by Chopin, she moved to Tchaikovsky and her own adaption for the piano of his 1812 Overture. She felt that this particular piece of music best reflected her own mood of love and war: stormy and melancholic. As she continued playing, she suddenly remembered something Hanna had said to her a long time ago. In every marriage, she had said, one partner always loves more than the other simply because no two people will ever feel quite the same. Alix now recognised for the first time that Hanna was right. Alix felt that in this 'marriage' it was she who loved more. She knew she loved Tansie unconditionally. She did not know whether she could continue to love her in the same way. Her thoughts saddened her yet, at the same time, she felt calmer than she had for some time.

Later on, Alix contemplated whether or not to tell Hanna about her ordeal with Tansie. In the end, she decided against it. It would only distress her she thought. She would be home soon enough where she would have people to talk to and to seek advice from. In due course, she hoped that she would forget the terror she had felt during those moments she believed that Tansie had actually hurled herself off the balcony.

The day before she was ready to leave Switzerland, Alix contemplated whether to ring Tansie and ask her to pick her up at the airport. Thinking that she couldn't face Tansie just yet, she rang Jesse instead. Jesse promised to be there and Alix felt an immediate calmness sweep through her body.

The following afternoon, Alix and the children caught their flight home. But it was nearly forty hours later before they landed in Melbourne. Their flight out of Hong Kong was delayed by ten hours and then, en route, the passengers were told that they would have to fly via Sydney. Alix all but despaired when they were delayed for another few hours in Sydney.

Everybody's temper was on a short fuse by the time they finally collected their luggage. An immediate surge of relief flooded through Alix when she spotted Jesse who was waving to her from the other side of the glass walkway. She was home.

Chapter 19

Jesse looked at Alix's drawn pale face and lifeless eyes, at the same time noting how unusually stooped her shoulders were and the lack of spring in her step. She knew that this wasn't just the result of the long journey. The simplicity of her attire – a pair of tight knee-length shorts and a white, silk polo shirt made Alix look slimmer and, most certainly, more vulnerable. Jesse had never seen her like this. Something was not right, she thought.

Jesse kissed Alix lightly on the cheek and said to the children, "How was your holiday, you guys? I heard you did some terrific skiing."

"We did, it was great," they said, as they visibly began to wilt in the oppressive heat which greeted them outside the terminal. After several weeks of mostly sub-zero temperatures in Europe, even they found the heat unbearable.

After dropping Alix and the children off at home, Jesse left for the surgery, promising to come back later.

Alix had a quick chat to Jenny who gave her an efficient run-down on the state of affairs and then she retreated into her studio. She had missed not having a piano in Gstaad. Now, more than anything, she needed music. Not just any music. With an inward smile she thought Mozart was too flighty for her unsettled mood. She started with her own loose adaption of the Adagio by Albinoni before proceeding to play Tchaikovsky and Beethoven.

Alix was still hammering away at the keyboard several hours later when Jesse sauntered in.

"Why don't you try some Liszt or maybe Mahler?" Jesse stated dryly.

"Mahler?" Alix groaned as though she was in pain. "I'll settle for Liszt," she added and gave Jesse a disarming smile. Seconds later, her hands flew over the keyboard and she played the first of the Liszt Hungarian Rhapsodies that came to her mind.

"Now we're getting somewhere," Jesse acknowledged and filled a glass from the open champagne bottle.

Alix continued playing for a while as she observed Jesse. She noted the light suntan which gave Jesse a healthy glow and seemed to enhance her sparkling blue eyes. Jesse stood leaning against the side of the grand piano, her feet crossed at the ankles, just as she had when she'd delivered her paper in Cambridge. Alix thought this posture most becoming, charming even. Both her elbows rested on the piano as she rotated the champagne glass with both hands.

Smiling, Alix said, "Your suntan makes me look pale and ill. Did you have some time off after you came back from London?"

"I did, I went up north for a few days," Jesse confirmed. She too smiled when she noticed that Alix had obviously lit a cigarette and then promptly forgotten it in the ashtray. Its smoke curled lazily towards the ceiling. Jesse had seen Alix do this once or twice before. In the past she had always assumed that Alix simply got carried away with the music. Now she thought it had more to do with her troubled mood.

Alix was about to ask if Jesse had gone up north on her own but caught herself just in time. She wondered, though, why she had even contemplated asking such a question.

When Alix finished, they both sat down in opposite corners of the couch. The french doors to the terrace and the garden were open, allowing the cooler evening breeze to gently billow the curtains. Normally when she returned from an overseas trip, Alix felt restless, missing the European scenery and wondering why she had even returned at all. Tonight, for the first time, she was glad to be home.

After a short pause, Jesse said gently, "I'd like to think that you asked me to pick you up from the airport because you couldn't wait to see me."

Alix was too preoccupied with her own thoughts to register Jesse's meaning and didn't respond.

"The moment I saw you, I knew something had gone wrong," Jesse continued, taking a sip of champagne.

"It did," Alix sighed.

"Maybe you had a wild and wonderful affair with a gorgeous Italian count and now . . ."

Despite how she felt, Alix laughed. A laugh that came from the lips but was not visible in her eyes. "I probably should have, but I didn't."

"Okay, what's troubling you?" Jesse asked. "Tansie?"

"Yeah," Alix replied. She needed no further prompting and the whole traumatic saga came bursting out. She did not engage in accusations or complaints, she simply related what had happened in Gstaad.

Concluding her story, Alix said, "You know what the worst thing of all was? There was nowhere for me to go for help. I felt as though I was the only person on this goddamned earth, alone and abandoned. It was the most devastating feeling."

"Do you have any idea why Tansie behaved like that?" Jesse asked.

"No, I don't," Alix responded. "Could it really have been the children as she said it was?"

"It's possible, but not because of anything they did," Jesse said. "From what little I know of Tansie, I think her behaviour is certainly in part motivated by jealousy. She probably feels threatened by them and the love you have for them."

"How could she be jealous of the children?"

"We're not dealing with a rational person." Jesse gave her a mild, thoughtful smile and raised her eyebrows.

"No, I suppose not," Alix replied. With some apprehension, she asked, "Can people lose their minds just like that? Temporarily or even for good?"

"It's possible. Often, something quite small and irrelevant can trigger a memory and cause such volatile behaviour," Jesse confirmed. "Tansie needs help . . . professional help and . . ."

"She told me that Dr Callahan didn't want to see her any more."

"I'd be surprised if that were true," Jesse pointed out. "You might have to put some pressure on to her to go back and see him no matter how much she dislikes the idea."

"I might have to," Alix replied. "I'm petrified that she will take her own life one day, or even lose her mind."

"Whatever you do, Alix, don't be too hard on yourself," Jesse replied, deeply troubled by Alix's horrible experience and the effect it obviously had had on her.

She also thought of Alix's relationship with Tansie. She appreciated that whatever experiences Alix had had with men in the past, she expected something different from a woman. Jesse felt immense sadness that Alix's very first intimate encounter with another woman was turning out to be so traumatic. But then, Jesse knew that love did not guarantee happiness irrespective of the partner's gender. Moreover, if the partner was as unstable as Tansie, it made it doubly difficult.

When Alix walked her to the car later, Jesse suddenly

laughed. "In my haste to come and see you, I forgot to bring in these books," she said, picking up three paperbacks from the passenger seat. "Remember you asked . . ."

"Of course," Alix interrupted. They were Alice Miller's publications on childhood trauma. "If I ever needed them, now is the time," she said. "Thanks."

"It's a pleasure," Jesse smiled. "I'll be in touch," she added, and revving up the small, light yellow BMW's powerful engine, drove into the night.

Alix watched the tail-lights disappear down the court and turn into the main street. She smiled. Until now, she hadn't known what sort of car Jesse drove. But, had she ever given it any thought, she would have picked the right one: powerful yet unpretentious.

She returned inside and went upstairs to her bedroom. Felix had been up earlier to turn down the bedspread and switch on one of the bedside lamps. The curtains were not yet drawn and the french doors to the balcony were open. The full moon seemed to hover just outside, watching.

After a quick shower, Alix ruffled her damp curls with her hands and then slipped into bed. For a moment or two, she languidly stretched her weary body. It felt good to be in her own bed again. She contemplated whether to start reading one of the books Jesse had given her but decided against it, knowing she would have a busy day tomorrow. She swallowed a sleeping pill and let her head sink into the pillow.

Quite automatically, she reached across the bed. It was cold and empty. She was gripped by an overwhelming feeling of loneliness. Suddenly Jesse's words came back to her. "In my haste to come in. . ." Jesse had said. Had she missed something, she asked herself, recalling not just Jesse's words but also her expression. It had been strangely caressing,

Alix now thought. She contemplated momentarily what it would be like to go to sleep in Jesse's arms instead of Tansie's. Would it be the same? No, she decided. She was in love with Tansie, not with Jesse.

When she had showered and dressed and was ready for work the next morning, Alix wandered downstairs to her studio. She was in a hurry to start working and had not yet put any make-up on. As she passed the large mirror in the main hall, she caught a glimpse of herself and stopped. For the first time, she noticed two fine lines running from the corners of her lips to the side of her chin. There were even a few finer lines around her eyes. She didn't know whether they had been there for some time or whether they were the result of her recent trauma. She sighed and walked on.

She was so absorbed in her work, she didn't hear John enter an hour or so later.

He took one look at her and commented with concern, "Considering you've just had six weeks holidays, you don't look very rested. Maybe the life of the idle rich doesn't agree with you?"

"John, you frightened me." Her back stiffened and she swivelled around to face him.

"And you're jumpy," he noted. "What happened? Some cute Frenchman broke your heart?" With a wide grin, he added, "Sorry, wrong gender!"

Alix laughed and rolled her eyes in a mocking manner. "Jesse thought I met an Italian, you think a Frenchman . . . or a Frenchwoman . . . I wonder who's next!"

"You tell me!" John grinned loftily. "Anyway, how was it?"

"It had its moments," Alix replied.

"I'm sorry to hear it. I take it your friend joined you over there?" John responded and, without waiting for an

240

answer, added, "as for the good news, we've been asked to compose the music for an Australian documentary on, guess what?"

"The typical Australian male?"

"You'd have a field-day with that one! But no, it's much better than that," he laughed. "It's a commission from the Wool Board . . . the Australian sheep industry!"

"That's right up your alley, John," Alix replied and headed for the door. "You're the good little colonial boy."

Stroking his blond, neatly clipped moustache, he rushed after her. "You're not going to get out of this that easily. We're going to work on this together."

"Mañana," Alix's response came quickly and she was gone.

He stared after her and shook his head. "I should have known she'd pick a bloody Spaniard," he grumbled.

It was not until later that day that Alix finally decided she could not put off her visit to Tansie any longer. She knew she couldn't work until something had been sorted out.

"Hi," Alix said evenly when she entered through the open back door at Tansie's house. The sitting room was bathed in semi-darkness with only the light from the setting sun illuminating it. As usual, it was chaotic. Tansie seemed to have unpacked her bags at random without bothering to put anything away.

Tansie flew from the couch where she had been sitting and into Alix's arms. "I'm so glad you're back." Her body moulded into her lover's, sensuously and seductively.

Alix wrapped her arms around her. She felt Tansie tremble and wondered what the cause was. Had she been frightened that Alix may never come back? She didn't know but, for a brief moment, she was able to forget the real purpose of her visit and held her tightly. It was with difficulty that she eventually drew away. "Let's sit down," Alix said and, lighting a Davidoff, added softly, "you know we have to talk, don't you?"

"I know but, before we do, let me give you your anniversary present," Tansie replied and went to fetch it. She returned and deposited the bronze sculpture on the coffee table.

It was even more beautiful than the photographs. The lines of their bodies and the way the two women stood together indicated such sensuous intimacy, Alix felt deeply touched.

"Do you like it?" Tansie asked timidly and buried her hands in the pockets of her red shorts. She drew up her shoulders as though she was suddenly cold and her body seemed to go limp.

Tansie's simple gesture of drawing up her shoulders immediately evoked sympathy in Alix. It was the childlike, charming vulnerability Alix had noticed when they first met. She reached out and drew Tansie down on to the couch. Gently stroking her cheek, Alix looked into her eyes.

"It's stunning," Alix barely breathed. "Thank you . . . I love it."

"You're welcome," Tansie murmured. She too had been especially pleased with it. In fact, it was this particular sculpture which had made her realise how much progress she'd made. She had also felt very close to Alix when she created it. Hesitant and apprehensive, she braced herself for what was yet to come. "I want to tell you how sorry I am." More slowly, she continued, "I don't know why I behaved like that . . . I just freaked out . . . I lost control and . . ."

"We can't undo what happened," Alix said. "But, you must understand that it cannot continue like this. I want to help you but I can't. I don't know what the problem is."

"I have already had one session with Dr Callahan and I've arranged to see him regularly for a while," Tansie informed her. "Mind you, he doesn't think that there is much wrong with me at all. Other than temporary stress, most likely to do with my divorce," she added.

Alix found that a little hard to believe as the divorce had been many months previously. She kept her thoughts to herself. She trusted that Dr Callahan would soon get to the real cause.

Alix and Tansie spoke until well into the night. But not having had any sleep other than a short nap on the plane between Geneva and Hong Kong, Alix was eventually too exhausted to go on. As Alix got up to leave, Tansie timidly suggested that Alix stay with her for the night. Instinctively, Alix turned her down. Her mind was too cluttered to even think about going to bed with Tansie.

Tansie walked Alix to the door and, after kissing her, she watched Alix drive off. Later, Alix wasn't sure whether she had really achieved a great deal. But at least they had talked and discussed the distress Tansie's behaviour had caused them both. She was pleased that she had started.

Although Tansie didn't like the idea of seeing the shrink, she knew if she did it would at least pacify Alix. She was comforted by the thought, however, that she would never have to tell Alix what she told him.

"Where do I start?" Tansie asked when she returned for her next session with Dr Callahan the following Monday. She didn't look at him but rather let her gaze wander through the open window and into the beautifully kept Victorian garden. She inhaled the scent of the roses which grew just outside the window and protruded over its sill.

"Start wherever you like," he invited her.

Tansie gave him a weak grin. "Okay," she said and,

drawing a deep breath, blurted out, "I've told you I'm in love with Alix, but I want to be married again and have children. I love children. That's all I've ever wanted."

Rubbing the bridge of his nose where the glasses had sat, he gazed at her with astute blue-grey eyes but didn't comment right away. He was an older man and after many years in practice he had learnt to be patient. He knew that sooner or later the truth would surface. "Why don't you tell me a little more about your relationship with Alix."

Tansie laughed. "That's the easy part. Don't get me wrong, Alix is a lovely wonderful person. It's just that I love men, you know."

"So, it was Alix who wanted more?" he asked evenly. There was something in her tone of voice that made him doubt her.

"Oh yes," she lied as easily as if it were the truth.

"This is now causing you some concern?" he asked and glanced at the notes he had made during a previous visit. This relationship was not a problem to her in the past.

"It bothers me a great deal and my relationships with men are suffering because of it."

"How does Alix feel about it? Does it worry her?"

"Why should it?" Tansie was perplexed by his question. "She has the children, they give her automatic protection from any gossip and she has plenty of men around as well." The latter part she added with just enough tremble in her voice to make it sound plausible.

"Have you thought about living together?" he asked.

"Alix would never go for it," Tansie gasped horrified, neglecting to mention that she had refused an invitation to do just that. "That would destroy her precious career and she doesn't like people thinking badly of her. She's very protective of her image."

"It may not be entirely socially acceptable, but people do it just the same, you know, with little repercussion to their daily lives," he told her.

"Anyway, her children would be flabbergasted. She's as protective of them as she is of her career."

"Children can be quite adaptable and are often more resilient to change than what we give them credit for. In fact, I have seen relationships between partners of the same sex working extremely well where children are concerned."

He made a few notes on the pad in front of him. Despite the fact that he was far from having a clear picture of the situation, he said, "If that is not acceptable, then perhaps you should tell Alix that you want out of the relationship."

"She'd never go for it!" Tansie cried aghast.

"How could she stop you?"

"Alix believes that money can buy anything, including love. She normally gets what she wants, including me." Tansie played the part of the innocent victim without blinking an eyelid.

But she didn't fool Dr Callahan. He was beginning to put the jigsaw together quite effectively.

"Give it a go anyway," he said. Tansie's cringe confirmed that at least some of his assumptions were correct.

"You know, I have a feeling that Alix loves you enough to wish you well in whatever you choose."

He was a big man, well over six feet tall, and yet there was something distinctly cuddly and comforting about him. He towered over Tansie when he walked her to the door. In a more pensive manner, he added, "Maybe next time you come, we might explore your childhood."

"Whatever for?" Tansie was shocked. "Look Dr Jim, whatever my background was, I have come to terms with it. My mother didn't want me, so I was shipped out here from England and ended up in an orphanage until I was sixteen years old. It's no big deal."

"If you have come to terms with it then that's all that matters," he replied and opened the door for her.

Tansie left with a new spring to her step, blinking against the bright sunlight outside. She was pleased with the outcome of her session. Dr Callahan would be an easy target for whatever stories she told him. So she thought anyway. As for Alix, she would never really know that she told one story to her and another to her shrink. Had Alix known the truth, she would have been devastated.

With screeching tyres, she pulled away from the curb and joined the other drivers at a red traffic light. Since Alix would be busy that evening and couldn't see her, Tansie decided to visit Julie. She hadn't seen her since her return from overseas and now felt a little guilty. She would invite both Julie and Margret to Brunswick Street for a bite to eat. Tansie chuckled to herself. Alix would probably freak out if she ever suggested that they visited that part of town. Tongue in cheek, Tansie thought that Alix wouldn't even know where Brunswick Street was. They had certainly never been there together.

Tansie had barely knocked on Julie's door when it flew open. "It's nice to see you," Julie said, an undertone of sarcasm in her voice.

"I'm sorry . . . I've been busy," Tansie smiled disarmingly and kissed her on the cheek. "Is Margret home from work yet? I'll take you both out to dinner . . . we'll go to that place in Brunswick Street you like so much."

Julie gave her a suspicious glare and was about to ask where her 'mate' was but thought better of it. "Yes, we'd like that," she replied instead. She walked towards the kitchen and looked over her shoulder. "I had a letter from

246

your sister," she continued. "She's worried. She hasn't heard from you for a while."

"Oh, yeah," Tansie replied, unenthusiastically. Tansie saw Arlene once a year if that. She lived on a large sheep station in the far north of New South Wales with her husband and children. Now that Tansie was divorced, she resented Arlene's life even more. "Tell her I'm fine," Tansie added and poured herself a straight scotch from the bottle on the kitchen bench.

The disastrous trip overseas caused Alix to have nightmares for several weeks afterwards. She started to read the books Jesse had given her. But it was hard going. What she read disconcerted her so much at times, she had to stop reading. She was determined to persevere though. She wanted to understand what Tansie must have suffered as a child.

Alix was pleased that Tansie seemed to take her sessions with Dr Callahan a little more seriously and that she seemed to be in a much better frame of mind. Perhaps naively, Alix had started to bank on him to not just help Tansie but to cure her. At least so far he appeared to have had a stabilising effect on his patient.

Tansie worked gruelling hours at times, perfecting her chiselling skills and producing some amazing sculptures. But she was still uncertain of her talent and often asked Alix to accompany her to the stonemason's yard to select new pieces of marble and granite. Alix's approval and encouragement always gave her a lift.

Tansie's positive spirits extended beyond her work and her lover. She started to entertain and gave lavish dinner parties. Sometimes she stayed in the kitchen all day, remaking a particular dish until it was perfect. As a hostess, she was delightfully charming and entertaining.

It was after one such dinner party that Alix told Tansie that she had to go back to Europe in a couple of days time.

"It's only a few weeks since you came back!" Tansie wailed. "I know," Alix replied. She wasn't happy either, but had no alternative. "Pierre wants the new movie score recorded with the French National Radio Orchestra and my stockbroker has just advised me that I am now the majority shareholder in Clemenger Pharmaceuticals. So, I'm also going head-hunting for a managing director. I've already done some homework on that. I found out that one of my old friends from boarding school, Johan Kunz, has been working for one of the big Swiss pharmaceutical companies for some years. If I can lure him away, I'll be right. I faxed him a couple of days ago and he has agreed to meet me in Basel next week."

"What do your brothers-in-law have to say about all this?" Tansie chortled.

"I'll find out when I tell them," Alix replied, loathing the idea of giving the Clemenger family the news.

"I'll miss you," Tansie said and put her arms around Alix. "Can we spend the weekend before you go in the country?"

"Of course we can," Alix confirmed. "We can leave late on Friday afternoon if that suits you, although I will have to do some work at some stage."

"That's okay," Tansie readily agreed. All she wanted was to have Alix to herself for a couple of days. Alix had been too aloof since their return from Europe for Tansie's liking. They had barely even made love since then. "I'll do some work as well. There is still a piece of marble at your house that I haven't even touched yet."

The weekend turned out to be one of the best they had ever had. Their time together was harmonious, filled with

248

laughter and affection. Tansie was relaxed and she felt deeply contented. Even the way she held the fine chisel and hammer reflected her carefree and more confident mood. When working with stone in the past, she had often hit too hard, all but ruining what she had tried to achieve. Now, she gently tapped away on the large piece of white marble.

In the meantime, Alix worked on a new piano concerto, her fifth. She had neglected it for far too long. She was to give the first performance in Honolulu during the concert tour of the Pacific Islands in July which she had finally agreed to do. Only a week or so ago, she had started to re-write the first movement which had been far too slow and sombre. Now, the piano solos were fast and bubbly, reminding Alix of the small creeks in the Swiss mountains she had often sat and watched during her years at boarding school.

When Alix walked into the kitchen late on Saturday afternoon, she stood for a while and looked at the statue Tansie was working on. She was mesmerised. The statue was a self-portrait and the likeness was so uncanny Alix gasped.

"It's you," Alix muttered and let her thumb run over the cool polished material. It traced the head which was flung back in a defiant manner and followed the curve of the slender neck and narrow shoulders. Underneath her warm fingers, Alix could almost feel the statue come alive. That simple touch brought back memories Alix could not now ignore. Memories of how beautifully their bodies fitted together and of what pleasures they could give each other. She was well aware of just how little physical contact they had had over the last few weeks and of how reluctantly she had gone to bed with Tansie. It was time to rectify that, Alix thought.

Slowly Alix turned to face her lover. Her eyes were clear and longing as she held Tansie's gaze.

That was the moment Tansie had been waiting for. "Why don't you do that to me instead," she whispered in a husky voice, covering Alix's hand with her own and sweeping her into her arms. "It's an awfully long time since you made love to me."

"Too long," Alix said softly and together they sauntered into the bedroom.

As though they were about to become lovers for the very first time, they lowered themselves on to the bed slowly and carefully and without their lips parting even once. It took some time until each piece of clothing finally landed on the floor and their bare bodies touched from head to toe.

Afterwards, feeling a closeness she had not experienced for some time, Tansie drew Alix tightly into her arms. "I am so glad you suggested I see a shrink," she said softly. "For the first time in my life, I think I'm getting somewhere. There are times when what Callahan says deeply distresses me and I come out of a session howling my eyes out, but I'm starting to understand how my mind works and how it affects my emotional welfare."

Alix's heart missed a few beats. She had seen the change in Tansie but had not been sure whether Tansie too had recognised it.

"It makes me very happy to hear you say that," Alix replied as she let her hand wander over Tansie's smooth back.

Alix left for Europe two days later. Her heart was lighter than it had been for some time. Maybe everything would work out now, she thought as she leant back into her seat.

It was late March, spring-time, when Alix arrived in

Paris. Most of the trees along the wide boulevards were covered with new leaves, their colour a vibrant fresh green. People started emerging from their winter lethargy, strolling leisurely in the many parks in the warm sunshine or sitting in one of the sidewalk cafes, sipping Pernod and chatting. Lovers stopped on one or another bridge, gazing into the Seine or each other's eyes. Small children leant dangerously close to the ponds in the Tuileries Gardens, squealing with delight as they coaxed their little wooden boats.

Alix's only regret was that Tansie was not with her. She missed not being able to stroll under the trees together or hold hands in one of the cafés or even pop a plump oyster into Tansie's mouth during a leisurely lunch.

But she consoled herself with her work, thriving on the excitement of working with the French National Radio Orchestra. She felt the adrenalin surge in a way that it hadn't for a while. The musicians were far more flexible with and adaptable to her wishes than the musicians in the local orchestras, other than when Boris was conducting. A faint smile appeared on her lips as she thought of how Boris could extract the most perfect sounds from the musicians.

The music she and John had composed over a relatively short period of time very much reflected the tragedy of the fall of Saigon to the communists and the capture and torture of the film's heroine. The music was both moving and exciting.

Towards the end of the first week, Alix confirmed her meeting with Johan in Basel. He was expecting her the following Thursday, he told her.

Alix was sitting in the lobby of the Hotel Drei Könige, when Johan arrived for his appointment. Alix saw him before he saw her, giving her time to look him over. She had done her homework and knew everything there was to

251

know about him, including the brand of cigars he smoked. Davidoff, she had noted with a smile, remembering that he had been the only boy who had smoked at school and had never been caught.

As Alix expected, Johan was dressed in a conservative pin-striped dark grey business suit. It was elegantly styled and hung perfectly on his tall frame. He carried his hat in one hand and a navy blue overcoat was folded over the other. His black slip-on shoes were some of the finest Bally made.

Since they hadn't seen each other for many years, their greetings were cordial, though formal. They proceeded to the bar, where Johan ordered drinks.

After they exchanged pleasantries, he came straight to the point. "Alix, you are a very successful composer and pianist. I'm intrigued as to what you could want from me. Science and music don't have that much in common."

Alix flashed him an easy smile and went on to explain in detail what she had in mind.

At the end of it, he said, "I'm very flattered. Why me?"

"You have all the right credentials." She drew deeply on a cigarette and then, as though deep in thought, gently ran her thumb along her lower lip.

"That simple?" he said more to himself than to her.

"That simple," she repeated. "Are you interested?"

When he confirmed he was, she shook his hand and added, "I'll have my lawyer send over the contracts. When can you start?"

Johan laughed. "You're still as impatient as ever! I won't be able to do it quite that fast."

She didn't reply immediately but stared at him instead. He was a very sensuous attractive man with intelligent light blue eyes and strong smooth hands. In the past, she knew she could quite easily have fallen for him. But being in tune with her own feelings, she was aware that her thoughts about Johan had more to do with her see-saw relationship with Tansie than with the man himself. Reaching for another cigarette, she asked again when he could start.

"I have some business meetings in Hong Kong next week so, why don't I fly down to Melbourne and have a look around?" he replied. "Can you wait that long?" he added, wondering whether she was just her normal impatient self or whether she had another motive for wanting to get this over and done with as quickly as possible.

"I can," she said. Had she known what he had been thinking, she would have told him that she simply wanted this over and done with today rather than tomorrow. She wanted to put Clemenger Pharmaceuticals to the back of her mind and get on with her real work.

After his visit to Melbourne, Johan needed no more prompting and promised to report for work at the beginning of September. Alix in return promised to have a house ready for him so that his wife and three children would suffer minimal dislocation as a result of being moved from one end of the world to the other.

Alix made the announcement to the Clemenger board after her return from Paris and after Johan's brief visit. It was just before the Easter break. Alix was the first to arrive in the board room and, as usual, she took her designated seat next to Joe, her father-in-law.

"I haven't seen you for a while," Joe said softly and gave her hand a quick pat.

"I know," Alix said. "But once this is all over, we'll have lunch. I think we'll both be more relaxed then."

Moments later, the other eight members filed in together. Alix watched with amusement as each one nodded in her direction, took his seat and deposited his fine-leather brief-case on the large table. Eight locks snapped open simultaneously. She thought any ballet company would be delighted with such a co-ordinated performance.

Once her father-in-law had worked through the items on the agenda, he gave Alix the floor. The rest of the meeting was as unpleasant as she had anticipated. When it was all over, she flew from the room and decided then and there that she hated corporate politics. In future she would leave it all to Johan who was more than competent with running the company.

Her father-in-law caught up with her just as she was leaving the building. "Thank you Alix, you did a great job," he said and put his arm around her shoulder.

"I don't like myself much for what I've done," she replied. "Did I have an alternative, Joe?"

"You didn't," he comforted her.

Chapter 20

The next three months seemed to simply disappear. Autumn was gone and another winter had started. Alix remembered other winters and how she had hated the cold, wet and impossible climate of a typical Melbourne winter. Quite miraculously, this winter was mild and sunny and reflected the relationship between Alix and Tansie. It too continued to thrive and gave them both great pleasure.

After a short holiday in Honolulu with Tansie and the children, Alix completed the music score for the documentary for the Australian wool industry. Now that she was less burdened by work pressures, she invited John to dine with her. He gladly accepted. They had both put in a great deal of effort over recent weeks and were looking forward to an evening together.

When they returned to Alix's house after dinner, he followed her inside. "How about a brandy before I hit the road?" he asked and sat down on the couch.

"Why not," Alix responded and reached for the Waterford decanter on the side-table. "Now that I have your undivided attention, I'll play you my part of the score for the 'sheep' movie."

"By the way, when do you start rehearsal for the Pacific concert tour? Is Boris back from Europe yet?"

"No, he isn't due for another couple of weeks. We'll start as soon as he returns," Alix replied and put some music sheets on the piano stand.

The composition began with a *fortissimo*, which gave it

a thunderous opening; just like the hot north wind which could so ferociously whip through the desert. Periodically she picked up speed, indicating that the shearers were working at a frantic pace, only to slow down to a gentle *adagio* when the sheep were set free, unharmed, yet floundering after the loss of their fleece. The finish commenced with a flourishing *allegro*, but before Alix could complete the last few bars, the telephone rang. Reluctantly, Alix got up to answer it.

"Hiii," Tansie murmured in her childlike drawl.

Alix immediately picked up the undercurrent in her voice but wasn't quite sure what it was. "Are you all right? I thought you were going out to dinner with Penny?"

"I cancelled it," Tansie replied, as her voice faded away even before she finished the sentence.

"Tansie?" Alix asked firmly, "have you taken anything?"

"I love you . . . don't ever forget that . . . I just can't cope any more . . ."

"Damn you," Alix yelled and slammed the handset down.

John was already on his feet and, grabbing his keys from the table, took her arm. "Come on, I'll drive you."

As Alix had expected, she found Tansie sprawled across her bed, fully dressed and out cold. Either she was sound asleep or already in a coma. Alix didn't know which. She grabbed her roughly under the arms and tried to stand her up, shouting at her at the same time.

"Wake up, for God's sake!" Her own words echoed in her ears, but all she got in reply was a faint groan.

"You can ring Douglas from the car," John said and scooped Tansie into his arms.

Slipping into the back seat, Alix cradled Tansie in her arms and reached for the telephone. Jesse was on call and she instructed Alix to bring Tansie to the Windsor Clinic.

Replacing the receiver, Alix wept and cried, "Why, Tansie, why now? You've been doing so well for months."

In between sobs, she urged John to hurry, fearing that her lover might die in her arms.

Jesse was waiting for them at the emergency entrance and arranged for Tansie to be wheeled away. She told Alix and John to wait in the room across the hall. Alix turned towards John and collapsed into his arms.

She gave him a desolate look and said, "Why, John? How can she do such a thing?"

"I don't know, love," he sighed with equal frustration. "Maybe if I knew what the woman wants from you, or from herself for that matter, we might have an answer," he added.

Alix didn't reply. If she didn't know what Tansie wanted how could anybody else know? She could not figure out what had triggered this drastic action. Since their return from Europe in January and, more recently from Honolulu, they had enjoyed months of relative calm. And now this.

Alix eventually went home. Just before she fell asleep towards morning, Alix had only a dim memory of Jesse telling her that they had pumped Tansie's stomach and that she would be all right.

Towards lunchtime the next day, Alix woke up with a jolt. Sweat was running down her back and her mind was blurred. She wasn't sure whether she had dreamt that Tansie had taken an overdose or whether she had actually done it.

It took her less than a second to realise that it wasn't a dream. "You bloody coward!" Alix shouted at the top of her voice. When she arrived at the clinic, Alix marched past the nurses' station and walked straight into Tansie's room.

Tansie was in a half-sitting position with several pillows propped up behind her back, her eyes fixed on the door. "Get out of here," she yelled, adding, "you brought me in here, didn't you?"

Alix felt a surge of relief. Tansie was alive. But the shock of nearly having lost her sat like a heavy weight in her stomach. Moments later, the relief was replaced by anger.

She was angry that Tansie had felt it necessary to do this to herself. She had tried so hard to understand Tansie and help her whenever she had had short-lived bouts of depression. At those times, Alix had dropped everything and rushed over in an effort to cheer her lover up. Sometimes she had been reluctant to do so, but she did it anyway. Alix would naturally choose an intellectual, rational approach to such a cry for help and yet, with Tansie, she couldn't do it and this surprised her. She had often surprised herself where Tansie was concerned, she noted briefly.

When Alix finally replied, her voice was unrelenting and left no doubt as to her seriousness. "Yes I did! You had better start listening because what I have to say, I'll only say once. Next time you take a bloody overdose, don't ring me!" Alix never swore, Tansie briefly registered. Seconds later, Tansie crumbled into a weeping mess. She flung herself into the pillows and buried her face.

Alix folded her arms across her chest and remained rigid at Tansie's bedside. It wasn't easy for her. She wanted to take Tansie into her arms and comfort her. But she thought that, if she gave in that easily, Tansie might well try again and perhaps succeed next time.

"Oh, Alix, I'm so sorry . . . I didn't mean to do it . . . I would never do such a thing, you know that . . . I didn't know you'd feel that way . . . please . . . you must believe me!" Tansie eventually said as she turned to face Alix.

"Why did you do it then?" Alix's words seemed unkind but, inside, she was devastated. How can this beautiful woman do such a thing? Why would she want to?

"I don't know," Tansie cried in despair. Then she changed her expression and became defensive. "Anyway, I don't know what you're making such a fuss about, it was an accident. I wouldn't ever jeopardise . . ."

"They pumped out your stomach and there were over thirty pills they could still count, so don't give me that nonsense!" Alix shouted. "You ever try that stunt again and I can promise you right now, I'll have you certified!"

"See if I fucking care!" Tansie shouted even louder. "You'll suffer more than I will!"

"That's just fine with me!" Alix turned and began to walk towards the door.

"I don't need you . . . I'm going to marry Herb!"

"That's just fine with me too!" This time Alix slammed the door with a bang. She had heard enough.

Blinded by tears, she didn't see where she was going and ran straight into Jesse in the corridor.

"Hey . . . take it easy," Jesse said.

"Jesse, how could I have said all those things to her? What if she succeeds next time, I would never forgive myself." A new flood of tears choked her voice.

Jesse draped an arm around her shoulders and walked her to her car. "I'll have a chat to Jim Callahan and see what's going on," she comforted.

A little calmer now, Alix stopped and looked at her thoughtfully for a moment. "I'm not sure I can take much more of this, Jesse. She is destroying everything we ever had. The harder I try, the worse she gets." After a short pause, she added, "Why is she doing this? To me, to us?"

Opening the car door for her, Jesse replied, "You shouldn't

have to take it. Alix, you are not her nurse-maid, no matter how much you may love her. Jim is there to help her but, if she doesn't want help, then there's nothing any of us can do about it." She didn't mean to be unkind to either woman but she knew that if she didn't make her views known, it would help them even less.

"I know that, Jesse. Still, I can't just desert her. Certainly not after she's done so well," Alix admitted with frustration.

"It might be an option you may well have to consider in times to come," Jesse said softly. Spontaneously kissing Alix on the cheek, she added, "If you're free one evening over the weekend, let's have dinner. Bring Tansie along, she might need to know that you do love her regardless."

Alix smiled. "Lately, I only seem to speak to you when I'm in trouble or when we talk about the benefit concert," she said, regretting that she hadn't seen Jesse socially. "How about Sunday night?"

"Sunday is fine," Jesse confirmed and watched as Alix reversed the car and drove off.

Love makes strange bedfellows, Jesse mused to herself as she walked back into the clinic. She had grown very fond of Alix. With an inward smile she acknowledged that, perhaps in time, something could develop between them.

Since Maxine had left her, Jesse had been on her own. That was entirely her choice and quite all right by her. It had given her a chance to spend more time doing research and to accept invitations to give papers around the world. But as time went on, the wounds started to heal and she started to think about a new companion. She did not intend to be on her own forever. She smiled, thinking what a shame it was that Alix was not available.

From the clinic, Alix went back to her studio and began to work on the composition for the movie *Eva*. Quite out of the blue, Germany's foremost female director, Marta Borg, had sent her part of the script. When she'd read it, Alix had noted that it was a love story between two women. Through her European agent, she had advised Marta that she would be delighted to work with her.

Given her lover's recent behaviour, Alix was glad to be able to bury herself in a new composition. She knew that the only way to keep herself from thinking about Tansie was to work to near exhaustion. Still, once or twice she picked up the telephone to ring her. She replaced the receiver before Tansie's phone started to ring. As much as she disliked it, she knew she would have to let Tansie come to her.

By Sunday evening, Alix was ready for some company. She looked forward to having dinner with Jesse. Once the two women were comfortably seated in Jesse's small dining room, Alix started to relax. As they chatted, Alix wondered why she did not spend more time with Jesse. Particularly given how much they had in common intellectually and how much she enjoyed Jesse's no-nonsense, yet charming company. Was she so preoccupied with Tansie that she couldn't even form new friendships, she wondered.

"How is Tansie?" Jesse asked as she ladled a rich vegetable soup into their bowls.

"I haven't spoken to her since I saw her in the hospital the morning after she was admitted," Alix replied miserably. It had only later occurred to Alix that had she extended Jesse's invitation to Tansie, Tansie may well have gone off the deep end over it. Jesse of course didn't know that Tansie had no love for her, hence her invitation was made quite innocently.

"If only I knew what to do about her," Alix eventually continued.

"Alix," Jesse said. "Have you ever considered living together? At least if she were to live with you, your mind would be more at ease and you would have a better idea where she was and what she was doing."

"I did suggest it once but Tansie didn't seem partial to the idea. But you're right, it probably would put my mind at rest," Alix replied. "Did you and Maxine live together?"

Jesse smiled. "We did, although she always kept her own house," she confirmed. "After a short pause, she continued. "To us it was like a marriage, we were partners."

"You mean you shared the highs and the lows and the bills?" Alix asked, giving her companion a cheeky smile.

"All of that . . . and more."

"You still miss her a lot, don't you?"

"I have my moments but, with help from friends, it is getting easier." Jesse let her gaze wander to the oil painting which hung over the ornate fireplace.

It was a portrait of Maxine that Jesse had commissioned. After Maxine had moved out, Jesse couldn't walk past it without tears in her eyes. It showed Maxine the way Jesse had loved her most: her head thrown back in laughter and her green eyes sparkling with mischief. Now, Jesse had reached the stage where she could look at the portrait and remember the wonderful times they had shared. The relationship had always been exciting and Jesse never knew which way Maxine was going to jump next.

"Did the fact that you lived together cause you any problems? I mean, was it difficult for you professionally?" Alix asked.

"For me personally, no," Jesse confirmed, turning to face Alix. "From time to time Maxine told me that some derogatory remarks were made by her parliamentary colleagues but nothing she couldn't deal with."

"Judging by what I've seen of her on television, I'm not surprised. I'm sure most of the time her colleagues don't know what she's up to until it's too late," Alix laughed. "She has style . . . it's just a shame that we don't have more women like her running this country."

"It is indeed," Jesse agreed. "Why don't you give it a go?" she added as she imagined Alix standing in parliament and delivering a speech so convincing her colleagues would believe black was white. The thought evoked a smile.

"Offer me the prime-ministership and I might consider it!"

"How modest," Jesse laughed. "I would have thought you'd want at least a title!"

"None of the eligible crown princes particularly appeal to me," Alix responded. "By the way, how are the preparations for the benefit concert coming along?" Alix asked.

"Thanks to you, it'll be a full house," Jesse beamed.

"That's fantastic." Alix was genuinely pleased to be able to contribute something constructive to help other women.

When it was time to leave, Alix gave Jesse a warm hug for the first time. "Thanks Jesse," she said.

Tansie checked herself out of the clinic the following morning and rang Herb to pick her up. For the next two days, Tansie didn't leave the house or answer the door. She did answer the phone but only to tell whoever it was that she was busy and would call back. Alix, the one person she desperately wanted to ring her, didn't. She drank herself into a stupor and fell into bed at odd hours. She got up only to start all over again. In a sheer fit of temper, she swept through her studio like a hurricane. Her only purpose was to destroy all her works. In the end she collapsed on the floor and cried hysterically at the destruction. For a brief moment, her mind was lucid and she asked herself why she had wanted to destroy something she had created? Something which had given her such incredible satisfaction?

The moment passed and she opened the next bottle of wine. Finally on the third morning and after having vomited for most of the night, she went to see Alix.

Tansie stood just inside the door to Alix's studio and glared across the room, but seemed undecided as to what to do next. "You're not going to make this easy for me, are you?" she blurted out.

"I can't," Alix replied and thought how awful she looked. Her hair hung limply around her drawn face. The once-yellow tracksuit was now grey and baggy. More than anything, Alix wanted to rush to her, take her into her arms and tell her she loved her regardless. But she didn't do it.

"Dr Callahan says I'm having a nervous breakdown," Tansie said.

Alix's heart went out to her and it was with great difficulty that she remained seated on the piano stool. Eventually she said, "I've been thinking, Tansie. How would you feel about living here with us? Maybe we both need some stability and . . ."

"Do you really mean that?" An instant glow appeared on Tansie's face. Although she had turned Alix down in the past, she would not do so now.

"Yes . . . all considered, I think it's a good idea. But, there is one condition to the offer."

Tansie lowered her eyes. "I'll do anything you suggest. You want me to continue to see Dr Callahan, don't you?"

"Him or someone else," Alix said. "I am very distressed by what happened and, as much as I want to help you, you need much more than what I can give you. What I can do is be here and support you."

Although Alix had spoken kindly, Tansie knew that she

had no alternative but to accept Alix's offer. She knew that she had pushed Alix as far as she probably ever could without losing her. That was really the last thing she wanted.

From the moment she moved in with Alix, Tansie behaved more rationally. Her visits to Dr Callahan were regular, but she remained close-lipped as to what they discussed. She attended all of her lectures at the college and rarely went out for lunch or dinner. She looked happier and healthier than she had in a long time and the works of art she created were better than ever. When Alix had asked about the sculptures she had destroyed, Tansie had told her she had given them away. She was relieved when Alix accepted the explanation. They had both been so excited about the works, how could she now explain to Alix that she had destroyed them in a fit of temper?

As Tansie began to bloom, Alix began to relax and enjoy the good times they shared. Although Alix had been worried about how the children would feel if Tansie moved in with them, she soon realised that there had been no need for it. They seemed happy with the arrangement. She was often surprised at the astuteness with which they handled Tansie, as though she was a delicate flower and needed nurturing. And yet, they never questioned the role she played in Alix's life. Or at least, they never commented on what they thought was going on and accepted Tansie as part of the household. Alix was pleased to see that Tansie seemed to be getting along with the children much better than she had in the past.

After their initial discussion, Tansie had only once again broached her suicide attempt. She had cried in Alix's arms, devastated by what she had done and why she had done it, admitting that she had been feeling so much better for such a long time. She could not explain her behaviour and, according to Tansie, neither could Dr Callahan. It was most likely depression, he had said, the cause of which he had not yet been able to discover. Alix had to believe her.

After Michael's death, Alix could not have imagined herself ever living with anyone again. Yet with Tansie, she had no trouble adapting and was delighted with the arrangement. She loved the idea of having her companion so close by where, at a moment's notice, she could drop in to see her in the studio especially set up for sculpting, or watch her through the french doors as she played with Christian and the dog in the garden.

Alix particularly loved the fact that they could go to sleep together and wake up together without having to drive from one house to the other at unreasonable hours. Tansie's warm body next to hers, gave Alix great pleasure and comfort.

When it was time for Alix to leave for her ten-day Pacific concert tour at the beginning of July, she was confident about leaving Tansie behind. During that time, the women spoke to each other on the telephone two or three times a day. Tansie was in a creative frame of mind. In turn, Alix performed to her maximum capacity and enchanted the audiences everywhere she went. When she played her own Piano Concerto No. 5 for the very first time in public, it was immediately acclaimed as one of the finest ever composed in the twentieth century. At the end of the tour, Alix returned to Tansie's welcoming arms.

The benefit concert the following week was not only a glittering affair but successful beyond anyone's imagination. The local bourgeoisie had not let them down. Every single seat in the concert hall was sold and the concertgoers arrived in gowns that would put any fashion show to shame. When Alix finally walked off stage, Jesse was waiting for her backstage.

"What can I say?" Jesse threw her arms into the air as though she wanted to embrace the whole world. "How can I ever thank you for that? Not just for the wonderful performance but for what it will do for the women's refuges."

"Jesse, it was my pleasure," Alix replied.

Chapter 21

Towards the end of winter that year, Alix prepared to go to Berlin. She had been fascinated by the movie script *Eva*. Now she wanted to meet the writer Marta Borg who was also in the process of directing the film.

However, when Tansie started to show signs of restlessness again, Alix was a little apprehensive about leaving her behind. She was concerned that all the good work might come undone during her absence. Alix could not think of a single reason for Tansie's shift in behaviour, slight as it was.

Dashing across the lawn with the torrential rain pelting down on to the large umbrella, Alix stopped in the doorway to Tansie's workroom. She jumped when another bout of thunder crashed in the distance and lit up the black sky. Folding up the umbrella, Alix slipped inside and watched Tansie from the doorway for a moment as she quietly shut the door.

Tansie was working on a clay sculpture, a portrait of a young girl Alix thought could well be a portrait of Tansie herself when she was much younger. The long hair was swept off the girl's face, leaving it exposed and vulnerable. The lips were parted into a sulky typically teenage pout. And yet, it was the eyes Alix was most fascinated with. There was a wildness in their expression Alix found just a little unnerving.

Alix hadn't moved when Tansie snatched one of her wooden scalpels from the workbench. For a second or two, it looked as though she was going to drive it through the girl's eyes.

The exclamation "Don't", froze on Alix's lips as she quickly took two steps towards Tansie and enfolded her lover's shaking body into her arms.

"It's okay," Alix whispered into her ear, although she had no idea what was going on. Tansie had obviously wanted to mutilate the statue but something had made her stop.

Tansie gave Alix a momentary blank stare as though she didn't recognise her. Somewhere at the back of her mind, she vaguely recalled how petrified she had been as a child in such stormy weather and how, very often, the nuns had been even more vicious with their beatings than normal. As though pulled by an inner subconscious force, she too tended towards violence and destruction in tempestuous weather conditions.

Turning her gaze to the bust, she burst into tears. "I was so frightened. I wanted to destroy it," she muttered.

"You didn't, Tansie. It's over," Alix comforted her. Even more distressed now at having to leave Tansie, she added, "Please, will you come to Berlin with me?"

"I can't," Tansie replied and wiped her clay-covered hands on her overalls. "You know your friend Marlow has set the date for the opening of my exhibition. It's in just over three weeks and I've got so much work to do beforehand. You will be back in time, won't you?"

"The exhibition, of course." Alix kept her voice even but she was disgusted with herself for having forgotten such an important event. An event Tansie had worked towards for so long. How could she?

"Maybe it's better if you're not here for the next couple of weeks. How can I concentrate on my work when I've got you around?" She emphasised her point by kissing Alix gently and snuggling her own body closer to Alix's.

When Tansie finally released her, Alix laughed. "You're

right, that way neither of us will get any work done!"

"Alix," Tansie murmured after a short pause. "How would you feel if I moved back home?"

"You are home," Alix pointed out.

"Please, Alix, don't be difficult," Tansie said. "I don't want people to start talking about us . . . I just couldn't cope with the gossip."

Alix wanted to tell her that there had been no talk about their arrangement but changed her mind. She doubted that Tansie would believe her and she didn't want to force an issue that Tansie was obviously apprehensive about.

"I don't want you to go but if you're happier back at your own house, then you'll have to go," Alix relented sadly. She hated the thought of not having Tansie close by any more and of having to sleep by herself again. And, she was frightened that Tansie's emotional welfare would deteriorate again.

"I do appreciate your concern but, truly, I'll be just fine at home," Tansie assured her.

At the end of the week, Alix helped Tansie move back into her house. When she was satisfied that Tansie was fine and happy in her abode, Alix went home. Later that day, she was on a flight to Zürich where she caught a Lufthansa flight to Berlin. When the pilot announced that the temperature in Berlin was around 22 degrees and sunny, Alix smiled. She had packed the right clothes for early European autumn days.

Marta Borg picked her up at Tempelhof. Alix had only ever seen black and white photos of Marta and was not prepared for the woman who now stood in front of her.

Marta was a little taller and heavier than Alix and appeared to be in her early forties. Her black hair was pulled off her face and tied back into a knot at the nape of her neck. Her eyes were a soft warm brown with specks of green in them. She was handsome rather than beautiful and, when she laughed, it came from somewhere deep inside her. Overall, Alix thought, there was something warm and lovable about her, yet she also appeared feisty and efficient. Marta was a formidable woman.

Marta gave Alix a wide smile, showing two rows of perfect white teeth, shook her hand energetically and noted, "You've grown since I last saw you!"

"I expect you're referring to the concert I gave in Berlin in 1965," Alix laughed. "I was still a kid then."

"You were a *Wunderkind*," Marta responded and motioned to a porter to fetch the luggage.

Although Alix had booked into the Kempinski Hotel, she now accepted Marta's invitation to stay at her house on the Wannsee, Berlin's famous lake.

Marta's parents hadn't survived the War but their villa had. Marta had since restored it to its full glory. Alix admired the magnificent music room with its high, dome-like ornate rococo ceiling and tall, narrow french doors which led into the magnificently kept garden. A full-size concert grand piano was placed to one side with numerous couches, arm chairs and tables arranged around it.

At dinner that evening, Alix was introduced to Marta's partner, Nina Jensen. The five children they currently fostered came from all over the world: India, Vietnam, Brazil, Cuba and, the youngest, a four-year-old boy from Alaska.

Nina was pretty in a delicate, lady-like way with large blue eyes, fair complexion and short, dark hair. She was petite with a keen intellect and a droll and unassuming sense of humour. And, quite obviously, she adored and worshipped Marta. Her partner's success was never a threat to Nina. She knew her own worth. Alix thought they complemented each other well.

Alix had expected to meet an interesting, even fascinating, woman but Marta was well beyond Alix's wildest imaginings. With Nina in charge of the household and the children, Marta had the freedom and the time to pursue her career. She was a woman with so much energy even Alix's head spun a couple of times. What fascinated her in particular were Marta's very precise views and ideologies and her courage to stand up for them. She could not think of a single conventional marriage where both partners cared for and shared with each other as those two women appeared to do. She was deeply touched.

Alix noted that Marta was very much respected for her views and not just from within the ranks of the world's feminists. As Alix learnt during her stay, Marta's formal dinners were legendary and were attended by many influential people from all over the world. They included politicians, artists and academics, film makers and industrialists, lawyers and doctors. Young and old people.

Although Alix missed Tansie, especially when she crawled into the massive four-poster bed in the guest bedroom, her thoughts often turned to Jesse. Jesse would love it here, she thought. She would feel as at home as Alix did and would enjoy sparring with Marta on women's issues.

When Alix's stay in Berlin came to an end, the two women parted as friends. They both looked forward to working together again. Marta's next project would deal with women who had to leave their native country and who were expected to settle on the other side of the globe often under difficult cultural and social conditions.

Although somewhat unsettled in her own house for the first few days, Tansie attacked her work with a new bout of creative energy. She was happy and confident that nothing could now go wrong with her relationship with Alix. However, with Alix out of the country and despite her best intentions, Tansie was soon on the phone to Herb inviting him over for a meal.

When the dinner was over and their conversation exhausted, Tansie contemplated sending him home. Instead she took his hand and led him into her bedroom.

Tansie saw him four more times during Alix's absence, but made no attempt to take him to bed again. She didn't want him to get the idea that this would be a regular occurrence whenever they were together. She didn't want to lose him but wasn't quite ready to get pregnant either, just in case someone else came along in the near future.

Two days before Alix was due to return, Tansie went to see Douglas for a thorough physical check-up. He declared her fit and healthy and said that there was no reason why she couldn't get pregnant whenever she was ready for it. After the miscarriage she had suffered, she had let Alix believe that she was no longer interested in having a child.

As Tansie was leaving the surgery, she collided with Jesse in the doorway.

"Tansie, how are you?" Jesse greeted her.

"Fine, just fine." Tansie gave her a wide grin and hurried off.

Later, Tansie contemplated whether or not to tell Alix that she had seen Douglas. In the end she decided she would. She didn't want Alix to find out from someone else.

"I went to see Douglas the other day," Tansie informed Alix when they drove home from the airport.

Alix gave her an alarmed glance. "Haven't you been well?"

"I'm fine. I told Jesse the same when I saw her in the corridor," Tansie chortled. After a short pause, she continued. "Tell me, what does Jesse specialise in? Douglas sort of said that I should see her for any women's problems, which luckily I don't have."

Alix smiled. "Jesse is primarily a GP but she also specialises in helping women who don't want to conceive a baby in the conventional manner. You know . . ."

"You mean artificial insemination and all that?" Tansie gasped. "That's disgusting! That's for women who can't get a man. Thank God we don't have that problem!"

"Who said I want a man?" Alix laughed. "I think it's rather nice to see women take charge of their lives. Why should they be deprived of children just because they'd rather not have intercourse with men. As far . . ."

"I don't want to talk about this!" Tansie cut her off.

Alix suddenly realised that Tansie had no idea of what their relationship was really about. Nor did she really have any idea about women who chose other women as partners.

After having spent time with Marta and Nina, Tansie's attitude saddened her. If those two women could live together in such obvious harmony, why couldn't she and Tansie? She smiled briefly. Marta would probably point out that Melbourne might not be quite as ready as Berlin to accept such liberal arrangements. Unfortunately, Alix would have to agree with her. In certain ways, Berlin and Melbourne were worlds apart.

"Speaking of Jesse," Tansie continued as she gave Alix a sideways glance. "I saw her the other day with another woman. They seemed very chummy, you know what I mean."

"I'm very pleased to hear it," Alix replied, wondering what brought this on. "She's a lovely woman."

"Why are you always defending her?" Tansie quizzed, suspicious of Alix's tone of voice.

Alix shrugged her shoulders and smiled. "As I said, she's a lovely person . . . that's all."

Tansie dropped it after that. Nothing would be gained by pursuing this conversation. If anything, she thought, it might just push Alix even closer to Jesse.

Tansie's exhibition opened three days later on a warm sunny afternoon in early spring. Tansie chose a simple, royal blue dress for the cocktail party. She knew that was her best colour. Her eye make-up consisted of delicate shades of amber and blue and her lipstick was a rich cherry colour. She had never looked better.

When two-thirds of the statues were sold on the first evening, Tansie was elated. She had finally made it as an artist, if the comments she received were any indication. She would never have to feel inferior again, not professionally anyway.

Sipping French champagne and chatting to some acquaintances, Alix excused herself when Jesse arrived with her friend Carol. She welcomed them both and took two glasses from the tray of an obliging waiter.

"I'm sorry I'm late," Jesse said. Letting her eyes rest on an eighteen-inch-high bronze statue of a small boy, its curly hair tousled and its eyes wide with wonder, she added, "What a shame the little boy is already sold. It's just beautiful."

"I think so too," Alix responded and smiled to herself. She had bought it only moments earlier.

As soon as Jesse and Carol wandered off to view the exhibition, Tansie appeared at Alix's side. "That's the woman I saw Jesse with. Remember I told you about her? Who is she, do you know her?"

"I've met her once or twice," Alix admitted. "She's one of Melbourne's leading architects and has just won a competition to design the new international hotel complex down by the Yarra. She's very well-respected in her profession."

"Do you know anybody who's not famous?" Tansie retorted ungraciously.

"Actually, I do," Alix laughed. "I always have a chat to Max when he collects my garbage bin!"

Tansie eventually laughed, seeing the humour in their conversation. Linking her arm with Alix's, she added, "Isn't it just wonderful? The exhibition is nearly a sell-out. Marlow has already suggested I have another exhibition before Christmas."

"That's fantastic, Tansie. I hope you said yes."

"I did," Tansie confirmed. After a short pause, she turned to face Alix. "You know you're the only one who's ever believed in me. You stuck by me even when I behaved like a spoiled brat. I am grateful for that, don't ever forget it."

"You have the talent, my love, I only encouraged it," Alix assured her. "I'm very proud of you."

"Maybe one day I'll be as famous as all your other mates and then . . ."

"As long as you never forget that I fell in love with you long before you were famous," Alix whispered into her ear and gave her a brief hug. Alix reflected on the fact that Tansie had to reach middle-age before she had the confidence to believe in her worth and her talent.

"I love you, Alix." Tansie didn't say the words aloud but rather formed them on her lips. Touching Alix's cheek with the palm of her hand, she murmured, "You know, when you're happy, you have the most beautiful eyes, like huge pools of clear sparkling water."

"And you have the sexiest body I've ever touched," Alix replied in a similar manner and ceremoniously swept her into her arms.

Before Jesse and Carol left the exhibition, Jesse invited both Alix and Tansie to her birthday party the following week. "I hope you're both free next Saturday," she concluded.

Alix looked at Tansie. "What do you think? I'm free as far as I know."

"I'm busy. I've got a date, but thanks for the invitation," Tansie said and bustled off to welcome some other guests.

"You'll still come, won't you?" Jesse asked.

"I'd love to," Alix replied, wondering whether it was her imagination or whether there had been some real antagonism in Tansie's response. It was the second invitation from Jesse that Tansie had declined. She couldn't understand why Tansie treated Jesse with anything other than the same dignity and respect as Jesse extended to her. Because Alix knew that she loved Tansie and was not looking for a new lover, it didn't occur to her that Tansie might feel threatened by Jesse.

Although Alix had bought the statue of the little boy for herself, a few days later when she picked it up she reflected on how disappointed Jesse had been when it was sold. Alix decided to give it to her for her birthday.

When Alix arrived at Jesse's on the evening of her birthday party, Jesse's face lit up as she ambled over to meet Alix.

"Happy birthday," Alix smiled, and kissing Jesse on the cheek, handed her a large and heavy, beautifully gift-wrapped box.

"Thank you," Jesse responded and proceeded to unwrap the present. "Oh, you didn't," she gasped as she carefully lifted the statue out of the box. Suddenly she gave Alix a puzzled frown. "You'd already bought the statue when I admired it at the exhibition, hadn't you?"

"Although I'd bought it for myself initially, I later changed my mind. I wanted you to have it," Alix replied honestly.

"It is very beautiful, Alix. Thank you," Jesse said and placed it on the mantelpiece over the open fireplace in the sitting room. She was deeply touched by Alix's extravagant gesture, although not surprised. After having shopped with Alix in Hong Kong and London, Jesse knew that Alix would buy one or another trinket for a friend for no other reason than Alix thought she or he might like it. It would never occur to her to look at the price tag. Alix's generosity was just one thing Jesse had come to like a great deal about her.

Taking Alix's arm, Jesse added lightly, "Come and meet my mother. She came down from the country especially for my birthday."

"What a shame!" Alix exclaimed. "Now I won't ever be able to say, 'When're you going to take me home to meet your mum'!" Alix drew up her eyebrows in a semi-seductive manner.

Jesse's response was quick. She said playfully, "There is still my father . . . you haven't met him yet!"

Alix laughed but decided to drop the subject. After Alix had been introduced to Jesse's mother and had chatted to her for some time, she moved on to another group of people. As she periodically let her gaze wander from one group of guests to another, she noticed how many attractive people were there, women in particular. As a lazy smile slowly crossed her face, she wondered how she would go about making a pass at one of them. With an inward chuckle, she noted that she was still quite naive where such matters were concerned.

Seconds later, Jesse whispered, "If you tell me who you fancy . . . I'll tell you who is available!"

"You're a real worry, Jesse. You're reading my mind!" Alix laughed. "I was wondering how I would go about making a pass at another woman."

"You did well enough a little while ago," Jesse responded smartly.

"That could be even more of a worry," Alix laughed, her eyes twinkling with mischief.

Jesse laughed too. She enjoyed their playful exchange of words. "Now, let me see," she continued, "There is Carol . . . she's on her own at the moment. Talking to my sister Anna is Maggie and over there leaning against the window is Sally. My other sister Josie is talking to Catherine."

"I'll keep them in mind," Alix replied with an amused glint in her eyes. Moments later, she strolled to the baby grand piano, opened the lid and started to play 'Happy Birthday'.

Alix drew an immediate response from the guests and they gathered around her. Much to everyone's delight, she played a repertoire of popular tunes which lasted well into the night.

Chapter 22

When Haig was in town a couple of weeks later for one of his fleeting visits, Alix dined with him. Running late from a conference, she met him at Maxim's Restaurant where they had arranged to eat. He looked suave as always and, although he was now just over fifty, the years had been kind to him. There were only a few fine lines around his amber eyes which enhanced his distinguished appearance.

With her back to the door, Alix couldn't see who was coming in but when she noted a sudden frown on Haig's face, she asked lightly, "You look as though you've seen the devil."

"Tansie has just arrived," he said.

Turning around in her chair, Alix briefly reflected that she had told Tansie where and whom she was dining with that evening. There had been no response from Tansie other than her wishing Alix a nice evening. Tansie's and Alix's eyes momentarily locked, then Tansie turned abruptly and followed the waiter to a table at the far end of the restaurant. Alix had no idea who Tansie's escort was. He was a handsome man, several years younger than Tansie. As for what this all meant, Alix couldn't imagine.

"Are you okay?" Haig asked with concern.

"Yes, I'm fine," Alix replied. "I was just a little surprised to see Tansie here."

When Alix and Haig left the restaurant soon after eleven o'clock, there was no sign of Tansie. Haig walked her to her car and kissed her goodnight. Moments later Alix backed out of the parking lot and drove home.

Alix was sound asleep when the telephone rang. Reaching for the handset, she noticed that it was three o'clock in the morning.

"Hello?" she said with some impatience.

"Is he still there with you?" Tansie shrieked.

"Tansie, what are you talking about?"

"Your lover . . . how can you do this to me?" Tansie shouted even louder.

Alix took a deep breath. "Haig is not my lover," she said sternly.

"Do you really think I'm that stupid?" Tansie responded and hung up.

Alix sighed as she too replaced the receiver. She was angry at having been woken up at this hour. But she was also puzzled at Tansie's behaviour. Had she known Tansie would feel like this, Alix could quite easily have refused Haig's invitation. She wouldn't have liked to do it because there was really no reason why she should, but she would have done it just the same.

When sleep still eluded her half an hour later, Alix got up and went into her studio. She might as well make use of the extra couple of hours she now had to work.

Later that afternoon, on the way home from a meeting with Laura, Alix called in at Tansie's house.

"What are you doing here?" Tansie greeted her less than graciously.

"Visiting you," Alix said evenly and, lighting a cigarette, added, "I told you that I was having dinner with Haig because I have absolutely nothing to hide. Haig and I are friends as you well know but that's all!"

"Why should I believe that?"

"Because I have never lied to you."

"Alix, don't you understand? I can't bear the thought of you in bed with someone else! I just go crazy thinking about it," Tansie said on the verge of tears.

"Now you know that I don't," Alix said and drew her into her arms. "You have been my only lover for a very long time and I intend to keep it that way."

"I'm sorry," Tansie murmured burying her face at the side of Alix's neck. After a short pause, she said meekly, "The man I was with, Tim, he's Penny's husband . . . while she's in hospital I thought it might cheer him up to go out for a meal. It doesn't mean anything."

The explanation sounded perfectly plausible. Alix believed her, particularly since there had been no evidence in recent times that Tansie had other lovers. The only man Alix had given some thought to from time to time as being a possible lover was Herb. Alix had eventually discarded even that idea. Tansie never had anything nice to say about him and therefore Alix could not imagine her sleeping with him either.

Much later, while undressing in Tansie's bedroom, Alix reflected that over three years had passed since they'd first met. Out of the corner of her eye, she caught a glimpse of Tansie who stood naked in the dim light. With a wry smile she recalled the dramatic change her life had taken because of Tansie. A change she could not have foreseen even in her wildest imagination. Periodically she still wondered whether she would ever regret that Tansie walked into her life and expanded it to a horizon she had never thought possible. No, she decided, she would never regret it. She smiled as she thought that, regardless of what the future held, with Tansie around it would never be boring. Moments later she slipped into bed and into Tansie's arms.

A few days later, Alix wondered whether or not to go to the Symphony Orchestra ball. Tansie had already said that she didn't want to go because she couldn't think of a suitable escort. She was in one of her contrary moods and nothing Alix would say or do could make Tansie change her mind. Alix's other regular escorts and friends were all busy that night. She smiled as she recalled that she had never taken the same partner twice to this particular function. Not even her husband.

But Jesse knew what to do when Alix told her that she had finally decided to give the ball a miss all together.

"If finding a partner is a problem, I'll be happy to escort you," Jesse laughed.

For a brief moment, Alix cast her a horrified look. She can't possibly be serious, she thought. Then she laughed. "You're on, Jesse! If you can do it, so can I!"

Jesse raised her eyebrows, teasing her just a little. "Now, on a more practical note . . . what are you going to wear?"

Alix smiled knowingly and, keeping up the playful mood, said, "You'll see . . . a little something I picked up in Berlin a few months ago. What about you?"

"I don't know . . . I'll have to think about it."

"Don't think," Alix said. "Wear that turquoise dress you wore for your birthday party." As though she could see Jesse right now as she had looked then, she added, "You have lovely eyes, you know, and that colour especially suits you."

"What a compliment . . . thank you." Jesse smiled as she tried to work out what had provoked Alix into saying something like that. But remembering that Alix had paid her other compliments, she decided that it meant nothing more than that.

Alix was delighted when she noted afterwards just how much fun she had had. During the evening, Alix had also noticed that they weren't the only single sex couple.

When Alix pointed it out to Jesse, Jesse laughed. "It just

shows you, people in the art world know how to live."

"So it would appear," Alix replied, wondering whether it would have been different in a gathering of parents from the exclusive private schools her children attended. Although she attended few of the social gatherings the school put on for the parents, she had a fair idea how they would react. With an inward smile, she thought maybe one day she would take a female partner to a function like that.

After the ball, Alix and Jesse tried to see each other once a week. They had much in common and Alix found her to be a stimulating and enjoyable companion. Alix also greatly admired Jesse for standing up for her beliefs and for the relentless work she did for women who did not have the opportunities she had. She had to admit that Jesse was far more her intellectual and emotional equal than Tansie. But the fundamental difference between the two women was her feelings towards them. In Jesse she had found her match but she was very much in love with Tansie.

Alix intermittently thought about the possibility of loving another woman if something ever happened between her and Tansie. At times, she thought she could not. At other times she believed she could and possibly would one day if her relationship with Tansie ended. Tansie had opened a door for her and had shown her the magic of a close relationship between two women.

Towards the end of October, Alix returned to Berlin to supervise the recording of the music for Marta's film *Eva*. At the last minute, John decided to accompany her, saying that he needed a break from his domestic bliss!

The moment they stepped outside Berlin's terminal, he drew up the collar of the overcoat Alix had told him to bring. A couple of days before their arrival, the city had experienced an unusually early snowfall and the temperature had dropped to below zero degrees. He grumbled about the freezing conditions but admitted as they rode into the city that the snow gave it a wonderfully romantic feel.

"Are you working up to something?" Alix laughed, recalling his endless pursuit of women.

"Maybe!" he said although he had already decided to keep an open mind where women were concerned.

Later when John met some of the actresses from the movie, he groaned. "How can you do this to me?" he wailed. "All those beautiful women and they don't even want to look at me! Let alone take their clothes off!"

"Shave off your moustache . . . it might help," Marta told him tongue in cheek.

For the first few days, the three of them sat in the auditorium of the Philharmonie, Berlin's concert hall. They listened to the Philharmonic rehearse and, from time to time, either Alix or John interrupted to discuss some changes with the conductor. When they eventually listened to the first tape in Marta's music room, they were all delighted with the result.

As soon as it was finished, John got to his feet. He formally shook Alix's and then Marta's hand. In a jocular manner, he said, "It was a pleasure working with you, ladies . . . now I have a date with Katarina Reichenbach!" Looking at Marta, he added, "Would you mind if I borrowed your Merc for the night?"

"Not at all," Marta said, and giving Alix a conspiratorial wink, added, "Good luck!"

"Do you know something that I don't?" Alix asked the moment the door had shut behind him.

"I've grown quite fond of him, you know, but I expect h can take care of himself," Marta mused in jest. "Katari lives with Candy Sassoon. I expect she'll be going to din as well!"

"The woman who plays Eva in your movie?"

"That's the one."

On the flight home, John told Alix that this would be his one and only trip overseas. He had seen and done enough, he informed her, and it had been too bloody cold for his liking.

"Maybe it was the temperature of your female companions rather than the weather that caused your drastic decision," Alix replied but did not seek further details. In her view, the trip had been most successful.

From the moment Alix returned from Berlin, Tansie became quarrelsome and contrary. Tansie gave one or another excuse for her behaviour but, in Alix's view, none of them had any substance. Generally, Alix listened but tried not to respond. Tansie continued to threaten suicide and Alix was fearful that she might do it yet. Her only comfort was that Tansie was still seeing Dr Callahan. Alix clung to the hope that Tansie's emotions would one day lead her down a more even path.

But after a time, Alix's patience began to be severely tested. She knew that she could not go on like this indefi-itely. Her love was still there, but not the willingness to sit ck and accept Tansie's irrational behaviour. She made v allowances for it but intellectually she could not ehend it. And, no matter how robust and resilient is, she had her own needs and vulnerabilities. At nt moment, they were not being met.

y through November, when it looked as though ng weather was finally improving, Tansie invited Alix, Felix, Kate and a number of children ouse for a weekend. Alix hoped that they w peaceful days together.

e didn't seem to be in a peaceful mood.

She was edgy from the moment they arrived. She disagreed with everything Alix said and regularly retreated to the guest bedroom to sulk. On Sunday night, Tansie stormed from the house and took off in Felix's Range Rover. Alix's efforts to try and stop her were useless. Alix had no idea what had actually pushed Tansie over the edge.

Alix went back inside and fell on to the couch.

"Why do you keep hitting your head against a brick wall?" Kate asked with exasperation. "Don't you think it's time you got out of this relationship or at least took a closer look at where it's going?"

"Where Tansie's concerned, I seem to have lost all rationality," Alix sighed.

"You have, pet," Kate sighed, deeply concerned with where Alix's and Tansie's relationship was really going.

Alix was still awake and pacing the floor when the call came at four o'clock in the morning.

"Where are you?" Alix asked.

"As if you bloody cared," Tansie shrieked, her voice already several notes higher than usual. "You ignored me all fucking weekend and treated me like shit . . . why did you even bother to invite me?"

"You wanted to come along," Alix replied and thought, well, at least she was safe. "We can't go on like this . . . enough is enough, Tansie," she said impatiently.

When Tansie continued to rant at the other end of the telephone, on impulse, Alix told her that she would hang up and did. She felt terrible about doing it but realised that it would be destructive to continue the conversation. Lying in bed later, she wondered why she was still hesitant about taking even more drastic action where Tansie was concerned. Was it guilt, she wondered, or the responsibility she felt towards Tansie? Had she not done everything she could to help Tansie? Suddenly she wasn't sure any more and a feeling of uncertainty about their relationship sat heavily on her shoulders. She loved Tansie and wanted to do the right thing for both of them. At the moment, severing ties seemed the wisest thing, though she did not want to do it. But, deep inside her, she knew that the day may well come when she would have no option.

Moments after Alix returned home from the beach house the following afternoon, Tansie rang. "I just wanted to tell you that Dr Callahan has put me into hospital for observation. He was very worried about me when I saw him this morning. I haven't stopped crying ever since I came home. He says I'm suffering from acute depression."

"I'm sorry to hear it."

"Oh, Alix, I feel so awful! What am I doing? What is happening to me? Am I losing my mind? Please Alix, help me."

"I care very much what happens to you, but right now I feel as though I'm drowning. I don't know how to help you any more," Alix replied, as a sudden thought struck her. "How would you feel if we both had a chat to Dr Callahan. Maybe . . ."

"He's my shrink, I won't allow it!"

"Maybe he can tell me how we can work on this together," Alix concluded the sentence she had started earlier.

"You won't let me lead a normal life, so how can I . . ."

Alix felt more than just a little exasperated but hid it well. "If that's how you feel, then let's part with some dignity before we totally destroy each other."

Alix hung up seconds after Tansie did. She picked up the receiver again and rang Jesse. Jesse was free after four o'clock and arranged to see Alix at home.

Over a cup of coffee, Alix related the events of the weekend and concluded, "In the end I just hung up on her but I never meant for her to end up in hospital."

"You couldn't have stopped it, Alix," Jesse assured her. "I think it's been on the cards for some time. Sooner or later she was going to suffer another breakdown. Her emotions are still very volatile despite Dr Callahan's good work. There is no such thing as a miracle cure." After a short pause, she continued, "But to get back to her behaviour, in order for Tansie to block out her horrendous childhood part of her mind has never grown up. It's probably still at the level of a four-year-old, although not in all respects. We're therefore not dealing with a rational, balanced adult."

When Alix remained silent, Jesse continued. "You have shown her great love and caring. However, if she believes she is not loved, she will repeat the behaviour she knows makes you most angry. When you finally lose your temper, it confirms in her mind that she is in fact unloved and unwanted. It would not occur to her that she pushed you in that direction in the first place."

"You know, one part of what I found very appealing about her was her childlike manner, her charmingly seductive powers." Alix replied softly. "At least, until I realised that she wasn't half as fragile and vulnerable as I thought she was. While I don't blame her for her volatility, there are times when I think that she actually knows what she is doing."

"You're probably right," Jesse said thoughtfully. She was just a little uncomfortable with this conversation. Douglas had told Jesse that Tansie's check-up some months back had been for the sole purpose of finding out whether she could get pregnant and that she was thinking about getting married. It distressed Jesse that medical ethics did not allow her to tell Alix what she knew. By not knowing Tansie's intentions, Alix's agony was only prolonged. Jesse couldn't change that, she knew. What she could try to do was make the fall a little less traumatic for Alix when it finally came.

"What are you thinking about?" Alix asked when she noted Jesse's far away look.

"Alix, the day might come when you have to accept that Tansie may never be what you want her to be," Jesse replied gently.

"Maybe I just haven't done enough," Alix sighed.

"Don't even think such a thing," Jesse said. As they held each other's gaze, Jesse added, "You must keep in mind that Tansie had little love shown to her in her youth and simply doesn't know how to deal with it regardless of how sincerely it is offered to her."

"You mean it wouldn't matter how much anyone loved her, she would never be comfortable with it?" Alix asked.

"Yes . . . something like that," Jesse replied. "You see, many people will repeat the emotional pattern they learnt in their youth in their adult life, whether it is an appropriate emotional response or not."

Alix shivered. "I have learnt many things reading those books you gave me and, yet, I can't quite comprehend what it really all means."

Jesse smiled. "Psychiatrists spend years analysing the mind and even then they don't always comprehend it."

"I suppose I am being rather impatient," Alix too smiled. "However, no matter where it will eventually lead me, I do need to understand whether Tansie's anguish is a result of early childhood abuse or whether it's me who provokes it."

"I understand that," Jesse said with some distress. "However, I must add that some people do recover from such trauma, in the sense that they are able to cope adequately with or without the help of a psychiatrist,"

Jesse continued. "Anyway, don't be too hard on yourself where Tansie is concerned. I'm sure you have tried everything humanly possible."

"I would like to think so but maybe I haven't," Alix replied.

Afterwards, Alix tried to ring Tansie at the hospital but was told that she was out to dinner. The next morning, she was told that Tansie had checked out.

"Thank you," Alix said and replaced the receiver. Chewing her bottom lip, she wondered what to do next. In the end she decided to go and visit her.

She found Tansie sitting at the kitchen table, staring out the window and nervously drawing on a cigarette. A half-empty bottle of wine stood in front of her. She looked at the slouched figure and, again, Alix saw what she had seen the day they first met. Despite everything she now knew, her heart involuntarily missed a few beats and she felt an uncomfortable tugging deep down inside her. How could she desert a child?

Alix approached the table and smiled. "How are you?"

Tansie's vacant eyes filled with tears and, as they brimmed over, ran down her hollow cheeks. Slowly she lifted her arms and, putting them around Alix's waist, she rested her head on her stomach.

"Dr Callahan only let me out of hospital today after I promised that I would check into Quentin's tomorrow. That's some sort of clinic where apparently the rich go for their nervous breakdowns. He has arranged it all . . . I'm supposed to stay for two weeks," Tansie murmured.

"I'll drive up to see you at the weekend," Alix comforted her, gently running her hand through Tansie's hair. Her own simple gesture reminded her just how their relationship had started and later progressed. Alix couldn't give up just now.

"No . . . you can't!" Tansie cried. "I mean, the clinic apparently has a policy that does not allow visitors or phone calls for that matter. We're not supposed to have any contact with the outside world. Dr Callahan said it would be detrimental to the patients."

Alix was surprised to hear that, but, because she didn't know any different she believed it. She trusted Dr Callahan. It didn't occur to Alix that Tansie might not be telling it how it was. "How do you feel about that?"

"I don't want to go but I'll go anyway," Tansie sighed. "Dr Callahan said there was an excellent psychiatrist there who could work with me on a more intensive level during my stay. Maybe that's what I need." Later she added, "I really want to sort myself out. I know I can't go through life living on a tightrope all the time and never knowing when I'll lose my balance. I've hurt too many people, you in particular. I want to rectify that." Tears began to brim in her eyes again. In her mind, she was convinced that she meant what she said. What she didn't know was that her mind was too cluttered to see any attempt successfully through to the end.

Alix was both surprised and delighted by Tansie's rational statement. Often in the past, Alix had felt that Tansie only saw the psychiatrist to please her and in fact had resented seeing him. And, if Tansie had had a particularly harrowing time with him, Alix felt responsible for putting her through the trauma. She wondered whether it would not have been better to keep the lid tightly on the box and simply accept Tansie the way she was. Initially, that had been an option. A soft option, Alix thought. Now it was too late to stop.

They walked to one of the Italian bistros in the Toorak Village for dinner and, afterwards, returned to Alix's house for the night.

Alix watched from her bed as Tansie bustled in and out of the bathroom, taking off her clothes as she went. She is such a beautiful and talented woman, Alix thought, and yet, she just didn't seem to be able to get her life together. It was so wasteful and most unfair.

When Tansie dived under the covers moments later, Alix closed her arms around her and held her tightly.

Tansie sensuously moulded her body into her lover's and gave out what sounded like a small child's happy gurgle.

"What are you going to do when I'm away at the 'nut' farm?" Tansie asked, breaking the silence between them.

"Nut farm?" Alix laughed. "That's a bit dramatic, don't you think?"

"I'm sure that is what every sane person calls it," Tansie chortled. "Alix, with Christmas coming up soon, do you think the two of us could go away somewhere for a holiday? We haven't had any real time together for far too long."

"Where would you like to go?"

"Anywhere, as long as it's just the two of us on a secluded island," Tansie replied.

"That shouldn't be too difficult. The children have decided that they want to spend their holiday at the beach," Alix smiled. "I have to go to New York just after Christmas. So, how about coming with me and once I'm through with the music publishers, we can fly down to Jamaica for a week or so. We can even go skiing in Aspen afterwards." With a wide smile, she added, "I think I'll take a whole month off."

"Oh, Alix, how wonderful . . . oh, I can't wait . . . and, you'll see, once I come back from the 'loony bin' I'll be everything you've ever wanted me to be," Tansie babbled.

Alix wanted to believe it and believed it. Later she asked, "How are the sculptures coming along for your next show? It opens on the tenth of December, doesn't it?"

"It does," Tansie confirmed. "As long as the foundry doesn't let me down, everything will be ready on time. I have three or four wood sculptures, several sandstone and marble ones and the rest are bronze."

"It'll be a great success," Alix said and, drawing Tansie closer, began to nibble at her earlobe. "You smell lovely, you sexy thing," Alix whispered.

"I splashed nearly a whole bottle of your Oscar de la Renta perfume all over me," Tansie giggled happily as she slowly let her hand wander over Alix's stomach.

Chapter 23

Masses of summer flowers lined the edge of the driveway leading towards the main building at Quentin's. A few people strolled through the gardens in no apparent haste.

Tansie liked what she saw and suddenly couldn't wait to check in. After a brief meeting with the doctor in charge, she went to her room and ran a bath. She lowered herself into the soft soap bubbles when an involuntary cry escaped from her chest and she called out Alix's name.

For no apparent reason, her earlier enthusiasm suddenly sapped right out of her. Slowly she submerged her body but came up spluttering when she felt herself being pulled up by the arms. "If you know what's good for you, you won't try that again," a soft female voice muttered. "This establishment doesn't take kindly to such behaviour . . . you'll end up in a real loony bin if you don't watch it. By the way my name is Tory . . . we're room-mates."

Tansie gave Tory a disconcerted glare. "What do you mean we're room-mates?" Tansie exclaimed angrily. "I'm not sharing a room with anybody!"

"Sorry," Tory grinned, showing two rows of beautiful white teeth. "House-rules dictate that no person is to be on his or her own. We're lucky they don't take away our belts!"

Tansie studied the young girl for a moment then she turned her back on her. Room-mates or not, Tansie thought, she didn't have to like Tory.

During the first week Tansie was at the clinic, she attended group therapy sessions, spent a few nights in Tory's arms, cried out for Alix in her sleep and slept with Herb at the local Motel when he came to visit her for the weekend. That she had lied so blatantly to Alix about not being allowed to have visitors was of little concern to Tansie. Alix would never know.

Tory was sitting on the fence when Herb pulled up to deliver Tansie back to the clinic after lunch on Sunday. He looked miserable and was not happy about leaving her for another week.

"Don't bother driving me to the house," Tansie snapped at him, oblivious to his distress. "I'll walk back with Tory." She was out of the car before he could reply and began to walk up the driveway.

It took Tory only a few seconds to catch up with her. "Is he the guy you're going to marry?" Tory asked.

"No!"

"Just as well, he looks like a real creep," Tory said and laughed. "How many other lovers have you got tucked away?"

"None of your business!"

"What's he got that your girlfriend doesn't have, other than the obvious?" Tory continued.

"The offer of marriage and a chance to lead a normal life," Tansie replied tersely, contradicting her earlier statement and regretting having told Tory about Alix.

"You're a fool, Tansie," she cried in disgust.

"Shut up, just shut up! What the fuck do you understand!" Tansie shouted and clamped her hands around the younger woman's upper arms and shook her violently.

"You're some screwed-up lady," Tory muttered, pushing Tansie away and rubbing her sore arms. "You don't have the guts to stand up and come to terms with your sexuality

. . . it's sad, real sad." She shook her head slowly. She couldn't believe that anyone could be stupid enough to give up love for supposed normality.

During the whole of their second week at Quentin's, the two women ignored each other, except for the polite smiles they exchanged at the dinner table or during group therapy.

Driving home at the end of her two-week stay at Quentin's Tansie felt calm and ready to do what she had resolved to do. After dumping her bags inside the door, she rang Herb and invited him over for dinner. Then she tried to ring Alix but was told that she would be in Sydney at least until the following Wednesday. Tansie took the news with more poise than she had expected.

Tansie had decided she would marry Herb straight after her holiday with Alix in Jamaica. Her only interest in the marriage was to become somebody again: a socially acceptable married woman – Mrs Herb Mullins. Despite the good work she had done with Dr Callahan, she acknowledged that he had been helpful in many ways, he would never convince her that she was a whole person without being married. Her belief that she was an outcast and a freak because of her deplorable background was so deeply ingrained, it would take a psychiatrist years to convince her otherwise. Tansie didn't have years to wait.

She was not unhappy about marrying him but did not look forward to the intimate aspects of the marriage.

Every time she went to bed with him, she reflected on how her body responded to women far more naturally than it did to men. During each encounter with Herb and despite his pawings and gruntings, she tried to eclipse thoughts of her women lovers and of Alix, in particular, but without much success. In the end, she used her vivid imagination to create a female lover in order to tolerate intercourse with

Herb. She hoped that she would get pregnant quickly. After that, she would find an excuse to no longer sleep with him.

Alix didn't miss Tansie as much as she had in the past, although she was never far from her mind. Deep down, Alix knew they needed a break from each other and comforted herself with the knowledge that they were soon to spend some weeks away together after Christmas. And, she never forgot that Tansie was at Quentin's for a specific purpose.

Two days before Tansie was due to return from her stint at the clinic, Alix prepared to go to Sydney. As it was, Jesse too was going to be in Sydney at least part of the time to give a conference paper.

As soon as she checked into the Hyatt Hotel in Sydney, Alix proceeded to the music room which had been especially set aside for her. Without preparation, she brought her hands down on to the keyboard with a deafening crash. She was cross with herself for having agreed to do this documentary on contemporary composers and the *presto furioso* she now played was well matched to her mood.

"Superb, superb," a male voice suddenly shouted.

Alix swivelled around to face the intruder. It was Silvan Moreau and his film crew.

Approaching her, he clapped his hands. "That's the best footage we've had in a long time," he cried in French. "You were magnificent, cherie." The twinkle in his black eyes suggested that he knew exactly what impact he had on women. He was as suave as only a Frenchman could be with some North African charm thrown in.

He extended his hand and said, "I am Silvan Moreau. I look forward to working with you, Madame Clemenger." His lips drew into a seductive smile.

"Enchanté," Alix replied returning his smile. Nobody

had called her Madame Clemenger for ages and it amused her that Silvan should use that formal term. "Please, call me Alix . . . Silvan."

Although the work turned out to be more exhausting than Alix had expected and, despite her initial annoyance, she began to enjoy it. She thrived on the challenge offered by this eccentric and often difficult director. She never knew what he wanted from one moment to the next. Silvan did not believe in scripts, he had told her right from the start. In the end she decided it had all been worthwhile.

Now that his work was finished, Silvan was much easier to get along with. When he invited her to join him for dinner the evening before she was to return home, she accepted. He was a charming and entertaining dinner companion and they had no problems communicating. After they'd left the restaurant and were back in his chauffeur-driven Rolls, Silvan leant across and said, "I would like you to come home with me."

"Thank you Silvan, but I won't," she replied.

"Is there someone else? Do you have another date this evening?" Silvan asked, a slight sullen line around his lips.

"I do."

"He is a very lucky man," he grinned.

Alix smiled. "I think so too."

Silvan kissed her outside the hotel and continued, "Maybe some other time. Please look me up when you're next in Paris if you're there before the film is finished. Otherwise I'll see you at the preview screening, oui?"

"Peut-être," she smiled.

As she walked into the lobby, she spotted Jesse with whom she had finally caught up earlier that morning and arranged to have a drink. So far neither had had the time even for a quick chat. With a smile, Alix noted that Jesse looked her usual dignified self in her light tan linen dress and jacket.

"I take it that was the famous Monsieur Moreau," Jesse commented, adding, "he's very sexy."

"You mean you actually notice men?" Seemingly automatically, Alix fluttered her long eyelashes at Jesse. Seconds later, she wondered what had possessed her to make that gesture.

"Noticing and doing something about it are two totally different things!" Jesse smiled.

"You're right . . . I didn't do anything about it either," Alix responded, a little unsettled. But given the jocular mood, she continued lightly, "Much to his chagrin, I might add."

Sitting in comfortable armchairs and sipping cognac, the women exchanged their latest news.

Eventually Alix spoke with unusual hesitancy, "When Silvan asked me if there was someone in my life I said 'yes' but without correcting his assumption that it was a man. By remaining silent, I feel as though I'm betraying my love for Tansie."

Jesse put her hand over Alix's. "No you're not," Jesse assured her. "You know you love her. Telling others serves no purpose except fuelling their greed for gossip."

"When I first met Tansie, I wanted to shout out to the world just how happy I was."

"Would you have done that had you fallen in love with a man instead of a woman?" Jesse asked.

"I doubt it," Alix replied.

"We can achieve far more for the gay community without hanging a banner around our necks or marching in the streets," Jesse said. "My aim is to change the view of the world at large and, although, if it has to be done I'd probably march with them, I believe radicalism generally only helps to substantiate the negative views people already hold. It is more important for people to see us as regular, loving and caring women who happen to prefer partners of the same sex."

"Maybe this is a rather romantic view but, as far as I'm concerned, love should not cause adverse repercussions to anyone's life."

"Who knows, maybe one day everyone will think like that," Jesse smiled.

From time to time during the course of the conversation, Alix's thoughts wandered to Tansie and the great times they had shared at the beginning of their relationship.

"What're you thinking about?" Jesse asked after a short pause.

"I was thinking how easy and comfortable it is to be with you." More slowly she added, "Just like it used to be with Tansie."

For a moment Jesse contemplated her response. In the end, she chose a casual approach. "It's always nice to start a new relationship. There are no emotional ties to complicate matters. It's a time of discovery and learning about another human being."

"Before boredom and complacency set in?" Alix smiled, raising her eyebrows in a teasing manner.

"Something like that," Jesse confirmed.

Resting her elbows on the table and cupping her chin, she held Jesse's gaze. "Maybe I just like the idea of being in love."

"That's not the worst thing you can do." Jesse smiled, an amused twinkle in her eyes. "Do you have anybody in particular in mind to fall in love with?"

"Not at the moment." To herself she thought, I am in

love, how can I fall in love with someone else? Alix wasn't sure how to respond to Jesse's question but decided to keep the conversation light and casual. "Jesse, did you always know that you were a lesbian?" Alix asked.

"After my first experiment with a young lad when I was at boarding school, I decided that was not for me!"

"With all the groping and fumbling that goes on at that age, no wonder you didn't like it," Alix laughed.

Jesse too laughed. "That did cross my mind at the time. Some years later, I allowed myself another faux-pas. After that men were out and I haven't changed my mind since."

"And, you have no regrets I take it?" Alix smiled.

"No regrets at all," Jesse confirmed.

Chapter 24

As planned, Tansie's exhibition opened on the tenth of December. Due to the publicity Alix's PR lady had organised for Tansie and the success of her last exhibition, Melbourne's establishment turned out in droves. Nearly a hundred guests mingled in the gallery, sipped icy cold champagne and delicately popped little savouries between their pursed lips. While Tansie wandered around as though in a daze and not quite believing some of the extraordinarily favourable comments she heard, Alix moved from group to group engaging in the necessary small talk.

When Jesse arrived, Alix excused herself and went to greet her. Handing her a glass of champagne, they strolled through the gallery together, discussing and admiring each work of art. Jesse particularly liked a bronze sculpture of a woman and a child.

"This is superb," she exclaimed. Noting a sudden flicker of knowing mischief in Alix's eyes and remembering the sculpture of the little boy Alix had given her for her birthday, she smiled. "Don't even think about it," she said and moved towards the back of the gallery where the sales desk was.

Alix followed her. "How do you know what I was thinking about?" she asked lightly, keen to prolong the recollection of Jesse's last birthday.

"Past experience."

"Fair enough." Their eyes momentarily locked as each smiled.

Before the evening was over, only two sculptures remained

unsold. This not only delighted Alix but convinced her that, having achieved such enormous success, Tansie would finally come to think of herself as a whole person. It had crossed Alix's mind once or twice that Tansie may have felt as though she was walking in Alix's shadow and that her volatile behaviour was due to resentment. It would be interesting to see whether things would change now that Tansie's second exhibition had been so successful.

Alix was convinced, nevertheless, that their relationship could only improve and stabilise and that they could both look towards a happy future together. Although Tansie had told Alix little of what she had done during her stint at Quentin's, given how happy and calm she had been when she returned, Alix could only assume that it had helped her enormously. Had she known what decisions Tansie had made, she would have been devastated.

Alix, Felix and the children left the city the day they finished their school year and went to the beach house. Tansie said she had a few things she wanted to do but would join Alix a couple of days before Christmas. Straight after Christmas, Alix and Tansie would fly to New York and Jamaica for their holiday.

The weekend before Christmas, Jesse rang to see whether she could wander down for the weekend. Alix told her she would be a very welcome visitor.

Jesse arrived early on Friday morning and, moments later, the two women were out on the tennis court. Alix could not remember another time when she had belted the balls to her partner as she did now. She showed no mercy, but then, Jesse was more than able to handle herself. Soaked with perspiration and gasping for air, they were even after four sets. They agreed to play the deciding set the following day.

Later they went waterskiing and, there too, Jesse was Alix's equal. Letting go of the rope as Felix drew the boat near the shore, Alix asked, "What other surprises do you have in store for me?"

"If I told you, it wouldn't be a surprise any more," Jesse replied.

"How silly of me!" Alix laughed and handed the skis to Felix to stow in the boat.

Dinner was eaten outside on the terrace and, given there were eight children of various ages, it was a noisy affair. Alix rarely ate with the children. More often than not, she was either out or was too busy to do so. But Jesse had requested that they join the younger members of the household. From time to time, Jesse and Maxine had seriously considered having a child together and discussed the possibility. In the end, nothing had come of it. Maxine had started to have second thoughts and Jesse hadn't pushed it. When the relationship finished, Jesse was glad that there had been no children. Now she enjoyed other people's.

During dinner, Alix noticed just how comfortable Jesse was around her offspring and how easily they accepted her. They bantered with her as though they had known her for many years. In particular, they responded to the cordial and genuine respect she showed them. She treated them as people with views and opinions as legitimate as any adult's.

After dinner, the two women retreated to the formal sitting room and Felix took the children for a spot of night fishing.

"Do you have any piano sheet music for four hands floating around?" Jesse asked casually.

Alix gulped. "No wonder you wouldn't tell me what other surprises you had in store!"

It took Alix a few moments to find some appropriate

notes and put them on the stand. They sat down on the stool together. "Let's go," Alix said to Jesse and rested her hands on the keyboard.

As they played, Alix occasionally cast Jesse a sideways glance. Her earlier surprise at how well Jesse played, soon turned into genuine pleasure and admiration.

"You're wonderful," Alix cried when they had finished and threw her arms around Jesse.

Jesse returned the embrace and, with a smile said, "Coming from a real pianist, that's quite a compliment." Her gaze was honest when it met Alix's as she took Alix's hand into her own and playfully stroked the inside of her palm.

In turn, Alix felt a warmth spreading through her that she had not felt for a long time. Alix was well aware what it meant but, since her love and loyalties lay with Tansie, she tried to ignore it.

Alix dropped her hands back on to the keyboard. Moments later, the room was filled with the most exquisite sounds of Chopin's stormy *Revolutionary* étude. Her touch was smooth and flawless as she used her own rhythmic freedom. She was half-way through a piece by Rossini when she noticed a smile on Jesse's face.

"Why are you smiling?" Alix asked without interrupting her playing and without taking her eyes off Jesse. The intimacy from moments earlier was still with them but, not quite sure what to make of it, Alix kept a straight face.

Jesse saw the twinkle in her eyes but she too decided to ignore it for the time being. "I'm just wondering why you're playing this particular music . . . it's not played very often," Jesse replied.

"Do you know what it is?"

"Rossini, *Sins Of My Old Age*," Jesse said. "What real

follies do you intend to engage in?"

"Never you mind."

Jesse raised her eyebrows but didn't reply. She was well aware how attached Alix still was to Tansie and how much she wanted that relationship to work. She would try not to confuse Alix further, although she now knew that she had grown more than just fond of her.

Alix was sorry when Jesse had to leave. She would have liked to have Jesse there when Kate, Jackie and her next door neighbour Debbie came to play tennis that afternoon.

It had been the first hot day of summer and the four women were exhausted when they walked off the tennis court. Rubbing various parts of their aching bodies, they complained about how unfit they were. Despite her workload, Alix was the only one who exercised regularly.

Remembering the work-out on the tennis court she had had with Jesse, Alix gave them a superior smile. "Wait until next year, I'll have a real treat for you then," she said.

"If it's Martina Navratilova you've invited, I'm heading for the hills," Jackie cried.

"Now that's a thought . . . I wonder if she's free?" Alix muttered in response and reached for a glass of champagne from the tray Felix had just brought out on to the terrace.

Downing it in one gulp, Kate cried, "You saved my life, Felix. What would any of us do without you!"

"What indeed, ma'am," Felix joked and filled her glass again before she could ask. Addressing Alix, he added, "Who is dining here tonight?"

"I think there's just me, but you'd better check with the kids as to how many of them are staying," Alix laughed.

"I already have, there are nine."

"We're light tonight!" Alix responded.

When Felix had retreated into the house, the four women

continued their banter. Suddenly, out of nowhere, Herb Mullins and Tansie appeared in the double doorway which lead from the main sitting room out on to the terrace.

Chewing on a bit of gum, Herb barely managed to utter a, "Hi". Flicking his wrist limply, he gave them the semblance of a wave.

Alix couldn't help but raise her eyebrows at the insufferable manner with which he had made his appearance. Fortunately for him, her impeccable breeding prevailed over her impulse to be derisive. She got up and, kissing Tansie on the cheek, said to Herb, "Would you like a cup of coffee?"

"Naaa . . . I'll be goin' then," he replied and departed the same way he'd arrived.

Alix shook her head and watched him leave. Herb was indeed insufferable and she couldn't help but wonder why Tansie still saw him. Surely, Alix thought, he had nothing to give Tansie.

"What a treat he is!" Kate groaned. "Next time I complain about my husband, remind me that there are worse than him!" Looking at Tansie, she added, "What are you doing with this bloke anyway? You're a very attractive woman and you're financially secure. Not to mention your two highly successful solo exhibitions and just about everything else you could want." The latter part she added with a twist in her voice, leaving no doubt that she meant Alix. "What can he possibly offer you?"

"Nothing much, I admit," Tansie replied as she sat down in the chair next to Alix. Lamely she added, "Nothing . . . except marriage!"

An immediate silence fell upon the women, as they glanced from one to the other. Kate thought she'd choke and reached for the water decanter, speechless.

"You're not seriously considering that?" Jackie rasped, horrified, as she too thought of Alix and what this could do to her.

"Don't be silly," Tansie replied breezily. With a throaty chuckle, she added, "I don't think there is any love lost between you girls and him . . . he thinks you're all snobs with nothing else to do but play tennis!"

"You had me worried there for a minute," Debbie chirped. "As for his views about us, I can live with that."

"Herb is a handbag and not even a good one at that . . . that's all." Tansie never blinked an eyelid as the lie fell from her lips.

Alix had listened to the exchange but remained silent. She wondered what Tansie was really up to and why she had arrived at the beach house sooner than planned. Had she perhaps been too confident too quickly after Tansie's successful exhibition? Or had she missed something? Alix wasn't sure as an inner tension began to grip her. She knew that it wasn't Mullins' presence which had unsettled her. Tansie had made it quite clear that she had no interest in the man.

As though she had at least guessed in part what was going through Alix's mind, Tansie leant towards her and kissed her lightly on the cheek. To the other women she announced cheerfully, "Let's drink to Alix. I want to thank her for my success as a serious sculptor . . . something only she ever believed was possible."

"We'll drink to that," the women responded in unison. "And, to Mullins' departure . . . take a double swig for that one, girls," Kate added and drained her glass.

Soon afterwards, Jackie and Debbie finished their drinks and rose to go. Groaning somewhat, Debbie exclaimed, "I won't be able to walk for a week . . . but thanks for the tennis anyway." Rounding up their various offspring, Debbie and Jackie left together promising to return the next day for a re-match.

Alix walked them to their cars, leaving Kate and Tansie behind. In her usual blunt way, Kate said, "I don't know what game it is you're playing now, Tansie, but to arrive here with that moron is not playing it fair."

"I don't know what you're talking about!"

"Alix adores you and has just about given you the world as you well know," Kate said, a touch of anger in her tone.

"Yes . . . she has," Tansie admitted with some embarrassment. Even she knew that it would be stupid to disagree. Especially after what she had said about Alix earlier.

"So what the hell is your problem?" Kate pressed on. The sad look in Alix's eyes earlier on had not escaped her.

"She's a woman!" Tansie cried.

"We both know you've had relationships with other women in the past. I assume you prefer women," Kate responded with impatience. "Don't you think it's time you accepted that fact and took your responsibilities more seriously?" Getting to her feet, she added, "But, if that's not what you want, then get the hell out of Alix's life . . . you don't deserve her!"

"How dare . . ." Tansie started but Kate had already turned her back.

Alix had barely sat down again when Tansie moved her chair closer and reached for her hands.

"I missed you," she said softly. "I hope you don't mind that I came earlier."

"Of course not," Alix replied, smiled and brushed the back of her hand over Tansie's cheek. "Let's go for a swim before it gets too dark."

Together they made their way down the narrow path to

the beach and dived into the cool water. Swimming beside each other, they quickly put distance between themselves and the beach. As they swam further and further out, Alix recalled the first time they had made love on this very beach and how she had subsequently swum out to sea.

Suddenly, Alix felt involuntary tears stinging her eyes. Nearly three years had passed since that first night and, during those years, she had experienced some of the happiest times she could remember. So, why was she now crying? Alix didn't know but obviously something was troubling her. Perhaps she had lost faith in the future! She was rarely pessimistic and those feelings alone worried her.

When they came to one of the boats some distance from the beach, they reached for a nearby anchor-chain simultaneously.

Holding on to the chain with one hand, Tansie put her free hand around Alix's waist. "I love you," she said and lowered her lips on to Alix's.

When they finally drew apart gasping for air, Alix gave Tansie a long, and somewhat sad, look. "Is this the beginning of the rest of our lives?" she asked softly.

"I hope so, my love," Tansie confirmed and drew Alix back into her arms.

After a short pause, Alix added, "You see, I can't live in fear for the rest of my life that one day you'll . . ."

"If you could only trust me then you'd find out just how committed I am to you," Tansie interrupted. "I love you, more than anybody or anything . . . we will never be apart." As though to confirm her words, she tilted her head forward and kissed the side of Alix's neck, tasting the salt water.

Alix closed her eyes and with her free hand reached for Tansie's breasts and gently began to caress one after the other. She smiled, a smile Tansie could not see in the pale moonlight. "You've put on weight," Alix chuckled softly. "You're breasts are getting bigger."

Tansie just stopped herself from gasping. Then she allowed a soft gasp to escape from her lips. "I always knew that sooner or later Felix's wonderful Christmas pudding would catch up with me," she exclaimed.

Alix laughed half-heartedly. "Yeah . . . maybe," she said, thinking that they hadn't had any Christmas pudding yet. What if Tansie was pregnant again? Don't even think it, she scolded herself silently.

Alix looked up into the sky. A few clouds had started to scuttle back and forth over the moon. "Let's swim back," she said. "It'll be pitch black soon and I don't fancy groping my way back to shore," she added lightly and let go of the anchor-chain and Tansie at the same time.

Later, Alix wondered what it really was about Tansie that rendered her incapable of terminating this relationship. Probably still very much what had attracted her in the first place, she noted. Her childlike charm, enthusiasm and unpredictability appealed to her sense of adventure, probably because she herself was so staid, she thought with an inward smile. In her view, Tansie always had been, and still was, a breath of fresh air breezing in and out at her leisure. Even if the breath of fresh air was sometimes a little fresher than she would have liked, Alix could do nothing to change her feelings.

Chapter 25

Three days after Christmas, a blistering summer wind swept through the city, swirling dust and litter in all directions. Alix hated those hot steamy days and couldn't wait to get out of town and catch the flight to New York. The plane had barely soared into the sky when Alix reached for the champagne the steward offered and clicked her glass with Tansie's.

"Here's to a wonderful holiday," she said and smiled.

"It will be wonderful." Tansie looked happy and confident. She was excited at the prospect of spending some weeks just with Alix.

Tansie's excitement was contagious and Alix allowed herself the luxury of being caught up in it. She too wanted this holiday to be special.

After their flight finally touched down at Kennedy International, they were greeted by a heavy snowfall and their breath caught in their throats. Tansie groaned as the freezing wind blew her hair into her eyes but Alix was in seventh heaven. She almost shouted with joy as she walked outside, catching the delicate snowflakes on her tongue.

As soon as they had installed themselves in a suite on the fourth floor of the Hotel Pierre, the two women moved into each other's arms. It was spontaneous, and yet that simple gesture of affection soon turned into a spark of electricity so overwhelming it left them breathless. It was as though no time had passed since they had first become lovers. The attraction between them was still strong and passionate and time had not diminished it. They trembled in each other's arms, overcome by the sheer power of their emotions.

"Let's make sure nothing ever comes between us again," Tansie murmured. Holding Alix in her arms, Tansie moved towards the bed. Soon their hands and lips sought out the other's warm tingling skin through the fabric of their shirts.

Alix was instantly lulled into believing in the strength of their love. She felt energised beyond comprehension. She could not bear the pain the alternative would cause her. Whatever minor doubts she still had at the back of her mind vanished. She was once again ready to accept the charm of their relationship, regardless of what had happened in the past. She gave no thought to the future. This was here and now and nothing else mattered.

Alix took care of business on her first day in New York. After that, she was free to be with Tansie around the clock. With their arms linked, the two women walked from one exclusive shop on Fifth Avenue to the next, dodging the heavy snowfall and laughing when the wind turned their umbrella inside out. Other pedestrians who sloshed through the wet snow often cast them frowning glances. How could anybody be this happy in such weather? Alix and Tansie were and they were oblivious to the many stares.

Four days later, they caught a flight to Montego Bay. They were met by a chauffeur who drove them to the private villa Alix had rented on the beach. The villa's cook, maid and butler stood on the large front porch by way of welcome.

The sitting room and the main bedroom both overlooked a vast stretch of near-white sand and the crystal-clear water of the Caribbean sea beyond. The sun was about to set in a bright ball on the horizon, bathing the lush flourishing vegetation in a glow of red and orange. Their villa was only a few steps away from the beach and secluded from anybody's view. Their immediate surroundings vibrated with different sounds, exotic scents and the brightest of colours even in the fading daylight.

"This is truly magic, isn't it?" Alix drew deeply on her cigarette as she ran down the few steps that led from the terrace to a stretch of lawn. "Do you want to go for a spin around the island?"

"Can we take the Mini Moke? It'd be so much more fun than the Jag," Tansie replied.

The moment Alix drove the Mini Moke on to the firm wet sand, Tansie stood up and leant over the windscreen. She threw her head backwards and let the wind toss her hair in all directions. Small happy noises escaped from her throat.

Having found a truly deserted spot, they left the Mini Moke and strolled along the water's edge for a short distance. The waves gently rolled over their bare feet. Alix loved the feel of the fine sand between her toes and the slight tickle it caused. Tansie walked alongside occasionally picking up a small pebble and skipping it over the sea's smooth surface.

They were two people truly in love, enjoying the solitude of their surroundings and each other's company.

"If there's a paradise, this is it!" Tansie suddenly cried, as she drew Alix down on to the sand and slid her left arm underneath Alix's head. Softly, she murmured, "Remember the night I seduced you? It's nearly three years ago." She didn't wait for a response and instead proceeded to caress Alix's body, from her neck all the way down to her toes.

Alix smiled as she too recalled that very first time and what it had subsequently come to mean to her. They had had their ups and downs, but the intensity of Alix's desire for Tansie and the passion with which she responded had not wavered.

What Alix did not yet know was that this beach would change her life.

Their idyllic love lasted for just over two weeks. Neither felt the slightest need to speak to or see anyone else. Alix took unrestrained pleasure in Tansie's passion and charming company. Nothing in Tansie's behaviour could have fore-warned Alix of what was to come. Only Tansie knew that Alix could never give her what she craved and needed most: a name and respectability. Herb Mullins could and was willing to do so.

For the first two weeks, Tansie put all thoughts of Herb and of what she had promised him to the back of her mind. For now, there was only Alix.

It wasn't until they were into their third week in Montego Bay that Tansie realised that she was running out of time. She would have to tell Alix that she was going to marry Herb. She started to agonise over where and when she was going to do the deed. She had an even less clear picture of how she was going to do it. All she knew was that she would have to do it soon and before they left Jamaica.

As they were lying on the beach late one afternoon, after having just made love, Tansie suddenly knew that she could not tell Alix either here or at the villa. She too wanted to be able to treasure these memories in times to come. Tansie drew Alix closer and held her in a tight embrace.

A restaurant, Tansie suddenly thought, would be much more suitable. She wanted a neutral place where nothing would remind her of the glorious time they had just spent together. Otherwise she may never go through with it. She suggested that they have dinner in town that evening.

"Why not," Alix agreed without further thought, drew

Tansie to her feet and into the seclusion of their bedroom.

Moments later, they playfully sprawled out on the king-size bed as they started to caress each other all over again. But it was Tansie who soon took control. She knew that this would be the last time they would make love, certainly for a while, and she wanted to savour every second of it. She also wanted Alix to remember just how wonderful it was to make love, not just with any woman but with Tansie. She believed that it would be those memories that would bind Alix to her forever no matter what Tansie did.

Alix was oblivious to Tansie's thoughts but she too wanted to savour every moment, every touch and every kiss. In her view, they were still on their honeymoon.

When they finally exhausted themselves and collapsed into each other's arms, they dozed for a while, listening to the soft humming of the ceiling fan and the birds that had gathered outside on the terrace.

Eventually Alix lifted her head and looked at her lover who lay next to her: so quiet, serene and beautiful. Alix knew that she would never get tired of looking at Tansie, of feeling her and of loving her. She took in the sweet scents of the island which the light breeze carried into the semi-dark bedroom and knew that she would always remember Tansie and the island scents together.

As Alix slowly let her hand wander over every inch of Tansie's body, she noted not for the first time that in the last three weeks Tansie's body had filled out a little. Her shoulders and hips were no longer as angular as they used to be and her stomach not quite as flat any more. Tansie looked much better for it, Alix thought.

As though she guessed what Alix was thinking, Tansie rolled on to her stomach. "Don't say it . . . I know I've put on weight . . . it's disgusting," Tansie said and, with some truculence in her voice, added, "it's all your fault . . . you made me eat all that food!"

"You look beautiful," Alix assured her softly.

Much later, they showered and dressed for dinner.

"It's such a glorious evening," Tansie said as they were leaving the house. "Let's take the Mini Moke, can we please?"

"Of course," Alix said and smiled to herself. Right now it wouldn't matter what Tansie wanted. Alix would turn the whole world upside down if that was what Tansie wanted.

With their eyes sparkling, their skin aglow and their hair tousled, they both looked radiantly happy when they pulled into the restaurant's carpark.

The statuesque maître d' ushered them to a large table outside on the terrace and underneath the blue and white striped awning, facing the beach and the sea beyond.

Neither spoke for some time as each one slowly sipped the Brandy Alexanders the waiter had promptly brought for them. Alix was at peace and engrossed in watching the waves which lapped on to the smooth sand, curled over and retreated back to sea. She recalled other times when watching the sea had had a similar effect on her emotions. It was those very feelings which now lulled her into a sense of security. From somewhere further up the beach, she could hear the sounds of the island: adults singing and children playing, and fishermen tying up their boats for the night.

Tansie was occupied with studying their fellow diners who, judging by their accents, were mostly Americans. Even after having spent considerable time travelling with Alix, she was still fascinated by the wealth and opulence of other tourists. Their elegant evening wear and their exclusive jewellery often left her, if no longer in awe, certainly a little uncomfortable. She began to think that she could not leave it much longer to tell Alix that she was going to go home sooner than planned. She had promised Herb that she would be back no later than the end of January. She looked at her companion, swallowed hard and sighed. Forcefully, she pulled herself out of her reverie. It would not help her to go all soft and sentimental now. Just how she was going to approach it, she still wasn't sure. And then fate played right into her hand.

Straightening her shoulders and lifting her hand, Tansie motioned the waiter to come. "If you don't have a table for the two gentlemen who've just arrived, ask them to sit here with us," she whispered. The two men could not have arrived at a more opportune time, she thought. Although she was well aware that her approach was callous and cowardly, she would have to make Alix leave her and not the other way round.

"You would not mind?" he beamed, flashing two white rows of teeth at her. "We are a little short of space this evening."

"Not at all," Tansie replied and gave Alix's arm a sharp squeeze. "We don't, do we?"

"I'm sorry, I wasn't listening," Alix apologised and smiled, unaware of what Tansie was about to do.

"Just bring them over," Tansie urged the waiter, before addressing Alix again. "I've just invited the two fellows at the door to come and sit with us."

"Why?" Alix asked just a little perplexed by Tansie's behaviour. "I don't really want company, especially not the company of strangers."

"Please, Alix?" Tansie pleaded. "It's only for a couple of hours or so. Come on," Tansie coaxed. "You can't always have me to yourself," she added with a seductive smile.

"Okay, if it makes you happy," Alix agreed. It never

occurred to Alix that Tansie's impulsive decision to invite the two men was anything other than a friendly gesture.

"Jolly good of you to have us here," the taller one of the two said in perfect Queen's English. "My name is Charles Montague and this is Mark Carlisle."

Despite her earlier hesitation, Alix quickly settled into a conversation with Charles on all sorts of topics. He was an orthopaedic surgeon at Guy's Hospital in London, as well as a classical music buff. He had heard her in concert on two occasions and told her how much he admired her talent.

After the initial, compulsory small talk with Mark, Tansie quickly became bored with his conversation. But, since that wasn't what she had in mind, she rapidly moved on to the next part. Even before their main course arrived, Tansie's hand, casually at first, slipped behind Mark's back. As though deep in thought and not aware of what she was doing, she began to slide it up and down his spine. It wasn't long before she leant closer towards him and gave him a peck on the cheek, accompanied by a throaty seductive giggle. Her words were spoken too softly for either Alix or Charles to hear. But the message came across loud and clear just the same.

Alix averted her gaze and looked out to sea. She had to be dreaming, she thought. This couldn't possibly be happening, not now. Had those last few weeks really meant nothing to Tansie? Had her words of endearment been spoken without substance? All conversation momentarily stopped as though each one of her companions guessed what was going through her mind.

"Alix," she vaguely heard Charles say. "Your dinner is getting cold."

Alix slowly turned around, saw Tansie's hand slide along Mark's thigh and felt sick. She knew she would have to get out right now or she would lose what little control she still had.

Alix folded her napkin and said, "I don't feel well, would you please excuse me?" As both men got to their feet, Alix turned her back and fled. Although it was barely an hour since she had strolled into the restaurant, looking cool and elegant and holding her head up high, her shoulders were now stooped and her step was heavy. She looked broken.

By the time Alix found the Mini Moke in the carpark, she felt her light summer dress clinging to her back. She didn't know whether it was the heat of the night or her disgust at what she had just witnessed that made her perspire like this. It didn't matter. She didn't care any more and slipped behind the wheel. Ramming the gear stick into reverse, she shot out of the parking lot. As tears began to well up in her eyes, she shouted, "How can you do this to me?"

She put her foot down hard on the accelerator at the same time as she saw a pair of headlights shoot straight towards her. With tears streaming down her cheeks, she pulled the wheel sharply to the left and hit the curb. The car literally bounced off its wheels on impact, flew over the curb into the sand-dunes where it rolled several times, before coming to a standstill upside down.

Tansie followed Alix outside but before she could get to the car, Alix had reversed it and taken off. When she saw the Mini Moke literally fly off the road and turn in mid-air, she froze momentarily.

By the time she shouted, "Alix . . . Alix . . ." people were already rushing past her. She followed them and, on all fours, scrambled down the embankment.

Tansie stood and stared as though in a daze as a man in uniform directed the Mini Moke to be moved. Alix lay still and ghostly white in the sand. Her eyes were closed and her left leg was twisted sideways.

"Can you hear me, Miss?" The man in uniform shouted as he gently patted her cheek.

Alix did not reply. She was unconscious.

"She's dead," Tansie shrieked and dashed back into the restaurant to get Charles and Mark.

By the time the ambulance delivered Alix to the hospital, she was conscious again but her face was contorted with pain and her eyes flashed with wild anger.

Charles organised the necessary X-rays and, later, setting Alix's leg into plaster. It was a relatively simple fracture and nothing he had not taken care of many times before.

Mark was dispatched to take Tansie back to the villa. She was hysterical and would do more harm than good at the hospital. Even before they arrived back at the villa, Tansie clung on to Mark's arm as she kept crying and begging, "Please, don't leave me."

In all of his adult life, Mark had never been able to resist a beautiful women. By the time he had carried Tansie into the bedroom and sufficiently calmed her down, her caresses had gone beyond any man's endurance.

The first rays of sunshine filtered in through the closed shutters when Tansie woke up the following morning. So as not to disturb Mark, she quietly packed her bags and asked the butler to drive her to the airport. She joked with the check-in clerk and bustled through customs as though this was the most natural thing to do.

It wasn't until she was strapped into her seat that she finally allowed herself a deep sigh. All she would have to do in Miami or Los Angeles was to ring Herb and let him know her time of arrival in Melbourne.

She knew she had made promises to both Alix and Herb

before leaving for Jamaica. But, as she had always known she would have to, she had now broken one. Her fear of being labelled a freak and an outcast, as she had been as a child, had finally won over everything else. Only another marriage could save her. And, she was over two months pregnant. Short of having an abortion, she no longer had any choice in the matter. Marrying Herb was not just the better alternative but the only one as far as she was concerned.

For a brief moment, she let her hand wander over her stomach. This was her baby growing inside her and nothing would stop her from having it. Not for the first time, she noted how lucky she was that she had not been plagued by morning sickness. She didn't think she could have explained that as easily as she had her swelling breasts and the fact that she had put on some weight.

She closed her eyes as the aircraft soared into the sky and allowed her thoughts to wander to Alix. The tears began to squeeze out fast and furiously from underneath her eyelashes. She had to make herself believe that once Alix got over the shock, she would come around. She did love her but, given her current condition, she had to marry Herb. Even Alix would have to see that.

The day after her return from Jamaica, Tansie moved in with Herb and his three sons. The local estate agent was told to put her house, including her furniture and artworks, on the market and sell it all to the highest bidder. She wanted nothing to remind her of the past. The jewellery and other mementos Alix had given her over the years were deposited in the bank safe deposit box. Her art materials and tools were stored at Julie's house. She knew she could not work until she had come to a satisfactory arrangement with Alix. Alix had believed in her talent, had been her mentor and inspiration. She could not sculpt without her.

When she told Herb that she was nearly three months pregnant, he was overjoyed. Being of quite simple mind, he believed that she was now his for good. He wanted to get married immediately but Tansie wanted an Easter wedding. Herb agreed without protest and the date was set for the end of March.

Chapter 26

"Where's Tansie?" Alix asked the moment she woke up the morning after her accident.

"Mark took her back to the villa last night," Charles consoled her and wiped her flushed forehead with a damp towel. "How are you feeling?"

"Okay," she said slowly, not yet quite comprehending what had happened the night before. "Would you take me home now?"

"I'd prefer it if you stayed another day, but I don't suppose I can convince you of that?" Charles responded with some concern.

"Not a chance, doctor!" she tried to smile but couldn't.

"I didn't think so," he said and arranged for Alix to be checked out of the hospital.

When Charles drove Alix back to the villa, she suddenly became quite anxious. She had to find Tansie before she lost her nerve. She needed to tell her that the relationship had to end now and for good. Alix could not take any more. Already, she felt the agony of that decision tearing her apart. But, she knew that if she waited much longer to do battle with her lover, she might never go through with it. As fast as her crutches would allow, she hobbled across the tiled floor in the main hall and towards the bedroom. Alix felt herself flush but inside she felt chilled as though she already knew what was waiting for her. It was a premonition so strong, her legs began to shake.

The words, "I'm home," had formed on Alix's lips as

she walked into the bedroom she and Tansie had shared for almost three weeks. But, the sound died in her throat.

The rumpled bed, an empty bottle of wine and the two glasses on the bedside table took her breath away. The doors to the wardrobe were open and the shelves and hanging spaces were bare. Everything Tansie owned was gone.

When Alix paled despite her deep suntan, Charles was quickly at her side and took her elbow. He led her to a chair on the terrace.

Alix pulled herself together and appeared casual, but inside, her stomach began to lurch. "Thanks for everything, Charles. Would you please ask Victoria to come outside?"

"Of course," he replied, adding, "I'll check on you in the morning. But if you need me, call me at the hotel. I'll be here for a few more days."

"I will." She gave him a brave smile. When the maid arrived, she asked, "Victoria, did Ms Landon leave a message?"

"No, ma'am. She packed and asked Alfredo to take her to the airport," Victoria volunteered.

For the next three days, Alix sat on the terrace and stared out to sea but never really saw anything. It was as though this place held no past and no memories. The pain, if she allowed herself to remember, would simply be too much to bear.

Alix directed her thoughts to what had gone so horribly wrong. Had she done something terrible to Tansie to make her want to leave? Had she not given her enough or not loved her enough? Had she made too many assumptions for too long? Had she been too complacent about Tansie's male lovers? Or had the bond between them simply not been as strong as she had thought. Guilt, pain and anger fought each other as she wondered, over and over, and still didn't know.

As soon as she thought Tansie should have arrived home, Alix tried to ring her. Despite trying almost hourly, there was no answer. After another day had passed, Alix was frantic. Where was Tansie, Alix wondered and felt sick. Maybe Tansie never got home. Maybe she had met with an accident. Panic gripped Alix. Her mind was uncomprehending, unable to accept that Tansie was gone.

Then it came to her and she knew with clarity where Tansie was. There was only one place she could be.

"Hello?" Herb's voice was nasal.

"Would you put Tansie on for me, please," Alix said, holding her breath and hoping against all odds that he would say she wasn't there.

"Why don't you just leave her alone!" he snapped.

"Put her on," Alix snapped right back at him.

She heard him put the phone down and, seconds later, Tansie's little-girl voice crackled over the none-too-good line.

"Hiii," Tansie drawled.

"What the hell are you doing back home?" Alix clenched her jaw and swallowed hard.

"Please don't speak to me like that, Alix. I can't bear it when you're angry," Tansie replied. "Don't you understand?"

All the pent-up frustration burst forth without warning. "Understand what? That everything you'd said over the last few months was a lie? You're a liar and a coward, Tansie Landon!" Something inside her snapped like a fragile branch in a storm. "Does Mullins know you went straight from my bed into Mark's before joining his?"

"It wasn't like that at all." Tansie was on the defensive now and her voice was shrill and ready to break. "Herb's mother's just had a heart attack . . . I had to come and see

327

whether there was anything I could do . . . you wouldn't understand!"

"No, I wouldn't put myself out for someone I called a prick as I remember you called him not that long ago. As for his mother, you can't stand her! You two deserve each other!"

"I never said that!" Tansie shouted.

Then the phone clicked and the line went dead. Alix slammed the handset back on to its cradle. She contemplated ringing her back but thought better of it. It would upset Alix more than it would Tansie. Already, she felt drained as though someone had stabbed her right through the heart and bled her dry. She felt herself go weak, fumbled for the packet of cigarettes and dropped it. Then with frightening suddenness, a variety of feelings attacked her: anger, fear and guilt, love and hate, remorse. She knew her emotions were balancing on a thin rope. The ground, seemingly hundreds of feet below her, was looming black and menacingly, like a gorge which would swallow her up for good if she let go. Alix hung on. She had to.

An hour later, Tansie rang back. Crying hysterically, she gasped, "I didn't hang up on you . . . you know I would never do that . . . he did . . . just come home so that we can . . ."

"You and I have nothing more to say to each other," Alix shouted. "Just get the hell out of my life!"

"I don't fucking care any more!" Tansie lost control. The thin ice had broken underneath her feet. "Just get it into your thick head that I'm going to marry Herb . . . and have his baby!"

The handset fell out of Alix's hand and clanked against the leg of the sun lounge Alix was lying on. Vaguely, she heard Tansie's voice screaming before everything around her swam out of focus. Slowly the last link of the chain fell into place and snapped shut. The betrayal was final, but the agony was only just starting. Tears began to sting her eyes but, even had she wanted to, she couldn't stop them from flowing. Then, as though looking for relief from the pain, she slipped from the sun lounge and passed out.

When she came to, Alix was propped up in bed, with several pillows in her back and one underneath her injured leg. She looked directly at Charles, who was sitting on a chair beside her, but her eyes were vacant and she didn't appear to see him.

"Alix?" He said and reached for her hand. It was icy cold, despite the late afternoon heat. "Alix?" he tried again, but no response came. He waved his hand in front of her eyes a couple of times, but still there was no response. She was either in deep shock or had sustained some head injuries which he'd overlooked at the hospital.

He leapt from the chair and went in search of the maid. "Where are Ms Clemenger's personal belongings, you know, her passport, tickets etc.?" Charles asked.

Ambling towards a mahogany chest, Victoria opened the top drawer and retrieved a travel folder. "Is this it, sir?"

"Yes, thank you, Victoria." He flicked through her passport and found what he was looking for. Dr Tom von Arx was listed as Alix's next of kin. It didn't take him long to locate him in his chambers in Zürich. Since Charles was due to go on home-leave in a few days anyway, he arranged with Tom to fly Alix to Switzerland.

For several days after her arrival in Zürich, a friend of Tom's at the University Hospital ran extensive tests on Alix. When Dr Ballmer could find no physical cause, he explained that the most likely reason for her seeming withdrawal was the trauma she'd suffered from the accident.

That, he said, was not uncommon.

"In that case, I think the best place for her is with me," Hanna, who had arrived in Zürich the day before, said. And then, as though a sudden thought had struck her, she asked, "Tom, who was Alix in Jamaica with?"

"Tansie." Tom gave his aunt a curious stare.

"I'll take her home, Tom," Hanna replied. There was no doubt in her mind that Tansie was responsible for Alix's predicament.

Several hours later, the chauffeur delivered both Alix and Hanna to her lake house outside Geneva. Still on crutches, Alix hobbled into Hanna's house. She slowly negotiated the marble floor in the entrance hall and entered the sitting room.

The concert grand piano was in the same place it had been since she was a little girl. The huge picture windows overlooked the lake and the French Alps beyond. Taking in the familiar surroundings, Alix felt as though she was waking up from a deep sleep. She was home. But why was she here? It had started to snow and she could suddenly feel the cold. She felt a chill deep inside. Where was the sand, the beach and the sunshine? This was all wrong.

It was then that she remembered. The whole nightmare came bursting out. She threw her arms around Hanna and wept uncontrollably as she recounted her trauma, re-living it all over again. The ups and downs of their torrid relationship, the three years of happiness, the many broken promises and the final betrayal.

Hanna held her niece in her arms and listened until Alix was too exhausted to go on and fell asleep. Covering her with a blanket, Hanna stroked her hot forehead. She wished she could simply make Alix forget that Tansie had ever been part of her life. That Alix would wake up and remember nothing, even if it meant that she would also never remember the good times she and Tansie had shared.

In her sleep, Alix looked peaceful. Her chest rose and fell at a rhythmic pace and her long eyelashes cast deep shadows on her sunken cheeks. There was no smile on her lips. Hanna shook her head. She was deeply saddened by what Alix would yet have to go through. She hadn't even started to come to grips with her loss.

Later, from her study, Hanna rang Tom. "She's going to be fine, Tom," she said.

"Should I ask what caused her distress?"

"It doesn't matter now, Tom," she said softly.

As each new day dawned, time, which in the past had been precious, suddenly meant nothing to Alix any more. On some days she didn't go to bed and on others she never got up. She wanted to stay asleep to side-step the emotional nightmare and turn it into the beautiful dream it had once been. Then she remembered Tansie. Aloud, she shouted, "Why won't you let me go? You left me, don't follow me around!"

In more lucid moments, her only solace was music. Music was her safety net. It had never betrayed or deserted her in the past and she started to compose a new symphony. She progressed well with it, but was not aware that what she wrote was dark and tragic. It had nothing of her normally exuberant vivacity about it. There were no trumpets or French horns, no piccolo or *fortissimo* trills on the keyboard to shout her happiness to the world. But, there were solo parts for the cello and the bass and the deep dark rolling sounds of the timpani, plus a long, slow, plaintive solo for the *cor anglais*. Through her music, she shouted her despair and grief to a world that might never hear that very music.

Alix existed rather than lived and, what solace she didn't find in her compositions, she found in an endless supply of champagne and cigarettes. When sleep eluded her, as it usually did, sleeping tablets became her bed companions.

Sometimes Alix stood at the window and glared across the lake for hours in one stretch. She only saw darkness, an endless tunnel that was swallowing her up. At other times she wandered aimlessly through the quiet house. She heard nothing and saw nothing. The vacuum she had created was infinite as she felt herself float into oblivion.

Feeling terrible at leaving her children for such a long time, she kept in touch with them by telephone. She knew it was hardly a consolation for them and missed them more and more as each day passed. Drew and his friends, relentlessly playing their own hard-rock music until the walls shook. Sara, forever an actress, playing for an imaginary audience in front of a mirror. And Christian, sweet and young, happily joining his mother at the piano. Still, she could not face going home.

Hanna heard and saw it all. For many hours, she sat with Alix and watched her. Her face was no longer fresh and open but rather sallow and closed as though it had been wiped clean of all emotions. The European winter was slowly coming to an end and yet there was no sign of optimism in Alix's step when she wandered through the house. Hanna heard all the despair and heartache in the symphony Alix was composing. Hanna remembered only too well the Fantasy in C major Alix had composed for Tansie. She hoped that one day, Alix would compose another piece of music as beautiful as that.

But Hanna had to let her niece find her own peace, in her own way and in her own time, just as Hanna had done when Alix's father had died. Hanna simply nursed and nurtured her as best she could. In the meantime she too kept in touch with Felix and the children to make sure they were all right. She was glad that Felix was there to take care of them. Alix needed time to grieve properly and accept her loss. Only then could she get on with her life.

It wasn't until the beginning of March when Hanna was out of the house for a short while and Alix answered the phone that she was finally forced back into reality.

"Listen, kiddo," John joked at the other end of the telephone. "If it's a new lover that's keeping you over there, bring her home, for God's sake!"

John, the children, her friends . . . and Tansie. Suddenly the real world began to dawn on her. She no longer had a choice but to acknowledge that Tansie was gone and she would have to get on with life without her.

"One more week, John, and I'll be home," she finally promised. When she hung up, she buried her head in her hands and wept.

How can I face being at home where everything will remind me of Tansie? Trying to forget that Tansie had ever existed became a monumental task. The idea of running into her made Alix's heart miss several painful beats. The agony of such an encounter would be overwhelming.

"I can't do it!" Alix shouted and slammed her hands on to the keyboard.

Returning from her outing, Hanna had heard the outburst and slipped into the room.

"Hanna, I can't do it!" Alix repeated and flung herself into her aunt's arms.

"You can and you will, darling," Hanna comforted her, adding, "you know, when Siggy died, I didn't think I'd ever get over it. I was angry and thought it was so unfair that a man with his talent and beauty should be cheated out of at least another twenty years. But, in time, I came to understand that he would have hated to live as a cripple for the rest of his life. In those circumstances, I had to let him go no matter how devastated I was."

"Tansie wasn't a cripple nor did she die!" Alix responded, truculent and unforgiving. "What she's done is shatter all our hopes and dreams, for a man she says she despises!"

"Still, my darling, it's what she wanted and you too will have to let her go," Hanna said. "Maybe she doesn't dislike him as she said she did. You see, she knows you don't like him and that you think of him as being crass and uncouth, so how could she tell you that she is in love with him? I do believe that she loved you too, in her own way and, probably because of it, she needs your approval." A smile creased the corners of her lips. "By the way, is he really that bad?"

"Worse," Alix said. "For all the cheating and lying she's done, she's still a very beautiful and talented woman and she is throwing it all away for someone who doesn't deserve her!" Alix puffed on her cigarette and blew the smoke towards the open window. "What does she need a man for anyway? She has a brilliant career ahead of her and . . ." She couldn't go on. Her voice broke and tears filled her eyes.

"Maybe from where you're sitting it seems he's got nothing to give her. But what if all she wants is a simple normal life, to be Mrs Herb Mullins?" Hanna replied thoughtfully. "Or maybe keeping up with you was just too hard for her."

For a brief moment, neither woman spoke. As Hanna looked at her niece, broken and devastated, she recalled how happy and vibrantly alive Alix had been. She wished she could wave a magic wand and give her back her equilibrium, the sparkle in her eyes and the spring to her step.

It was Hanna who broke the silence. "Maybe she really can't come to terms with loving another woman . . . the loneliness of such a relationship and the social implications. You and I and many other women around the world would not agree with that but, in the end, it's she who has to live her life. We can't ever change that."

Alix became calmer as she thought about Hanna's words. "Even if what you say is true, did she have to violate everything we shared in such a cruel manner?"

"No, she didn't have to, but she did and you'll have to come to terms with it just the same. I think she did it in the only way she knew how." After a short pause, she added, "At least in leaving the way she did she made a clear break without prolonging your agony. You must now look to your own future, my darling."

Alix arrived in the breakfast room early the following morning, to find Hanna and Jesse sipping coffee and chatting.

Not quite sure whether to laugh or cry at seeing her friend, Alix threw herself into Jesse's open arms. Hanna left the room, smiling to herself.

Jesse held Alix close and stroked her hair. "You certainly manage to get yourself into some awkward situations."

"And what do you know about my 'situation' as you call it?" Alix laughed, for the first time in many weeks.

"Enough," Jesse replied softly. "Anyway, I was in the States at a conference when I decided that it was only a short hop and a skip across the Atlantic . . . so, here I am."

"I told John that I would be home in a week . . . can you stay for a few days?" Alix asked. Giving Jesse a momentary hopeful glance, Alix suddenly averted her eyes and let them wander over the smooth surface of the lake. She stood up and walked towards the windows. "You know, I've been here for weeks and I haven't once looked at the scenery. Because everything reminds me of Tansie and the wonderful times we had here."

"I know, Alix," Jesse said and went to stand next to Alix. Quite naturally, she gathered her into her arms. After a short silence, she added, "I can stay a few days. We'll go home together when you're ready."

During their stay with Hanna, Alix and Jesse talked for hours and, on most evenings, until well into the night. If at times Alix was too distressed to go on, Jesse simply held her in her arms. She knew that no words could take Alix's pain away. But she hoped that she might be able to ease it just a little.

Although the plaster had come off and walking was still difficult for Alix, most afternoons, they strolled through the vineyard down to the lake. Periodically they stopped and looked across the still water. Then they moved on and talked some more. The air was still crisp and clean but the sun shone, allowing the vines to slowly bud again. Each day, more and more tiny new shoots broke open, their fresh, light green leaves unfolding and growing. Alix too could feel herself become calmer and more rational. Whether it was because of the new life which had started to grow around her or Jesse's presence, Alix didn't know. It didn't matter anyway, she thought.

One evening, Jesse drove them into Geneva where she had made a dinner reservation in the small, cosy restaurant Hanna had suggested. Alix cringed at the thought of leaving the house and walking into a restaurant without Tansie, but she knew she had to do it just the same.

During dinner, Alix reached across the table and took Jesse's hand. She could feel the warmth from her hand seeping into her own, soothing her, relaxing her. To expect to be happy would be unreasonable, Alix thought. But she felt comfortable and was glad for Jesse's endless support.

"Thanks for being here, Jesse." Alix looked at Jesse and into her dark blue eyes. They reminded Alix of the Caribbean Sea at sunrise: rich in colour and sparkling in the first light of a new day. By simply being here, Jesse had given her that new day, she thought. The pain of remembering walking with Tansie and watching the sunrise over the Caribbean seemed not quite as bad any more.

Jesse smiled and said that she was glad to be here. She too had been lost in her own thoughts. She sighed and watched the intricate interplay of the light from the candle and the shadows it created on Alix's face. For the first time, Jesse noticed how graceful Alix's neck was. Her eyes travelled further down to the cleavage between her breasts and lingered for just a moment as she indulged herself in Alix's beauty. She had to fight the urge to touch her, to love her and to feel her respond. But Jesse knew that it was far too soon for that. She knew that Alix would have to grieve and she wanted to give her that time.

Driving back to Hanna's villa later that night, Alix leant her head on Jesse's shoulder. After a long silence, she said, "You know, over the last few weeks I had moments when I seriously doubted that I would ever be able to do something as simple as walk into a restaurant again. The thought of socialising petrified me." Alix put her hand over Jesse's. "I'm glad I was with you . . . you'll never know just how much you've helped me." She smiled a little as a few tears began to brim in her eyes.

Alix showed no embarrassment about her display of emotion. She never had, Jesse thought. It was an instance of honesty and Jesse found it immensely appealing.

"My motives for coming over here were not entirely

selfless. I started to miss you." Jesse too was honest.

"Thank you for coming," Alix replied. Over the last few days, she had become well aware of how deeply Jesse cared for her. Alix too cared a great deal about Jesse.

The following week, Alix bid Hanna a teary farewell at the airport and, holding on to Jesse's arm, boarded the jet. As soon as they were in the air, Alix leant back into her seat and closed her eyes.

For a while she tried to concentrate on a novel, but her thoughts kept wandering to what awaited her at home. More than anything, she wished that Tansie would just disappear, never to be heard of or seen again.

As the jet taxied towards the terminal building in Melbourne, Alix said, "Thank you, Jesse." She reached for Jesse's hand and held it as though this was her last link to sanity.

Chapter 27

As soon as Alix stepped off the aircraft, she began to shake. A searing pain shot through her whole body. Her eyes began to blur and, swaying from side to side, she thought she was going to pass out. She had expected to feel terrible but not that terrible.

Jesse grabbed her elbow and steadied her. "Are you okay, Alix?" she asked with concern.

Alix gave her a weak smile. "I just felt faint for a moment . . . it's probably the heat."

When they finally emerged into the arrival hall, Alix was instantly bowled over by the children scrambling for attention. Felix gave her a wide grin. "I hope you don't mind, I allowed the children to take the day off," he said, adding, "it's good to have you home."

Despite the early evening, it was still very hot and Alix gasped. After the many weeks of clean, crisp winter air in Switzerland, she found the heat more oppressive than ever.

"Why did I come back here?" she said in mild disbelief and shook her head.

Drew laughed. "Why don't we just go and live over there and be done with it? At least I could leave school then."

She draped an arm around his shoulder. "If only it were that easy." What she didn't say aloud was that she had entertained that idea many times over recent weeks and had not altogether discarded it.

When they delivered Jesse to her house, Alix embraced her warmly. "Thanks again, Jesse . . . I'll ring you later."

They had all just finished dinner and were sitting outside on the terrace, when Kate rang to say that she would be over soon.

"Where are you?" Kate called as she came through the back door into the kitchen half an hour later.

The two women hugged one another. "It's great to have you home, you old tart," Kate chirped.

"Thanks for the compliment," Alix laughed and, armed with glasses and a bottle of champagne, headed for the sitting room. Kate filled Alix in on all the news which Alix was quite happy to hear. It gave her a little more time to prepare herself for what she knew would come, sooner or later.

"Anyway, so much for the local gossip. Now let's talk about you," Kate concluded. "Alix, what happened?"

Her voice shaking, Alix murmured, "Exactly what you and Jesse warned me about . . . Tansie left me for Mullins!"

For the next hour, Alix recounted what had happened. She finished by saying, "She violated everything, even our friendship!"

"Yes, I'm afraid so," Kate replied. "I know how passionately you loved her and it'll take you a long time to get over it."

Alix only nodded for fear of bursting into tears again. Time – she needed time, and silently she prayed that Tansie would at least understand that and stay away from her.

After a short pause, Alix said, "Now I feel as though the last few weeks have simply disappeared."

"Maybe that's the only way our minds can cope with pain," Kate replied. "Otherwise, surely half the world would be insane." Kate remained quiet for some time, but sipped her drink rather hastily. Alix wondered whether there was something else on her mind that she hadn't yet come out with.

"Kate, is there something that you know and I don't?" Alix asked, breaking what she thought was an unusually uncomfortable silence between them.

Kate took a deep breath. She hated to be the bearer of bad news but felt that it was better for Alix to know now. Before she replied, she suddenly noticed that Alix was wearing a black T-shirt and shorts. Alix very rarely wore black, she recalled, and wondered whether it was deliberate or accidental. Either way, she thought, it didn't suit Alix's normally vibrant energy. "Tansie is getting married at the end of next week," Kate eventually said.

"So soon," Alix muttered.

"Yes, I'm afraid so," Kate confirmed. "I expect she wants the wedding over before she starts to show." When Alix gave her a perplexed glance, she added, "You know she's pregnant, don't you?"

"No!" Alix responded and hurled herself into her friend's arms. She had no recollection of the fact that Tansie herself had told her that. "Please, Kate, tell me that's not true," she shouted and clamped her hands around her ears. "It's not true! It's not true!"

Kate put her arms firmly around Alix and held her to her chest as Alix murmured, "How many months?"

"It's due around the middle of August."

Alix shook her head. "So, she knew even before we went away!"

"It looks that way," Kate said.

"You know, no matter how much I loved her, I couldn't ever have given her a baby. Not in the conventional way," Alix said softly. "But had she told me she wanted one, I would have been prepared to go to any lengths. We even discussed the possibility at one point."

"I know you would have," Kate agreed, adding, "But,

341

given the way things have turned out now, I'm glad you didn't."

"So am I."

"What are you going to do now?"

"As you said, it's over. Tansie's gone and I have to get on with my life," Alix muttered. With a weak smile, she continued, "Maybe I'll write my memoirs."

"If you call it, 'Follies of a middle-aged woman', it'll be a bestseller for sure," Kate grinned.

"You're very helpful today!"

"How about a permanent seat on Haig's jet for a few months?" Kate suggested. "An endless supply of French champagne and caviar should make it quite pleasant."

Alix smiled. "If that were at all practical, I might consider it."

"How about an extended concert tour?" Kate asked.

"Before I went on holidays, Boris asked me to tour Europe and America with him later this year and early next year."

"That's fantastic, tell him you're going," Kate instructed. "Anyway, what's one lover less if you can have the whole world at your feet?"

"I'll think about it," Alix promised, wary and unsure.

Despite the early autumn evening, the weather was humid and it started to take its toll on Tansie. Standing at the kitchen sink and peeling vegetables, she wiped a strand of matted damp hair from her face. She hated her hair like this, long and shapeless and in desperate need of a new tint, but she could not be bothered doing anything about it. There were many things she could not be bothered doing any more. Her waistline had started to thicken, she felt fat and ugly. Her clothes didn't fit and she hated that too.

Since she had moved in with Herb, Tansie had been

moody and suffered many bouts of depression. They came upon her without warning and pitched her into sullen silences. On those occasions, she didn't want to speak to anybody and snapped if someone spoke to her. All she wanted was for Alix to come home.

"Fucking house," she muttered under her breath and threw a carrot into the saucepan. It missed and slithered across the floor.

"What do you want?" she snapped at David when he walked in moments later. She hated him too. As Drew's friend, he still had a privilege that she no longer enjoyed: walking in and out of Alix's house at his pleasure. She should have that privilege, it wasn't right that she didn't! It never entered her mind that such thoughts were totally irrational. After all, Alix should understand that she had to marry Herb. Alix couldn't give her what she wanted most: a name, an identity and a baby.

David watched her for a moment. He felt, at most, ambivalent about her. On the rare occasions when he saw Tansie's vulnerability, although he didn't understand it, he felt sorry for her. He wondered why she had always been happy in Alix's house and yet, since moving in with his father, she hadn't even smiled, let alone laughed. He didn't understand that either.

"Drew told me that his mother came back yesterday. Apparently she had a car accident in Jamaica and has been recuperating in Switzerland ever since." David gave her a long hard stare.

"Don't ever mention her name in this house again!" Tansie shouted and chased him out.

As David was leaving, Herb collided with him in the doorway. He stared after him and then put his arm around her shoulder. "Why are you so angry with David?"

"It's none of your goddamned business!" she told him and returned to her task of preparing dinner. She knew if she started to talk about Alix, she would blurt everything out: their relationship and how she was now suffering because it was all over. Although in a fit of temper she had told him about her real liaison with Alix, she was sure that it had gone over his head. Just like most other things, she thought angrily. But, reminding herself of his sole purpose in her life, she calmed down a little. With her progressing pregnancy, she needed him and was prepared to go to extreme lengths to protect herself and the unborn child.

The wedding took place a week later, but had it not been for the narrow gold band on her finger she would not have remembered that the ceremony took place. Tansie was drunk even before lunch was served.

For several days afterwards, Tansie pondered over how to contact Alix. She wanted to talk to her, explain and make up. Late the following night, Tansie slipped out of the house. She parked the car in Alix's driveway and wandered around the back of the house. Faint rays of light still filtered through the partly drawn curtains.

Tansie made no noise when she pushed the curtain aside and stepped into the studio. Alix was sitting at the piano and seemed absorbed in what she was doing. A full glass of champagne stood on the side as did a half-empty bottle. Memories of the many happy hours she had spent in this house, this very room, came flooding back and filled her eyes with tears. For a moment or two, she wondered whether she had made a mistake in marrying Herb. Alix would have loved her and always looked after her, she knew. Tansie shook her head as though to rid it of such thoughts. Alix could never give her a name and that was all there was to it.

Tansie cleared her throat and murmured, "Hiii," as she

watched her former lover gasp and her back stiffen.

The pencil Alix had held in her hand dropped from her grip and, as though in slow motion, she turned to face her visitor. Her heart began to race and she had trouble breathing. Catching her breath, Alix said, "I have nothing to say to you."

"I know you don't mean that, but at least hear what I have to say."

"No! Get out!"

Tansie took several small steps towards Alix. "I want you to know that I never meant to hurt you . . . I love you . . . but, I need to live a normal life."

"You could have told me that. I would have let you go," Alix replied. "You let me believe that we were bound together by a special force and then you violated it without warning."

"Oh, Alix that's not true. When I found out I was pregnant, I had to marry him, don't you understand?" Tansie cried.

Alix took a few steps towards Tansie and gave her a menacing stare. "Give me my keys and then leave!"

Out of sheer fright, Tansie dropped the keys and her eyes filled with tears. "You know how much I suffered because I never had a father . . . I never even found out who he was . . . how could I inflict the same pain on my baby?"

In a moment of compassion, Alix thought, yes I do know that. Although she nearly choked on the words, aloud she said, "To get pregnant was entirely your choice, Tansie!"

Tansie averted her gaze. Could she now tell Alix that it wasn't just the baby that made her marry Herb? That she needed a name and an identity Alix could never give her and that without it she was a nobody? She decided that she couldn't. It would take Alix only seconds to work out that, if that were so, Tansie had lied to her during most of their relationship. Tansie too experienced a brief moment of compassion. She really didn't want to hurt Alix any more than she already had. At the same time, she had to look out for herself. She still loved and wanted Alix. She couldn't bear the thought of a life without her.

In an effort to at least shift part of the blame on to Alix, Tansie said, "Do you think I didn't know that you and Haig were lovers?"

"Whether Haig and I were lovers or not was of absolutely no consequence to our relationship. We've been friends for over twenty years and will still be friends in another twenty years . . . unlike us!" Alix lit another cigarette and eyed her former lover. God, she looks awful, Alix thought and felt pity. Nothing could convince her that Tansie's marriage had been made in heaven. She felt sad, for Tansie and for herself.

"Please, Alix, don't give me a hard time, it's bad enough without you adding extra stress," Tansie suddenly pleaded.

"You have what you wanted, don't you?" When Tansie didn't reply, Alix asked again, "Don't you?"

"I love him . . . he's a wonderful person and wouldn't hurt a fly. I'm just sorry that you can't see that."

"What made you change your mind about him?"

"I didn't know him then!"

Alix fought with herself to keep control. This conversation had to stop, she told herself.

"He's a wonderful person . . ." Tansie started again.

"You're repeating yourself! Who are you trying to convince . . . yourself?"

"Alix, I love you . . . nothing has changed . . . everything inside me aches for you. Don't you think I've suffered enough? All those weeks you were away and nobody told me where you were? I nearly went crazy."

"You didn't deserve to be told!" Alix shouted and shook

her head in frustration, as she wondered why she had allowed herself to be drawn into this insane situation; it was over, they had nothing more to say to one another.

"He made me do it, don't you understand?"

Alix turned away and sat down on the piano stool. With a thundering crash, she dropped her hands on to the keyboard and began to play a *fortissimo* so fast and loud, she hoped to drown out Tansie's voice, her presence. But she stopped as suddenly as she had started and swung around to face Tansie again.

"He made you do what?" she yelled, near hysteria now. "That's baby stuff, Tansie, and it won't wash any longer. Nobody can make you do anything you don't want to do yourself!"

As though she hadn't heard Alix, Tansie said, "He's forbidden me to ever see you again!"

"Then do as you're told and go home!"

"Don't treat me like a child!"

"It suited you only a minute ago."

For a moment the two women glared at each other and caught their breath. Flashes of their good times simultaneously swept through their minds. It made them tremble. This couldn't possibly be happening, not after what they had shared for three years.

"I can't live without you . . . I want you . . . but I had to marry him," Tansie murmured, her voice soft and mellow, childlike.

Alix gave her another sad glance as Tansie's words began to intrude on her thoughts. "Find another 'ménage-à-trois'!" Alix said, turned her back on Tansie and began to hit the keys again. "I'll always love you," Tansie muttered and then fled from the room. She disappeared into the darkness of the night as though a cavern had swallowed her up.

Chapter 28

What little reserve Alix still had left, vanished the moment Tansie was gone. She collapsed on to the piano stool and wept. She wept for herself and she wept for Tansie. For what they had shared and for what was no longer there to be shared. She began to dread the days, weeks and months ahead. Although she had done much of her grieving in Switzerland and had accepted that Tansie would never be part of her life again, she was still in for a rough time.

Alix walked to the french door Tansie had not bothered to shut when she left. She stood for a moment, gazing into the darkness of the garden and remembering how she had often stood on this very spot watching Tansie. Invariably, Tansie would come around the back when visiting and stop for a moment to play with the dog. Those moments had been rare and now became precious beyond reason.

In the days that followed, Alix threw herself into her work with hyperactivity. With Tansie she had valued her solitude and privacy, but now she gathered people around her again. She had no wish to spend even short periods of time in her own company. Much like she had felt during her marriage to Michael, she recalled bitterly.

Alix had moments of regret no matter how fruitless such feelings were. Had Tansie not walked into her life, she would not now be in this dreadful situation. With Tansie, she had allowed herself to explore and travel a path she had never dreamed of. She knew she had welcomed that romance and, yet, if she could make it all go away as though it had never happened, she would.

When she was alone, mostly late at night, and when she was too exhausted to continue working, she could not stop her mind from replaying every devastating moment of their last night in Montego Bay. And worse, their very last intimate encounter and Tansie's words of everlasting love. She tried hard not to think about the sensuous pleasures they had shared for three years.

At other times she was gripped by guilt when she recalled how terrible Tansie had looked the last time she'd seen her. Tansie had always referred to Alix as her spiritual mentor and creative muse. And then, Alix had gone and withdrawn all support.

In more lucid moments, she remembered the torrid times and the pain Tansie had caused her. She could almost make herself believe that she was glad to be rid of the cause. Certainly towards the end, the relationship had often been destructive for both of them. But the pain of truly letting go was almost intolerable. Her passions for her first female lover continued to smoulder deep inside her. But the fire was no longer out of control and she felt occasional relief from her anguish.

Her friends noticed that she drank a lot more and seemed to sleep even less than normal, but they didn't comment. They knew the cause of her distress and offered her what comfort they could. Kate and Jesse were always there when she needed a shoulder to cry on.

Arriving unannounced in Alix's studio for coffee one morning, Kate positioned herself at the piano where Alix was pounding away at the keyboard.

"Alix," she cried, "I've just met this great chap and, since he too is all alone in this world, you might as well meet him."

A brief shimmer of light appeared in Alix's smouldering eyes. "And?" she asked.

"I'm doing you a favour, pet. If I weren't married, you'd never even get a look in," Kate responded smartly. With a wide grin, she added, "Julian's got the cutest little backside you've ever seen!"

"They're your speciality!" Alix pointed out.

"I have a small problem . . . Richard . . . you know, my husband?"

"After nearly twenty years, it's time you traded him in!"

"I happen to love the silly bugger," Kate laughed. "Anyway, Julian's got a lovely house in Toorak and . . ."

"So have I!" Alix interrupted.

Kate ignored her friend. "He's also got a house in the South of France and an apartment in New York . . . four grown-up children who rarely visit and three ex-wives who never visit . . . two luxury cars and a butler who's divine and calls him dear!"

"Even I can't afford him!" Alix threw her hands in the air. "I've invited him to your house for dinner this coming Saturday," Kate continued nonplussed. "Richard and I, of course, will be here too, and so will Jackie and her new lover Anton."

"Anybody else?" Alix asked. "If I'm going to entertain, I might as well do it properly and invite half of Melbourne!"

"That's the spirit, pet," Kate agreed. "I ran into Boris in the Toorak Village the other day, so I invited him and his wife, and Jesse. I've lined her up with a date too," Kate informed her. "One of Richard's mates, Geoffrey Beaumont-Wilson."

"What did Jesse have to say about all this?" Alix couldn't help but ask.

Kate gave her a puzzled stare. "She was delighted and

said she'd love to come."

"Fair enough," Alix laughed. "By the way, who's doing the cooking?"

"Felix of course."

"It's his night off," Alix said.

"I'll do it then," Kate replied, and, blowing her friend a kiss, added, "Now I've got to fly. It's time for the beauty parlour!" Kate dashed out as quickly as she had arrived, leaving a wave of her newest perfume behind.

When Saturday came, Alix stood in front of the mirror and applied her make-up. It was then that she noticed the new lines beneath her eyes. Tansie was responsible for those lines, she thought. With a sigh she returned to the dressing room and selected a silver-grey, body-hugging dress. She was not in the mood for colour.

Later, she noticed with a smile that Julian Grosvenor was everything Kate had said he was. And even she had to agree that his backside was indeed quite cute!

Due to Kate's cooking, dinner was delicious.

As the evening progressed and became noisier, Alix too started to relax a little and took part in the vivacious conversation which flew across the table. Occasionally Alix gave Julian a sideways glance, thinking that if she were looking for someone, certainly in the past, he would have fitted the bill very nicely. She had grave doubts that she would ever try it again. The pain at the end of a relationship would never compensate for the joy of a new romance.

From time to time, she also allowed her gaze to wander to Jesse, who was sitting opposite her. Alix recognised how relaxed she always felt in Jesse's company, maybe because Jesse was so at ease with herself, she thought. Looking at her, bathed in the light of her immense dignity, Alix felt a brief rush of passion sweep through her. It was then that

Alix realised that she might never want to go to bed with another man again.

It was well past midnight, when the phone suddenly rang. Despite the late hour, Alix went to answer it in the study.

"Hello?"

"It's me!" Tansie murmured.

Alix took a deep breath. She could do nothing else but hang up. She felt as though the fragile barriers she had erected around herself were blown to pieces with the simple statement, "It's me." What do you want from me, she asked silently, wondering whether she would ever really understand what was going on inside Tansie's head.

"Is everything all right?" Julian asked when she returned to the dining room.

Alix nodded and took a big gulp of wine, followed by several more. Not long afterwards, the first couple rose to leave. The others soon followed.

Lingering at the door for a moment, Julian said, "Thank you for a wonderful evening. Would you have dinner with me one night?"

"Why don't you ring me?" she asked. She didn't mean to be ungracious, but she wasn't sure whether she could cope with going out with him.

"I'm leaving for San Francisco and New York tomorrow, so I'll call you when I get back," he suggested.

"That's fine," she said, thinking that if she wanted another globe-trotting lover, she might as well return to Haig.

When Alix found herself alone with Jesse, she took her arm and said, "Let's go and play the piano." She felt so lonely, she could not actually face being alone.

Sitting down on the piano stool, Alix asked, "How did you get on with Mr Geoffrey Beaumont-Wilson?"

"Very well." Jesse smiled, an amused glint in her eyes as she sat down next to Alix. "He was the last man I ever went to bed with . . . and what's more . . . he knows why!" she added.

"You're kidding?" Alix shook with sudden laughter. If Kate only knew, she thought. "How did he take your change of 'heart', so to speak?"

"At the time, not all that well," Jesse replied. "Many years later, he told me that he was not altogether surprised that women chose women partners given the unattractive characteristics of a large number of men."

"Coming from a man, I suppose that means a lot," Alix said and continued playing. Slowly the earlier loneliness dissipated and left Alix feeling calmer once again. Jesse always had that effect on her, she thought.

Jesse accompanied her and Alix never took her eyes off her companion's hands. They were beautiful hands, slim and gentle as they moved gracefully over the keyboard. She wondered what it would feel like to have those very hands touch her, roam over her body and caress her. As that thought surfaced in her mind, Alix sighed. She remembered only too well what Tansie's hands had been able to do, what feelings and responses they had evoked in her. Alix couldn't allow herself to become vulnerable, not so soon in any event. The pain and the disappointment were still very much with her.

Later when Jesse eventually got up to leave, Alix embraced her. For a second or so, she rested her cheek against Jesse's and then brushed a light kiss over it.

Jesse smiled. She knew for sure that she was in love with Alix. Alix's simple gesture of affection gave her hope that Alix might feel the same one day. Now she could wait, Jesse thought, and left.

When Tansie rang again the following day and the day after, Alix continued to hang up on her. Eventually she installed an answering machine with a pre-recorded message that said that she had gone on an indefinite fishing trip.

A couple of weeks later, Kate told Alix that she'd heard that Tansie had lost the baby. Alix took the news with mixed feelings and, although a part of her wanted to ring Tansie and convey her sorrow, she didn't. She decided that for both their welfare, it was better not to have any contact at all.

Early one Saturday morning, after a heavy night drinking alone, she attempted to compose the music for the movie *Endless Dusk*. She tried many different melodies and occasionally jotted down some notes, but, neither her heart nor her mind were able to create even a simple tune. She gave up and lit a cigarette. As she momentarily watched the dog chasing a bird around the garden, it slowly dawned on her why she felt so unsettled; other than the constant reminder that Tansie was no longer part of her life. She had hoped to spend a weekend with Jesse but Jesse had left for a conference in the States a couple of days earlier. Alix admitted that she was disappointed and missed her. She was well aware of how much she enjoyed Jesse's companionship, her sharp intellect and the warm friendship she continued to offer. Don't even think about it she checked herself, frightened of her own feelings.

With sudden determination, Alix shook her head and got up. She walked through to the sitting room, picked up one of the books from the unread pile on the coffee table and strolled outside. It was unusually warm for the late autumn season and, discarding her T-shirt and jeans, she stretched out on a sun lounge.

Lost in thought, she looked up sharply when the pool gate opened. Squinting against the bright sunlight, she stared at Julian, who stood towering above her and smiling.

"I'm sorry to barge in on you like this, but when nobody answered the door, I thought I might find you out here," he said. With a wide grin, he added, "Do you always welcome your guests in such sexy attire?"

Alix blushed. "Only the good-looking ones!"

"Thanks for the compliment."

For the first time in weeks, she began to feel a little more human, being able to exchange light-hearted pleasantries and to enjoy some adult conversation, particularly with someone who knew nothing of the sorrow she was experiencing.

When he embraced and kissed her later, her body stiffened instantly and went icy cold. She had not made love to anyone since Tansie had left her in Jamaica and although she accepted how much she missed the comfort and warmth of another human being, she could do nothing to accept Julian's offer. She had been starved of affection for an eternity and desperately needed to be held, caressed and even made love to. But, she couldn't bring herself to do so.

"I'm sorry . . . I can't," she whispered and drew away. Julian left moments later, promising to ring her in a day or two.

Already half-asleep when the phone rang, Alix slowly rolled over and reached for the handset. "Hello?" But no voice greeted her. All she could hear was someone sobbing. "Tansie, is that you?" she asked, annoyed with herself for forgetting to put the answering machine on.

"Alix, I can't bear this, I'm so miserable without you," Tansie cried in between sobs. "Isn't there anything I can do to make you understand that I'm slowly dying inside?"

Alix gripped the receiver with such force a sharp pain shot up her elbow and into her shoulder. "It was your choice!"

"Herb was the only chance I had and I took it. Are you going to make me suffer for the rest of my life because I did what I had to do?" Alix didn't reply and Tansie continued, "I haven't been able to work in weeks . . . I can't face it, not without your encouragement and. . ."

Alix momentarily tuned out and didn't hear the rest. She had two choices. She could either scream and yell and tell Tansie to leave her alone, or she could simply hang up. As she had done before, she chose the latter.

"Goodnight, Tansie." She replaced the receiver and curled underneath the sheet.

Although Julian had temporarily relieved her distress simply by being there and not pressuring her into something she couldn't do, it only served to bring home to her how deeply she was still in love with Tansie, and what joys her female lover had given her. She closed her eyes and saw Tansie's face as it used to look down at her. She smelt her scent and felt her hands as they used to sweep over her body. Tingling sensations invaded her body with such force she cried out. She wanted to recapture what they had once shared. But the memories of Tansie began to mingle with thoughts of Jesse. Then she wept into the pillows. It was all too hard and she was afraid.

Her thoughts of Tansie continued to invade her jumbled mind, particularly Tansie's comment that she could not work without Alix's encouragement. Had she built up Tansie's career and now destroyed it? The thought made her shudder. Silently she cried, "I gave you everything I could. Don't make me responsible for your failures as well. It was you who didn't want me!"

Much later, when she was calmer, Alix started to wonder whether she would ever have had a relationship with a woman had Tansie not walked into her life, or whether she would simply have continued to have male lovers. Alix couldn't know but thought it probably would have been the latter. However, Tansie had changed her life forever and there was no point speculating about it.

Alix felt as though there were two separate beings within her and each pulled in a different direction. One was desperately in love with Tansie, needing and wanting her and refusing to accept that she was gone. The other, almost as desperately, wanted to let go so that she could build a new life and perhaps find someone else in due course. But, for the moment, there seemed to be no reconciling the two.

Ever since she had become Tansie's lover, except the one time with Haig, she had not sought to go to bed with anyone else. Would she, could she, ever fall in love again?

When she aired her feelings to Jesse some time later, Jesse smiled.

"Give yourself time, Alix, and you will eventually find someone who will love you as you deserve to be loved," she said, adding, "there's always room for love."

"Don't tell me you made out with Geoffrey after all?" Alix asked in mock innocence.

"How did you and Julian get along the other night?" Jesse laughed.

"I expect the same as you did with Geoffrey!"

Jesse heard the sadness which lurked just below Alix's surface and she drew her into her arms. "Don't despair . . . it will get better." When Alix didn't move out of her embrace, Jesse continued to hold her. She wanted much more than that but Jesse was too sensitive not to realise that now was not the time. If, or when, Alix came closer to seeking a more intimate relationship then it would be quite early enough to start the real romance.

At the end of the following week, Alix told John that she

had finished the music score for the movie *Endless Dusk*.

"Well, what do you think?" she asked.

"If you're looking for a compliment, you've got it, pal," he smirked. "It is quite exemplary . . . it has Mozart's light-hearted charm, Tchaikovsky's melancholy moods and even Paganini's wild eccentricity."

"That good, hmmm?" she asked with a playful glimmer in her eyes. Even the dimples in her cheeks appeared for the first time in months.

John twirled his moustache between his fingers and looked as though he was deep in thought. The fact that her creative energy and sharp wit had taken a severe beating had not escaped him. And since he guessed rather than knew that Tansie was the cause of it, there was no need to ask her for an explanation. He felt sorry for her and because he was aware that he could offer her little comfort, he didn't even try.

Instead, he gave her a cheeky smile. "Welcome back." Moments later he sauntered from the room.

Alix returned to the piano and sat with her hands in her lap and stared out the window. She watched a few birds twittering and hopping from branch to branch and thought, if only I could fly away; as far away as possible. How she envied them their freedom.

She was still in a pensive mood when Kate arrived just before lunch.

"Welcome home," Alix smiled, giving her friend a peck on the cheek. Kate had been overseas for a month and Alix had missed her.

"How is it all going, pet?" Kate asked, noting that Alix was becoming very thin.

"I have my moments," Alix mused. "Most of the time I wonder whether things would have been different if I had . . ."

"You couldn't have changed anything," Kate interrupted. "But, if you really want to know, why don't you go and have a chat to someone professional?"

"You mean a psychiatrist?"

"Yes, just for a little while," Kate said. "I don't think you'll ever be free of Tansie if you don't do something drastic. Maybe a shrink might be able to explain Tansie's behaviour to you so that you don't have to keep wondering about what could have been, but wasn't."

"You might be right," Alix sighed. "I'll ask Jesse, she might know someone suitable."

Clapping Alix on the shoulder in an affectionate manner, Kate cried, "That's the spirit, now, let's get down to some real gossip. Did you hear from Julian again after the dinner at your house?"

"Hmmm," Alix muttered, as a slow twinkle appeared in her eyes.

"And?"

"And . . . nothing . . . I couldn't do it."

Kate shook her head in near despair. She had so hoped that if anyone could help Alix get over Tansie, Julian could. She gave her a long sideways glance as it suddenly dawned on her that maybe it wasn't a man Alix might want.

"Alix . . . would you be happier with a woman?"

Alix shrugged her shoulders. "I'm not sure but that is not the issue right now," she replied. "The way I feel at the moment, I don't want anybody. I'm not saying I don't need love and affection, I do very much. But I can't allow myself to be this exposed again . . . not now."

"Alix don't say that," Kate implored her. "Look, I understand how hurt you are but don't shut out love for good. We both know that you're far too sensual to ever go without . . ."

"Sex?" Alix laughed.

"Yeah," Kate confirmed, adding with a smirk, "it's good for the complexion, didn't you know?"

"Then I must look absolutely dreadful." On the surface she was casual about it but inside she hurt and was frustrated. Why couldn't she just accept what was offered to her from Julian and, Alix thought, probably from Jesse too if she wanted it? It was then that she made the first real rational decision since Tansie had left her. Yes, she would ask Jesse to refer her to a psychiatrist and she would make every effort to get over Tansie and put her where she belonged: in the past.

Chapter 29

When Alix saw Jesse a few days later, she asked her about a suitable psychiatrist.

Jesse gave it some thought. "Dr Kim Elliot is one of the best," she eventually said. She had a lot of admiration for Kim. Her reputation was flawless and her academic achievements were remarkable.

"Where do I find him?"

"Her!" Jesse was amused that Alix would automatically think that Kim was a man. "Her rooms are in South Yarra. I'll give you a referral and make an appointment for you if you like," she added smiling and thinking that Alix would be too impatient to wait, which she might well have to do if she rang herself.

"I'd appreciate that," Alix replied, grateful for Jesse's help. Now that she had made the decision to see someone, there was no need to delay the first visit.

"Come in, please," Kim greeted Alix when she arrived for her appointment two days later. "Have a seat," she invited her. She motioned to the armchair on the far side of the fireplace and sat down in the chair opposite. "Your name is very familiar," she continued, "But I can't quite place it."

"Do you like classical music?" Alix's eyes had a glimmer of mischief.

"Of course," Kim laughed and lifted the old-fashioned teacup to her lips. "You're a pianist and the composer of the Rostoff Symphony among others, correct?"

"Correct," Alix said.

"By the way, call me Kim. Most of my patients do," she invited Alix.

"Okay." Alix was hesitant and not quite sure where to start; she studied the doctor.

Kim appeared to be in her late forties and, in Alix's view, looked as any psychiatrist should: a little vague, a little untidy, a little old-fashioned but exuding warmth and compassion. Her rich honey-coloured hair was piled on top of her head in a mass of wild curls and was held in place with three or four wide tortoise-shell combs. She was not very tall, but slim, and dressed in a cream-coloured linen suit. It was her light brown eyes Alix felt herself most drawn to. They were alert, intelligent and inspired confidence.

"How can I help you?" Kim asked.

Alix took a deep breath. She began by recalling the time, over three years ago, when she and Tansie had first met. Slowly she recounted the story of an accidental meeting and the friendship which had slowly developed and become an intense love affair. She concluded by describing how the love, the passion and the friendship had all been shattered. Alix left nothing out. At times Kim made notes and asked her the occasional question if she wasn't clear about something.

Although she tried to remain calm in order to give Kim an accurate background, there were moments which were simply too distressing and tears would find their way down her cheeks. Silently Kim handed Alix the box of tissues and waited.

It took three further sessions, with three or four days between each one, before Kim knew the substance of her patient's and Tansie's relationship and had a clear picture of what it meant to Alix. At the end, Alix felt wrung out and Kim suggested she wait a few days for her next visit.

When she returned for her next session, Kim gave her a friendly smile. "You know, Alix, people don't die of broken hearts. Sooner or later we all get over it."

Alix smiled and for a fleeting moment, her eyes twinkled. "What about Romeo and Juliet?"

Kim acknowledged her comment with a chuckle and went on to ask how Alix thought she could assist.

After a moment's silence, Alix replied, "In order for me to put this relationship into perspective, I need to understand what Tansie is all about and whether I could have changed anything."

"That sounds reasonable," Kim agreed.

For several weeks afterwards, Alix saw her on a regular basis. As she slowly came to understand Tansie's intricate and complex character, the motivation for her behaviour and the fact that she could not have changed the course of events, she became calmer. Although there were times when she resented having to see her, she learnt many things from Kim.

Her sessions with Kim were only interrupted when Alix had to go overseas at the end of May. Marta Borg had asked her to compose the music for the film they had already discussed. Alix was delighted to accept the commission. She also welcomed the idea of spending some time with Marta and Nina.

At the same time she also had to make a decision as to whether or not she would accompany Boris on the concert tour. After several discussions with Boris and John, she decided that she would. Boris was delighted and arranged for their agent to make the necessary bookings. He wanted to perform in most European capital cities and then the United States. All in all, the tour would take about four months. He planned a short break over Christmas. Alix was pleased with that. She would arrange for Felix and the children to meet her somewhere in Europe.

Over many weeks, Alix began to find more and more comfort in Jesse's supportive companionship. Jesse also helped her to gain a better understanding of lesbians and their varied reasons for entering into such relationships.

As often as time allowed it, the two women spent evenings and the occasional weekend together. They talked endlessly. About music and politics, about people and how they interacted, about places they had visited around the world and about their childhood experiences. They talked about their work, their hopes and their dreams. Although their relationship continued much on the same intellectual level as it had started, some playful affection between them seemed inevitable. Both women were naturally affectionate and their passions always smouldered just below the surface. Neither of them was made to be celibate for any length of time. Jesse still felt, however, that Alix was not ready for an intimate liaison. Instead, she saw it as a time they could get to know each other better.

It was towards winter that year when Alix found out from her older son that all was not well in the Mullins household and that Tansie was pregnant again. She was deeply troubled by the news. Alix was sorry, particularly for the boys, but she was not surprised. However, there was nothing she could do. Tansie had made her own choice and Alix could no longer help her.

When Alix arrived for her next session with Kim the following week, they chatted for a while about her work and the children before getting down to the real reason for the visit.

"I hate to say this, Alix, but it was extremely unwise of

you to continue to grant Tansie her wishes, particularly over such a prolonged period," Kim told her. "Don't misunderstand me, I'm not sitting in judgement, I'm merely saying, had you said 'no more' a long time ago, it would have been a lot easier for you."

Alix reached for a tissue and wiped her eyes. "I know that now, but because I loved her so much, I wanted to believe that she loved me too."

"I understand and I'm sure she did love you," Kim replied. On the surface, Kim noted, Alix mostly appeared cool, aloof and in control, and yet underneath that layer was a very fragile woman. A woman who wanted and needed to be loved and nurtured and couldn't quite understand why she wasn't and why she had been let down so badly by Tansie. "However, I honestly believe that you were never meant for each other and not because you're both women. I think she did you a favour when she left."

"So you keep saying," Alix sighed.

When she left soon afterwards, Alix had to admit that she felt a little better. She had come to like Kim a great deal and trusted her judgement implicitly. Alix knew that it was her own impatience which got in the way from time to time. She wanted to be free of her emotional ties with Tansie, sooner rather than later.

Although Alix regretted it later, she had promised her son Christian that she would go to his and Drew's school fair the last Saturday before the July holidays. The closer the date came, the more distraught she became. All she could think about was how to avoid Tansie who would surely be there, as David had a scholarship at the school. Driving out the driveway, she convinced herself that Tansie, being Tansie, wouldn't turn up.

As soon as they arrived there, Christian went to find

Felix who would by now have finished his round of duties on the merry-go-round. Alix ambled about aimlessly for a while. Occasionally she stopped and exchanged pleasantries with other parents she knew but had not seen for some time.

Not quite sure what to do with herself, she had just swung herself on to a seemingly deserted trestle table when she froze. Tansie was less than five feet away and stared straight at her. They were so close, they could almost touch. A blind panic gripped Alix and she had to take several short shallow breaths of air. For a few seconds only, their eyes locked and a tentative smile appeared on both their faces in acknowledgment of the other's presence.

Tansie was the first to avert her glance and turned her attention to her three female companions: her mother and sister-in-law and her friend Julie.

In Alix's view, Tansie looked positively awful and it was quite obvious that she was less than happy.

With sorrow, Alix realised how much she still loved her. Her body was vibrantly aware of Tansie's closeness. She was so close, yet too far to reach. She cried silently for the woman who was no longer hers to love.

"Had I known you were going to be here, I would have warned you that Tansie was around," Jesse said as she appeared at Alix's side and put a protective arm around her shoulders.

Only moments earlier, Jesse had observed the two women from afar. It was with great sadness for Alix that Jesse noted how difficult this meeting was for her and how deeply attached she still was to Tansie. She wondered whether she had hoped too soon that Alix might in time return her love.

Alix gave Jesse a weak smile. "Short of popping myself on the top of some mountain, I'll have to learn to cope with such unexpected meetings. She's not going to simply disappear just to please me," Alix murmured without taking her eyes off Tansie. "Anyway, what are you doing here, Jesse?"

"As you know my sister's four boys are at school here, so I promised to help out," Jesse replied, searching Alix's face. "Maybe we can have a coffee in the Toorak Village later?"

"Yes, I'd like that," Alix said as she watched Tansie's group preparing to leave. They all turned towards Alix but, without so much as a sideways glance, started to march past her, although they all knew her. Alix was not surprised by their display of bad manners. Herb didn't have any, so why should the rest of the family be any different? What she found harder to understand was how Tansie could bring herself to stoop to such depths.

Tansie trailed behind the three women and looked as though she too was going to walk past. Then she stopped directly in front of Alix, but ignored Jesse.

Staring at her former lover at close range now, Alix was curious to find out if her sessions with Kim had helped her at all. Not feeling nearly as distressed and agitated as she had the last time Tansie had visited her at her house, Alix decided that her sessions with Kim had indeed not been wasted. Alix was very pleased with herself.

As Tansie came nearer, Alix noted that her eyes were dull and expressionless and her lips were drawn into a thin, sulky line. Although she wore a shapeless, overly bright maternity dress, Alix noticed Tansie's rounded stomach underneath. On impulse, Alix wanted to yell at her that what she was doing was all one big mistake and that this marriage would never work.

Instead, she remained determined not to let Tansie guess what she was thinking or feeling deep inside. To all outside appearances, she stayed aloof and the look in her eyes bore an element of indifference.

Scrutinising Alix, Tansie asked with greater concern than she had displayed at other times, "Are you all right?"

The words, "Of course I'm not all right," were already forming on Alix's lips but died instantly. Involuntarily, she lowered her gaze to the ground. Fleeting shock set in as she noticed that Tansie was still wearing the ring which matched her own: the pair to the one Tansie had given her on the plane from Vienna to Paris during their first overseas trip together.

"Alix?" Tansie asked softly when no response came.

Alix slipped the ring from her middle finger and handed it to Tansie. "Give it to Mullins, I have no more use for it!"

Tansie paled and gasped. "Alix, please, don't do this to me." Swallowing hard a couple of times and holding back tears, she added, "If you'd only understand what a wonderful person Herb really is. He's kind and considerate and quite prepared to give me the world. He truly loves me."

Alix wanted to say that she was all those things, and more, but that was obviously not enough. Instead, she said tightly, "He sounds perfectly irresistible . . . what a pity I let him slip through my fingers!"

Tansie glared at Alix. "Is that meant to be an insult?"

"Take it as you like," Alix replied. "Among many other things, you called him an uneducated peasant!"

Tansie's cheeks blushed bright red and she was about to reply, when Alix cut in first.

"Take care," Alix said. She slipped from the table and, taking Jesse's arm, drew her away.

Jesse gave her hand a gentle squeeze. "You did very well . . . I'm proud of you."

"I'm not sure that I'm proud of myself," Alix looked

crushed and miserable. "You know, when I gave her back the ring, I wanted to hurt her and . . ."

"Thank God for that," Jesse replied. When Alix gave her a bewildered glance, she added, "You are human, and you have as much right as anybody else to be angry and hurt and even to want to hurt others. I'm sure if you told Kim about this encounter, she would tell you that what you did is hardly the end of the world."

"You're probably right," Alix sighed. "I just never thought that I would ever want to hurt Tansie, that's all."

After a coffee and a toasted cheese sandwich in the Village, Alix rang Felix to tell him that she wouldn't be home until after dinner that evening. Instead she went to Jesse's house. Just like its owner, it displayed a great deal of dignity and elegance. Its high Victorian ceilings, panelled doors and large windows gave it an air of openness. It was comfortable and inviting. Anybody who walked through the door felt immediately at home, including Alix. The sun had finally broken through the clouds and now filled the sitting room with light and warmth.

They sat on the couch and, as they talked and laughed, they leafed through Jesse's photo albums. As though guided by an inner force, Alix surprised herself by suddenly wanting to know everything she didn't already know about Jesse. What sort of kid she had been at school. Was she a good attentive student or did she make smart comments during classes? Alix's questions seemed endless.

Jesse happily supplied all the answers. Her face had a light flush, her eyes sparkled when she spoke and her smile was warm, the lips parted just a little. As she spoke, she rarely took her eyes off Alix, thinking what a beautiful woman she was. A woman who excited her like no other woman had for a long time. Alix's insouciant air and her flattering attention warmed Jesse's heart.

Alix felt a lurid flush spreading through her and a small ache gripped at her soul as though it wanted to shake her back into reality, to tell her that whatever it was she wanted, she could have it. It was there for the asking. Involuntarily, her eyes twinkled and smouldered at the same time and, unbeknown to her, gave out messages of slow seduction.

"Jesse?" Alix didn't say the name but rather exhaled it as though not to break the spell. Their glance was mutual, searching each other's souls. Alix leant forward, her lips touched Jesse's, lightly kissing them. Then she drew away, feeling suddenly shy, and lowered herself on to the pile of cushions on the floor. She drew her knees up underneath her chin and wrapped her arms around her legs. Although she had to admit that it felt good kissing Jesse, Alix was just a little rattled by her own impulsiveness. She wondered what had induced her to kiss Jesse. Was it just the heat of the moment?

Smiling, Jesse let her hand run through Alix's lustrous curls and then kissed the top of her head. "It's okay, Alix," Jesse murmured, then moved her hands to Alix's shoulders and gently massaged them.

Alix leant her head against Jesse's legs and let her gaze wander to the large french doors and into the garden beyond. A smile curved her lips upwards as she became aware that the sun always made her act impulsively.

Later, they played the piano and the mood between them became light again. Each knew there was something smouldering below the surface, leaving them just a little breathless every time their eyes met.

When Alix finally left, she drew Jesse into her arms, just for a moment. "Thanks for a lovely evening," she said, turned and sauntered down the few steps. She felt happier and calmer than she had for a long time.

The following week, Alix and Felix took two car-loads of children to Portsea for their winter holidays. The days had suddenly turned cold and wet and the wind blew viciously over the cliff top. The sea just below savagely crashed over the rocks, spraying white foam high up into the air.

At first when the children had asked whether they could go to the beach house for the holidays, Alix had baulked at the idea. The mere thought sent a wave of despair through her. Tansie wouldn't be there. She suggested that they all go to Bali or somewhere; to the sun. In the end, she decided she would not disappoint them.

When she was not out with her offspring somewhere, Alix worked at a frantic pace or simply sat for hours in front of the blazing fire, staring at the flames licking the logs and remembering the times she and Tansie had shared together in this very same spot.

Once in a while, when her thoughts were less lucid, she felt as though her memory was playing tricks on her. She wondered whether the love between them had not been as intense as she thought it had. But invariably, she came back to the same conclusion: their good times had been perfect. After her many sessions with Kim, the one thing she was now sure about was that she could not have changed the course their relationship had taken. Given Tansie's temperament, insecurity and unwillingness to explore her inner self, it couldn't have gone anywhere else but where it did.

Very often now, when she thought about Tansie, invariably her thoughts also strayed to Jesse. She missed her. It was that simple. During the second week, Alix rang her and invited her to visit.

"I've been coaching the girls in tennis . . . they're ready to take you on," Alix said over the telephone.

Jesse laughed. "I'll be there, say, Thursday lunch?"

Jackie and Kate, who were waiting for the fourth person to show up, briefly glared at Alix when Jesse arrived.

"Knowing how much you like winning, Alix, I'm not sure about your choice of partner," Jackie commented.

Kate as usual was more blunt. "No offence, Jesse, but are you sure you want to take us on? You just don't seem the sporty type."

With a soft smile around her lips, Jesse replied, "The stakes are your earrings, right Kate? And, should you and Jackie win, each of you gets to have Felix for a week."

"Hey, wait a minute," Alix cried. "What am I supposed to do without him?"

"Maybe a stint at a domestic college might help. I'm sure even you can be taught such menial tasks!" Kate quipped and strolled towards the tennis court.

As they warmed up, Jackie glanced at her partner and gave her a conspiratorial wink. "The best of five should sort out the chaff from the grain, don't you think?"

"I expect so," Kate grinned.

"As you wish," Alix said and gently hit a ball back to Kate. There was no need to start the assault too early or too quickly. She was confident that Kate and Jackie had little hope of winning this game.

And five sets they played. Almost staggering off the court and gasping for air, Kate removed her diamond earrings. "One for each of you," she cried and handed them over to the winners.

"Felix?" Alix called as soon as they went inside. "Since I haven't gambled your services away, could we please have some drinks?" To Jesse who had taken the seat next to Alix on the large leather couch, she said, "We did well, partner . . . thanks for your help."

"The pleasure was mine, partner!" Jesse raised her eyebrows with nonchalance.

"Right away, ma'am," Felix called in jest from the kitchen and promptly arrived with a tray.

Later, when Alix and Kate were on their own for a moment, Kate asked casually, "What's the story with Jesse? You've grown very fond of her, haven't you?"

"I have," Alix replied. "She's an excellent sportswoman!"

"That's not what I asked," Kate pointed out.

With an amused smile, Alix continued, "She also has three university degrees, is a world-wide authority on . . . hmmm . . . women's matters . . . loves five star hotels . . . and . . . she's a great pianist to boot!"

"That makes her your perfect match, doesn't it, pet?"

"It does," Alix agreed. "If or when I'm ready for it."

For a moment, Kate glared at her friend, dumbfounded. "You mean she could be interested?"

"Possibly!"

"Alix, you're driving me crazy!" Kate exclaimed with exasperation. Shaking her head as the full meaning of Alix's statement sunk in, she gasped. "I had no idea . . . I would never have guessed! Oh my God, I lined her up with a date!"

"I'm sure she has forgiven you your faux-pas!"

"Is there a possibility that the two of you might get together then?" Kate asked after a short pause.

"I don't know, Kate." Alix absent-mindedly traced her lower lip with her thumb.

"Good grief, Alix, what are you waiting for?" Kate cried. "She's beautiful, warm and generous, never mind all the credentials. What more do you want?"

"You're right, what more could I want." Alix readily agreed. "But, as you know, I'm not emotionally free yet.

And I certainly don't want to hurt Jesse any more than I want to get hurt. So, for the moment, I'll bide my time."

"That's fair enough," Kate said. "Just don't wait too long. I want to see you happy again, Alix."

Alix smiled but didn't reply. Instead she sighed as she wondered whether she would ever be free to love again with all the passion she knew she had. Maybe with Jesse it would be possible.

Chapter 30

Towards the end of winter, Alix decided that she would have to go to her country property. She had not done so since Tansie had deserted her. Not wanting to be alone that first time, she invited Jesse. She needed the tranquillity it offered her but wasn't ready to be by herself. Jesse seemed the most logical companion and the only person she knew she would be comfortable with. They left town early on Friday morning so as to have a full weekend.

Alix cringed inside when she first walked into the bedroom she had so often shared with Tansie. She walked straight out again and, opening the doors from the sitting room to the verandah, stepped outside.

It was a cold, but clear, beautiful winter's day. The sky was blue, the grass in the paddocks was lush and green, the massive tree trunks were a rich dark brown colour and the Victorian Alps in the distance were covered with snow. The contrast of the four colours was quite startling.

Jesse had followed Alix but stopped just inside the door and watched her for a moment. How beautiful and serene Alix looked and what a pleasure it was to see her like this. She stepped up behind Alix and quite naturally wrapped her arms around her shoulders.

Alix just as naturally leant into Jesse's body and covered her hands with her own. Neither felt it necessary to speak nor were they in a hurry to move or do anything at all.

Slowly, Alix's earlier distress dissipated and she managed to put the old memories to the back of her mind. Tansie is gone forever, it's over, she reminded herself with considerable impatience. This is here and now, and you have to get on with your life.

Jesse was well aware of Alix's apprehension and kept Alix as busy as possible that first day. She suggested a long walk through the woods and an even longer ride into the hills. When they did so, she talked about her work, her research, the papers she had been invited to give and the work she did for women's causes. Jesse was pleased to see that, judging by her response, Alix was able to keep her mind off Tansie most of the time.

However, when it was time for bed that first evening, it was different. An hour or so after having said goodnight to Alix, Jesse still heard her hammering away at the piano.

Eventually Jesse got up, pulled on her silk dressing gown and wandered into the sitting room. Lowering herself on to the piano stool next to Alix, she drew her into her arms.

"Jesse, how can I sleep in my room when everything reminds me of Tansie?" Alix exclaimed as tears filled her eyes. "It was here in this very house that we first shared a bed . . . although not as lovers, I still feel that it started right here."

Jesse cradled Alix's face in her hands and said, "Then you will sleep in the guest room. You can't stay up all night." When Alix didn't reply right away, she added, "If you're more comfortable by yourself, I'll sleep in one of the children's rooms."

"Do you like single beds?" Alix asked with a weak smile.

"Not particularly."

Holding Jesse's gaze, Alix added, "Then don't sleep in one. If it's okay with you, we'll both share the guest room."

When they slipped into bed, Alix murmured, "Would you just hold me?"

Jesse drew Alix into her arms and said, "Sleep well."

Comforted by Jesse's presence, Alix went to sleep shortly afterwards. Even though she was now well aware that it could lead to something else, Alix was no longer frightened by the fact that she found solace in another woman's arms. Although she was not ready for another relationship, the thought that there might be one in the future did not daunt her as it had previously.

Jesse was comfortable just holding Alix. She smiled, as she thought that they had a long future ahead of them. She was confident of that and she could wait.

At the end of the weekend, Alix noted with pleasure that she did not feel nearly as distressed as she thought she might. As Kim had predicted, memories of Tansie had started to take a back seat.

During her next session with Kim, Alix told her about the weekend and not just how much better she felt but that she actually felt quite good. She had found an inner peace she had thought she would never experience again. Alix also told her that Jesse was largely responsible for the change in her emotional state.

"What would you do if Tansie were to leave her husband now?" Kim asked.

"I don't know," she said softly. "But I do know that I couldn't ever go back to her. In time she would destroy both of us." After a short pause, she added, "You see, Tansie was still leaving messages on my answering machine, telling me how much she missed me, loved me and wanted me back. Finally I changed the number."

"I think that was very wise."

When Alix remained silent, Kim continued, "By the way, I heard on the grapevine that you're playing with the MSO shortly."

"No secrets in this town," Alix smiled fleetingly. "Boris can be very persuasive. When Alicia Bartoli cancelled her concert at short notice, he asked me to fill in for her. Since I'm already preparing for the concert tour later in the year, an extra performance is no trouble really." Raising her eyebrows in a teasing gesture, she added, "And, I do rather like to be on the stage and have the world at my feet!"

"You most certainly feel better. Six months ago you wouldn't have said that." Kim beamed. She was most pleased with Alix's progress.

"You see, Alix," she continued, "because you allowed Tansie to abuse you, she never had to deal with any of the real issues. By that I mean she behaved like a spoilt brat and you pandered to her whims. In the long run that was not healthy for either of you."

"It wasn't always like that. We had periods of extreme happiness . . . she wasn't all bad."

"No, she wasn't," Kim replied. "But as I've said before, you just weren't meant for each other."

Alix had two more sessions with Kim who then informed her that she should try and get along without her. But, there were a few things she wanted to say to her before they finished their regular appointments.

"You may ask yourself why she didn't modify her behaviour, knowing that her behaviour was so destructive. In order to change anyone's behaviour, we have to find the underlying cause of the pattern," Kim explained. "Tansie has buried a great deal. It would have been extremely painful for her to bring it out into the open and it could only be done with long-term intensive therapy. Unfortunately Tansie chose the easy way out which, by the way, is not that unusual."

Kim went on to explain that, in her view, Tansie's

devastating childhood had so traumatised her that at times she barely knew right from wrong, or good from bad. She was one of the unfortunate victims who constantly experienced a feeling of powerlessness and yet at the same time, because of the pain, constantly struggled to achieve some sense of power.

Kim concluded by saying, "Now, when we fall in love we effectively lose control over our emotions . . . we lose some of that power we have fought so hard to gain."

"You mean I had such power over Tansie?"

"Not now, the balance has tipped in her favour again," she replied. "Initially, of course you did. She fell in love with you. In order to regain her dominance she became abusive and cruel, and because you allowed her to get away with it, she had no reason to change. You were always in a no-win situation where Tansie was concerned."

"Had I withdrawn my support earlier would it have changed anything?"

"Possibly, but there is no guarantee," she replied gently. "However, I would not have advised you to wait for any transformation, bearing in mind that other things may have surfaced that still would have hindered any healthy and lasting relationships, whether with men or women."

Kim studied her for a moment and then continued. "In my view, Tansie only married to be Mrs Somebody. Unfortunately, that is the only thing you could not have given her. The relationship was, as I've said before, doomed from the outset."

"I understand that now." Alix took Kim's explanation with relative calm. But then her aim had always been to understand Tansie and, once she did, she could put her into the past and get on with it. She was satisfied that Kim had helped her to achieve that goal.

Alix shook Kim's hand when her last session came to an end. As much as she had hated these sessions at times, she was glad she had pursued them. She had worked through her relationship with Tansie and had come to a satisfactory understanding of it.

Jesse also helped her a great deal. Although they both travelled extensively and often in opposite directions, they still managed to see each other frequently. Gently, but surely, Jesse had swept into the empty space Tansie had left behind.

In her new found state of calm, Alix gave Brahms' Piano Concerto No. 2 a new meaning when she played with the MSO ten days later. The fact that this particular piece of music was one of the longest and most demanding in the repertoire, didn't seem to phase her.

The music had all the strength and passion which most suited her own character. It was in the concluding movement, with its airy and childlike cheerfulness that she felt really free again. Her spirits lifted and she gave it the solid yet carefree interpretation she thought Brahms had intended.

Her delivery had an extraordinary effect on the audience and they responded accordingly. They repeatedly called her back to the stage. In wasn't until after the third encore that she threw her hands into the air, blew several kisses into the crowd and took her last bow.

As she had often done in the past, Alix invited the whole orchestra and a number of journalists and friends back to her house afterwards. The party was still in full swing when the speculation began amongst the journalists as to whether or not she would accompany Boris on the European and North American tour.

Alix smiled when she overheard two journalists arguing about it. One was adamant that she wouldn't. The other one was just as adamant that she would. Alix knew that

Boris had only told one journalist that she was indeed going on tour with him. The rest would have to read it in the paper like everybody else, she thought and moved on.

Despite the late night, Alix was up early the next morning. She bought all the newspapers, visited the local bakery to pick up fresh bread and croissants and went to Jesse's house.

"I'm so proud of you. Last night was one of the finest performances I have ever heard," Jesse cried and kissed her on the lips. Reaching for one of the papers, she added lightly, "Let's see what everyone else has to say about it."

Alix could not have hoped for better reviews. They were excellent, bar one. As she read it, Alix drew her face into a grimace and threw the tabloid on to the table.

"I should have known Geoff would do that!" Alix exclaimed. She was angry with herself for even having spoken to him when he had appeared at rehearsal one afternoon. "He has completely distorted everything I said!"

"Listen to this," Alix continued, picking up the paper. "Although Ms Clemenger remained tight-lipped about her extended stay in Europe earlier this year, we have reason to believe that she suffered some sort of breakdown which necessitated that stay." The article went on to insinuate that it had something to do with either a romance that had gone horribly wrong or professional burn-out. Alix wasn't sure which comment infuriated her more but they both added to her anger.

"They have no right to impinge on my privacy like that!"

"Unfortunately for you, it makes you more human for the reader," Jesse pointed out.

"I'd rather be inhuman!"

Jesse laughed. "That's more like the old Alix I know, a little stubborn and a little contrary!"

"They'd have a field day if they ever found out the truth," Alix muttered.

"They won't," Jesse assured her. "Have you decided when you're actually going to leave for Europe?"

"We start the tour in Vienna at the beginning of December, so I thought I might leave early in November and stay with Hanna for a couple of weeks," Alix said. "I'm also half-tempted to accept an invitation to stay with Marta and Nina in Berlin for a while."

"Why don't you? That's a great idea," Jesse responded enthusiastically. Suddenly her eyes lit up. "Why don't you go to Switzerland now? You could prepare for the tour and you'd have time to visit Marta."

"I have thought about going earlier but I'm reluctant to leave the children for that length of time," Alix said. "At the moment I have arranged for them to meet me in Madrid for Christmas."

"Why don't you take them with you?" Jesse asked. "Switzerland is renowned for its excellent schools, I'm sure you could find one to suit them, don't you think?"

"Now that you mention it, I'm sure I could," Alix confirmed. "In that case, I suppose there is no real reason why I couldn't go in a couple of weeks or so," Alix replied. On impulse, she added, "Is there any chance that you might come over to Europe, maybe for Christmas?"

"The thought has already crossed my mind," Jesse admitted with a smile. "If I can organise myself I'll even meet you in Vienna for the opening night of the concert tour. How would you feel about that?"

"Oh, Jesse, that would be wonderful," Alix replied, genuinely happy about the prospect. She had not liked the idea of a prolonged separation from Jesse but didn't quite know how to approach her about it.

The following day, she told John her plans. "John, how would you feel if I deserted you earlier than I had originally planned? I thought I might leave for Europe in a couple of weeks and prepare for the concert tour over there. I'll take the children with me and . . ."

"Go for it, love," he assured her. "You've had a rough time with Tansie, a break will do you good. And, with you out of the country, I might get to take things a bit easier!"

"Enjoy it while it lasts!" Alix replied. "I'll be as normal as ever when I return."

John rolled his eyes and winced. "Geniuses are never normal!" With a sly grin, he added, "If you know what's really good for you, you'll take Jesse along with you."

"You're turning out to be more astute than I realised," Alix smiled.

"I see many things," he responded loftily.

The children too were excited when she told them of her plans.

"Can I take Felix with me?" Christian asked.

Before Alix could reply, Drew did. "Mum wouldn't know what to do without him. Of course he's coming!"

"Thanks for the confidence, chum," Alix laughed.

Chapter 31

Quite by accident, Tansie came across the magazine that carried a long story about Alix and Boris and the concert tour they planned in Europe and America. Her heart sank when she realised that Alix would be out of the country when the baby was due.

For some time Tansie simply sat and stared at one of the photos that appeared with the story. It was obviously taken at Alix's house and, given that Alix was still wearing an exquisite, but simple, yellow and black designer dress, she assumed it was taken after the concert with the MSO a couple of days earlier. For a change, Alix had swept her curls off her forehead and held them back with a band to match the dress. She looked young and vibrant, just like Tansie remembered her. But it was her eyes Tansie was mesmerised and enthralled by: they were large and luminous as she had often seen them in the past, particularly when they had made love.

"Alix, my love," Tansie sighed and wiped a few tears from her face. It was at that very moment that she knew that she had to see Alix before she left Melbourne.

When Herb rang her during the day to see how she was, Tansie told him that she was on her way to see Alix.

"What for?" he asked. He was not pleased at all.

"I just want to," Tansie snapped. "But before I go and see her, I want you to promise me that when the baby comes you'll ring Alix and tell her."

"Why would I want to do that?" he asked. He was even

less pleased with the prospect of having to speak to Alix.

"Because I ask you to," Tansie said.

"If it makes you feel better, I will," Herb said. "I'll be home late for dinner," he added and hung up.

Within the hour, Tansie arrived at Alix's and, without a word to Jenny, walked straight into Alix's studio.

Alix looked up from the piano where she was gathering some music sheets when she heard the footsteps.

"Please, Alix, don't throw me out!" Tansie begged. "I need to talk to you."

"Okay, talk!"

Tansie sat down on the couch and said, "Don't you think we have both suffered enough?"

Not sure where this conversation was leading, Alix remained aloof. She couldn't allow herself to slip into something she might not be able to control no matter how confident she had felt in recent times. Seeing Tansie at such close range made Alix feel quite vulnerable.

"What do you want?"

"Alix, I love you and I'm slowly dying inside," Tansie said. "I can't bear the thought of having this baby without you being there to hold my hand." Before Alix could say anything, Tansie added, "I know you'll be in Europe some- where . . . that's why I had to come and see you now."

Alix remained silent.

"Why are you going on this concert tour, Alix? You hate to be away from home for such long periods of time," Tansie said. When after a considerable pause Alix still failed to reply, Tansie continued. "Have I done this to you?"

"Don't flatter yourself!" Alix said, keeping her voice low and pleasant.

"I am so sorry," Tansie replied and lowered her eyes as they filled with tears.

Alix took a deep breath. Now that Tansie was here, there was one thing Alix needed to know. "Why did you let it go on for so long, Tansie? You must have known that sooner or later you would leave me. Why did you come to Jamaica with me?"

"I love you, Alix . . . I couldn't stop it," Tansie murmured. "I couldn't then and I can't now. As far as you and I are concerned, nothing has changed, I want you more than ever."

"Go away!" Alix could barely get the words out. Her emotions were so close to the surface, she thought she would burst if she said anything else. She remembered the very first time she had met Tansie: an exotically beautiful woman with a childlike charm Alix had eventually been unable to resist. A talented woman who with Alix's encouragement had made it to the top only to discard her success for a worthless man. As far as Alix was aware, Tansie had not produced a single sculpture since she had married Mullins.

Instead of leaving, Tansie took a few steps towards Alix. She was so close, Alix could feel her breath on her cheeks. As though in slow motion, they seemingly automatically moved towards each other. Their arms reached out as if it were the most natural thing in the world. They were gripped by an instant electric current. When Tansie's lips found Alix's, what little control either still might have had, vanished in seconds.

That barest touch had an instantaneous and devastating effect on both women. Neither could deny the magical desire which passed between them and all but swept them off their feet. How easy it would be, Alix thought, to make love right here and now. That very moment suddenly became precious beyond comparison. But it had to stop – now.

Alix managed to call upon her reserve of strength from somewhere deep within.

"No, Tansie!" She pushed her away. "What the hell do you think you're doing here? Get out . . . just get out of my life."

As soon as Tansie was gone, Alix sat down at the piano. Suddenly she felt calmer and more at peace than she had for a long time. Truth and love have so many faces, she thought. Finally she understood and accepted that it had not been within Tansie's capacity to comprehend either. As though she had needed Tansie's visit, Alix now knew that she would be able to bury the ghost and the dream. It was all over. It had to be over. What was left was some guilt at having totally withdrawn all help. However, as she remembered Kim's many words of advice, she knew even that would eventually slip into the background.

Three days later and after having brought her departure to Europe forward by nearly another two weeks, Alix had only one more thing to do before she could leave. She rang her florist.

"Paul? Would you please send two dozen apricot roses to Mrs Herb Mullins," she asked.

"What message would you like on the card, Ms Clemenger?"

"Message?" Alix repeated as though far away in her thoughts. "No message, Paul," she said softly and hung up. If Alix knew Tansie at all then she expected Tansie to understand the gesture: I have forgiven you, but now I must leave you and your life for good.

The house was locked up and Alix, Felix and the children left for Hong Kong and Geneva early the following afternoon. Autumn had started in Europe and turned whole forests into masses of warm reds, yellows and oranges. The mild afternoon breezes, which came up from Lake Geneva, rippled the lake's surface and gently swayed the tree tops, making them whisper as though they were speaking to a lover. The many vineyards were awash with excitement. Men, women and children, all grape pickers, moved through the vines, picked the fruit and laid it in the wooden barrels they carried on their backs. They sang, they talked and they laughed. It had been a good season and the fruit was plump and heavy, ready to be made into wine.

From the moment the family arrived at Hanna's house, they all thrived. Almost daily, Alix wandered into the vineyards. She chatted to the locals and joked with them as though they were old friends. She felt freer and happier than she had for many months.

It was with fond memories that she recalled the only time Haig had visited her at her aunt's house. It had been harvest season, like now, and the two of them had lain underneath a grapevine, popping grape after grape into each other's mouths, wanting time to stop. Suddenly she thought of Jesse. She could imagine Jesse, with her long willowy body stretched out underneath the grapevines, her deep blue eyes sparkling and the sky reflecting in them. Her lips would be moist and sensuously parted as she slowly drew the grape inside her mouth. Sadly, Alix thought, Jesse would not be here for another few weeks and would miss the harvest.

The children took to their new schools with enthusiasm and not even their lack of French could dampen their spirits. Soon they competed with one another as to who had learnt the most that week. Drew and Sara attended the English-speaking school in Geneva and Christian went to the small village school near Hanna's house. Hanna's house began to vibrate with noise and energy from Alix's three offspring and their new friends.

Felix too loved his new environment, particularly the quaint foodstalls in Geneva on market days. With Hanna in tow, he roamed the market for hours on end to find the freshest tomatoes or the best zucchini. Hanna was delighted with Felix's company. She never tired of spending hours in the kitchen with him. He taught her the finer points of cooking, a skill she had never had time to acquire and, in return, she taught him to speak French.

Alix too began to come alive. Her thoughts turned to Tansie less and less. When they did though, it was no longer with the same pain. She remembered the good times as well as Kim's assurances that they were never meant to be together.

When the children had a short break in October, she took them and Felix to Berlin to visit Marta. When Felix emerged from the car outside the lake house, Marta gasped and said in jest, "I'm not sure this household can cope with a real man . . . male children are one thing but . . ."

"What about him coping in an all-female household?" Alix grinned.

"That's a point," Marta laughed and stretched out her hand to welcome Felix. "Don't take any notice of what I said. It's a pleasure to have you here."

During the day, Nina took Felix and the children sight-seeing and Marta and Alix worked in the music room. But whenever they needed a break, they took long walks along the lake or through the nearby Grünewald forest. The weather in Berlin had not been as mild as it was in Geneva and the trees had lost their colourful foliage much earlier.

Observing Marta and Nina together, Alix, from time to time, thought of Tansie and of what they would never have again. But more often she thought of Jesse and of what they might have one day.

"What are you thinking about?" Marta interrupted Alix's train of thought.

"I was thinking of a former lover, who left me earlier this year."

"Only a foolish man could leave a beautiful woman like you," Marta observed with dry humour.

"It was a woman," Alix responded with a smile.

"Mein Gott," Marta cried and, sweeping her ceremoniously into her arms, gave Alix a hug. Releasing her, she added, "And now? Has someone else captured your heart?"

"I don't know, maybe," Alix said slowly. She briefly wondered why she had never mentioned Tansie or Jesse to Marta before. As they continued walking, Alix told her about her relationship with Tansie. In doing so, Alix realised that, for the first time, she could talk about Tansie rationally rather than emotionally. Later and without realising it, when she spoke about Jesse, her words came right from the heart.

"And how come you have not seduced this Jesse yet?" Marta asked with a wicked glint in her eyes. "If you don't, you must know that someone else will!"

Alix laughed and linked her arm with Marta's. "I'll think about it," she said.

Ten days later, Alix and the children returned to Switzerland. Despite the early onset of winter and the colder weather, she played the piano for hours with the windows wide open. Wrapped in a heavy woollen sweater, thick socks and ribbed leggings, she loved to feel the cool breeze on her cheeks. It seemed to unclutter her mind, leaving it open to magnificent inspirations when she started to compose a new piano concerto. For the moment, she simply called it the Jesse Piano Concerto in E flat major. It was to have three movements: *allegro con brio*, *adagio un poco mosso* and *rondo vivace*.

The first movement opened with a formal chord before the piano entered with a fast passage which was full of *bravura*, *arpeggios* and trills with short solo passages for most of the orchestra's instruments.

The second movement, the *adagio un poco mosso*, was deeply expressive. When the piano entered on the ninth bar, it immediately launched into a dialogue between itself and the orchestra – much like two people would explore each other's personality after a first meeting.

In the third and last movement, the *rondo vivace*, her flow of inspiration was unstoppable. The basic theme could only be described as jolly: a roller-coaster ride with many merry and prolonged trills for the piano as it teased its way into a new, exiting relationship. The concerto finished with a volcano-like explosion from the piano and the orchestra, representing the final union of two people.

Alix was pleased with her efforts. When she played parts of it for Hanna, she was so enthralled tears brimmed in her eyes. She remembered only too well the symphony Alix had composed earlier that year which had been full of pain and melancholic memories.

"It's wonderful, darling," Hanna exclaimed and gave her niece a hug. She smiled when she asked, "By the way, when is Jesse arriving?"

"You are the most intuitive woman in the world," Alix laughed and threw her arms around Hanna. "She's coming soon, very soon."

Alix had kept in touch with Jesse either by way of letters or telephone calls. She particularly enjoyed Jesse's letters. They were full of humour and the jocular, teasing affection which had very much become part of their friendship. During the many hours she had spent composing the Jesse Piano Concerto, she had often caught herself thinking of Jesse and admitting that she missed her, especially after her conversation with Marta.

Towards the middle of November, Alix flew to Vienna where she was to start rehearsals with the Philharmonic under Boris Rostoff's baton. Hanna, Felix and the children would fly over for the opening night of the concert, on the second Saturday in December. Kate was to fly over from Melbourne for the first performance and then on to Zürich for a spot of Christmas shopping as she called it. She was sure to find the appropriate trinkets for her family and friends on Bahnhofstrasse.

It was a beautiful clear winter's day, with the sun shining from a bright blue sky and a thin blanket of snow on the rooftops, when Jesse arrived in Vienna three days after Alix. She had missed Alix a great deal and was pleased that she had been able to organise her own holidays and her schedule so that she could join Alix much earlier than planned. Wanting to surprise Alix, she had not told her of her arrival date. Jesse took a cab into the city and to the Imperial Hotel. She smiled at the doorman when he opened the massive doors for her, but stopped when she caught a glimpse of Alix.

Alix had returned from rehearsal only moments earlier and still stood at reception, conversing in rapid German with the concierge and flicking through a bundle of letters he had obviously just handed her.

As Jesse slowly approached her, she noted how young and energetic Alix looked despite the usual Davidoff she held in her right hand. She was dressed in a pair of tight jeans and a green roll neck sweater which matched her eyes. A green and red silk Christian Dior scarf was casually draped around her neck and her navy coat was flung over her left shoulder.

"Alix?" The word had barely been breathed from Jesse's lips when Alix spun around and flew into her arms.

"Jesse . . . you're early . . . when did you arrive . . . you didn't tell me." Alix's eyes shone with pleasure and without a single thought, she kissed Jesse on the lips. Drawing away, she added, "I'm so glad you're here."

"I couldn't wait another day to see you." Jesse's gaze was so charmingly honest when it met Alix's, on impulse, Alix kissed her again. This time, she lingered just a little and, although only their lips touched, Alix felt as though her whole body was invaded by excitement and anticipation.

Catching her breath, Alix drew away, reached for the key on the counter and took Jesse's arm. "Let's get out of here," she said breezily.

As soon as the door to Alix's suite on the first floor had shut, Alix ambled over to the baby grand piano which had been especially installed for her. "I have a surprise for you," Alix said as she sat down. "Would you like to freshen up first?"

Jesse smiled. "No . . . I'll have the surprise first." Normally after such a long trip Jesse always had a shower the moment she arrived in the hotel, but today she made an exception. She didn't want to spoil the mood, still feeling Alix's lips on her own.

Alix immediately started to hum the first few bars and then, without taking her eyes off Jesse, leapt into the solo part from the first movement of the Jesse Piano Concerto.

Jesse took off her coat and then ambled over to the piano. Leaning against its side, her eyes never left Alix's as her expression changed from surprise, to delight to utter astonishment. She had never heard a piece of music as exciting and beautiful as what she heard now. Since the tune was not familiar to her, Jesse assumed that it was one of Alix's compositions. Of course there was no orchestra to accompany Alix but Jesse could almost hear the violins and imagine a wind instrument leaping into a solo of its own, as though teasing the composer's quick wit. It simply had to be one of her own works, Jesse decided, totally mesmerised by the music.

"I called it the Jesse Piano Concerto in E flat major," Alix said softly when she finally dropped her hands into her lap.

Jesse was momentarily speechless. What words could possibly express what she felt right now?

Both women remained motionless. The air was thick yet vibrantly alive with an electric current that seemed to flow between them. Their eyes were touching from afar, each trying to figure out what the other was thinking.

Jesse knew what it all meant. She took two steps towards Alix, reached for her hands and drew her into her arms. It was the most natural thing, the only thing, Jesse could do. Holding her, Jesse lowered her lips to Alix's and kissed her. Jesse closed her eyes and savoured each precious moment.

The first, bare touch of Jesse's warm lips on her own, made Alix tremble in her embrace. It felt wonderful beyond comparison. Alix responded with such hunger and pleasure, she surprised herself. For many months she had believed that she could never feel like this again.

She had not felt as close to anybody for a long time as she did now to Jesse. But right now, she could not think beyond wanting to be held. Whatever was going to happen between them would happen anyway, she was sure of that. They had all the time in the world.

For what seemed an eternity, neither moved. With night approaching, the room became darker and the silhouettes of their bodies stood in contrast to the light from the street lamps.

Slowly, Jesse was the first to draw away. "It's time to freshen up," she said softly, adding, "and then I'll take you to dinner at Sacher . . . we have a reservation for seven-thirty."

"You're very droll," Alix laughed. "However, now that we're talking about more practical matters, hmmm, are you comfortable sharing my suite or would you rather . . ."

Putting a finger gently on Alix's lips, she replied, "I'm very comfortable with that. Now, if you direct me to the bathroom, I'll get out of these grotty clothes."

Laughing together now, they wandered down the passage to the bedroom. While Jesse unpacked, Alix ran a bath for her.

Moments later, Jesse appeared in the doorway, removed her dressing gown and gingerly lowered herself into the warm, scented water. She sighed contentedly as she rested her head on the rim of the tub and closed her eyes.

Alix sat down on the low stool and reached for her cigarettes. She lit a Davidoff and, as she slowly inhaled, her eyes fixed on Jesse. Alix took in Jesse's fine features with the lips just slightly parted and half-smiling, the straight line of her shoulders, the gentle roundness of her breasts, the flat stomach and narrow waist and hips. Jesse's legs were long and well-shaped. An urge to touch Jesse, to let her hands caress her, kiss her, gripped Alix with such force, she felt herself starting to shake inside. She took a deep puff on her cigarette, stood up abruptly and returned to the bed-room.

Discarding her clothes and leaving them where they fell, she stalked into the shower and turned the tap on. As the hot water started to sooth and calm her, she knew for sure that a relationship with Jesse was now inevitable. She was in love with Jesse.

Out of sheer joy, Alix began to sing, her voice clear yet mellow and very passionate. Although this aria was for a tenor, Alix didn't care. She sang Rodolfo's aria to Mimi from the first act of Puccini's opera *La Bohème*. She felt that this piece of music was most suitable for her current mood: she was free to love again.

Wrapped in one of the hotel's dressing gowns, Jesse stood at the shower stall holding a huge towel when Alix turned off the tap and slid open the door. "You have a lovely voice," Jesse smiled and gave Alix's dripping wet body an open, appreciative glance. She didn't just notice the slender torso, the small breasts and the long legs but rather the sparkle in her green-grey eyes and the soft smile on her face.

Kissing the tip of Alix's wet nose, Jesse pulled the towel around her. Lightly, she said, "If you don't get dressed soon, we'll never make it to the restaurant."

"No sense of romance!" Alix rolled her eyes again and sauntered into the bedroom.

The streets were covered with a thick white blanket when they stepped underneath the canopy outside the Imperial. Fat snowflakes danced in the streetlights before coming to rest on the road. It looked like fairy land and Alix's spirits lifted even higher.

A momentary attack of guilt began to tug at her as she remembered the first time she and Tansie had been in Vienna together. She felt guilty because she now knew that she could care for and love someone else. She felt guilty because she had stopped mourning for Tansie and was about to open her heart to someone else.

As though she had guessed what Alix was thinking, Jesse put her arm around her shoulders. "It's okay to remember but do it without guilt. You loved beyond comparison and you cried and mourned just as much," she murmured softly. "It's time to let the ghost go."

"I know," Alix said, adjusting her coat and linking her arm with Jesse's, "Sooner or later, the overture must finish and the real symphony has to start."

"Spoken like a true musician," Jesse smiled and squeezed her hand.

The moment they climbed into the back seat of the cab, Alix snuggled into Jesse's side and leant her head against her shoulder. "I'm going to be okay . . . we're going to be okay," she said simply and meant it.

Chapter 32

The restaurant Sacher was elegant, although a little frilly, the food was prepared and presented perfectly and the wine had been chilled to just the right temperature. Alix and Jesse's fellow diners were luxuriously clothed and glitteringly bejewelled. Heavy furs were carelessly spread over the bench seats. Waiters occasionally addressed guests as Baron or Countess. The muffled sounds of many languages drifted to their table. All in all it was a sight to behold and they both agreed that it would be a perfect evening even before it started.

Alix and Jesse talked, sipped the French champagne from crystal flutes, nibbled at the food they ordered and gazed and smiled into each other's eyes. Everything was divine. They were both lost in each other, wanting to touch and taste each other's lips again. Neither was ever meant to be on her own.

When they returned to the hotel, they collected the key to their suite, ordered hot chocolate and headed towards the massive staircase. The light on the answering machine flashed in the semi-darkness. Alix pressed the play button.

"Alix?" Boris' voice boomed. "I've changed tomorrow's rehearsal schedule. I'll let you sleep in . . . how does a two o'clock start sound to you? Sleep well."

"You're a real treasure, Boris," Alix laughed.

After several beeps, a female voice said, "Jesse? . . . I just called to see whether you arrived in Vienna all right . . . let me know how you're getting on when you have a moment

. . . I'm going to miss you, you know. . . take care . . . bye."

When no other messages came, Alix re-set the machine, her hand trembling just a little. Who was the woman Alix wondered, anxious. Her earlier mood dampened. She looked at Jesse and wanted to smile but couldn't.

Jesse reached for her hands. "Sally and I spent a bit of time together before I came to join you."

"Jesse, you don't have to explain."

"I don't have to but I want to," Jesse smiled, thinking that she could never be anything less than totally honest with Alix. "Sally would like to be more than just friends but I told her that was not possible!" Jesse said.

"How can you be so sure of that?" Alix asked. She thought she knew the answer, hoped she knew the answer, but needed to hear it.

"Because I am much more interested in someone else," Jesse said and squeezed Alix's hands. She wanted to see the woman she had first met; the woman who wandered through the world confidently believing that she belonged wherever she went. Earlier tonight, during dinner, she had seen just that woman. "I love you, Alix," Jesse murmured.

Jesse had said what Alix wanted to hear but, still, she felt herself tremble.

"Alix, don't be frightened. Nothing is going to happen unless we both want it to happen," Jesse said and folded her into her arms. "I'm ready for it but if you're not, then . . ."

"Oh, Jesse. The thought of ending up in the same emotional mess again makes my skin crawl, and yet I do want your love and everything it brings with it," Alix exclaimed, weeping and laughing at the same time.

Moments later, she continued in an unusual outburst of volatility, "No . . . I couldn't face that pain again." As soon as the words had left her lips, Alix realised that Jesse might well think she had been turned down. She sighed, took a deep breath, and started again. "Jesse, what I meant to say was that I couldn't face losing another lover . . . not after Tansie." She stopped and, with fear, frustration, anxiety and happiness all rolled into one, Alix tightened her arms around Jesse and added, "You see, I am in love too . . . with you."

For a moment neither woman spoke. Being much the same height, each tilted her head sideways just a little as they moved closer towards each other and kissed.

Alix knew that she wanted much more than just a brief kiss. She wanted to touch Jesse, to trace the lines of her delicate cheekbones, to feel her breasts in the palms of her hands. She wanted to reassure herself that neither her feelings, nor Jesse, were a figment of her imagination and would disappear again at dawn.

Without letting go of each other they wandered into the bedroom, Alix walking backwards drawing Jesse with her. Button by button, they undid each other's shirts and slipped them off the shoulders. Seconds later, their slacks and silk panties were gathered at their feet. Jesse kissed the soft flesh at the side of Alix's neck and reached around her back to undo her bra.

As Jesse fumbled trying to find the clasp, a soft laugh emanated from Alix's chest. "It's in the front," Alix murmured and reached around Jesse to undo her bra.

"I obviously haven't done this for a while," Jesse smiled. Both bras joined the rest of the clothes on the floor.

Encircling Jesse's waist with her hands, Alix drew her closer until their naked bodies touched. That first moment was enough to make Alix's head spin and wish that time would simply stop. She wanted to engrave the memory of that touch forever in her heart.

Kissing and holding each other, they slowly lowered themselves on to the king-size bed. Bending over Alix, Jesse let her lips wander over her smooth neck, along her collarbone and to her breasts. Her kisses were light yet she could feel Alix shiver in her embrace.

It was with clarity that Alix knew that nobody, not even Tansie, had ever stroked her the way Jesse did. She touched and caressed her like nobody else had done before. Alix felt whole again as all of her passions burst forth. She knew she had found her true soul-mate, friend and lover.

Later, Jesse cradled Alix at her side. Judging by Alix's passionate response, Jesse knew that Alix had buried the shadow of her recent past. They were two people in love. Two people who were truly meant for each other. In Alix she had found what she had been looking for all of her adult life.

Alix only slowly came back to earth. Eventually, she said, "Jesse, I love you."

Even before Alix was awake the next morning, she felt Jesse's hands sliding over her stomach. She kept her eyes closed, just a little fearful that, if she opened them, the dream may be gone. The pale winter sunshine streamed into the room and lit their glowing faces. They heard the traffic rattle by in the street outside. A new day had started.

During the three weeks leading up to the beginning of the concert tour, their routine changed little from day to day. When Alix was busy rehearsing, Jesse often sat in the auditorium and watched and listened to Boris and the orchestra. She smiled to herself as she recalled Alix telling her exactly which seat to take so that they could always look at each other without disrupting Alix's play and concentration.

When Alix had free time, they took long walks in the

Stadtpark or sat over leisurely luncheons in one of Vienna's quaint restaurants. But invariably and, on sudden impulse, they rushed back to the hotel. They dived into each other's arms to explore whatever yet remained undiscovered. If Alix had a whole day off and the weather was favourable, they hired a car and drove out of the city to the Lainzer Tiergarten and to Rohrau, Josef Haydn's birthplace.

Two days before Alix's first concert, they rode in a large limousine to the airport to pick up Kate and Alix's family. It was one of the happiest reunions Alix could remember.

Felix and the children were installed in a large suite on the third floor of the Imperial Hotel. Hanna had her own down the hall and Kate moved into the second bedroom in Alix's and Jesse's suite.

"You have been holding out on me, Alix!" Kate exclaimed when she saw Jesse's gear in Alix's room.

"I have indeed." Alix smiled and nibbled Jesse's earlobe.

"Say no more . . . I get the message." Kate rolled her eyes in jest.

After dinner that first evening, when Alix's family had returned to their rooms for the night, the three women sat together in Alix's suite and talked. Alix asked Kate whether she had heard anything about Tansie's baby. Kate said she hadn't. It wasn't until later that Kate told Jesse, when Alix was out of the room, that Herb had rung her to tell her Tansie had had a baby boy a few days earlier. And although, Kate said, the baby was fine, Tansie had tried to slit her wrists but they'd found her in time and she was okay. Together the two women decided that Jesse would tell Alix during the Christmas break which they intended to spend in Madrid.

The next morning Kate was up first and, drawing her silk dressing gown around her waist, casually ambled into

Alix's and Jesse's room. Standing next to the bed for a moment, she looked down at the two women who only slowly appeared to awake.

Alix felt Kate's presence and, without opening her eyes, casually rolled on top of Jesse, at the same time drawing the eiderdown over both their heads.

"That's not playing fair!" Kate grumbled but with a wide grin on her face.

Seconds later, Alix's head appeared again. She laughed and her eyes sparkled. "If you hadn't crept up on us like this, you'd never know what goes on in here."

"Give me some credit for my imagination, pet," Kate responded loftily, adding, "Shall I order breakfast?"

"Please," Jesse's muffled voice came from somewhere underneath the comforter.

The concert that night was an overwhelming success. Alix had not performed in Vienna since studying there some twenty years before. But the Viennese people had not forgotten her. They gave her the acclaim she deserved. For the first encore, she played Liszt's *Liebestraum*, a piece of music she particularly liked because of its romantic theme. When Alix finished the second encore, a loose adaption of the first movement of her own Jesse Piano Concerto in E flat major, the audience went wild. Although, generally speaking, the Viennese reacted conservatively to anything new, tonight there was no holding them back. They clapped and shouted for more.

Alix responded accordingly and played three more encores, short pieces by Chopin, Liszt and Rossini. When she walked off stage for the last time, Jesse was waiting for her in the wings and swept her into her arms. She had been deeply moved when she first learnt that Alix had dedicated her newest piano concerto to her. But now that

Alix had played it in public for the very first time, she was overwhelmed. It was a truly priceless gift.

Chapter 33

Alix's family and Kate returned to Switzerland after the weekend. Alix and Jesse travelled on to Budapest, Prague, Warsaw, Helsinki, Stockholm, Oslo, Copenhagen and eventually to Hamburg which was to be their last stop before the Christmas break. Although the concert schedule was gruelling, Alix thrived on it. She had the world at her feet but, at the end of each performance, she had Jesse in her arms.

The morning after Alix's concert in Hamburg, the two women sat at a small table in the window of their suite at the Vier Jahreszeiten Hotel, having a leisurely breakfast and reading the latest reviews. Alix had her legs stretched across Jesse's lap, enjoying Jesse's gentle caresses. She loved the way Jesse ran the palm of her hand over her bare thighs.

There was no need to rush that morning. Their flight to Madrid would not leave until later that day. From their window, they had a magnificent view over the hotel garden and the Alster Lake beyond. It was another beautiful winter's day with the snow-covered scenery glittering in the sunshine. Alix smiled and, leaning forward a little, kissed Jesse on the lips.

"That's nice . . . what was it for?" Jesse peered over the rim of her reading glasses.

"No special reason," Alix said and kissed her again. "I just thought that if the weather we've had is indicative of our relationship, then we can look forward to lots of sunshine in our life."

"I expect nothing else." Jesse smiled, confidently. Moments later, she chuckled. "Listen to this," she said, reading from one of the glossy German tabloids. "'Many artists have played on Germany's concert stages but rarely have we had the pleasure of not just an exceptionally talented but also beautiful woman like Alix Clemenger.' Then it goes on with a few more compliments I'm sure you've heard before." Jesse stopped, raised her eyebrows as she glanced at Alix, and smiled. There was a photo of Alix and Jesse which had been taken one day when they were leaving the Musikverein in Vienna. Jesse's arm was casually draped over Alix's shoulder and their long overcoats flapped around their legs as they strolled off. Jesse continued reading aloud, "'Ms Clemenger's equally beautiful travelling companion is Dr Jesse Carrington from Melbourne, Australia where Ms Clemenger has been living for nearly twenty years.'"

Alix swept Jesse into her arms as she glanced at the photograph. "This outfit, small as it is, might just work as long I get to be the prima donna," she muttered in jest, her words muffled against Jesse's chest.

"I can cope with that," Jesse laughed and kissed Alix leisurely.

Hanna, Felix and the children were waiting for them in the Palace Hotel lobby when Alix and Jesse arrived in Madrid that night. Alix had had some misgivings about Christmas, remembering that a year ago Tansie was still with her. But then, Alix reminded herself, she now had Jesse.

On the morning of Boxing Day, when Alix and Jesse were having a quiet breakfast in bed, Jesse told her what Kate had said about Tansie and the baby.

As tears began to glisten on Alix's long eyelashes, Jesse drew her into her arms and held her tight. Alix seemed fragile and vulnerable as Jesse drew her head against her chest and cradled it.

Finally Alix said, "Tansie trusted me, Jesse . . . I know we fought and battled, but there was a bond between us . . . and then I wasn't there to protect her." Alix stopped for a moment and wiped a few tears from her face with the back of her hand. "Because I hurt so badly, I closed my mind to her pain and withdrew. I never returned calls she left on the answering machine and I repeatedly hung up on her." Again Alix stopped and, lifting her head, looked at Jesse. "Could I have prevented her attempted suicide if I'd been there for the birth of the baby?" Alix asked.

"I don't think so," Jesse replied softly. "She's been hovering on the brink for a long time, you know that. You also know that giving birth is often traumatic. Depression is inevitable for some women."

"Yes . . . I do know that," Alix sighed, a deep heart-felt sigh. "I loved her Jesse but, still, I couldn't save her."

"No, you couldn't but not because of anything you did or did not do, Alix," Jesse comforted her.

For a long time, neither spoke. Then Jesse asked gently, "Are you okay?"

"Yes . . . I'm okay," Alix said.

After spending a week in Madrid with their mother and Jesse, the children, together with Hanna and Felix, returned to Switzerland. Alix and Jesse continued to tour for another three months. They travelled from Europe across to the United States and back to Europe.

Jesse had been able to schedule at least some of the papers she was asked to give to coincide with Alix's performances. Neither could bear the idea of being apart even for a short period of time.

As it had turned out, Alix's very last concert was to be in Berlin. When Alix rang Marta from Paris to announce

407

her imminent arrival, she told her that she was bringing a surprise with her.

As usual, Marta was waiting at the airport.

"Hello, Jesse," Marta grinned. "You have indeed brought a surprise," she winked at Alix. "A wonderful surprise."

"Am I going to be let in on this little conspiracy?" Jesse asked.

Alix smiled and kissed her. "When I was here last October, I told Marta about you. She advised me at the time that if I didn't seduce you, someone else would."

"I'm glad you took her advice." Jesse too smiled and returned Alix's kiss.

When they were finally on their own in the vast guest room, they leisurely moved into each other's arms. Standing close together and glancing across the still lake, Jesse asked softly, "Are you happy, Alix?"

"Very happy."

Epilogue

It was Autumn the following year when Jesse arrived home late one evening. She looked drawn and deeply distressed as she wandered into Alix's studio.

Alix poured them both a drink. "Cheers," Alix said. "You look as though you need it." When Jesse didn't reply, Alix asked, more alarmed, "What's wrong? Did you have a bad day?"

Jesse took a swig of cognac and cleared her throat. "It's Tansie and it's not good news," she said softly and reached for Alix's hand. Before Alix could catch her breath, Jesse added, "Her little boy died early this morning . . . Tansie took an overdose of sleeping pills and is now in a coma."

As though in slow motion, Alix withdrew her hand and sat down on the couch. No, not the little boy, she thought and burst into heartbroken sobs. When Jesse came to sit next to her, Alix moved into her comforting embrace.

It was a long time before Alix could speak. Her voice was still weak and shaky when she finally began. "It's not right, Jesse," she said. "Tansie had a raw deal from the day she was born . . . have we all failed her?"

"Compared to you and me, yes, she had a raw deal," Jesse agreed softly. "But you must try and remember that she experienced periods of light from time to time. Maybe that's all she could have ever had."

After a short pause, Alix continued. "You know, I never even found out the baby's name . . . I never asked anybody."

For a brief moment, Jesse contemplated whether or not

to tell Alix or to pretend she didn't know. "Tansie called him Alexander . . . his father called him Mickey," Jesse finally replied.

"Tansie would have hated that," Alix stated.

"I believe she did," Jesse confirmed.

"How did he die?"

"He had a heart disorder which he could have survived had it been picked up in time. But when the doctors realised what they were dealing with, it was too late. He couldn't be saved."

What Jesse could not bring herself to tell Alix was that Herb Mullins was not the child's father. Even Tansie wasn't sure who he was. In not quite telling Alix everything, Jesse hoped that Alix would always have some fond memories of her time with Tansie.

Tansie was still in a coma when the baby was buried. Alix did not go to the funeral but wrote a short note to Herb and his son, David, offering them her condolences.

Tansie remained in a coma for ten days. When she came to she remembered nothing and recognised nobody. Her mind was gone for ever. Nobody would know for sure what it was that finally sent Tansie over the edge, an edge she had precariously balanced on for most of her life.

"What's going to happen to her now?" Alix asked Jesse when she brought her the latest news.

"She will be put into one of the state's mental institutions," Jesse said softly. "Herb has already made arrangements for her transfer. It appears she is no longer his responsibility. I believe he has also filed for a divorce."

"He can't do that!" Alix was devastated at the prospect of having Tansie end up in a public mental hospital and took matters into her own hands. Over many months, she sought to have Tansie put into a private institution. Despite his earlier claim that she was no longer his responsibility, Herb changed his mind when he found out that Alix wanted to move her.

For the first time in her life, Alix used both her power and her wealth to get what she wanted. After many months, a judge eventually ruled in Alix's favour. Tansie was to be placed in an institution of Alix's choosing.

It was during the court-hearing that Alix was finally, truly able to put her relationship with Tansie into the past. As she was leaving the court room, she suddenly stopped and paled. For a split second, she thought she had seen a ghost.

"I'm sorry, I didn't mean to startle you," Tansie's sister Arlene said, adding, "You are Alix Clemenger, aren't you?"

"Yes, and you must be Tansie's sister." Alix smiled weakly. Except that she was a few years older than Tansie, Arlene could have been her identical twin.

Over a cup of coffee in a nearby tea room, Arlene told Alix how grateful she was for everything Alix had done for her sister. All the things she herself could not do because Tansie had never allowed it. It was only in more recent times that Tansie kept up some sort of regular contact with her sister. Whether Tansie had had a premonition of sorts about her future, Arlene didn't know. But what she did know and now told Alix was that Tansie had genuinely loved her.

Watching the smoke from her cigarette curl over their table, Alix listened without interrupting.

"You see," Arlene said, "Tansie's greatest fear was to be ignored and invisible again just like in her childhood." Clearing her throat and taking a sip of coffee, she continued. "While I believe that you gave her everything humanly possible, she felt she was walking in your shadow and, in a strange sort of a way, she felt she was a nobody again. Sadly, she could never live with that."

"While it helps me to understand her a little better," Alix said as she traced her bottom lip with her thumb. "It does make me very sad to hear you say this."

"I thought you deserved to know," Arlene said.

"Thank you," Alix replied and watched Arlene leave. Even if nobody had been able to help Tansie, Alix was glad to see that, despite the despicable background they had both shared, at least Arlene had come out of it, if not totally unscarred, certainly able to cope quite well.

It was spring again, and three years since Alix had seen Tansie, when the final ruling was made about Tansie's future. She was immediately moved to the institution Alix had chosen.

The day after Tansie's admission, Alix pulled the car into the visitor's carpark and walked towards the main hospital building; a large Victorian mansion set in a huge, well-tended tranquil park. Tansie would like it here, Alix thought, remembering the times they had walked through a spring park somewhere and how happy Tansie had been.

Alix slowly walked up the few front steps and into the main reception area.

"Ms Tansie Landon?" she asked the sister at the desk.

"Turn left at the end of the corridor. She is on the back verandah."

Dressed in a navy, light wool pullover Tansie sat in a wheelchair, a blanket wrapped around her knees, staring into space. She was painfully thin, her eyes were vacant, but a slight smile played around her lips. It was the forlorn smile of the small child Alix had fallen in love with.

Bending over Tansie, Alix gently kissed the top of her head and murmured, "I loved you, but I couldn't help you."

As soon as the words had left her lips, Alix turned and slowly walked back along the terrace. Tears welled in her eyes, as she thought how ironic it was that Tansie had to lose her mind before she could find peace and that her life would end one day much in the same way it had started: as a helpless child locked away in an institution.

From that day forward, Alix tried to visit Tansie once a week and, when she couldn't be there in person, she sent flowers. On each such occasion, Alix kissed her and told her that she would always love her. In time, Tansie came to smile when Alix visited. But other than that, there was never the slightest sign that she knew who Alix was or that she remembered anything from her past.

But even if Tansie was not capable of remembering, Alix was. Alix could never forget that it was Tansie who had shown her a different world and a path she had never thought she would walk. Now, with Jesse at her side, she walked it daily with great joy.